THE GOOD NEARBY

The Good Nearby

NANCY MOSER

TYNDALE HOUSE PUBLISHERS, INC.
CAROL STREAM, ILLINOIS

Visit Tyndale's exciting Web site at www.tyndale.com

Check out the latest about Nancy Moser at www.nancymoser.com

TYNDALE and Tyndale's quill logo are registered trademarks of Tyndale House Publishers, Inc.

The Good Nearby

Designed by Beth Sparkman

Edited by Kathryn S. Olson

Published in association with the literary agency of Janet Kobobel Grant, Books & Such, 4788 Carissa Avenue, Santa Rosa, CA 95405

Scripture quotations are taken from the *Holy Bible*, New Living Translation, copyright © 1996, 2004. Used by permission of Tyndale House Publishers, Inc., Carol Stream, Illinois 60188. All rights reserved.

Library of Congress Cataloging-in-Publication Data

Moser, Nancy.
  The good nearby / Nancy Moser.
    p. cm.
  ISBN-13: 978-1-4143-0162-4 (pbk.)
  ISBN-10: 1-4143-0162-6 (pbk.)
  I. Title.
  PS3563.O88417G66 2006
  813'.54—dc22   2006013396

Printed in the United States of America

12 11 10 09 08 07
7   6   5   4   3   2

In memory of Judy Hainline;
To her husband, Dallas, and son, Zach,
and to other hopeful and courageous recipients;
And to all the generous organ donors and their families
who give others the gift of hope and life.

❧ ❧ ❧

To the world you may be one person,
But to one person, you may be the world.
ANONYMOUS

PROLOGUE

There is a time and a way for everything,
even when a person is in trouble.
ECCLESIASTES 8:6

Mama sat on the bed, going through her wallet. She pulled out a piece of money, looked at it, then wadded it up and threw it down. "This is ridiculous."

I stood at the foot of the bed and watched. I put my thumb in my mouth, then pulled it out and hid it behind my back. It wouldn't do no good to get Mama mad about that too.

She turned her purse upside down. A comb, lipstick, keys, cigarette case, and some coins fell onto the sheets. She shook it hard. A few more coins came out. "Ah, come *on . . .*"

Money. She was after money. I ran after a few pennies that had rolled onto the carpet and brought them back to her. "Look, Mama. Here's more."

She glanced at the coins and flipped a hand at them. "Worthless. Just like everything else in my life."

I tried to think of something to cheer her up. "I can count."

Mama started looking through the drawer of Daddy's bedside table. "I would certainly hope so."

"Want to hear me?"

With a sigh she sank onto the bed and lit a cigarette. She took a long puff before saying, "Sure. Why not? Go for it."

I took a deep breath. "One, two, three, four, five, ninety-six, seven—"

Mama blew the smoke out. "It's six, Gigi, not ninety-six. You're almost four now. I can't have you being dumb. You know how it goes. Four, five, six, seven."

I shook my head. "Ninety-six."

"No, it's—"

I stomped a foot on the floor. "Mama! Ninety-six!"

Mama raised an eyebrow, and for a second I was afraid I'd get hit. But then she said, "You are a stubborn little thing. Just like your father."

I didn't know what stubborn was. I didn't care as long as I could count—my way.

I skipped out of the room. "One, two, three, four, five, ninety-six, seven . . ."

1

He makes the whole body fit together perfectly.
As each part does its own special work, it helps the other parts grow,
so that the whole body is healthy and growing and full of love.

EPHESIANS 4:16

I was happy.

Sitting between Mama and Daddy in the pickup, driving to Great-Grammy's for Thanksgiving dinner . . . I wondered if Grammy would have a turkey with funny legs on it, with even funnier socks like I'd seen in pictures. My friend Susie had told me what her family was having for dinner, and though I didn't know what yams were and couldn't imagine eating a pie made out of a pumpkin, I nodded and said, "Me too. I can hardly wait."

From the sounds of Mama and Daddy's arguing, Grammy had been asking us to come for years, but we'd never gone. I wasn't sure why we were going this year, except I heard Mama say something about Grammy being gone soon and us needing to get in good with her. Was she taking a trip? I'd sure like to go with her.

They also talked a lot about an in-her-tence. Daddy said we shouldn't expect one of those, but Mama said we'd better get it because she'd married him to move up in the world, not down. "You promised," Mama said way too often. "You promised me the world and I'm tired of settling for less."

Daddy got real quiet when she brought up the promise thing. He'd been kind of sad lately. He'd gotten laid off from his office job. I *did* like having him around more but it made Mama huffy. Last week Daddy got a job as a gofer for a house builder. Now, when he comes home from work he's so sore from lifting and moving things he can barely move. Mama says it's beneath him. I just wish it wouldn't make him so tired.

Mama may have worried about getting in good with Grammy, but I didn't have to worry about that 'cause Grammy always smiled when she came to visit me. And today, going to her house for the first time, I imagined her giving me one of her very biggest hugs. "I'm ever so glad to see you, Gigi girl. And my, my. Seven years old and getting so big!"

I couldn't remember ever seeing my parents hug Grammy. I liked hugs a lot, but I knew Mama and Daddy didn't care much for 'em because whenever I tried to hug them, they'd pull away and say, "Go on, now. There's no need for that."

There was, but I couldn't argue with them. At least I'd be hugging Grammy soon.

I dug in my coat pocket and got out a slip of paper to look at Grammy's address. Daddy had made Mama write it down: *96 Maple*. When I first saw that number, that 96, I got all excited. Grammy lived in a house that had my special number on it! I knew right then this was going to be a good day.

Mama was reading one of her fancy fashion magazines, *Vogue*. The clothes were way too weird and fancy for anything she'd ever wear so I wasn't sure why she liked looking at it. Besides, she didn't need many clothes. She sold makeup at a department store and wore a pink smock every day. And we never went anywhere that made us get dressed up. Except today. Today Mama had told me to put on my red jumper and a blouse because Great-Grammy was old-fashioned. I didn't know what one had to do with the other, but I was glad enough to wear it. 'Cept it was hard sitting like a lady in a truck, in a jumper.

Mama liked helping the rich ladies who came in the store spend tons of dollars on face cream and eye shadow. I thought spending that much was dumb, especially when they could get a lipstick at the drugstore for cheap. But what did I know? ChapStick was enough for me. How I loved the smell of that stuff.

Even if Mama would never be wearing the magazine clothes, she did know how to use makeup. Her skin was soft and creamy, the color of a fresh-peeled potato. Her eye shadow was blue, and she had a brown line drawn around her eyes and a red line around her lips. I loved watching her put her makeup on. She was an artist. I thought she was every bit as pretty as the women in any old magazine. Especially when she was all done, when she smiled in the mirror and posed. She looked happy right then.

I looked out the window at the world whizzing by. The snow peeked through dead plants in the fields and was piled along the edge of the road. Part of the road was covered with it, and I liked watching the snow slip across the highway in front of us like it was running to get away from the tires. I'd run too. We were going really fas—

S-l-i-d-e . . .

The back of the truck went right.

The front, left.

We headed into the other lane—

"Watch it!" Mama yelled.

The truck got straight again with a jerk like the road had reached up and grabbed the tires.

"You're going to get us killed," Mama said.

"Don't even start." But then Daddy flicked his cigarette out the window and put two hands on the wheel. That made me feel a little safer. Daddy usually drove with one hand on the top of the steering wheel, not really holding it, but his arm just resting there, bent at the wrist. I wasn't sure how a wrist could drive a truck, but Daddy seemed to make it work.

But now he was using two hands and was sitting up real straight. I saw the muscles in his jaw twitch. Mama sat straighter too. I held on to the corner of Mama's coat, but I don't think she noticed. Anyways, she didn't tell me to let go or anything.

"It's this stupid truck," Mama said. "No weight in the back. I will never understand why you traded your car for this piece of—"

"I need a truck for work."

"What you need is different work. Office work. You do *not* need to be a delivery peon."

"A job's a job."

She huffed. "You going to tell your grandma about your new job?"

"Maybe."

Mama laughed. "That'll impress her."

Suddenly, Daddy slammed on the brakes, making the truck slip and slide some more, until we stopped right there in the middle of the highway.

"Jay!"

I looked over my shoulder and was glad to see there was no one behind us.

Daddy glared at Mama. "It was your idea to go to my grandma's today. We've never gone before. I don't know why we have to go now."

She slapped her magazine shut. "You know very well why." She tapped a pink-painted fingernail on the model's face. "If I'm ever going to get a life like in these magazines, we need some real money."

"I'm working my tail off."

"So am I." She shook her head. "But it's not enough. You need to be a vice president or a manager to make the bucks we need."

"Things like that take time."

"Gigi's seven. She needs the best schools. Private schools."

"Since when?" Daddy started driving again. "I'm doing the best I can, Joyce."

I was glad Mama didn't repeat her line "It's not enough" even though I knew she was thinking it. Nothing was enough for Mama. Ever.

After a few miles Mama sat up straight and pointed out the front. "Look! Lights. There must be an accident."

I saw the lights too. Red spinning lights on a cop car and a white van.

The cars on the highway in front of us slowed down and we had to slow down too. There was a blue car upside down in the ditch. People in dark coats were bent over a person in the snow.

"Ewwwww," Mama said. "That one's dead." She pointed to a person lying every which way by the edge of the field. The snow was red.

I sat forward and leaned on the dash to see better. I wasn't interested in the person with the people around them, but the dead one off alone, by themselves. "Why isn't anyone with her?" I asked.

"Because she's dead," Mama said.

"You shouldn't be so blunt," Daddy said. "She's just a kid." Daddy pulled on the back of my coat. "Sit back, Gige."

But I didn't want to sit back. I had to see the person who was dead. "What does *dead* mean?" I asked.

Mama snickered. "Dead, dummy. Not alive. Gone. Outta here."

"Cut it out, Joyce," Daddy said.

"You want me to lie to her? Tell her some baloney story about being asleep, or being up in heaven, or turning into an angel? Give me a break."

"You don't have to be so crude, that's all."

"Where's heaven?" I asked.

Mama snickered again. "Not anywhere near here, so don't think about it."

But I did think about it. If the lady was dead and dead people went to heaven, then heaven had to be close. Didn't it?

The line of cars was moving now, and I got on my knees and turned around to see out the back window. I looked past the lady all crumpled in the red snow and looked for heaven. Shouldn't I be able to see something going on between here and there?

Mama yanked on my coat. "Sit down! Little girls aren't supposed to want to see things like that."

I sat.

"Stupid crash," Mama said. "Now the traffic's all bogged up. Stupid crash."

"They didn't do it to make you mad," Daddy said.

Mama called him a nasty name and told him to shut up.

Mama was right. Heaven wasn't any place close to here.

❧ ❧ ❧

Grammy did just what I'd imagined Grammy would do: she hugged me and even gave me three kisses instead of the one I'd expected. She tried to hug Mama and Daddy, but ended up touching cheeks with them more than giving them a real hug.

The turkey didn't have socks, but the food was yummy. And I could eat pumpkin pie every Thursday from now on.

I'd never seen Mama so helpful. She kept saying, "Let me get that, Grandma" and was between the table and the kitchen a dozen times. At home she always sent me to get things. Grammy seemed glad to let her do it. She looked kinda pale and sank into her chair more than just sat on it.

There was lots of laughing and good talk until Mama brought up the accident we'd seen.

"Don't talk about that," Daddy said.

"There was a dead person in the snow," I said.

"Gigi!"

I hadn't meant to say it, but since Mama had started the whole thing . . .

"I'm sorry to hear that," Grammy said.

"Is there a heaven?" I asked.

Grammy reached across the table and put her hand on mine. "Of course there is."

"Mama says it's no place around here."

Mama's jaw dropped. "I said no such—"

"It isn't," Grammy said. She sat back. "And yet, it is. Heaven doesn't have any boundaries like the walls of a house, or even a neighborhood." She spread her arms wide, crossing them over her head. "It's everywhere."

"You shouldn't tell her things like that," Mama said.

Daddy chimed in. "*You'd* rather not tell her anything."

"As if you have all the answers?"

Daddy looked at Grammy. "I do know a few things about heaven and stuff. I learned 'em. Way back."

Grammy smiled at him. "I know you did. Your parents and I tried to teach you . . ." She looked at me. "So you could teach *your* children."

Daddy took another helping of yams. "These sure are good."

"I could give you the recipe if you'd like," Grammy told Mama.

Mama just sat there, shaking her head. "Who cares about yams?" She sighed loudly. "We've gotten way off track. I brought up the accident because I wanted to make a point." Grammy passed her the cranberry salad. Mama set the bowl down hard, making a bit of cranberry jump over the side. "My point was . . . that one never knows when the end will come. That's why it's so important to have your affairs in order. So your loved ones will be taken care of."

Daddy cleared his throat.

"Well, it's true," Mama said, glancing at him. She passed him the salad. "That poor woman in the snow . . . what will her family do?"

"Do you have a will?" Grammy asked her.

"Us?"

"Have you written a will so Gigi is provided for in case—"

"We're not going to die!" Mama said.

"But you yourself just said one never knows."

Mama tossed her napkin on the table next to her plate. "I wasn't talking about us!"

Everybody was quiet. I heard the furnace kick on and felt a whoosh of warm air creeping up the floor behind my chair. We didn't need it. It was plenty warm.

Then Daddy stood. "I think we'd better go."

"No! I don't want to go!" I said.

Grammy patted my hand again. "Sit down, Jay. There's no reason to leave. I'm not offended." She looked at Mama. "I just wish you'd said it plain. The only thing beating around the bush gets you is a messy yard and sore muscles."

Daddy sat back down and Mama put a hand to her chest. "I wasn't beating—"

"You want to know if I have a will? I do. You want to know whether you're in it? You are. But so is the Plainview Baptist Church, the Red Cross, and a few other charities. Not that I have that much to leave anyone, but I figure you and my grandson are doing just fine. You both have good jobs, and—"

"Not anymore," Mama said.

Daddy shook his head and spoke under his breath. "I can't believe you sometimes."

"You have something to tell me?" Grammy asked Daddy.

He rearranged the fork on his plate. "I lost my job—but I've gotten another one."

"As a gofer for a house builder."

"It pays the bills."

"Hardly."

Daddy stood again and pointed at Mama. "You want too much. Why don't you accept that we are never going to go on fancy vacations, drive new cars, or live in a big house like this."

Mama looked around the room. "You call this big?" She tapped her temple. "This is nothing compared to the house I have in my head."

"I wouldn't dare guess."

"There is nothing wrong with having dreams," Mama said. "Just because you don't have any."

"I have plenty of dreams. I'm just not obsessed with pipe dreams."

"That, you're not. You're just intent on making us live a nightmare."

"What's that supposed to mean?"

Grammy got out of her chair, took my hand, and led me into the kitchen, leaving my parents to duke it out alone.

"They're loud," I said as we moved to sit at the little table by the back porch. From a chair she picked up a red pillow with fringe on it that said Home Sweet Home and held it in her lap.

"I'm sorry you have to hear them."

I glanced toward the swinging door leading to the dining room. "Oh, that's nothing. You should hear 'em when they really get going."

Grammy looked toward the door too and we both listened. There was a deep crease between her eyes. Then she patted her lap and drew me onto it, letting me hug the silky pillow to my chest. Her lap was warm. She smelled like flowers.

"I don't want you to die, Grammy."

I expected her to tell me she wasn't planning on doing any such thing. Instead she talked softly into my hair. "Dying ain't so bad. Not when a person knows where they're going. We're all born to die."

Born to die? What did that mean?

I felt her shake her head, then hold me extra close. "I may not have money to give you, child, but know this: I love you more than anyone in the world, and I want you to know you're special. You're going to do something important someday. It may not change the entire world, but it'll change the world of the people around you. You'll be the good nearby."

"The what?"

"The good nearby. People don't realize good is closer than they think. Good people. Good things. And chances to *do* good." She nodded once. "The good nearby. That's you, Gigi. I know it."

I moved back an inch to look at her. "How do you know it?"

"Because God said so. He said, 'I knew you before I formed you in your mother's womb. Before you were born I set you apart.'"

"Set apart how?"

She looked me right in the eye. My, she had a lot of wrinkles around her eyes. Mama should get her some fancy face cream for Christmas. "That's for God to decide. But you listen to me, child. You grow up, find yourself a wonderful husband, and have beautiful babies. That's a good place to start. You have some babies that have already been set apart in *their* own special way."

I giggled. "Me? Have babies? Grammy, I'm only seven."

"But someday you'll be grown. I want you to be happy, Gigi. I want you to feel your life means something. I want you to have bigger dreams than those of your mama and daddy."

It seemed to me Mama and Daddy had big enough dreams for us all.

She seemed to read my thoughts because she added, "I'm not talking about a fancy house or vacations or bigger cars. I'm not talking about *wanting* more; I'm talking about *giving* more. I'm talking about really big dreams . . . of making a difference in this world. Of being that good nearby because you *can* be. Anyone *can* be, if they keep their eyes open to chances. I want you to take care of the here and now the best you can so you can rest easy in the hereafter." She let me go and gave me one of her special smiles. "I wish big dreams for you, Gi—"

She stopped talking when Mama yelled extra loud, "You don't like the way I'm doing things, then I'll leave. Is that what you want, Jay?"

Grammy pulled my head to her chest, covering my outer ear with a hand. She started rocking and began to sing. "'Abide with me; fast falls the eventide; the darkness deepens; Lord, with me abide!'"

With one ear against her chest and the other covered by her hand, it was like hearing the singing from the inside out. I could listen to her forever. Her voice and the words were like a blanket making me warm and safe. And hugging the Home Sweet Home pillow tight to my chest and peeking out into the pretty red-and-white kitchen with the black-and-white-checkered floors made me feel safer still.

"'When other helpers fail and comforts flee, help of the helpless, O abide with me.'"

She stopped singing but kept rocking and humming the tune. I was glad Mama's and Daddy's voices weren't as loud anymore, yet I was content to let them scream as much as they wanted to as long as I could stay right there in Grammy's lap. Maybe it's good they screamed, for it got me where I was, hearing good things from Grammy, about the good nearby.

"You'll be fine, Gigi. Everything I said will come about because you have Jesus to abide with you. You'll be fine. I know it." She pulled back to look at me and flicked the tip of my nose. "And ninety-six out of a hundred times, I'm right."

Ninety-six! I wanted to believe Grammy. I really did.

❊ ❊ ❊

After spending Thanksgiving at Grammy's and coming all the way back home, I was tired, but I still had trouble getting to sleep—even after hugging the red satin pillow Grammy had given me to take home as my very own Home Sweet Home. I kept thinking about things: the dead lady in the snow, heaven, and Grammy saying she had big dreams for me, that I was going to do something important with my life and be the good nearby. It was like they fit together.

I didn't feel scared about any of it. It was like it was part of a plan that made sense to somebody. Just not to me.

I heard someone in the hall outside my room. "Mama?"

She opened the door wide enough to see inside. "Why aren't you asleep?"

"Can I ask you something?"

"It's late. Ask me in the—"

"Please?"

Mama came in but stood by the door. I saw the glow of her cigarette in the dark. "Hurry up. I got things to do."

I didn't know how to say what I wanted to say. . . . "What's being 'born to die'?"

"What?"

I sat up in bed. "Grammy says everyone is born to die."

Mama took a drag on her cigarette. "Crazy old woman." She let out the smoke.

"But what about that lady we saw today?" I said. "Was she born to die?"

"Don't talk stupid."

I took a deep breath, needing to get it all out at once. "But Grammy said God knew me way before I was born, and I'm going to do something good, and dying's not a bad thing if you know where you're going, and everyone's been born to—"

Mama let out one of her disgusted sighs. "Great. Between you staring at that dead woman at the accident and listening to the wild talk of a senile old woman . . . I suppose you'll have nightmares and wake us up."

I stroked the pillow. "No, I won't. I promise. 'Cause when Grammy talked, she didn't act afraid of the dying part. So I'm not afraid of it either." I remembered something that might make Mama happy. "She said I was special and I was going to do something good and have babies."

Mama snickered.

"She said dying ain't a bad—"

Mama let her air out in a puff. "So you think dying's a good thing?"

I was getting confused. "Well, not all the time, but Grammy has big dreams for me and says I'm going to be the good nearby for some people."

"The what?"

I swallowed hard. How had Grammy explained it? "Good things are nearby if we just look for 'em."

Mama came in the room and looked behind the door, then returned to her spot. "I don't see nothing good."

I hated that she'd made fun of me—and Grammy's words—but I had to finish. "Grammy says I can do something good in my life—and

I want to. But then I keep thinking about heaven and that lady in the snow and—"

She came over to the bed and picked up the red pillow. I was afraid she was going to take it away, but she just looked at it, then tossed it down. "Then stop thinking. That'll take care of it."

I couldn't. Not yet. "Grammy used my number. . . ."

Mama rolled her eyes. "Ninety-six this, ninety-six that. You think that number's magic or something?"

"No, but—"

"No. That's it. No. Now, get to sleep and quit talking crazy." She closed the door on her way out. "The good nearby . . . you find any of it, you let me know."

Her laughter followed her down the hall.

❊   ❊   ❊

Dr. Kordo settled in behind his desk with Mama and Daddy in the chairs in front of him. He'd sent me to the play area in the corner that had blocks, puzzles, and books. I pretended to read a comic book, but I wasn't really reading.

I was listening.

"So?" Mama said. "What's wrong with her?"

Dr. Kordo cleared his throat and picked up a pen. "Gigi is a healthy, happy, normal—extremely bright—child."

I was?

Mama leaned forward in her chair, whispering, "Cut the bull, Doctor. Tell us what's wrong with her."

He pointed the pen at them. "Gigi's a healthy, happy, normal, extremely bright child who is focused on being the good nearby—"

"I hate that phrase. Drives me crazy," Mama said.

"She just wants to do some good in the world," the doctor said.

"As if she can . . ."

The doctor took a deep breath. "Gigi is focused on being the good nearby, on the number ninety-six, and with the thought that she's been born to die."

Mama lifted her hands then let them fall into her lap. "That's it?"

"That's it."

"We knew *that*," Daddy said with a sigh. "I knew coming here was a mistake."

"We wouldn't be here at all except her stupid school is insisting on it," Mama said. "She's telling everybody stuff about ninety-six, and talking about wombs, dreams, God, and that nearby and death stuff, and it's creeping out the other kids. You need to tell us why she's weirded out on us. There's got to be an -*itis*—some name for it."

I didn't like their words. Did they truly think I was weird and creepy?

"There isn't an -*itis*," Dr. Kordo said. "I've never come across anything like this before—and from what I can research, no one else has either."

"But the death part's unnatural," Daddy said. "A kid shouldn't think about death."

"There, you're wrong. Gigi is neither consumed with death, nor morbid about it. In fact, she's got the most healthy attitude about death of anyone I know. We're the ones who are strange. We live our lives fearful and panicked, trying to cheat death, when all along, it is the one fact we all must face, the one fact that we all should be able to embrace and accept. In that way, yes, we all have been born to die. Yet we do everything in our power to push it away, deny it exists."

"She's not normal," Mama says. "And it scares me."

Dr. Kordo leaned forward, making me strain to hear him. "I've spent a lot of time with your daughter, and I can say without hesitation that Gigi is not a child of death but a child of life. The fact that she's come to terms with death could be considered a good thing." He paused and took time to look at each one of them in turn. "She'll be fine. If you let her."

I'd be fine. I'd be fine.

"How do we let her be fine?" Daddy asked.

"You let Gigi be Gigi."

Mama said, "Humph."

Daddy spoke. "But what about her idiotic fascination with ninety-six? Every time that number comes up she acts like she's won the lottery. What's all that about?"

"I have no idea."

"You're no help whatsoever," Mama said.

The doctor continued. "And more importantly, neither does she. When I ask her about it, she merely says, 'It's my number.'"

It was my number.

"That's what she tells us too."

"Then let it be." Dr. Kordo stood. "Take your daughter home. Stop and get some ice cream and make a nice day of it. Read a book together tonight before you tuck her into bed. Then move on. Treat her like you would any child whom you love."

Daddy stood. "Well, this was worthless."

The doctor said, "You have a very special daughter."

Mama stood too, hooked her purse on her shoulder, and waved me over. "Having her be good at math or drawing—something normal— *that* would make her special."

I wished I was good at math or drawing. . . .

I straightened up the comics in a just-right stack, then joined them. We left. I acted all innocent like I hadn't heard a thing. When we got in the elevator I asked, "So, what did the doctor say?"

"He said you're a sick girl and need to stop talking about death and dying." Mama pointed a finger in my face. "And we never want to hear another ninety-six thing again. Understand?"

That's not what the doctor said at all. I wanted to cry.

"Understand?" Mama said again.

I nodded. But in truth, I didn't understand. That . . . or much of anything else. Nothing had been explained. Nothing.

I was a freak.

2

My problems go from bad to worse.
Oh, save me from them all!
PSALM 25:17

Margery Lamborn hated to lie. And yet . . .

What choice did she have?

She looked at her husband as he lathered his face to shave. Mick was waiting for her answer to the question "What are you doing up so early?" As a cocktail waitress at the Chug & Chew she rarely got up before nine.

Except today.

She couldn't risk meeting his eyes so she turned her back to the mirror and folded the bath towel that he'd wadded into the space between towel bar and wall. She adjusted the volume on the radio that sat on the clothes hamper. She didn't need any competition from Kelly Clarkson even if the girl was singing about playing it safe by staying on the sidewalk. Margery could certainly relate to that one.

"I have a few errands," she finally said.

"Don't write any checks. Rent's due."

"I won't."

"Speaking of money . . . can I have twenty from your tip stash? I owe Barry on a football bet."

She hated when Mick bet on sports, because he lost

more than he won. If only he'd realize how hard she worked for that twenty dollars' worth of tips . . . what she put up with. The comments, the hands, the stares as she wore her skimpy bar-girl uniform. And a week ago, the drunk guy who'd pushed her up against her car when she was leaving and nearly—

"Marg? The money?"

She couldn't stall with the towel any longer. She faced him. "Sure. I'll leave it on the dresser."

"Good girl." His hand found her behind and he pulled her close enough to kiss. She pushed away, wiping the shaving cream from her face. So much for her carefully applied lipstick. Mick laughed.

Very funny.

She left the tiny bathroom of their double-wide and headed out before he could ask any more questions. If she'd been smart she would have made the appointment for later in the morning, long after he'd left for his mechanic's job. But when Dr. Quigley, the pharmacist at the drugstore, had said eight, who was Margery to argue?

Margery didn't *do* arguing. "Keep the peace" was her motto. Sometimes she felt as if the bulk of her life were spent in one continuous preventative act—looking ahead, checking the possible outcomes, guessing the consequences, constantly weighing and choosing the path of least resistance so the boat wouldn't be rocked and peaceful waters would cover the earth.

Mick never thought that way. He just lived. He just was. He didn't spend a moment thinking of what he would say, or how she would react to anything he might do. He just did it.

It was upsetting. How dare he coast through life clueless to the delicate balance between trouble and calm? Since he didn't care what effect his actions had on her, why should she care?

But she did. And amid her anger, she often envied him. To be so certain of his space, his identity, his moments . . . Margery took one moment at a time and weighed each one, hoping—just hoping—she'd get it right and wouldn't cause too much trouble *or* be called to suffer through something she'd messed up.

Her habit of walking the baseline made her current road risky. It wasn't that she hadn't looked ahead and imagined Mick's reaction to her trying to get a new job—that was as inevitable as a drunk spilling his drink—and if she told anyone else of her worry, they'd think she was overreacting big-time.

Which she probably was, but so be it.

Fifteen minutes after leaving the house, Margery parked in front of the drugstore, shut off the car, and leaned against the steering wheel, trying to find the courage to open the door and get out. Maybe she should forget the whole thing. Go home. Keep things as they were.

She fumbled putting the keys back in the ignition.

"Margery?"

She put a hand to her chest and sucked in a breath. An older woman with pumpkin-red hair and thick glasses peered in the open passenger window.

"You scared me," Margery said.

"It's a lifelong trait," the woman answered. "If you *are* Margery, I'm Gladys Quigley." She stood up straight, then stooped low again. "Actually, even if you aren't Margery, I'm still Gladys Quigley. Can't escape that if I tried. So now that we know who *I* am . . ."

"I'm Margery. Margery Lamborn."

"Punctual. Two brownie points." She jangled a crowded key chain.

Margery followed the woman inside Neighbor's Drugstore.

Dr. Quigley flipped on the lights. "Follow me to the office. We'll chat back there."

The office was tiny and contained a metal desk with a computer, two chairs, and a four-drawer file cabinet. What made it unusual were the travel posters that lined the room floor to ceiling, covering every inch of wall like wallpaper. Venice ran into Paris, which butted up to the Alps, with half of Mozambique cut off at the ceiling.

"You like?"

Margery turned full circle in order to see every wall. "Have you been to all these places?"

"Most." She pointed to the upper corner above the file cabinet. "Still working on Australia and New Zealand. If only they weren't so drattedly far away. Thirty-three hours on the plane. Though I love to fly, that one's pushing even my tolerance button. I mean, how many movies and pretzels can a person tolerate?"

"Movies?"

"On the plane. They'd probably show four. Maybe five."

"I didn't know they had movies on airplanes. 'Course, I've never been on a plane at all."

"You afraid of flying or something?"

"I don't think so. I just haven't had the chance to go anywhere."

"Anywhere *yet*," Dr. Quigley said. "You'll have a chance one of these days. If you make it a priority."

Priorities were rent, utilities, and food. Margery couldn't see how travel for fun would ever override any of that. Especially now since she was applying for a job as a checkout clerk that would mean a cut in pay. She and Mick would never have a better life if she took a step backward like this. Maybe the Chug & Chew wasn't so bad . . .

Suddenly full of doubt, Margery took a step toward the door. "I'm sorry, Dr. Quigley, but I've changed my mind. I can't apply for this job after all. I'm sorry for taking your time and—"

Dr. Quigley signaled time-out. "Whoa there, girl. What happened in the last five seconds that's making you run? I didn't scare you that bad, did I?"

Margery stopped in the doorway. "No, it's just that . . ." She ran a hand along the doorjamb.

"Out with it."

She didn't want to explain. She didn't even know this woman, though she sensed she might *like* to know her. "I really can't go into it."

"Oh pooh." Dr. Quigley pulled the guest chair close and patted it. "Sit. Though people have accused me of going over my allotted words per lifetime, I do know how to listen if I've a mind to. Which I do right now. So take advantage of it, girl. Sit and tell me what's going on."

To leave now would be rude. Besides, if Gladys Quigley had been around the world, maybe she knew a thing or two about life. What could it hurt? Margery was always open to suggestions.

She sat down and Dr. Quigley took a seat in the wheeled desk chair. "All right. Step one completed. Now fire away. How about starting out by telling me why you wanted to apply for this job in the first place."

Margery hesitated. Why *did* she want this job? "I . . . I like people."

"That's a job-interview answer. I want a real one."

Put off guard, Margery dug out the truth. "I want to quit my other job. I want a regular job."

"This other job is irregular?"

Margery looked past Dr. Quigley and focused on the Eiffel Tower. "I'm a cocktail waitress at the Chug & Chew."

"Can't say as I've partaken of their cuisine."

"Burgers, nachos, beer . . ."

"And . . . ?"

Margery sensed Dr. Quigley wasn't wanting an extended menu. "And skimpy outfits, guys hitting on me, me coming home smelling like booze and smoke, long hours, and never seeing Mick."

Dr. Quigley pulled Margery's left hand close and peered at the ring finger. "Mick's your boyfriend?"

"Husband."

She pointed at Margery's vacant ring finger. "No ring."

"We were only seventeen. There wasn't money for a ring."

Dr. Quigley's eyebrows rose. "You're a ways from seventeen now."

"I'm twenty-seven."

"There hasn't been a chance for him to get you a ring in ten years?"

It was a sore point that went far beyond lack of money. "He says he's bought me one."

"Where is it?"

Margery looked at the Roman Colosseum. If only she could escape there right now . . . "He has it. He told me he has it. He just hasn't found the right time to give it to me yet." *I haven't earned it yet.*

Dr. Quigley rubbed her forehead. "I'm guessing a discussion regarding your husband's lack of romantic skills would best be held another time. Let's get back to your job at the bar. You want to quit."

"I do. But I make decent money—with the tips." She looked at the purse in her lap. The stitching on the strap was coming out. "This job here . . . from what you said on the phone, this job pays less." She looked up and offered a smile. She didn't want to offend. "But it does have normal hours. I'm hoping Mick would like that." She shrugged, knowing he wouldn't care. "I'm hoping."

"How's your eyesight?"

It seemed an odd question, but maybe it had something to do with Dr. Quigley's thick glasses. "It's good. Real good."

The woman studied her, as if thinking things through. "To be honest it's not like I've had a lot of applicants. And if you've been handling the punks and jerks at the Chug & Chew I figure you can handle the normal folk who come in here for TUMS, film, and prescriptions. I like the idea of getting you away from that place. What if I pay you a bit above what I quoted before? How about eight bucks an hour to start? We'll talk about getting more after you've proven yourself."

Margery wanted to cry. She shook Dr. Quigley's hand vigorously. "I won't let you down. I won't."

"I know you won't, and call me Gladys. Later, you'll meet Bernice, the other checkout clerk, and King. He's my partner and fellow pharmacist."

"King?"

Gladys rolled her eyes. "Dr. King Marlowe. He doesn't like the name much, but in his own way, it suits him. Not that he's high-and-mighty. Just the opposite. There's not a more down-to-earth, dependable partner than King. He's a widower with a son in college. Why another woman hasn't snagged him is a mystery he'd prefer I stop trying to solve—though I do my part by connecting him with eligibles."

"How old is he?" Margery asked.

Gladys smiled. "And here I thought you were married."

"I—" Margery felt herself blush—"I'm sorry. I shouldn't have asked."

"Oh, ask away; there are few secrets round here. King is fifty." She paused a moment. "Seems he pretty much spans the difference between your twenty-seven and my sixty-five. You'll like him. Most do." She stood. "Now, back to the basics . . . the hours vary, but most evenings we'll get you home to have dinner with your darling hubby. Can you start today?"

"Now?"

"Now is always good."

She had a job. A regular nine-to-five job.

Mick would be furious.

❈ ❈ ❈

Gladys filled the prescription and was just putting it into the envelope for pickup when King walked in.

"What are you doing here?" she asked.

He started to take off his jacket. "I work here."

"Not in the mornings, you don't."

He shrugged and put his jacket back on. "You want me to leave, I'll—"

"Don't be silly. Work your fanny off; that's up to you."

Lately King had been coming in above and beyond the times when they'd decided he would be in charge. Not that she minded his company, but . . .

Actually, this morning Gladys was glad to see him. She wanted to hear all the juicy details about his blind date last night—a date Gladys had arranged. Mandy Thomason: pretty, witty, and successful. Combined with King's qualifications—handsome, witty, and successful—they'd surely hit it off.

She waited until he'd hung up his jacket. "Well?"

"Well what?"

"How was it?"

"How was what?"

She groaned. "Don't make me work for it."

"Work for—"

"King! Your date. How was your date with Mandy?"

He slipped a white pharmacy coat over his plaid shirt. "It didn't happen."

"Why not?"

"I called it off."

Gladys made a dramatic show of finding a stool to catch her as her legs gave out in shock. "Why would you do a dumb thing like that? She's a beautiful woman. She's smart, funny . . ."

He grinned. "What do I need with her? I have a beautiful, smart, funny woman right here."

She crossed her arms. "Very funny. Honestly, why didn't you go?"

"Since you've handily ignored the main reason, you're making me resort to reason number two: I don't want to date. I don't want a girl-friend. I don't want a woman who's looking to become a wife."

"But Carla's been gone five years. And Jason's off at college now. You're in that house alone."

"You're in your house alone."

"Because I choose to be. I was never married. I never had what you had."

"*Had* being the key word. My life with Carla was wonderful. God was very generous to give me such a great wife then, and a great son now. I'm not going to be greedy and want more, nor am I going to try to re-create what was." He buttoned the last button on his white coat. "So, Dr. Quigley, I'd appreciate it if you close up your yenta shop."

She stood and pushed the stool out of the way. "You're no fun."

"You know that's not true."

She whipped toward him. "Exactly! Which is why I'm trying to get you to share the wealth."

He took hold of her upper arms. "I'm fine, Gladys. Really. I like my life. I like working here with you."

But he was such a catch. It was such a waste.

"Changing the subject, which desperately needs changing . . . what are you working on, Red?"

Only he could call her that.

Gladys pointed at the pills for Bonnie Philips, then nodded toward the stack of prescriptions left to fill. "It's not that busy."

King picked up the filled prescription. Then he looked at the doctor's note that she'd put in the basket. "Gladys . . . this isn't right."

"What do you mean?"

He held the bottle close. "The prescription says Zyrtec. This is Zyprexa."

"No . . ." Gladys adjusted her glasses. If she angled them just right she could see the mistake. This was not good. Zyrtec was an ordinary antihistamine, and Zyprexa was a potent antipsychotic with lots of side effects. Both were 10 mg—at least she'd gotten that right.

But she couldn't kid herself.

This could have been a catastrophe.

She took the bottle back. "I would have caught it." *But I wouldn't have. I was ready to put it in the bag.*

"Are your eyes bothering you again?"

"They are never bothering me, young man. They are what they are. And I always double- and even triple-check the prescriptions before they go out. If you think you're pulling a George Bailey on me, implying I'm Mr. Gower filling a prescription with poison, I'll give your ears a boxing just like Mr. Gower gave George." She assumed he was familiar with the movie *It's a Wonderful Life*.

"I'm not accusing you. I'm your partner. I'm just trying to help. And if your eyes—"

"I'm fine." *But I'm not fine and that was way too close.* Gladys shoved the twinge of fear away. To deflect the conversation she pointed into the main part of the store toward Margery. "Do you see we have a new clerk? Her name's Margery Lamborn. She started today."

They watched as Margery worked the register. "Thank you, Mrs. Connors. You'll like that shampoo. I promise."

If Margery could handle Adele Connors, she could handle anyone.

"Will it make my hair shiny like yours?" Mrs. Connors asked.

Truth be told, Adele's hair had stopped being shiny twenty years ago.

"If you don't like it, you bring it back and I'll personally give you a refund."

Oh dear. One didn't offer save-a-dime-save-a-dollar Adele a way to get something for free.

"I'll do that," Adele said.

I bet you will.

"Have a good one," Margery said.

"Refunds?" King said to Gladys. "Since when do we do money-back guarantees on shampoo?"

Gladys leaned through the pharmacy window. "Margery? Can you come here a minute?"

Margery came close. "Yes?"

"It's probably not wise to offer someone their money back. Especially Adele Connors."

"But it's good shampoo. And it does make hair shiny, and she was wanting something to make her hair look better and—"

"Her hair can't look any better," Gladys said. "Glum and dour. That's Adele's personality *and* her looks." Gladys had a fleeting thought that perhaps she was being unfair. Maybe the woman was softening in her old age.

Nah.

"Just watch the refund offers, okay?" Gladys turned to King and made the introductions. He and Margery shook hands.

"Glad to have you with us, Margery," King said.

"Me too. I'll try to make you proud." She started to leave, then turned back. "I was wondering if it would be all right if I made a new display in the cosmetics section? Maybe use some of those cute cosmetic bags with the fall leaves on them and a few pieces of jewelry?"

Gladys was impressed. "Have at it, girl. I give you free rein."

Margery was going to work out just fine.

Gladys's eyes were another matter.

❊ ❊ ❊

Gennifer Mancowitz slipped into work as unobtrusively as possible— as she did every Monday, Wednesday, and Friday when she came in late. Gennifer was a lawyer at Chasen, Grieb, and Caldwell. A good lawyer.

A good lawyer who had a secret. But didn't everybody?

Although her coworkers—and even her bosses—knew she would be late on these days, she always made her entrance as discreet as possible: once out of the elevators, she took the right aisle around the center island of paralegals and office managers, past her bosses' offices—which were always empty because they religiously met with each other on M-W-F mornings in the east conference room. Until 9:15. Gennifer had perfected her entrance to take place between 9:08 and 9:09. By the time they were done with their meeting she was deeply engrossed in work at her desk. She had the whole thing down to a science—which suited her just fine. She had enough iffiness in her life. What she could control she *did* control.

One office, two offices . . . just one to go.

"Gennifer, would you come in here a moment?"

At the sound of her boss's voice she suffered a surge of adrenaline.

She went inside Charles Chasen's office, her mind racing with reasons why he was there at this time of day, as well as wondering why he would want to talk to her. She usually dealt with Kyle Grieb—*after* safely slipping into work.

Chasen tossed his pen on the desk and leaned back in his leather chair. "I hear you've refused to be in court Friday at eight."

Her heart did a double flip. "*Refused* is a pretty strong word, sir. I *can't* be there at eight."

"*Can't* is a pretty strong word."

Gennifer wasn't sure what to say—which for a lawyer was not a good thing.

Chasen retrieved the pen and tapped it on his hand. "I guess my main question is whether you *can't* or you *won't?*"

More semantics. "I have morning commitments three days a week that prevent me from getting to work—or court—before nine. It's been this way for a year now."

He looked at his watch. "It's 9:10."

Exactly. Which begs the question of why you are in your office. "Excuse me. I'm not available until 9:10."

When he leveled her with a look, Gennifer had a flash of fear that she'd come off as too defensive—which considering she was a defense lawyer, was appropriate. In court.

"You mentioned commitments. What kind of commitments? If you don't mind my asking."

I do mind. But in response she brought forward the excuse she'd been using. "My daughter has special needs. She goes to the tutor first thing on those mornings. I drop her off at school and then come to work."

His right eyebrow rose. "How old is she now?"

"Seventeen."

"Does she drive?"

Oops. "Yes, but . . ." Gennifer hated to extend the lie but he was giving her no choice. "She can. But she doesn't have a car."

"Your life will be simplified when she does."

"I suppose." She risked one last comment. "When the time comes."

Chasen sat forward and pulled a file front and center. "Partners need to be available, Gennifer."

Partners? The carrot was suitably dangled. "Yes, sir."

He didn't say she was dismissed, but merely opened the file and began to read. She slipped out; her heart was racing. When her thrice-weekly dialysis had first started she'd thought her story about Sarah and a tutor was the perfect excuse—especially in a firm that embraced education. The fact that Sarah *had* her own car and was doing fine in school without *any* tutor . . . what was she going to do now? Chasen clearly expected Gennifer to be more readily available to the firm. *"Partners need to be available, Gennifer."* The implication was clear.

Yet coming up with a new excuse for her dialysis schedule wouldn't be easy, or even feasible.

As she passed her secretary's desk, Mary looked up and asked, "Is something wrong?"

Just everything. Gennifer pasted on a smile. "Not a thing."

She went into her office and quietly closed the door, took her seat, and tried to wait out the pounding in her chest.

She noticed the flip calendar where she'd painstakingly written *Sarah—Tutoring* in the first space on every Monday, Wednesday, and Friday. She tore off today's sheet and proceeded to dissect it into long strips. Then crosswise strips, then small squares.

Before she realized what she'd done, she'd created a pile of confetti. *I don't even remember tearing off the page. . . .*

It wasn't surprising. Subterfuge was new to her. It had *not* been a part of her life until a year ago when her kidneys had given out. Nor was it the norm for sufferers of kidney disease. Most patients didn't try to keep their dialysis a secret. Most people let others know about whatever disease was racking their bodies. Most people let others *in*.

She was not most people. Never had been, and wasn't about to start now.

Logic said that people *would* help. They wouldn't think badly of her just because her kidneys were bad. Surely she could trust her friends and family.

But what if she couldn't? What if they started treating her differently, making her feel sicker than she was by their pity routine? Since she wasn't completely sure how they'd react she didn't dare risk it. Just as you couldn't unring a bell, you couldn't untell a secret. Hence,

Gennifer's thrice-a-week trips to the dialysis center at 4:30 in the morning were necessary. Get it done before the world was up.

And before she had to be at work.

Until this morning it had been so far so good. *She* was good. She was superwoman. *Hear me roar.*

Wanting to maintain her superwoman status was the main reason Gennifer hadn't told even her family about this flaw in her health. It wasn't that they wouldn't have given her sympathy or supported her. Douglas was a good husband and seventeen-year-old Sarah was a good child. Good, good, good. The trait was epidemic in the Mancowitz household.

Her husband and daughter were not the main cause of her keeping the secret. The problem lay in her nearly obsessive revulsion to feeling out of control. There was no way she could show them her weakness. She'd spent way too many years establishing her competence and self-sufficiency. She couldn't throw that away. At least not yet. Not until it was absolutely necessary.

As it was, she was handling things. She had fit the dialysis into her schedule with neither work nor family the wiser. She'd adjusted her eating habits with nary a comment. And she'd even finagled things so Douglas had not seen the implanted port in her arm. All of this gave her yet another reason to be proud of her ability to run things her way.

Her intercom buzzed. "Call on line one, Ms. Mancowitz," Mary said.

"Thank you." Gennifer pulled out her trash can and with a swift swipe of her hand, swept the confetti debris out of sight.

If only the current problem could be handled as easily.

· Her life was complicated. But it worked.

Yet as she told herself that lie, an oft-repeated truth wagged its finger: *What a wicked web we weave when first we practice to deceive.*

One of these days she'd get caught and would have to come clean.

But not today.

❀ ❀ ❀

Angie Schuster paused before opening the door of her SUV in order to check her lipstick in the rearview mirror. Not that the people at the city shelter cared whether her face was on just so as long as the back of her car was filled with donations, but being well-groomed was not a habit she felt compelled to break. Years ago, her husband, Stanford, had informed her that her facial features completely washed out without lipstick, so she had made every effort to honor his tutelage and direction by being properly made-up on every occasion.

Satisfied her Coral Reef lipstick was not spotting her teeth, she slipped the car keys into the small shoulder bag that bisected her chest from shoulder to hip, and got out of the car. On the way to the entrance she passed two disheveled men smoking cigarettes. Such a nasty habit. It wasn't good for them. Stanford had stopped recently—though certainly not because of *her* influence.

"Good afternoon, gentlemen," she said with a nod.

Their foreheads dipped a bit in confusion. One nodded, then looked away. The other said, "Hey."

Then, at the last minute the Hey Man rushed toward the door and opened it for her.

"Why, thank you," she said.

He beamed.

Angie loved when the goodness in people burst out. Although she often worked with those who were down-and-out, she refused to adjust her actions to their level. Raise them up. That was the way to change the world. That's what Stanford had done with her.

Once inside, Angie looked for Josh Cashinski, the man in charge of the shelter. She saw him by the pass-through window of the kitchen, giving instructions to a bearded man with long stringy hair. The white cleaning rag in the man's hand was in stark contrast to the dirt and drudge of his grooming. Was it a flag of hope that would lead him out of the hole he'd been living in? Such thoughts fueled her. Hope. It was all about hope.

Josh saw her and quickly finished his conversation in order to greet her with a customary hug—which, considering the muscles in his torso looked like he could be the poster boy for a gym, was like receiving a hug from a grizzly. "Angie, oh reigning queen of compassion."

She pointed at a red stain on his gray T-shirt. "Marinara?"

"What can I say? The cook's recipes are rubbing off on me. Literally."

"It's not your own recipe?"

"Me? Cook? Joe does the cooking. I stir. And open the cans." With a fingernail, he attempted to chip away at the edge of the stain. "What can I do for you today, Angie?"

"I come bearing gifts." She crooked her finger at him, led him out to her vehicle, and opened the back of the SUV. "Blankets," she said. "I found a good sale on fleece and put a binding on them. Since it's fall, I thought you'd be needing them."

Josh fingered the piles. "There must be two dozen."

"Twenty-eight," she said. She pulled out a pink one, patterned with teal stripes. "I hope some of these aren't too garish. But I thought they were pretty. Some of the homeless women might like them."

"They'll love them." He put his arm around her shoulders. "Once again, you are my Lady of the Good Deed."

"Only giving a bit of what I've got, m'lord."

Josh moved to the curb and called to the two smoking men. "Jordie? Rashaun? Come help."

Hey Man flicked his cigarette away immediately, while the other took one last drag before coming forward.

"Take a gander at these blankets Mrs. Schuster made for you guys. Aren't they wonderful?"

Hey Man fingered the edge of a navy one then looked at Angie. "You made these? For us?"

"You like that one? It's yours. It's very long," she explained. "I made some of them a good eight feet long, with a tall man like you in mind."

The man's eyebrows touched each other, and he nodded but seemed unable to say anything.

Josh broke the moment. "Consider that one yours, Jordie. Now, let's get these inside so Mrs. Schuster can be on her way."

The three men took all the blankets in one trip. Angie held the shelter door for them but did not follow them inside. She hurried back to her car. She didn't want to risk another thank-you from Jordie. She'd cry; she knew she would.

She pulled away, but in her side mirror spotted Jordie coming back outside. He spotted her, took a few steps toward her car, and raised an arm.

She looked away. *I know, I know. You're welcome.*

More. She needed to do more.

※ ※ ※

Talia Soza strapped her two-year-old son into the car seat after picking him up at the sitter's. "How was your day, sweetie?"

Tomás bounced in his seat. "Hop! Hop!"

"You learned how to hop today?"

"Bunny hop!"

"Very good. When we get home you can hop for Papa."

"Hop! Hop! Papa hop!"

No, Papa won't hop. They'd be lucky if her husband got out of his recliner. It wasn't Nesto's fault. He had a congenital heart defect that his own father had suffered from—and died of—when he was only forty-two.

Nesto was thirty-five.

As Talia drove home she mentally rummaged through the refrigerator. The October day was cold so soup would be good. Taco soup even better. She thought they had half of the last batch she'd made in the freezer. She'd whip up some Jiffy corn bread. Tomás had devoured three pieces last time she'd made it—though Talia realized the toddler probably liked the honey more than the bread itself. In that respect he wasn't much different from Talia, who only used french fries as a way to eat ketchup, and lettuce as a vehicle to scoop up ranch dressing.

Her mind moved on to the other to-dos of the evening. There was laundry to finish, the living-room carpet needed a daily vacuuming for Nesto's sake, and there was new weather stripping to put on the front door. Last weekend during a cold snap they'd practically had a wind coming through. They couldn't afford to have Nesto catch cold.

They couldn't afford a lot of things. Ever since Nesto had been told to quit his job as the foreman of a six-man landscaping crew (on doctor's orders), Talia had been forced to reenter the workforce, something she'd not wanted to do. Ever. She loved being a stay-at-home mom. It was enough for her. Plenty. But now, doing the housework, taking care of her family, plus working full-time outside the home . . . the gloss had been rubbed off the homemaker title.

Talia was the assistant to the events coordinator at the Royal Park Hotel. She was highly *un*qualified—except for her waitressing experience back in high school and a short stint in retail management before she'd gotten married. But she had hit it off with the head honcho, Wade Hampton, and had somehow ended up being hired.

She enjoyed her job. Sometimes. Yet the hours and the responsibility, added to the hours and the responsibility of taking care of Tomás and Nesto, and the house, and the yard, and the bills, and, and, and . . .

And a new baby on the way. Talia patted her seven-months'-pregnant belly, forced the pity party aside until it could do some good, and pulled into the driveway.

Life called.

🥀 🥀 🥀

It was weird being home for dinner. Margery was used to leaving for work at the Chug & Chew at four and never getting home until after 1 a.m. Even on her nights off she and Mick rarely sat down and ate a meal together. She wasn't sure whose fault that was, but heating something from the fridge and eating in front of the TV was the norm. And more often than not, Mick had a reason he couldn't come straight home after work at the garage. She'd asked why a few times, but he'd never given her a straight answer. She'd had to be satisfied with "stuff."

But she *wasn't* satisfied. Not that there was much she could do about it.

Margery checked the pasta water she'd put on to boil, then dipped a spoon into the red sauce in the other pot and stirred. She'd positioned the empty Ragu jar at the bottom of the trash can, not wanting Mick to see that the dinner wasn't made from scratch. Not that he'd taste the difference, but sometimes Mick was weird that way. It was best to cover the bases, think ahead. So much of her life was spent anticipating what *might* happen if she did or didn't do thus and so.

She glanced at the tiny kitchen table set for two. Although they didn't own china, she'd dug out the two wineglasses Mick had stolen from the Chug & Chew the first time he'd gone in while she was working. And she'd folded each paper napkin into a fan shape and set them under the forks. She'd even lit a vanilla candle. It was as nice as she could make it. She'd even made Mick his favorite strawberry Jell-O cheesecake. *Food soothes the savage beast?*

That didn't seem exactly right.

Music. Music soothes the savage beast.

Toward that end Margery moved to the stereo and looked through the CDs. Mick's favorites were Gretchen Wilson or Hank Williams, but she wanted music without words. Romantic background music. She walked her fingers over the CD titles, stopping on a Mannheim Steamroller disk: *Fresh Aire V.* It had been years since she'd played it.

Once the music started she took a quick detour to the bathroom to check her hair and makeup. Today at work at the drugstore she'd splurged and purchased some new light orange Passion lipstick from the cosmetics display she'd created. Her peachy lips looked nice. But her eyes looked old. Tired.

She smoothed her hair, which was pulled into a low ponytail. She never wore it down anymore. Quick and easy, out of the way. Maybe she should get it cut off in one of those flippy-dippy styles people wore.

Mick would kill her. He liked it long and made rude comments about women with short hair. At least he used to like long hair. She couldn't remember him saying much of anything about her hair lately. Or her looks. Or . . .

She let her hand fall. She couldn't remember the last time he'd said anything nice to her.

Leave. Just leave.

Margery saw her reflection shake its head. This wasn't the first time she'd had such a thought. The urge to walk out came in waves. Sometimes she thought about it daily, and other times she could go weeks without considering such a thing. Did other wives think such thoughts? Most of the friends she had at the bar were divorced. The owner was on his third wife. Ten years was a good run, wasn't it?

But I want a baby.

She pulled the fabric of her flowered skirt tight over her belly, imagining it plump with child. There'd been a baby there once. A baby conceived out of wedlock, but no other since they'd made things legal.

How ironic that the baby they hadn't wanted turned out to be the only one they'd had.

Or nearly had. The baby had been born too soon—on their wedding day. Another irony. To get married because of a baby and then suddenly to *not* have that baby.

I should have left back then.

Such thoughts did no good. She had to think of the present. Of the future. If they had a baby, things would be better.

Yet not having a child didn't seem to bother Mick. Margery ached from the need of it. Having a baby would be proof she existed, proof there was a reason she was here in the first place. She couldn't think of anything else she'd done that was worth mentioning. *Margery Lamborn, wife of Mick, clerk at Neighbor's Drug.*

Whoop-de-do.

There had to be more to life than this.

She heard a popping sound from the kitchen and ran to the stove. The tomato sauce was sending volcanic bursts over the top of the pan. She turned the heat down and stirred, relieved it wasn't burned at the bottom.

Mick's truck pulled into the driveway and Margery's stomach clenched. *Help. Please help it go okay.*

He came inside, making the door hit the closet behind it. She could gauge his mood by whether or not the door hit the closet.

"Hi, hon," she said, presenting herself in the living room. She hoped to catch him for a hello kiss on his way to the bedroom to change. But since that was not the usual scenario, when she came close, he balked, then gave her a once-over.

"Why aren't you at work?"

"I—"

"And what are you so dressed up for?"

She put on her best smile. "I got a new job. Started today."

He stopped unbuttoning his blue mechanic's shirt with MICK embroidered on the pocket. "You're working two jobs?"

She never imagined he'd think that. "No . . ."

"Surely you didn't quit the Chug?"

"I did. I—"

"Why would you do a dumb thing like that?"

Needing distance, she walked toward the kitchen, then remembered the dinner. She turned back to him, trying the smile again. "I want us to spend more time together, Mick. Eat together. Spend evenings together."

"I like things the way they are."

She didn't know what to say. "But . . . but we don't see each other."

He shrugged. *He shrugged!* As if it didn't matter? She wanted to flail at him, beat his chest, and demand he take the shrug back. Demand he care about this marriage as much as she did.

Instead she said, "I made us a special dinner." She presented the set table as a game-show prize.

"What is it?"

"Spaghetti. And salad. And garlic bread."

He pointed to the glasses. "You blew money on wine? You know I don't like wine."

"You can have beer in yours." She opened the fridge, presenting the topper. "I also made a Jell-O cheesecake."

"Strawberry?"

Her stomach relaxed. "Of course."

Mick pulled his shirt out an inch. "How long till dinner?"

"Ten minutes?"

He nodded and headed for his usual shower.

This would work. It had to.

※ ※ ※

Margery was glad when Mick turned over because the movement stopped his snoring. When she couldn't sleep his snoring was salt on her wounded nerves.

Although the romantic evening had ended as she'd intended, getting there had been like traveling a rutted road. Just when she'd thought things were moving along smoothly, Mick would say something that jarred them into a pothole.

He was mad about her quitting the Chug & Chew—but not for the reason she'd expected. She'd braced herself for an argument about the wage difference, but Mick had skimmed over that and had focused on the fact that she would now be home in the evenings. It had taken a good five minutes of back-and-forth for her to pinpoint the reason for his objection, but finally he'd come out with it.

"I like having time alone, Marg. Is that plain enough for you?"

Too plain. Yet not plain enough. Why did he like having time alone?

"Can't a man have a moment to himself?"

"Sure, but—"

"Too much togetherness can be a bad thing."

And not enough togetherness can kill a marriage.

Mick started snoring again. She extended a hand to nudge him into silence, but stopped short.

What good would it do? Mick would do what Mick wanted to do when Mick wanted to do it.

She wrapped her pillow around her ears and sought the oblivion of sleep.

3

*We pleaded with you, encouraged you, and urged you to live
your lives in a way that God would consider worthy.
For he called you to share in his Kingdom and glory.*

I THESSALONIANS 2:12

I put the brand-new box of crayons at the top of my desk
and positioned the piece of paper just so. The teacher had
told us to draw a picture of something we'd done during
the summer.

There was something so special about a brand-new piece
of paper with nothing on either side. The paper Mama let
me draw on usually had typing on one side, making all my
drawings look smudgy with lines peeking through like cross-
outs. We had to be real careful with money now. That's just
the way it was, and I'd better get used to it.

I looked across the aisle and saw that Mary Margaret
was drawing a picture of a swimming pool.

I'd never been swimming.

Sitting in front of Mary Margaret, Timmy was drawing
a picture of horses. I'd never seen a horse—except on TV.

On my other side, Eddie was drawing a house.

We had a different house now. We'd had to move. I
didn't have my own room anymore. I shared it with Daddy's office. He'd quit his gofer job a few months ago when

he got a nail in his foot and it got infected and he couldn't walk. Now, he was trying to sell stuff on the phone. He slammed it down a lot.

I took out the red crayon. I wasn't sure what I would draw with it, but since it was my favorite color . . . what could I draw about my summer?

The move. But that wasn't anything special. In the last year we'd moved a lot. When I heard "Rent's due. Come on, Gigi, time to move," I got out my two brown boxes and filled one with clothes and one with everything else I wanted to keep. I always made room for Grammy's satin pillow.

Last Christmas Grammy had also given me a dollhouse she'd found at a garage sale, but Mama made me give it away because it didn't fit into my everything-else box. "One pickup load is all we can take. You know that."

I knew that. And so I'd given the dollhouse (with a pink plastic washing machine and a blue plastic toilet) to a girl named Laurie who lived two blocks down. Laurie had lived in that one house all eight years of her life. I couldn't imagine.

I felt real bad giving away the present Grammy had given me. I never told her about it. Nothing—but nothing—would make me hurt Grammy's feel—

Grammy! That was the special thing I did last summer!

I looked at the pretty red crayon. As much as I liked it, it wasn't right for the picture I was going to draw, so I pulled the brown crayon out of the box and started.

Mrs. Taylor walked up and down the rows of desks, stopping to say, "That's very pretty, Diane," or "Did you go to the mountains, Mike? How fun." I hurried to get my picture started so Mrs. Taylor would say something nice about my drawing.

I drew a long rectangle, then realized I *could* use the red crayon to draw Grammy's dress. I colored fast, wishing there were a flesh-colored crayon so I could fill in Grammy's face. All I could do was outline it in black, coloring what should have been her gray hair black too, because there was no gray crayon in the box. I wondered what color Grammy's hair really was before she'd got old. I couldn't remember seeing any pictures, and without them, I couldn't imagine Grammy young. She was *Grammy*.

Mrs. Taylor stopped right between me and Mary Margaret and asked her, "Do you like to swim?"

I positioned my paper so Mrs. Taylor would get a good look.

The teacher turned my way. But instead of a question or a "You're a good artist, Gigi," Mrs. Taylor took the drawing. Was she going to show the whole class? My heart beat really fast. Maybe Mrs. Taylor would put it on the front bulletin board. Mrs. Garcia, my first-grade teacher, had done that with nice art projects—but only did it to mine once.

"Gigi? Please come with me."

Having me go up to the front of the class while she made a big to-do about the picture was too much. I didn't like being up front. Besides, I wasn't finished.

Mary Margaret poked Timmy in the shoulder and they whispered as I walked by. Mrs. Taylor didn't stop near the bulletin board. With her hand on my back, she led me into the hall.

Only bad kids got sent to the hall. Everybody knew that.

We walked halfway between our second-grade room and the third-grade room. Finally, Mrs. Taylor stopped and held the drawing in front of her stomach. "What's this, Gigi?"

"It's a picture."

"Don't be impertinent. What's in the picture?"

"My grammy."

Mrs. Taylor sighed. "What's your grammy lying in?"

"A box."

Mrs. Taylor rolled her eyes. "A casket. It's a coffin, right?"

Yes, that was the word Daddy had used. "Daddy wanted it to have satin lining, but Mama said it was a waste of money." I sighed. "I know Grammy would've liked satin. She had a pillow that was shiny like satin. She gave it to me. I still have it. I'll always have it." I put a hand to my cheek. I wanted satin in my casket someday. But red, not white.

Mrs. Taylor bit the inside of her cheek like she was thinking real hard. I didn't interrupt. I'd learned the hard way not to do that. Mama's ring had left a mark on my cheek once. I glanced at Mrs. Taylor's hands. She had two rings.

Mrs. Taylor squatted down to my level. "I'm sorry your grammy died, Gigi."

"Oh, it's okay. Grammy told me everybody is born to die, but it's okay if you know where you're going. And she told me the last time I saw her that she was bound for glory, so I know that's where she is." I didn't know exactly where "glory" was, but I didn't tell Mrs. Taylor that.

And Mrs. Taylor didn't ask, which must have meant that she knew where it was anyway. "It's a very nice picture, Gigi, but you were supposed to draw something special you did last summer. Something good special."

I didn't understand. Dying wasn't a bad thing. Especially since Grammy had died when she was ninety-six years old. That made it all right. That made it perfect.

Then Mrs. Taylor did something that nearly made me scream out loud: she folded the drawing in half. Folded the perfectly good piece of paper—with no typing on the back and no wrinkles in it—in half. Creased it between her fingers.

I wanted to cry and held out my hand to save the picture, but my teacher held it just out of reach. "Why don't you go back and draw something else about your summer."

"Like what?"

"Something special. Good special. I'll give you a brand-new piece of paper."

I agreed—in order to get a fresh piece of paper.

I drew a horse like the one in Timmy's picture—even though I'd never seen one in person. I put a red bow in its hair.

4

We can rejoice, too, when we run into problems and trials,
for we know that they help us develop endurance.
And endurance develops strength of character,
and character strengthens our confident hope of salvation.

ROMANS 5:3-4

"This is Douglas. I can't answer your call right now; please leave a—"

Gennifer's thumb pushed the Off button on her cell phone. What good were cell phones if her husband had his off more than on? Yes, he was in meetings; yes, he was often out of range in some obscure podunk town that needed the paper products he sold (as well as more cell towers), but the point was, when Gennifer needed him she needed him. Period.

Gennifer's boss, Charles Chasen, hadn't mentioned her late arrivals again, but she knew something had to change. Every day that went by without further comment from her superior made her nervous. Maybe he wouldn't ask next time. Maybe he'd just fire her.

After trying Douglas for the fifth time she stared at the phone. What was she doing? Douglas couldn't help her come up with a new excuse for her late-arrival times at work because *he* didn't know about her dialysis either. She had to figure this one out on her own.

But what else was new? Truth be told, that *was* her preference.

The intercom on her desk startled her. "Someone from Visa on line one, Ms. Mancowitz."

"Thanks, Mary." Gennifer picked up the line. "This is Gennifer Mancowitz."

"This is a courtesy call from your Mid-State Visa. We've seen some unusual activity on your card and we wanted to verify it's legitimate."

Warning bells rang. Someone was using her card? She got out her purse, then her wallet, seeing if the card was there. It was. "Yes, go ahead."

"There's a purchase yesterday from a store in Sioux City, Iowa."

She relaxed. Douglas was traveling in Iowa. "What brought it to your attention?"

"The amount. It's for $4,823.59."

That didn't sound like the amount of her husband's usual business expense. "What store?"

"Girabaldi Jewelers."

She didn't know what to say.

"Ma'am?"

"I think you need to call my husband about that." She gave the Visa rep his cell-phone number, told the woman not to mention that they'd contacted Gennifer first, and hung up.

Douglas had spent nearly five thousand dollars at a jewelry store? A worst-case scenario popped into her thoughts, annoying her by its very presence. She shook her head against the sordid thought and replaced it with the knowledge that she herself had a birthday this week. . . .

That's it. That had to be it.

She deemed her lack of excitement circumstantial and inadmissible.

❀ ❀ ❀

Talia entered Neighbor's Drugstore, list in hand. She hated the days when her lunch hour had to be spent on errands, but it couldn't be helped.

She made a beeline for the pharmacy counter.

Gladys looked up from her work, squinting. "Hey there, Talia. How are things going?"

"Horrible." She handed Gladys the prescription slip.

"Is Nesto—?"

"He's fine. Or rather, he's the same. But I'm swamped at work with three conventions coming in next week and way too much to do, and—"

"Then I'll hit my fast-forward button. Just let me call this in to your insurance company for verification."

Talia didn't like how Gladys had cut her off, but at least there was hope she'd get out of here quickly. She readied her shopping list.

Gladys smiled as she punched in the phone number. "Have you met Margery, the new girl?"

Talia turned around and saw a twentysomething woman with droopy blonde hair stocking the shelves in the Cold Remedy aisle. She smiled at Talia. "Hi."

"Hi." Talia didn't have time for this. She turned to start her shopping, but then—

"Oh, Talia," Gladys said, her ear to the phone. "Hold up a minute." She spoke into the phone, "Hold please." She covered the receiver with a hand. "The insurance company has a question."

Great. Just great. The insurance company was always ragging about something. Talia looked at the list in her hand. Maybe she could stop back after work, before she picked up Tomás.

"Do you have a list?" It was Margery.

"Yes, but I'm running out of time so I'll have to come back and—"

Margery held out her hand. "Let me help." When Talia hesitated, Margery said, "I'm a thrifty shopper."

"Better let her do it," Gladys said, laughing. "She's a doer, that one."

Talia had never had anyone shop for her before, but she handed the list over.

After a quick glance at the list, Margery asked, "Do you like any special brands?"

"Get me the bargains."

"Can do." And she was off.

By the time Talia and Gladys had taken care of the insurance company Margery had collected all the items on the list and had them sitting in neat rows at the register.

"If you don't like something, I'll run back and get another brand," Margery said.

"Everything's perfect. Thanks a lot."

Margery began ringing things up. "How old is your baby?" Margery nodded toward the baby shampoo.

"Tomás just turned two."

"How fun. And you're expecting number two?"

"In December."

"That's lovely." She sighed deeply as she sacked the purchases. "I want a baby more than anything."

"It'll happen."

Her head shook no. "But Mick and I keep trying." She took Talia's money. "Hey, if you ever want a night out with your hubby, I'd be happy to babysit Tomás. There's no such thing as a terrible two in my book."

"You haven't met Tomás."

"I mean it," Margery said. "Ask Gladys. I'm good with the kids who come into the store."

Gladys called out from the back, "You're good with everybody, Margery. Take her up on it, Talia. You and Nesto could use a break."

Maybe that's exactly what they needed. . . . "How about Friday night?"

Margery clapped. "Tomás and I have a date!"

And so would Nesto and Talia.

🌺 🌺 🌺

Even though Margery was new at the job, Gladys was confident about leaving the front register in her care. With King in the back, it would be just fine.

It had to be. Gladys's eye-doctor appointment was not something she could miss, nor that she dare postpone. It was hard getting in to see Dr. Moss and this appointment had been set for over a month. Yet until the incident the other day when Gladys had nearly sent out the wrong prescription, she'd thought it was just routine. She couldn't ignore it any longer. Her sight was getting worse, and she wanted Dr. Moss to tell her what to do about it—and fix it like a good doctor.

The bad part about these appointments was the waiting. There was the normal wait just to get in to see the doctor (who consistently ran at least forty-five minutes behind) but then there was the added wait caused by the drops the nurse had put in her eyes to dilate them. *If* the nurse did a good job and *if* Gladys didn't blink the drops away, she'd be presented to the doctor in thirty minutes. If not . . . she closed her eyes, willing the drops into action.

A little boy of about four played noisily across the waiting room, banging a toy car into the metal arms of a chair. Repeatedly. His mother read a magazine next to him, oblivious, the foot of her crossed leg bouncing to the beat of the gum she was chomping. And when the woman turned the pages of the magazine, she didn't just turn them, she slapped them over.

Car-*bang*, foot-*jostle*, gum-*click*, page-*slap*. Over and over it went, forming an inane rhythm that tortured Gladys's nerves.

Didn't the woman realize how her actions spilled into the public domain? Didn't she realize that not everyone found loud children cute? that the constant motion of her foot signaled a lack of deep thought and a nervousness Gladys found especially annoying? that chewing gum with her mouth open was the epitome of rudeness? and that it *was* possible to turn the page of a magazine without it sounding like the snapping of a crackling fire?

Apparently not, because the woman continued her one-woman show unabated and unfazed by even the most scathing of Gladys's repertoire of sour looks. Gladys was thankful the doctor wasn't going to take her blood pressure because she knew it was on the rise. She had to get out of there or blood would be spilt.

Gladys stepped up to the reception desk. "My eyes feel plenty dilated. Is there any way I could wait in an examination room?"

The receptionist looked past her to the little boy who was now using two vehicles in his crash tests. "I'll see what I can do." She disappeared through a door leading to the back.

Gladys didn't like that the receptionist had witnessed this less-than-stellar aspect of her personality. She shouldn't let people bug her so much. It was just a sound. Just a dumb mannerism. Why couldn't she tune them out?

Because I'm an observer. I'm astute. I'm a detail person. Only the less intelligent are oblivious to what's happening around them and their effect on others.

As Gladys was waiting for the receptionist to return she glanced toward the little fiend and his feckless mother. In midpage-*slap* the mother looked up. She didn't smile and Gladys didn't either, but there was a look in her eye that told Gladys the woman was well aware of the effect her actions were having on the older woman.

And didn't care.

Which, of course, made the whole thing worse. For even worse than rudeness or living in a state of oblivion was apathy.

The receptionist returned. "We can take you now, Ms. Quigley."

She was saved. Once in the examination room she soaked in the silence. Yet the subdued light and solitude left her mind open to worry. What would Dr. Moss say about her diminished eyesight? Was there a cure? Or was she going to be faced with an ever-worsening condition, leading—

"No!" She shut out the traitorous thought. She crossed her legs, and even though she couldn't read it, picked up a magazine.

She slapped the pages one on another.

As she bobbed her ankle.

If only she had some gum.

❧ ❧ ❧

Gladys's throat was dry, but she needed to get the question asked. "What are my options?"

Dr. Moss sighed, and for once she was glad she wasn't able to see his features clearly in the subdued light, to see his bereaved, pitying face. . . . The sigh said enough.

"As I've told you before, your best option is a corneal transplant."

"We've been through this. I don't need it. I'm handling things."

When he didn't reply she answered his unspoken objection. "I am."

"By handling things I assume you're implying you're doing something to improve your condition? You're stopping the degeneration of your eyesight by sheer will?"

She opened her mouth to speak, then closed it.

"You've proven yourself to be a strong woman, Gladys, capable of leaping tall buildings in a single bound but—"

"Only on Tuesdays."

"What?"

"I only leap tall buildings on Tuesdays."

He sighed again, obviously not in the mood for her jokes. "But in spite of your amazing abilities, you are not strong enough to stop the inevitable."

Her throat was like the Sahara. "Who says it's inevitable?"

He gave her a stern look. "Medical science does not lie."

"So there's no such thing as a miracle?"

It was Dr. Moss's turn to open his mouth to speak, then close it. "A miracle, by its very nature, is something against the norm. And though I will never rule one out, I have to treat you on the basis of science."

"Bummer thing, science."

"*Au contraire.* Science can save your sight."

He was back to the transplant thing again. She sighed. "*If* I got a corneal transplant, who, pray tell, is going to cough one up for me?"

He hesitated a moment. "Someone who no longer needs it."

She knew this. "Someone who's dead."

"An organ donor."

She shuddered. "I don't like the idea that I'd be seeing with someone else's eyes."

"Not their entire eye. That's impossible because the retina and optic nerve are attached to the brain, so until we can do brain transplants, we can't do eye transplants."

Too much information. "But you *can* take the corneas."

"Exactly. The success rate is very high. I've given you a brochure . . ."

Which she'd only glanced at. She still didn't like the idea of it. "Can't you just do some laser surgery, or put in a synthetic cornea, or something miraculous like that?"

"No, we can't. The miracle will come from the donor."

There had to be another way. "I'd rather go blind."

He took her hand. "Now, Gladys, you've fought your blindness every step of the way. Don't stop fighting now."

"But I wouldn't be fighting anymore; I would be taking. From someone else."

"You would be accepting their gift. People who are organ donors do so willingly. It's a choice *they* make. It's a choice they share with their family. It's a way for them to go on living by helping someone else live, or at the very least, live more fully."

She hoped the lecture was over. "I'll think about it."

He studied her a moment. "If you're troubled because of religious concerns, don't be. Every major religion condones organ transplants— some even encourage them—so you wouldn't be going against any church—"

"That's not an issue."

He blinked, obviously out of reasons. "Think about it. But don't wait long. I'd like to get your name on the list. The good thing about corneal transplants is we don't have to worry about matching blood types. The bad thing is, the waiting list can be lengthy." Dr. Moss moved toward the door. "Do you have any other questions?"

"Not now."

"Call me anytime. I want this to happen for you, Gladys. I want you to see clearly again."

So did she. But at what cost?

⁂ ⁂ ⁂

When Gladys worked in the pharmacy she faced outward, toward the store. She and King had positioned the display racks so they could see the front door and the checkout from this position.

But this afternoon, after getting the news from the doctor, she didn't feel like seeing anyone.

Seeing. Ha. Not much longer. So saith Dr. Moss. Not unless she agreed to the transplant. Not unless she agreed to take someone else's sight.

"That they aren't using anymore. You're not taking anything from them. They're giving you a gift."

The thoughts swam, causing Gladys to turn toward the back wall and lean against the counter for support. She closed her eyes. How could she do this? How could she *not* do this?

The clearing of a throat caught her attention. "Now this is a new one. Napping while standing?" King said.

"It's an art. You should try it sometime."

Back from lunch, he hung up his red Kansas City Chief's jacket. "You do look tired. Fill me in on what's going on and you can head home."

She was going to protest, then thought better of it. "Maybe that would be best."

She headed for the door, but King stepped in front of it, barring her way. He put a hand on her arm and whispered, "Gladys. What's wrong?"

His shoulder was inches away but she couldn't take advantage of its comfort. Theirs was a working relationship.

"Tell me," he said.

He *did* deserve to know. She stepped back. "I need a corneal transplant."

His eyes widened. "I hadn't realized it had gotten that bad."

"I'm not blind—yet. But it's only going to get worse."

"Then condolences and congratulations are in order," King said.

"What?"

"Condolences on the fact that you need a transplant, but congratulations on the fact that you're a candidate for one."

It was an interesting way to look at it. "Doesn't it bother you that in order for me to get what I need, someone has to die?"

"It's not like you're killing them."

Gladys was taken aback. This wasn't helping. "I'm going home."

He touched her arm. "Sorry if that was too blunt. *We'll* work through this, Gladys. I'm not going anywhere."

Good to know.

❊ ❊ ❊

Talia went through the checklist for the anesthesiologists' convention that was beginning today. Tomorrow there would be two catered dinners in the ballroom, the need for ten small meeting rooms with various audiovisual requirements, and coffee-break drinks and pastries to be set up while the attendees were in meetings.

"You look intense." Her boss, Wade, stood in the doorway leading from her desk to his office. She loved the way he wore suspenders with his suits. On an older, portly man it would look fuddy-duddy, but on a handsome man like Wade, it looked *GQ*.

"There's work enough for three people—but I have it covered," Talia said.

"I'm sure you do."

She gave him a second look. His tone was often hard to read.

He moved next to her desk and she handed him the list. He averted his head and sneezed—twice. "Excuse me," he said. "Stupid cold." She must have made a face because he said, "What's wrong?"

Her thoughts were forced into words. "When someone's sick . . . Nesto can't afford to be sick. So germs and such . . ." She shrugged, hoping he'd fill in the blanks.

Wade took a step back. "I'm sorry. I never thought . . . I'll try to keep my distance until it's gone."

She nodded. Was she being paranoid? Nesto's doctors had said to be careful, but how could she? Her job brought her into contact with hundreds, if not thousands, of people.

Wade finished checking the list and put it back on her desk. "It looks fine."

"Thanks." When he went back into his office, she picked up the list then suddenly let it go. He'd touched the list after he sneezed.

With a glance toward his office, she hurried to the restroom and turned the water on full blast. Hot, hot water. Lots and lots of soap. And when she was done she started over. *No germs. No germs. I can't bring home germs.*

Suddenly Talia caught sight of herself in the mirror. Her forehead had deep furrows far beyond her thirty years, and a crevasse bisected her blonde eyebrows. You'd think she was disinfecting her hands after touching something vile—not just a piece of paper. Yet one germ, innocent to most, could be deadly to her husband.

She raised her wet hands, taking the stance of a surgeon in post-scrub position. She looked ridiculous. The whole situation was ridiculous. Absurd. Thirty-five-year-old husbands shouldn't need heart transplants. And their wives shouldn't have to worry about touching a piece of paper or shaking hands, or whether or not their toddler would bring home some bug from day care. Life revolved around people, yet Talia felt that the best thing for her family would be if they could be isolated from the world. Move to Timbuktu. Wherever that was.

The baby kicked, reminding her that the family would soon be greater by one.

Add one, lose one . . .

She shook her head vehemently. No. Everything would be all right. They'd have the baby, and they'd get the heart transplant Nesto needed.

There would be four in the Soza family. Four.

※ ※ ※

Angie paused with her fork in midair and watched her husband chew. "Do you like it?"

Stanford closed his eyes, gave her a sigh, then chewed some more. He shrugged. "It's okay."

That's it? "It's chicken with a special hoisin sauce—with raspberries." Yet, Angie *had* burned the sauce. She always burned something. When they were first married Stanford had told her he wouldn't be surprised if their children came out burned.

He kept eating, and didn't add anything to his "okay" opinion. Then he looked up. "What's wrong?"

She set her fork down. She was on the verge of doing it again. Pushing too hard. Wanting more. Aching for him to give her a full-blown compliment. She tried so hard to please him, but there was little joy in it. She changed the subject. "I talked to Talia today. She's doing okay but tires easily. And with her having to work full-time now, I—" she immediately realized her mistake at mentioning . . .

"Women should stay home. It's a crime she's having to work. That's Nesto's job."

Angie didn't want to get into it. Stanford had a long list of grievances against their son-in-law, not least of which was that he was *not* Martin Madsen.

In her teen years Talia had been all set to marry Martin. They'd been school chums since eighth grade, and had gone steady since they were old enough to know what that meant. The Madsens were a good family. The father owned a bank.

The Schuster photo album was full of pictures of Martin and Talia in various tuxes and gowns, as they attended school dances arm in arm. They'd been inseparable. They'd known each other's schedules by heart and had both planned to go to Notre Dame, where they'd change their "steady" to "engaged."

That had been the plan.

But then, the summer after graduating from high school, Talia worked as a camp counselor. There, she met Nesto Soza. He was a Portuguese immigrant, working with a landscaping crew, putting in a fancy camp entrance with elaborate plantings. Ironically, Angie had worked on the fund-raising for the camp improvement.

While Nesto worked on the project, he and Talia began a serious flirtation—though how Talia had managed romance while overseeing her twelve-year-old charges was something Angie had never asked.

At the end of the summer any thought of going to Notre Dame with Martin Madsen was forgotten. Talia couldn't leave Nesto. And since they did live in the same town and since he had a good job, Talia hung around.

Their relationship did not go over well with Stanford or Martin, though in truth, Martin seemed less upset about it than Angie thought he should have been, considering the two young people—and both sets of parents—had always considered the kids' union a done deal.

Angie liked Nesto from the start and understood a portion of her daughter's heart. But Stanford was adamantly against him. To punish Talia for giving up her college dreams, Stanford had kicked her out of the house, saying she had to get a job and support herself. As if that was a bad thing? Talia was thrilled to be free of her father's oppressive thumb. Angie admired her daughter's gumption. Coming from nothing, Angie knew the excitement that could come from the challenge of making do—though Angie *had* periodically sent Talia money and brought her groceries on the sly.

Talia got a job as a clerk in a dress store and got promoted to assistant manager of Better Dresses in six months. Evenings were spent with Nesto, and ten months after they started dating, they were married.

Unfortunately, it was not the social event of the year that Stanford had always hoped for. Just a normal-sized wedding. Very middle class. Stanford had pouted through the Portuguese dance music at the reception and didn't even attempt to try the yellow sponge cake, the *pão de ló*, or the *queijadas de nata*, the lemon-tasting pastry tarts filled with whipped cream. Angie had found the music, the food, and Nesto's family—who'd come over from Portugal for the event— delightful.

Since the wedding Angie's biggest wish was that Stanford would put aside his could-have-been dreams, see how much the kids were in love, and accept Nesto into the family. But the fact that they'd named their firstborn son Tomás instead of good old American Thomas, didn't help matters.

She got up to refill his water glass. "I was thinking of going to Talia's tomorrow and doing a little housecleaning for her."

Stanford laughed. "You? Houseclean?" He pointed to the counter that was spotted with clutter. "I don't know why you can't get the hang of organization and cleanliness. I've never asked for perfection, Angela. Just some semblance of order."

She started to gather up the coupons and mail that had a way of spreading across every flat surface like leaves in the wind.

"Don't do it," Stanford said.

She stopped.

"Don't go over to Talia's. You'll end up fighting."

"No, we won't."

"Yes, you will. Because you'll try to help, but you'll end up being a hindrance, and then she'll get frustrated because you aren't doing things her way and you'll stress her out more than she already is."

Angie felt tears threaten. "You act like I'm this hurricane, causing destruction wherever I go."

He opened his arms wide. "Category four."

The house wasn't that bad. . . .

Angie tried again. "She needs help. She needs me . . . us."

Stanford stood, carrying his plate to the sink where he dumped the rest of his food down the garbage disposal. "Let it be, Angela. You can't handle this house, much less helping Talia with hers."

He left her alone in the kitchen, holding the coupons and the mail.

She opened a drawer and stuffed them out of sight.

※　※　※

Mick went through the mail as Margery made hamburger patties. "You don't have anything planned for Friday night, do you?" she asked.

He looked up, suspicious. "Why?"

She shrugged, but it was a dumb gesture. She was committed to Talia. She couldn't go back on it now. "I offered to babysit."

"For who?"

"A friend." Acquaintance. She realized she didn't even know Talia's last name.

"Why'd they ask you?"

She swallowed the insult. "I'm good with kids. You know that."

"How would I know that?"

Good point. "I love kids. You know *that.*"

He tossed the mail so it spread over the table. "Bunch of bills. Why don't they leave us alone?"

They would if we paid them. "Could you get out the hamburger buns?" she asked.

"Where are they?"

He knew. If he'd only think a minute, he knew. "In the bread box."

Mick dragged the bag of buns onto the counter and banged the bread box lid shut. "I like my burger rare, you know." And he was gone.

Which all in all was a relief.

5

Let the children come to me. Don't stop them!
For the Kingdom of Heaven belongs to those who
are like these children.

MATTHEW 19:14

"You make them take you out to lunch after, understand?"

"Yes'm."

I looked out the window, watching for the blue car that belonged to my friend Susie and her family. I could hardly wait to get in the backseat of Susie's car because she'd said we could pretend we were on an airplane and her daddy was the pilot.

Mama looked up at me from the couch where she'd been sleeping every night since we'd left Daddy and moved to this apartment. She said she didn't like an empty bed, but I didn't understand that, because if Mama was in it, it wouldn't be empty. Besides, it had been her choice to move. I sure hadn't wanted to.

Mama tucked a corner of the blue-and-pink afghan under her chin. "You don't have any money with you, do you?"

"No, ma'am."

"Because I know those churches. They get you sitting down, play a couple songs, and even get you enjoying yourself, but then they pull out the collection plate and expect you to pay up or get out. The rich taking from the poor, that's what it is. So I don't want you having even a nickel in your pocket. Don't want you tempted. They can pay for their own come-to-Jesus parties. They don't have to rip off people like us."

I saw the car pull in the parking lot and ran to the door.

"You understand me, girl?"

"Yes'm. No money."

Mama snuggled deeper in the pillow. "Bring me back one of those doggie bags too. Order enough to feed us both."

What was a doggie bag? I ran out to the car, pulling the door to the apartment shut with a slam. Mama would be mad because it made her head hurt, but I'd forgotten to close it quiet, and it was too late now.

Susie's dad had gotten out and had opened the car door for me.

"Morning, Gigi," Susie's mom said. "You're looking pretty this morning."

"Thank you." I'd tried, even though the dress I was wearing was too small. I'd taken a wet washcloth and rubbed the stain off the front the best I could. And I'd taken a black marker and filled in the places in my shoes where the shiny part had worn away. I'd bought the shoes for a quarter at our neighbor's garage sale before we moved. Mama thought it was dumb, but I'd always wanted Sunday shoes. I wore them around the house sometimes when Mama wasn't around because they made me think of Grammy. I wasn't sure why. . . .

Susie patted the seat beside her. "Hey-de-ho, Gigi! Hurry up! Daddy's flying us to Paris!"

Susie's dad got in the driver's seat. "How about a stop in London first?"

"Yay! London!"

Susie clapped and I clapped too. We giggled all the way to church. It was then I decided I was going to see the world someday and have posters of the places I'd been all over my wall.

❈ ❈ ❈

Mama had been right about the plates they passed around after a bit of music. But wrong about Susie's family making me give up whatever money I had. In fact, Susie's mama gave both Susie and me a quarter to put in the plate. *Clink. Clink.* I wished I had another quarter and they'd send the plate back so I could do it again.

Maybe that's what Mama meant. They got you in there and you ended up feeling good and wanting to give everything you had.

I wish I had more to give.

I liked the music part best. I'd never heard real people singing real music so close. The music in the church . . . it rushed right past where Susie and me were sitting, did a U-turn, and came back on the other side, wrapping me up in the notes and the words. After a few lines I recognized the song as one Grammy had sung: "Abide with Me." I missed Grammy. And her singing. Everything was perfect when I saw that the song was number 96.

> *Abide with me; fast falls the eventide;*
> *The darkness deepens; Lord, with me abide.*
> *When other helpers fail and comforts flee,*
> *Help of the helpless, O abide with me.*

I didn't feel quite so helpless anymore. Not here, not in this place. It was almost as if Grammy were sitting nearby, holding my hand, smiling and singing along to the music, making the world good and right. The good nearby.

I gasped. Grammy had been *my* good nearby! Why hadn't I ever thought of that before?

And suddenly, it wasn't like Grammy was just sitting next to me; I saw her in the pretty glass windows that showed a cross and a plate and a cup, and in the red flowers on a stand, and in the gray curls of a lady's hairdo, two rows up.

But it wasn't Grammy's hand that touched mine and asked, "You okay?" It was Susie's. But there, just for a second, I saw Grammy's eyes in the hazel eyes of my friend.

The money plates were taken up the center aisle to the front by the money people and everybody stood and sang, "Praise God from whom all blessings flow. . . ." Susie knew all the words. Everybody did, all looking straight forward, singing loud. I wished I knew the words because I certainly felt like praising God for blessings. I had a lot of 'em. So much good. Nearby.

We sat back down, but Susie leaned toward me and whispered, "It's almost time."

"For what?"

"Shh." Susie pointed up front.

The man in the black robe stood in the center of the up-front place and spread his arms. "Children? Come join me."

Before I knew what was happening, Susie took my hand and pulled me toward the Robe Guy. At first I tried to pull her back, but when I saw bunches of other kids going too, I let myself be led.

We all sat on a step, right next to the Robe Guy. He smiled at Susie, "Morning, Miss Susie."

"Morning, Pastor Bob."

He looked right at me and Susie said, "This is my friend, Gigi. She's visiting."

Pastor Bob held out his hand and shook mine. "Nice to meet you, Gigi. Welcome."

I felt my cheeks get hot, but it was a nice hot. I'd never had a grown-up shake my hand before. Then Pastor Bob got out a funny-looking frog. He was scrawny and stuffed, and he had a cowboy hat on, which made me smile. He sat on Pastor Bob's knee.

"Frog says hey. Say hey to Frog."

I was surprised when all the kids said, "Hey, Frog" right back. I was too late saying it, and wished I would've caught on quicker. I would listen real careful from then on and be ready.

Pastor Bob told a story about a Good Some Martian, but he didn't pronounce it quite right. And then Frog decided he wanted to be the kind of frog who would stop on the road to help someone, no matter how icky and gross they looked. It was the kind of person Grammy had wanted me to be—just so the guy on the road wasn't covered with throw-up or anything. I'd cleaned up way too much of that on Mama when she got drunk. Slimy, stinky stuff. Even a Good Some Martian would be in the right to pass that kind of icky by.

Too soon, Pastor Bob was telling everyone to say, "Bye, Frog," and this time I was ready to say it with the other kids. Me and Susie went back to sit with her parents, and I listened to everything Pastor Bob said after that, but was kind of disappointed Frog didn't come out again. But Grammy was there. I felt her round me all through church.

Afterwards, I remembered what Mama had told me, and when Susie's dad asked if I wanted to go to lunch with them, I said I would. But I didn't do what Mama said about ordering a lot and bringing it home. When Susie ordered pancakes and when her mama said, "You want some of those too?" I didn't have the nerve to order something different. And before I knew it, I'd eaten every bite. I liked the strawberry syrup the best and Susie's daddy got us two glasses of chocolate milk—each.

I was a little scared about what Mama would say when I came home without any doggie food—and Mama *did* scream at me and call me a selfish no-good—but eating every drop of that strawberry syrup . . . I'd do it again—if Susie asked me again.

I'd have to make sure she did. I'd have to be real good. Strawberry-syrup-and-chocolate-milk good. And next time when Pastor Bob said, "Say, 'Hey, Frog'" I'd say it real loud.

6

A ringing woke her. It took a few seconds for Margery to realize what it was, realize Mick wasn't in bed next to her, realize the time—4:33 a.m.—and reach for the phone.

"Hello?"

"It's me."

"Mick, where are you? I tried to wait up and—"

"It's a mistake, all right?"

She sat upright. The *Us* magazine she'd been reading before she fell asleep slid to the floor. "What's a mistake?"

"I'm in jail."

Not again. "What did you do?"

"Nothing. I need you to bail me out."

She checked the time again: 4:34. "Now?"

"You want me to stay in this stinkin' place?"

"No, of course not. But how much are we talking about?"

"Ten thousand."

Her heart nearly dropped right there on the bed. The

last time he'd been arrested for drunk and disorderly had cost much less. "That's a lot. What did you do?"

"I didn't do . . . just some drug charge. It won't sti—"

"Drugs?"

"I'm not getting into it. Get me outta here."

"But ten thousand . . . we don't have that much."

"A bond, Margery. You know how this works. You need to get a bond. You only need 10 percent."

One thousand dollars. "We don't have that much either."

"So you want me to stay here? You'd probably like that."

"No, no, of course not. I'll think of something."

"You do that. First thing in the morning. I'll be waiting."

Margery hung up and looked around the bedroom, mentally adding up their cash. She hadn't received her first paycheck from Gladys yet. They didn't have any savings and their checking account was rock bottom.

She got out of bed and pulled out the top drawer of the dresser. All the way out. There in the back she found her stash, an envelope of money she'd held back from Mick. Last time she'd counted there was $185. But as her fingers pressed on either side of its bulk, she knew he'd found this secret place and had helped himself.

She went back to the bed and opened the envelope under the glow of the bedside lamp. There were seven five-dollar bills: $35. Margery stared at the money and turned the envelope over, hoping she'd missed some hundred-dollar bill hiding among the fives.

She hadn't.

※ ※ ※

Margery stared at the key in her hand. Just two days earlier, Gladys had made a big deal about presenting her with the key to the store so she could open up or come in early to stock or do a display. Margery wasn't used to people trusting her so much.

She wasn't used to blowing that trust.

She hated what she had to do.

She hated that she had no choice.

Margery unlocked the door and slipped inside. She considered keeping the lights off, but if anyone spotted her slinking around in the dark they'd think she was a thief.

Which she was.

Yet the lights were intimidating. How could she take money from the register when the lights would showcase her crime? She shut them off before their buzzing reached full glow.

No wonder criminals chose the dark. Was it to hide their crimes from themselves as much as from others?

Margery hugged the edge of the shadows and moved to the register. But as she pulled the drawer open, she saw there wasn't a thousand dollars inside. More like a hundred. And if she took that, Gladys would see. She'd know.

Then she remembered the little strongbox in the bottom drawer of the file cabinet back in the office. She'd seen Gladys put money in there.

Margery hurried to the office. There were no windows so she risked turning on the light. The file drawer was locked, but she remembered Gladys taking the key from under a potted philodendron on the desk.

Margery unlocked the cabinet and pulled out the bottom drawer. The gray metal box tempted her. *Please, God, let there be way more than I need inside so Gladys won't notice.*

It crossed her mind that praying for God to help her get away with a crime was probably not kosher, but she hoped he would overlook it this one time. It was for a good cause. Wasn't a wife supposed to bail out her husband?

Most wives never had to think of such a thing.

Enough of that. She opened the box and picked up the neat stack of twenties. Her fingers walked through the bills, counting . . . *one, two, three, four, five. One hundred. One, two, three, four, five. Two hundred. One, two, three*—

"Margery?"

Her heart dropped, as did the money.

Gladys stepped into the room. She picked up the pack of twenties. "What are you doing?"

Margery wanted to die. This couldn't be happening. Her legs gave way and she crumpled to the floor. "I'm so sorry, so sorry. Please don't call the police. Please." Two Lamborns in jail at the same time . . .

Gladys looked toward the phone, then back at Margery. "I trusted you. I gave you a key."

"I know. I know . . ." Margery scooted backward until her spine met the wall. She pulled her knees to her chest. "I'm so sorry. I would have paid you back."

Gladys pressed a hand to her brow, shaking her head. "I don't believe this."

"I know, I know . . ." It was all Margery could say.

Suddenly, Gladys spread her hands and froze in place. "Why were you taking the money? Why?"

"Mick needed it."

"Your husband?"

"It's an emergency."

"What kind of emergency?"

Margery brushed her lips against her knees. She couldn't stop her head from shaking no. "I'd rather not say."

Gladys put her hands on her hips and squawked like a game-show buzzer. "Sorry. Does not compute. You gave up your right to 'rather not' anything when you made the decision to steal from me. Out with it. All of it. Now."

Margery forced herself to uncurl and stand up, but kept the wall close at hand for support. "Mick's in jail. I need money for bail."

"What's he in for?"

Margery decided to offer Mick's answer to that very same question. "He didn't do it."

"Do what?"

Oh, well. There was no use lying. "Drugs."

"Using or dealing?"

She wasn't sure. "Uh . . . I don't—"

Gladys's eyebrows rose. "Has he been in trouble before?"

"Twice. But never for drugs. Being drunk, brawling, that sort of—"

"Does he take drugs?"

Margery shook her head vehemently, even though she wasn't for-sure sure. "I don't think so. And if he did deal, I'm sure he just did it for the cash."

"Which of course makes it just fine and dandy, right?" Gladys pulled out the desk chair and sat. "This changes things, Margery. I guessed you had trouble with your husband, but I didn't think he was scum."

"He's not!"

"So he's a pillar of the community?"

She didn't respond.

"Do you take drugs, Margery?"

"Never!"

"You just steal."

Margery slid the store's key onto the desk. "I'm really sorry, Gladys. You've been nothing but kind to me and—"

"Does Mick have a real job?"

Margery nodded. "He's a car mechanic. A good one too."

"A car mechanic who deals drugs on the side."

What could she say? She'd seen many sides of Mick's character since they'd married ten years ago. She'd witnessed Mick beat up more than his share of people who crossed him. He'd driven drunk a few times too. He had one DUI—that she knew of. And now drugs? "He can be a really good guy." *Pitiful. Absolutely pitiful.*

"Hmm." Gladys ran a hand over her face. She looked weary. "You're not the only one who has problems, you know."

She couldn't imagine Gladys having a problem. She was so with it, so on top of things. She was about to ask what Gladys meant, when the older woman sighed deeply, tossed the bills back into the money box, and closed its lid. "Never mind that. Why didn't you just ask me for the money? I would have loaned it to you."

"You would have?"

"Well . . . probably."

"I didn't want you to think badly of Mick."

"Unfortunately, he is what he is."

"He can do better . . . be better. He's been better. He just gets off track."

Gladys's eyebrows came together. "Let me get this straight. This is the man you want to father your child?"

"He'd be a good . . . a baby might change him."

Gladys raised a hand. "Hold it right there. You do not play Russian roulette with children by purposely putting them in the middle of a bad situation. You do not use them to make yourself feel better, feel loved, or to mend a broken relationship. They need you to be strong from the get-go. You're the adult with the power to make *their* life better—or worse, if you mess it up. If Mick's having trouble in his life, now is not the time for you to force him into being a father."

Margery began to cry. "I can't force him into anything. It isn't happening—pregnancy, I mean. We try and try and nothing happens."

"Which might be a good thing."

"Don't say that!"

Gladys stood and put calming hands on Margery's arms. "There, there. You and this quest for a baby . . . I didn't mean to stir the pot. I can see having a child is very important to you."

Margery nodded and wiped her cheeks. "And I can't have a child if Mick is in jail."

"A few days might not hurt him, you know."

She shook her head. "He'll just get mad—madder. I have to get him out. He called me early this morning and told me to do it. I have to do it."

Gladys made a face. "You don't *have* to do anything. I don't like how he calls and you jump."

"He's my husband."

"Hmm." Gladys let go and pulled the money box close. "How much do you need?"

"Ten percent. One thousand."

Gladys counted out the money and pressed it into Margery's hand. "I *will* get this back. Mick's not going to skip out, is he?"

She shook her head, hoping she was telling the truth. "So I still have a job?"

Gladys kept her hand on the money. "I should fire you."

Margery's throat was dry. "*I'm* an honest person. Really I am."

"A desperate person."

"That too." She put a hand on top of Gladys's. "You'll get the money back. I promise."

"I have my eyes on you, Margery."

Point taken.

❀ ❀ ❀

Gladys had threatened to keep her *eyes* on Margery.

Ha! What a joke.

She'd decided to come in early that morning to get some extra work done because she couldn't sleep. But now, with all that had happened and with Margery off to set her loser husband free, Gladys wasn't up to doing anything more than sit at her desk and stare into space.

Bad things came in threes. Isn't that the way it worked?

If so, Gladys wasn't sure she could take number three. The doctor's bad news and the disturbing thought of a transplant was number one, an employee stealing was two . . . what was next? A fire? Car crash? A flood, blizzard, twister, or other act of God?

Actually, she didn't want to give God credit he didn't deserve. She had the life she had because *she'd* worked hard, and *she'd* overcome whatever obstacles came her way. She was an independent woman who was responsible for herself. God was there when—and if—she needed him, but until then, she could handle things well enough on her own (thank you very much).

She didn't understand women like Margery who were so pliable and easily used by others. Especially by men. Margery's extreme loyalty to her husband was not commendable. It was dumb. Talk about blind.

Of course, Gladys realized *she* had not had the most normal experiences men-wise so her opinions were probably skewed.

She looked at the poster on the wall that showed architect Gaudi's bizarre Temple de la Sagrada Familia in Barcelona. Men. Spanish men . . .

Caballero Medina. After working her fanny off getting her pharmacy degree—with no help from anyone but herself—Gladys and a few friends had taken a trip to San Francisco in a VW van and experienced the Summer of Love, 1967. Sergeant Pepper, Peter Max, and all things psychedelic and groovy. There she'd met Caballero and fallen in love—or at least in lust—with his dark looks and alluring accent. They'd gotten married. Kind of. Sort of. They were stoned at the time and Gladys never saw any paperwork.

Yet the drugs she consumed with Caballero took her places she didn't like to visit, and after six weeks she decided to beg off and try reality for a while. Then, when she caught him sleeping with another flower child, she decided to cut her losses. She headed back to her mother's and—like her—vowed off men forever. Vowed off love. She got her head together and realized utilizing her own smarts was the way to change the world. Peace, flower power, love, indeed.

Gladys let her eyes graze across the posters, taking her on a world tour. She loved to travel. Every year starting ten years ago, Gladys, her mother, and her aunt June went on exotic trips. They'd scrape money together all year to do that. They were three women who handled life as it was thrown at them—and came out on top, laughing and having a great time. And each other.

Which up until recently had been enough. There hadn't been any trips for two years now. Her mother's health was an issue, and she and Aunt June had moved the two of them into a nice retirement establishment. Gladys blamed her mother's health for the end of the travels of the Terrible Trio. But now, with her own eyes going out on her . . .

She wished she had someone to blame for that. Not that it could make her condition go away, but to have lived a healthy lifestyle and still have her body rebel . . .

God. I could blame God.

She shook her head and stared at the top of the desk. If she didn't give God credit for the good things she certainly couldn't dump the bad things on him. Because she'd gotten through on her own guts and gumption she was quite willing to be held fully accountable for her failures as well as her successes. She hated people who believed it was someone else's fault—or someone else's glory.

Her thoughts turned to Mick and Margery. She wasn't sure about Margery yet, but she would bet the rest of her eyesight that Mick was the sort who never tied even the thinnest thread of blame around his own finger—which is what made him a loser.

With a slap of her palms against the desk, she forced any thought of Mick and Margery away. She'd already helped to untangle their life as much—if not more—than she should have. Now it was their decision to sink or swim. She had her own tangles to straighten out, her own decision to make.

Should she tell Dr. Moss to put her name on the transplant list, or go blind?

She snickered at the absurdity of the choice but couldn't bring herself to make the decision.

She stood. Enough. She had work to do.

Yet as she left the office one thought remained . . .

Bad things come in threes.

🌿 🌿 🌿

Happy birthday to me, happy birthday to me . . .

Gennifer found herself humming and stopped, not wanting Douglas to hear her while he took his shower. He'd come home last night from his Iowa trip and hadn't mentioned her birthday. It had taken all her willpower not to remind him. The $5000 purchase from Girabaldi Jewelers would be proof enough he remembered. No need to nag.

She heard him singing Elvis's "Love Me Tender." He had a nice voice.

But then she realized that since he was occupied in the shower she didn't have to wait to see her present. Not if she was quick about it. His suitcase was on the floor by the window. Still packed. Still containing the gift. Her gift. Yes, her gift . . .

With one last glance toward the bathroom she rushed to the luggage, being careful not to disturb his neatly folded clothes. Her fingertips searched for a sack or a small box or—

She felt a leather case. Eureka! The treasure was found. Gennifer pulled out a large burgundy box with a fleur-de-lis embossed in gold in the center of the hinged lid. It was way too big for a ring—which was fine with her. She found rings bothersome. It was even too large for a bracelet—which also met with her approval since bracelets annoyed her when she gestured with her hands in court. The box was the size of a necklace. She smiled in expectation and opened it.

It was a choker made of . . .

Pearls.

The heat of her excitement was doused as if she'd taken a cold show—

The shower—and Douglas's song—stopped. She quickly closed the jewelry box, slipped it between the folds of the clothes, and shut the top of the suitcase.

Douglas came out of the bathroom wrapped in a terry robe. "Glad to see you're up." He came to her and kissed her cheek. "Birthday girl."

"Thanks."

"I assume you want to go to Cleveland's for dinner tonight?"

"That would be nice."

He smiled, revealing perfect teeth that had cost them another five thousand dollars just a year earlier. "I bought you something special," he said.

"Really."

"Something I think you'll love."

Really.

She headed for the shower—a hot, steaming shower.

❈ ❈ ❈

"But I have to be careful, honey," Nesto said, kissing the top of her head as he lay beside her. "The doctor said."

She knew that. At least her brain new that, but the rest of her body had trouble with it. Nesto was a beautiful man. Initially Talia had been attracted to his dark Portuguese looks, his luscious accent, and his way of looking at her as if . . . to quote Scarlett O'Hara, "As if he knew what I looked like without my shimmy." Talia ached to be with him, and practically trembled when he was close. When he used to brush his gentle hand against her skin . . .

Their initial sexual attraction had grown into a healthy married sex life. That's why the lack of sex now was so painful.

He nestled her close, burrowing his nose into her short, curly hair. "Women like to cuddle, don't they?"

She nodded against his chin. And she did like to cuddle. Nesto was a great cuddler. But sometimes she wanted more. Was that so wrong?

Talia pulled back the covers and got out of bed.

"You don't have to get up for ten more minutes," he said.

Talia headed to the bathroom. "I have to get to work early."

It was a lie.

※ ※ ※

If she had to plaster on one more smile . . .

Talia fled from the convention's check-in table and detoured down an empty hall that led to empty meeting rooms.

Where there were no people who needed her.

Where there were no responsibilities.

She chose the first room on her right, went inside, and closed the door. She didn't even turn on the light. Through the small window in the door, she could see enough to find a chair and claim it as her oasis. If only she could stay here and never venture into the world that demanded too much from—

She started when the door opened and stood when she saw it was Wade.

"Talia? I thought I saw you slip in here."

She didn't know what to say.

"Who are you hiding from?" he whispered.

Even though it was dark except for the light from the hall, she only shrugged and shook her head.

But he saw. He reached out and put a hand on her shoulder. "Poor Talia. Poor girl."

Upon hearing the sound of her name said with such compassion, tears appeared. She backed away from him into the shadows. "I'm sorry. This is silly and highly unprofessional."

"Is it your husband? Is he worse?"

"Not worse. The same. But still bad."

He removed the handkerchief from the pocket of his suit coat and handed it to her. "I hate seeing you overwhelmed with the burden."

She carefully dabbed under her eyes, trying not to ruin her makeup. "He does what he can."

"Which obviously isn't enough."

She sniffed and tried to regain her decorum. "It's fine."

The silence between them was intensified by the darkened room.

"I need to get back to work," she said.

His hand brushed her shoulder at she passed. "Remember, I'm always here if you need me, Talia. Any time. Any time at all."

She nodded and escaped into the hall.

※ ※ ※

If Margery had her choice, she'd evaporate into nothingness. Escape to never-never land. But the day offered neither choice. Later, at work, she knew she would feel uncomfortable under the watchful eye of Gladys, and here at the jail, waiting for Mick to appear—knowing she'd just spent a thousand dollars they didn't have—her most avid wish was to become invisible. Only then would she be able to avoid the disgusted looks from the police officers as if she herself was guilty. Maybe she was. Guilty of having a husband who was dumb enough to get himself arrested.

Not that she blamed them for judging her. Most women didn't have to deal with such things. Most women didn't pick losers.

She shut her eyes. It did no good to call her husband names. Life had dealt her Mick. She had to handle it. Handle him. It's not like she had a lot of options. A woman with only a high school education, no job experience that looked good on a résumé, no talents, few skills, fading looks, an expanding waistline, and no hope. Why was she even *here*?

The door leading to the cells opened and Mick came out, his chin tight, his eyes red, his hair a mess. He shoved his arms into the sleeves of his jacket.

She moved to kiss his cheek, but he brushed past her, making her kiss fall on dead air. "Let's get outta here." He grabbed her hand and pulled her out the door.

"See ya soon, Mick," called an officer.

Mick gave him the finger just as the door closed. Margery hoped he couldn't get arrested for that. She tensed as they walked to the elevator, but no policeman stormed after them.

Mick jabbed the Down button repeatedly. Margery stood half a step behind, wishing she could take a different elevator, or at the very least hoping it would be full so she wouldn't have to be alone with him.

No such luck on either account. The elevator doors opened to an empty car. Mick went in first.

Margery hesitated.

"Get in here."

She did as she was told.

❦ ❦ ❦

Margery had tried to perfect the art of not caring about the silence between them, had even tried to embrace it as better than the ranting-raving alternative. But the drive between jail and home made her wish she'd tried harder.

If only she didn't care.

If only he did.

As they drove block after block she thought about telling him where she got the bail money, yet had mixed feelings about whether he should know. Would he think more of her because she was willing to steal to set him free? Or would he get after her for botching the job by getting caught? The loan from Gladys would have to be repaid. Stolen money didn't.

She checked her watch. She needed to get to work. She'd told Gladys she would be back as soon as possible. It was going to be a long day. It had been a long day already.

Mick pulled in front of their trailer and got out, slamming his door. He stomped inside, letting the screen door fall back upon her. He drilled his jacket into the chair and fell onto the couch, grabbing the remote on the way.

"Aren't you going to work?" she asked.

"It's too late."

"No, it isn't," she said. "Better some hours than none. You should at least call."

He flashed her a look. "Don't nag."

"I'm n—"

"Got anything to eat?"

She was stunned to silence.

He looked away from the TV, directly at her. "Food?"

"You could at least say thank you."

"For what?"

"For bailing you out."

"For doing what a wife's supposed to do?"

The weight of the morning crashed around her. She moved to the edge of the coffee table and tried—unsuccessfully—to get her voice under control before speaking. "Most wives don't have to bail their husbands out of jail."

He looked away. "Sorry to inconvenience you."

She shifted her weight to the other foot. "It . . . it wasn't easy getting the money."

He snickered. "What'd you do? Rob a bank?"

Suddenly, she was at the couch, yanking him to standing. "Out! Get out! I want you out—now!"

Once he got his balance, *he* became the one who did the pulling, and within seconds pulled her down on the couch on top of him. She sprawled, one foot on the floor, her arm desperately seeking something to keep her upright.

Mick wrapped his arms around her, binding her in a vise grip. "Don't you dare talk to me like that."

"Let go!"

He held her more tightly and whispered in her ear. "You think you're in control? Think again."

He had her. There was nothing she could do to get away, nothing she could do to make the whole situation *go* away. Why had she provoked him? It was a battle she couldn't win. Had never won. What had she been thinking?

Held captive, she grabbed a breath and forced her voice into a whisper. "Let me go, Mick."

"Let you go? Let you go? I think that's a perfect idea."

He pushed her off, making her fall between the couch and the coffee table. Her elbow hit the edge hard, but she didn't have time to even wince because a second later he wrenched her to her feet, forcing her to high-step over the table, making her turn her ankle as she sought solid ground. He propelled her toward the front door— which he swung open, nearly making it collide with her face.

He shoved her outside, where she fell off the small stoop and down three steps, sprawling onto the gravel drive. "Let you go, you say? Gladly. Go. Get outta here!"

Only then, finally free of his physical contact, did she realize what all the scuffle had been about. "You're kicking me out?"

"Hey, you wanted *me* out. I think you're the one who should go. Besides, you asked for it."

She attempted to stand but her ankle balked at the weight. "I didn't mean that, Mick. I just wanted you to stop. . . ."

He made a gallant bowing gesture like a gentleman in court. "Your wish is my command."

Margery looked behind her, suddenly aware that their trailer-park neighbors were watching through parted curtains. "Let's go inside and work this out."

Mick disappeared into the trailer, leaving the door open. Margery started up the steps, leaning on the railing for support. But before she could reach the landing, he returned with her purse. He threw it at her, making the contents scatter on the gravel. "Here you go. Have a nice life."

With that, he slammed the door and yanked its curtain shut.

What just happened?

She heard the volume on the television rise. The inane clapping of *The Price Is Right* fell upon her like evil applause for their scene.

Margery gathered her things, shoved them back in her purse, and drove away. To where, she wasn't sure.

🌺 🌺 🌺

Margery had to get to work. But first she needed to figure out where she would go *after* work. She drove around town, weighing her options. There weren't many.

At a stoplight she went through her billfold: forty-three dollars. With its negative balance the checkbook was useless. The credit card was maxed out. She passed a motel whose sign read Single: $24.99. Cheap, but she couldn't waste her funds on sleeping.

Friends . . . what friends would take her in?

Most of her friends were waitresses at the Chug & Chew. None close. And now that she'd quit, they certainly wouldn't feel beholden to take her in.

Mick had never been interested in going out with other couples, so that avenue was out too. Her thoughts moved to Gladys, but quickly backtracked. There was no way she could impose on Gladys even a smidgen more than she already had.

So. There was no one who could be her savior. No one who would take pity on her and comfort her. She was totally on her own.

An idea began to form and she glanced over her shoulder into the backseat. She'd always hated this old boat of a car Mick had bought from someone's mother at the garage. It was far more car than Margery needed to run around town.

And yet it was just enough car to stretch out in, to sleep in.

Home sweet home.

※　※　※

Looking in the rearview mirror moments before she headed into the store to work, Margery noticed her eyes were swollen and red, and her makeup washed away by tears. Sadly, she had nothing in her purse except some powder and lipstick. They helped, but could not cover up the trauma she'd been through in the past few hours. Hopefully, Gladys wouldn't notice.

With one last look in the mirror, Margery took a deep breath. "It's showtime." She headed inside, the jangle of the door's bell announcing her entrance.

Gladys looked up from the front register where she was giving a man change. "Come again, Al. Hope that allergy medicine works for you."

Margery nodded to the man as they passed.

Gladys raised her eyebrows. "Good morning, or should I say good afternoon."

"Sorry. I'll get right to work." Margery came toward the register. Her sore ankle buckled and she stumbled.

Gladys came around the counter. "What happened to you?"

Margery sidled past her, put her purse under the counter, and pinned on her name tag. "I twisted it. I'll be okay."

Gladys leaned close to study her face, but Margery turned away, straightening a counter display of ChapStick.

"Odd word, *okay*," Gladys said. "It can mean just the opposite."

Now it was definitely showtime. Margery dug deep and found strength enough to smile. "Not this time."

"So, the bail's been paid and Mick is set free?"

"Home safe." She noticed a blue stripe on the receipt roll. "This roll needs changing."

"It had to have been traumatic for you—getting him out and all."

Margery shrugged. "I got through it." For the first time she turned her attention to her boss. "I want to thank you again for the loan and for your forgiveness this morning. You won't regret it."

"Make sure I don't." The phone in the pharmacy rang and Gladys headed in that direction.

Saved by the bell.

❈ ❈ ❈

Angie Schuster parked in front of Marlo's Coffee Shop. As usual, she was early. That was all right. It gave her time to get out the little red notebook that contained her to-do list. She took much satisfaction in checking things off: *Volunteer at hospital 9–11, Meals On Wheels 12–2, Haircut 2:30, Meet new mentee 3:30.*

Mentee? Was that the correct term? Angie was going to be the *mentor*, so that made the girl the *mentee*? Just to be safe she'd avoid using the term at all.

She was a little nervous about meeting the girl. Although she'd dabbled in nearly every other kind of volunteering, Angie had never done anything so one-on-one. But the idea of helping a teen in need appealed to her. Now that her own children were grown and gone . . .

Their son, William, was a lobbyist in DC and they rarely saw him. At twenty-six he was still single. Wasn't even dating anyone. Not that he'd tell them if he was.

At least Talia was in town. Angie was often thankful that if one of her children had to live far away, it was single William. Angie loved having Tomás close enough to cuddle. And now with the new baby coming . . . she could hardly wait.

She spotted a lone teenager walking toward the entrance of the coffee shop. Angie thought of the yearbook photo she'd received from the school that pictured a pale girl with mousy brown hair and a few extra pounds. The girl on the sidewalk fit the bill. She looked hesitant, even indecisive, as if she were considering not going in at all.

Angie got out of her car. "Sarah?"

The girl looked in her direction and nodded.

Angie locked the SUV and walked toward her, hand extended. "Hi, I'm Angie Schuster."

The girl offered a halfhearted smile yet shook Angie's hand strongly. But her eyes looked away. Was she shy? Angie hoped not. There was nothing worse than talking to a person who didn't want to talk. Especially a teenage person.

"Shall we go inside?"

Sarah shrugged.

Angie led the way and chose a table by a window. A waitress in jeans and a blue Marlo's Coffee Shop T-shirt took their order.

That done, Angie took a fresh breath. "Well then. I'm so glad to finally get to meet you. I've heard a lot about you."

Sarah's eyes flashed. "From who?"

Whom. Angie hesitated. "Mrs. Miller. Your counselor. She's the head of the mentoring program."

"Oh."

Actually, "a lot about you" was an exaggeration. There hadn't been much to tell. Mrs. Miller hadn't known much about Sarah beyond the bland details of a grade transcript. The girl did okay in school, but was not a stellar student. And there were no extracurricular activities listed except participation in a food-bank promotion the previous year. Information about her home life was limited to knowing that she had working parents. Actually, Mrs. Miller had expressed surprise that Sarah had agreed to join the mentoring program. Mrs. Miller's only advice to Angie had been *We think Sarah would benefit from having someone to talk to.*

As long as Angie could get her to talk.

Their coffees came along with a plate of biscotti.

Sarah fingered one tentatively. "I've never had these."

"They're Italian. You dip them in your coffee." Angie demonstrated and Sarah followed suit.

"They're good," Sarah said.

"I come here for the biscotti more than the coffee."

Sarah traced the edge of her mug. "I've never had coffee before either."

Angie had a sudden thought. "Your parents haven't forbid you from drinking it, have they?"

"What?"

"Saying it stunts your growth? Not wanting you to have the caffeine?"

She snickered. "They can't object. They drink it."

The girl had provided a segue. "What do they do for a living?"

Her eyes looked down. "They work."

Angie suffered an inward sigh. "Doing what?"

Sarah bit her lip, as if carefully gauging her answer. "My dad is a traveling salesman for a paper company."

"Traveling . . . that must be hard on all of you. How many days a week is he gone?"

"Uh . . . actually he doesn't travel anymore. Used to. But not anymore. He's home every night. We play chess together. Right after dinner."

"Knight to queen four, eh?"

"Uh. Yeah. That."

"How about your mom?"

"She's a lawyer."

"What's her specialty?"

"Huh?"

"Is she a criminal lawyer, corporate, divorce . . . ?"

"She does it all. She's almost famous. Everybody wants her to defend them. She was on TV once after defending a big-criminal guy."

"Who was she defending? Maybe I saw her."

"I . . . I don't remember. But you'd know the name if I said it."

Hmm.

Sarah wrapped her hands around the warm mug of coffee. "She and I are real close. Like that *Gilmore Girls* program on TV. We talk about everything. We even share the same clothes."

"That sounds nice." If it was true, it gave Angie hope. A good home life was important in the teenage years. Yet if Sarah's home life was so idyllic, why was she in need of "someone to talk to"? She decided to change the subject. "What are your favorite classes?"

"Lunch and recess."

"No, really."

Sarah tried a sip of her coffee and made a face. "This is bitter."

Angie plucked a blue envelope from the sweetener container. "Try one of these." She waited until Sarah stirred it in and sipped again. "Better?"

"Better."

"Your classes?"

She shrugged. "I'm kinda good at math."

"Want to teach me how to balance my checkbook?"

"I could."

Angie changed the subject again. "Do you play an instrument? sing? act? draw? knit? play sports?"

"I sing. I like to sing."

"Do you sing with the chorus at school?"

She shook her head.

"Why not?"

Sarah shrugged. "I sing on my own. At home. When I'm alone."

"Talent is meant to be shared, Sarah."

"I don't think so. My mom heard me singing with a CD once— I hadn't heard her come home—and she told me to shush, she had a phone call to make." She seemed to catch herself. "Then later, she asked me to sing the whole thing and applauded, right there in the living room. Dad did too."

"How nice of them."

"Yeah, they're great. They wanted me to be in chorus too. You're not the first one to say that. But it didn't fit in my schedule."

Everything Sarah said made sense, yet didn't, as if Angie were seeing the girl's life through a smoky veil.

Or rose-colored glasses.

"So what do you do?" Sarah asked.

Angie was taken aback—and impressed that Sarah had asked. "I . . . I do . . ." She laughed at her own ineptitude at explaining how she filled her days without having it sound high-and-mighty. "I do stuff."

Sarah's laugh was a lovely tinkling.

"I do stuff. For people," Angie explained. "I try to help people."

Her face brightened. "Cool."

No one had ever given Angie that reaction before. "I do a lot of volunteer work."

"Like what?" Sarah seemed genuinely interested.

"Fund-raising for various causes, and I volunteer at the hospital, and at the shelter downtown."

Her eyes widened. "You get to work with real poor people?"

It was an odd question. "Yes, I suppose I do."

Sarah nodded once, with emphasis. "That's what I want to do. Help the poor, make things right, change the world."

Angie felt her own eyebrows rise. "It's a lofty ambition. But not very glamorous. My husband doesn't like me being down there with that kind of—"

"Can you get me down there? To the shelter? With the poor people?"

"I suppose so. If you really want to go."

"I do."

Angie had never imagined that *this* would be their common ground. "I'm going to serve lunch on Sunday. You could probably—"

"Yes! Count me in."

※　※　※

For the fourth time since coming to work that afternoon, Margery dialed home. If she could just talk to Mick . . .

For the fourth time, the receiver was picked up, then set down hard. Stupid caller ID. He knew it was her. The fact that he didn't ignore her call, but repeatedly took the time to answer and immediately hang up on her, told Margery his anger hadn't passed. And wouldn't.

Why did she even try? When Mick was mad, he was mad for ages. And nothing helped. Not crying, pleading, yelling, leaving love notes, making his favorite cookies, sending flowers, cleaning the house extra clean, seducing him . . . nothing worked. Even when Margery's transgression was small, even when she was innocent, Mick held total control of his anger and wasn't about to relinquish it because she wanted him to—*especially* because she wanted him to.

And so, after this fourth rejection, her mind moved into survival mode. In between customers she compiled a list of items she needed in order to function away from home: toothpaste, toothbrush, deodorant, lotion, makeup, shampoo . . . working in a store where she could get all these items at a discount was a bonus. But considering that Gladys or King had to ring her up, how could she get all these things without drawing suspicion?

And bathing? Where would she take a shower?

With that question in mind, Margery checked out the restroom, looking with new eyes. It was a unisex bathroom back by the office and was extra big to handle the handicap requirement. The floor and walls were completely covered with one-by-one-inch tiles. One sink. One toilet. Very functional—with an added perk: there was a drain in the middle of the floor.

Fueled by the possibilities, Margery took a stroll down the medical-supply aisle and spotted a handheld showerhead that attached to a faucet. With a little ingenuity, she could create her own shower and clean up the restroom afterward . . . if she had towels. She needed towels.

Then there was the issue of clothes. She couldn't wear the same thing to work everyday. Plus, in order to sleep in the car she needed a pillow and a blanket. Neighbor's Drugstore had none of these things.

Home did. She had no choice but to sneak home. But when? Usually, Mick would be at work during the day, but after getting out of jail this morning he'd made it clear he was taking the day off. And she couldn't count on him going out at night. To be safe she'd have to wait until tomorrow. Surely, he'd go back to work tomorrow.

If he still had a job.

She shuddered at the thought of him losing his job. What bitter poison would *that* be to his mood? Jail, kicking his wife out of the house, then losing his job? Surely, he'd go back to work tomorrow. Even Mick wasn't that dumb.

Margery saw the lights in the pharmacy section go out. She checked her watch. It was six. Quitting time. Time to go home.

Home sweet Oldsmobile.

❊ ❊ ❊

Gennifer never thought she would be one of those people who practiced expressions in the mirror, but throughout the day, she'd done so in the firm's restroom. By dinnertime, as she and her family entered Cleveland's restaurant, she'd nearly perfected the surprised look of pleasure she would activate when she opened the jewelry box and saw the pearl necklace. She hated pearls. She would never, ever wear pearls.

But Douglas doesn't know that.

Douglas didn't know a lot of things.

And maybe it was time she got over it. A five-thousand-dollar necklace was a five-thousand-dollar necklace.

Gennifer didn't need to open her menu. She always ordered the same thing: Fontina Chicken, no potato, and a house salad with raspberry vinaigrette. Protein was very important while on dialysis. Since it was her birthday she might splurge on the Death by Chocolate. What a way to go.

She guessed Douglas would get the prime rib, but Sarah . . . she looked at her mousy daughter, with her dark and heavy hair, skimming the menu. You could never tell about Sarah. She'd been known to just order dessert, or order two appetizers, or something fried.

Which was the last thing Sarah needed to eat. Celery and carrot sticks would have been good.

"They have really good salads," Gennifer suggested.

No reaction.

"Leave her alone, Gen. This is your birthday," Douglas said.

My birthday. Not her birthday.

The waiter came to take their order. "Anything to drink, ma'am?"

"Water's fine."

"How about wine?" Douglas asked. "To celebrate."

Gennifer shook her head, regretting the absence of most beverages in her life. While on dialysis liquid intake was restricted to a quart a day. For someone who had lived on coffee and Diet Coke, it had been a difficult transition—but one Douglas hadn't noticed.

Gennifer ordered her Fontina chicken . . .

"And for the young lady?"

Sarah closed her menu with a snap. "I'll have the fettuccini . . ."

Pasta. Pasta is good.

". . . alfredo."

Great. Add a million grams of fat to my daughter's burgeoning hips.

When the waiter left them, Douglas grinned. "Ready for your presents?"

"Sure." *Look of surprised pleasure ready. Set . . .*

Douglas pulled a gift-wrapped box out of a small shopping bag and presented it to her. The shape was slightly off. So was the weight. She tore the paper away, revealing . . .

"A new PDA," Douglas said.

"A new PDA," Gennifer repeated. A gadget. A handheld, organizing gadget.

"You said you needed a new one."

She *had* said that.

"Don't you like it?"

So much for carefully orchestrated looks of pleasured surprise. "Thanks."

"She hates it, Dad. Look at her," Sarah said.

"Do you hate it?"

Yes. Completely. She didn't want an office supply for her birthday. Not that she wanted a pearl necklace either, but—

Which led her to the main question: where was the necklace?

And worse yet: who was getting it?

Somehow she managed a smile. Somehow she did a better version of pleased while opening the Il Divo Christmas CD Sarah had gotten her (which she *did* like.) Somehow she ate dinner and said the right things at the right times.

But the questions remained, making even the temptation of dessert impossible.

❦ ❦ ❦

While Douglas was in the walk-in closet getting ready for bed, Gennifer took a risk. As quietly as possible she pulled out his dresser drawers and felt around for the necklace. Nothing. She scanned the room, wondering where the box could have gone between this morning when she'd found it in the suitcase and—

The suitcase. She whipped around. It wasn't by the window anymore. She moved to the closet. There it was, on the floor, opened, with a pair of khakis hanging out. Then she remembered. "You're leaving again tomorrow, aren't you?"

He hung up his suit coat. "You knew that."

She knew that.

"Where are you going again?"

"Chicago. The main office. I may stay over. I may not have to."

She looked at the suitcase. Was the necklace still inside? She took one of his favorite shirts off its hanger. "I'll help you pack."

He pulled her arm. "No. I'll do it. I always do it."

"But you get things wrinkled."

"Since when?"

She had no defense. And no excuse to look in the suitcase.

He took her by the upper arms, and she started. A few inches down and he might have felt the dialysis portal in her arm. Long sleeves and dark rooms had kept it a secret so far. . . . "Are you coming to bed?"

It was the last thing she wanted to do. And yet . . . they'd always had a good sex life. She couldn't mess with that.

"I'll be there in a minute."

Rats.

※ ※ ※

Gennifer held her breath, gauging the breathing of her husband beside her. She jostled slightly to see if he reacted. When he didn't, she slipped out of bed and went into the walk-in closet. She closed the door behind her and flipped on the light. She even draped a blouse against the bottom of the door to keep the light from showing through to the other side.

The carry-on suitcase was upright, ready to roll out the door. She set it on its back, and started to unzip it. Should she do it quickly or inch the zipper along? Her nerves decided for her. She unzipped the case in one movement, then paused, listening for any sound from the bedroom. Douglas's snore was a balm.

She opened the case. Her fingers began their exploration, pausing on the red herring of his grooming kit. But then they found their mark, halfway down, amid the carefully folded shirts and pants. The burgundy box. Opening it was salt in the wound, but she did it anyway. The pearls shone back at her. The question of her husband's choice in jewelry was moot. *Her* preference was moot.

Because these gems were not for her. He'd bought them for someone else.

And bought her a Palm Pilot.

"Gen?"

She slid the box in between the clothes and dropped the lid. She kicked the blouse into the corner, slipped off the light, and opened the door. "What?"

"What are you doing? It's one fifteen."

"I'm getting a sweatshirt. I'm cold. Go back to sleep."

He mumbled something and turned over, satisfied. She closed the door most of the way and went back to the suitcase, zipping it shut an inch at a time. She set it upright, grabbed a sweatshirt, and pulled it over her head.

She was cold all right. Cold and very confused.

※ ※ ※

She was cold and very confused.

Margery lay on her side in the backseat of the car, thankful that unlike newer models, this old clunker had a flat bench. She could even tuck the seat-belt clasps into the seat, out of the way. Small blessings.

With one last check of the parking lot of Hilltop Park, she tucked an old jacket she'd found in the trunk over her bare knees. Next, she adjusted her purse to use as a pillow, moving the straps out of the way. She tried it out with her hand, and when she felt her comb poking outward, she adjusted it so the surface was as smooth as possible. That prepared, she draped the sleeves of her jacket over a shoulder and carefully descended into a sleeping position. A position for sleep—if sleep would come.

Her mind raced. Her to-do list had moved far beyond the usual list of daily living to include such things as *Win Mick back* and *Pay Gladys back* and *Get back home.*

Back. Back. Back. If only she could rewind the past week and go *back* before any of this had caused her to be curled in the *back* of a car, trying to sleep.

Yet even if she could go back in time, Mick would still have been arrested. He would still have needed bail money—that they didn't have.

And they probably would still have had the argument that had gotten her kicked out of the house. Which meant . . .

It isn't my fault.

Her eyes were wide-open now, and though she did not sit upright with the revelation—not wanting to ruin all her hard work—mentally, she stood at attention, paced, and even punctuated the air with a finger, emphasizing the truth. "This isn't my fault!" she said aloud.

Then why do I act like it is?

With a sigh she closed her eyes. The answer was simple: she was a wimp. Confrontation must be avoided at all cost. Don't rock the boat, keep the peace, blessed are the peacemakers . . .

And worn are the doormats.

She forced herself to keep her eyes closed, hoping to keep herself blind to the truth.

Good little doormat.

❧ ❧ ❧

Tap, tap, tap! "You there. Wake up."

Margery shot to wakefulness and squinted at the beam of light coming in the back window of the car. She put a hand in front of her eyes.

The light moved away from her face and she spotted a police uniform. "Get out of the car," the officer said.

She did as she was told and felt cold air brush over her as the jacket-blanket fell away. Her foot got caught and she stumbled upon exiting, making her already sore ankle scream in pain. The officer righted her with his free hand.

"You okay?"

"I'm fine." She brushed some stray hair away from her face.

"Do you have some ID, miss?"

"In my purse."

"This your car?"

"Yes, sir."

"Registration too, please."

She got out the paperwork.

He checked the names, then handed it back. "Why are you sleeping in your car?"

Margery was relieved she could tell the truth—or part of it. "My husband and I had a fight."

"So he gets the warm bed and you get the cold car?"

She shrugged.

"I'm sorry for your troubles, Mrs. Lamborn, but you can't sleep in the park. It closes at midnight."

She wanted to ask, *Then where can I sleep?* but sensed it wasn't a good question.

"The Super 8 over on Grant has inexpensive rooms," he said. "It's in a safe neighborhood. They might even give you a reduced rate since it's so late."

"What time is it?"

"Two-thirty."

She still had half the night to get through. "Thanks. I'll go there."

"You do that," he said. "Then make up with your husband, all right?"

Although he stepped toward his police cruiser, he did not get inside. He was waiting for her to leave. She got in and drove toward the park's exit. He followed. At the intersection onto the main street, she had no choice but to turn left, toward Grant. Unfortunately, he turned left too.

After two blocks it was obvious he was going to follow her all the way to the Super 8. Was it wrong for her to wish he'd get an emergency call that would take him elsewhere? No way could she waste money checking into a hotel. Every penny was precious.

She spotted the brightly lit Super 8 sign on the right. She checked her rearview mirror. Mr. Cop was still following her. She put on her blinker and waved to him as she turned in and he kept going straight.

But now what? If the cop drove around the block and saw that her car was gone would he put out an APB and go searching for her?

There was a parking place three spots from the office door, just out of any hotel clerk's sight line. She pulled in. The overhead light of the parking lot was like her very own spotlight. She turned off the car and looked back at the street, watching for the cop. There wasn't much traffic, but after a couple minutes she decided he'd forgotten about her.

But then she realized his intervention might be a blessing. The parking lot of the motel was well-lit and held enough cars to make her feel safe. And there was a person awake in the office close by in case of emergency.

It was worth a try.

With one last scan for witnesses, Margery climbed over the front seat and settled in for the long night's journey into day.

7

He will wipe every tear from their eyes,
and there will be no more death or sorrow or crying or pain.
REVELATION 21:4

I shared my secret on a perfect night. It was my first
sleepover ever. Susie and me planned it for a week. She
insisted we make a list of special foods we wanted to eat
and special things we wanted to do.

"Mom will go to the grocery store just for us, and she
said we could stay up real late."

I couldn't imagine my mama spending money on the
junk food on our list: potato chips, Oreo cookies, orange
slices, Hershey's kisses, and root beer. Actually, the only
food that had been my idea was the root beer. The rest
were Susie's, but I knew I'd love all of it. We were both ten
now, and Susie hadn't steered me wrong yet.

That night, after eating broiled peanut-butter sand-
wiches and chips, we settled into the family room with the
goodies, lay on our stomachs, and watched slides of Susie
when she was little. She was such a cute baby. Grammy
had told me I'd have a baby someday. . . .

Then we moved to Susie's room, and she taught me how
to play Monopoly and even let me be the banker. At one
in the morning, Susie's mom came in and asked us to be

quiet, and we went to bed. Her mama even kissed me good night, just like she kissed Susie. "Sleep tight. Don't let the bedbugs bite."

Susie had the neatest bed—a trundle, she called it. She slept in the regular bed and I pulled out the hidden bed and slept right beside her. I'd brought Grammy's pillow along and it looked real pretty on that trundle. Even though the lights were out, that didn't mean we stopped talking.

That's when I decided to tell Susie my secret. If anyone in the world could be trusted with it, it was her. "Want to know a secret?" I asked after we'd played flashlight tag on the ceiling.

Susie's flashlight went off. "Of course."

I nearly turned my flashlight off too, but didn't want to do the telling in the dark—plus I wanted to see Susie's face when I told her.

As if knowing what I was thinking, Susie turned on the bedside lamp. I switched off my flashlight and we both turned on our sides, facing each other.

I decided to start with the best part of my secret. "I have a special number in my life."

"What do you mean, special?"

"A number that comes up over and over and over."

Susie leaned her head on her hand. "What number is it?"

"Ninety-six."

Susie didn't say anything at first, then, "Why ninety-six?"

"I don't know. But it's always been that way." I told her a few of the times when number 96 had appeared in my life. The Highway 96 that took me to Daddy's house when he came and got me for a visit. The 96 on our license plate last year. And Grammy living at 96 Maple, and dying at age 96.

"That's weird," Susie said.

Which made me ask the question I desperately wanted answered. "So . . . does that make me weird?"

Susie sat up and pulled my satin pillow into her lap, tracing the edge of the fringe, making it flip and dance. "I'm not sure. Maybe it just makes you special."

I didn't expect the tears.

She crossed from her bed to mine and hugged me. "I'm sorry. I didn't mean to make you cry."

All I could do was shake my head. I didn't want Susie to feel bad, because these weren't bad tears. They were happy tears. Relieved tears.

Suddenly, she must have realized it too because she pushed me to arm's length and said, "I said you were special. There's no reason to cry about *special.*"

I sniffed loudly. "It's just that Mama and Daddy don't think it's special. That's part of why they broke up. I heard them arguing about how Mama didn't like Daddy ignoring my weirdness. She wanted a normal child and said I'd never have a chance to be normal if he kept ignoring my problem, pretending it was okay."

"They broke up over a number?"

I hesitated. The number was only part of it.

"What?" Susie said. "What else?"

This would be harder to explain, but since I'd come this far . . . I pulled my knees up to my chin and tucked my nightgown under my feet. "Death. Mama says I have a sick view of death."

Susie scooted back to her bed. "What sick view?"

I hated the look on my friend's face, like she was disgusted or, at the very least, scared of something I might say.

But I said it anyway. "I'm okay with it. Grammy said we are all born to die." That's about as simple as I could put it, but by the blank look on Susie's face, I had to say more. Maybe I'd talk about the other thing Grammy had told me. "Grammy said I'm going to be the good nearby for somebody and get married and have a baby. That I was born to do some—"

"Born again. Maybe that's it," Susie said. "I've heard Pastor Bob say that in church. We have to be born again."

Born to die? Born again?

I was confused.

Susie moved close again. "It's something about needing to be born again so you can go to heaven."

"But how do we do that?"

Susie shrugged. "I want to have lots of babies."

Then suddenly, it hit me. The answer. "Since Grammy told me I was going to have a baby, and Pastor Bob says we need to be born again, then maybe we need to have babies so there's another one of us running around in the world. Another Susie. Another Gigi. A better one."

Susie's shoulders dropped. "That doesn't sound quite right."

No, it didn't. Would I ever get this figured out? It was all such a mishmash. I tried again. "But maybe having a baby, being born again, that's the way to heaven and—"

"Dying's peaceful," Susie said. "Calm. Like taking a breath of fresh air. And when you let it out, everything's different."

I smacked my hands on the blanket, relieved we agreed on something. "That's what I've always thought."

Susie pulled her knees to her chest just like me. "Mom says when we die we take our last breath here then take the next in heaven, with Jesus. And everything's okay there."

"No more crying," I said.

Susie's eyes widened. "That's right. Where did you hear that?"

I couldn't remember. Maybe Grammy? "So it's true? There's no more crying?"

"That's what the Bible says. Dad told me that when Grandpa died."

Since Susie knew about heaven stuff . . . "So what else do you know about heaven?"

Susie bit her lower lip while she thought. "You see your relatives there, the ones who've died. I'll see my grandpa. And you'll see your grammy."

"Really?"

"And there's angels and seraphim and stuff."

"What's a seraphim?"

"I think it's a band. I know there's music. Lots of music."

"I like music."

Susie's feet popped out from under her nightgown. "I wonder if they'll have dancing there."

"No way," I said.

Susie climbed off the bed and started dancing around, twisting and gyrating until I laughed.

"Come on!" She grabbed my hand and pulled me off the bed. We danced together.

I thought it was odd there wasn't anything ninety-six the whole, entire evening.

'Cause there should have been.

8

*Just as you cannot understand the path of the wind
or the mystery of a tiny baby growing in its mother's womb,
so you cannot understand the activity of God, who does all things.*

ECCLESIASTES 11:5

Talia unlocked the door to the Events Office, flipped on
the light, and was immediately assaulted by the sight—
and smell—of flowers.

She beamed at the sight of them: yellow mums, orange
lilies, and purple asters. She dropped her purse to the floor
and bent down to inhale their fragrance. Heavenly.

She spotted the card and was thrilled to see her name
on its front. She'd assumed the flowers were for her, but
until one saw the card . . . *Nesto, my darling Nesto, you've
really come through for—*

Hope these lighten your load. Wade.

Wade?

He popped his head in the office door. "I see they came."

She slipped the card back into its envelope. "They're
lovely. You shouldn't have."

He took off his coat and put it on the rack near the door.
"I want to keep my best employee happy."

"I'm your only employee."

"But a happy one, yes?"

She had to admit it. "Yes. Thank you."

He put a hand on her arm. "You're welcome."

He went into his office and got to work. She, however, had a harder time of it.

☸ ☸ ☸

Going past their trailer without letting Mick see her was tricky. The Country Cousins Trailer Park had only one entrance. One exit. One gravel-covered street with homes on either side. Mick had often complained that he could have lobbed an empty into Mrs. McCraedy's trash can across the narrow drive as easily as he could his own. He'd even done it a few times when he was less than sober, and Margery had had to go apologize. They had nice neighbors all around. Good people. Good people with a well-established grapevine who surely knew all about the current troubles going on in the Lamborn household.

Actually, when it came to friends, Margery probably could have gone to one of these neighbors and pleaded her need for temporary shelter. They'd all witnessed Mick's temper—sometimes directed at them. But the proximity to Mick would be too much, the interior space too tight, and the threat of Mick's anger being directed at her good Samaritan . . . it was not an option.

Margery slowed the car at the entrance to the neighborhood, mourning—not for the first time—that she couldn't see the front of their trailer from here, couldn't see if Mick was home or not. He should have left for work by this time, but she couldn't risk being wrong. Her only choice was to park a block away and walk in.

So that's what she did, making sure she had her list of needed items in her pocket. But as she walked past the second set of homes, as she saw the face of Meyer Collins in the window of Lot 4 watching her, she decided her exit had better be out the back way, cutting through the shallow woods that divided their neighborhood from the bordering, more traditional residential areas.

Once she got to the fourth set of homes, she saw Mick's car was gone. She walked faster, readying the key to the front door. With a look toward Mrs. McCraedy's—luckily, the woman was a late sleeper—Margery was inside, the door closed behind her.

How odd to be home yet not be welcome there. The living room showed evidence of Mick's day at home: dirty dishes, a pizza box, beer cans, the *TV Guide* on the floor near the remote. It was obvious he hadn't missed her.

She felt one of the cans. It was half full. She was on her way to the kitchen to empty it out when she realized she should leave as little evidence of her visit as possible and hope Mick wouldn't notice. Depending on the depth and length of his anger, she might have to sneak back in again. She put the beer can back.

Retrieving her list, Margery got to work. She'd thought about using a suitcase, but since they were in the storage unit out back, she went with the next best thing: a black garbage bag. Being the heaviest items, clothes had to go in first. Conservative clothes. "Boring clothes," Mick would call them. But the clothes he liked seeing her in—short skirts, tight tops, and high heels—were not appropriate at Neighbor's Drug. She dug deep in the back of her closet and found khaki and navy pants, some longer skirts, and some tops that covered her midriff and didn't wrinkle. A few pairs of shoes with lower heels, underwear, and even some hose. Towels, blanket, pillow . . .

The bag was nearly full.

She went into the bathroom and gathered her toiletries, adding a few things she hadn't thought about like aspirin, face cream, and soap.

Margery moved back to the living room, her eyes scanning, assessing, making decisions. A box of Ritz crackers caught her eye. She hadn't even thought about food.

She left the Ritz where they were but dove into the cupboards. Saltines, a jar of peanut butter, raisins, a bag of chocolate chips, a box of Velveeta. She longed to fill her bag with canned goods and an opener, but it was already heavy, and she had the trek through the woods ahead of her. She finished her scavenging with a plate, eating utensils, bowl, and cup. And a roll of paper towels.

Margery noticed the clock on the microwave. Gladys would be at the store in forty-five minutes, and Margery still needed to get cleaned up and changed for work.

She looked longingly at the shower but didn't dare risk it. She compromised by setting her sack down, freshening up in the bathroom, and putting on clean clothes. She put the ones she'd been wearing at the bottom of the clothes hamper. As if Mick would notice . . .

She gathered her long hair into a low ponytail, hating that it needed washing. Tomorrow. She'd get a proper shower at the store tomorrow.

She laughed. Proper? Hardly. But it would have to do. So much would have to do.

With one last look at her home, she locked up and headed into the woods.

❧ ❧ ❧

Pro bono work was the pits. Not that Gennifer found the rest of her clients to be lovely people, but the ones who didn't have the money to hire their own lawyer often made her skin crawl. If she never had to defend another drug case . . .

Best get it over with ASAP. It was hard enough dealing with the dialysis, her paid work for the firm, and her suspicions about Douglas—who might be coming back from Chicago tonight—much less have to sit across the desk from a guy with tattoos running up his arms, grease under his fingernails, and the glazed look of a man who didn't care two hoots about anything.

She opened the file. "So, Mr. Lamborn."

His smile changed him from menacing to safe. "Mick."

"Mick." She read the charges. "Possession with intent to sell."

"I was framed."

Gennifer looked up. "By whom?"

He added a shrug to his grin. "I always wanted to say that."

Gennifer was unsuccessful in containing her smile, but tried to cover it by looking back at the file. "You've been arrested twice on a drunk and disorderly and an assault."

"Bar brawl. I won." He winked. "I always do. And I will here too. With your help, right, Gennifer?"

"Ms. Mancowitz."

He shrugged. "You'll get me off, right?"

"I'll do my best."

He reached across the table, nearly—but not quite—touching her hand. "The deal is, I got a wife and two kids to support. I can't go to jail. I admit I had the drugs, but they weren't mine."

"A friend gave them to you?"

"You bet. An unlawful friend who doesn't realize the damage drugs can do to a life."

"So you don't personally use."

He made a cross over his heart and raised his right hand. "Can't say I've never partaken of the product, but I can say I don't do it anymore. I won't touch the stuff. My family is too important to me. This is a genuine case of being in the wrong place at the wrong time."

"In possession of the wrong thing."

He touched the tip of his nose. "Right-on, Ms. Mancowitz. Right-on. Now we're on the same page."

Speaking of, she looked through the rest of his file. She knew his type: wild, fun-loving, but a mean drunk. Yet not a huge threat to society. And since drugs hadn't been involved in any of the other offenses . . . she closed the file with a snap and pushed her chair back. "Let me see what I can do."

He came around the table and shook her hand. "Thank you, Ms. Mancowitz. I'll be waiting to hear from you." As he left the office, he turned back and winked. "You're a good lawyer. I can tell. You're worth every penny I'm paying you."

She nodded and gathered her things. Only on her way out did she get the joke.

Very funny.

❧ ❧ ❧

Gladys picked up the phone. "Neighbor's Drug, may I help you?"

"Gladys."

It was Aunt June. "What's wrong?"

"Your mother . . . she's sick."

"How sick?"

"A bad cold. A cough now too. You know how it always goes deep in her chest."

"Bronchitis?"

"The doctor says no, but I think it is."

"What's his number?" Gladys heard a relieved sigh. June gave her the number. "I'll call him right away. You want me to come down there?"

"No, no," June said. "Wait till she's better. Then we can have a proper visit."

"You take care of her, June."

"I always do."

Gladys called the doctor.

🦋 🦋 🦋

In spite of the flowers on Talia's desk *not* being from her husband, they did lighten her mood. For the first time in ages, she felt special. All day.

Which gave her a positive attitude for the evening's festivities. Tonight, she and Nesto were going on a date. She'd already made reservations at Palomino's, and if Nesto felt up to it, there was a string quartet playing downtown.

Spurred by Wade's kindness, she'd made a point to think of every detail. There was only one glitch. Although she'd made arrangements with Margery to babysit, she'd never gotten Margery's phone number and they'd never finalized a time. So on her lunch break, she ran over to Neighbor's to make sure everything was set.

Talia found Margery arranging Rolaids on the antacid shelf. "Just the woman I want to see."

Margery stood, knocking into the shelf, making four bottles fall to the floor. "Oh, dear . . . hi, Talia. I'm all thumbs."

A trait that was not a good thing when dealing with a two-year-old. Talia let it pass and handed Margery a Rolaids bottle that had rolled across the aisle. "I just stopped by to finalize a time for tonight."

"Tonight?"

Talia tried not to gawk. "You promised to babysit?"

"Oh!" Margery fumbled another bottle of Rolaids. "I'm sorry. I forgot."

Talia saw her beautiful evening dissolve. "Can you still do it?"

Margery looked over the racks toward the pharmacy. "This was going to be at your house, right? I mean, I was coming to your house."

"Yes, that's usually easier when there's a baby involved."

Margery let out a breath. "Good."

Talia suffered doubts. "Maybe we should do this another time."

"No, no. You can trust me, Talia. I'll be there. You'll have a lovely time out with your husband, and you'll give me the pleasure of being around a baby. I love babies. They're so full of joy."

Talia laughed.

"What?"

Only in hindsight did she realize the punch line to her laughter was the word *joy*. "Tomás is full of lots of things: energy, orneriness, mischief, and stubbornness, but joy?"

Margery's face was serious. "Absolutely."

This young woman's positive attitude overrode Talia's wariness. It might do Tomás some good to be around a person who saw the good in his feisty little soul. "How's seven sound?"

❦ ❦ ❦

"Gog!"

"Dog, that's right!"

Impatient with the current page of the book, Tomás turned to the next page where his finger pegged a cat. "Ki-ee!"

"Kitty." Margery cuddled his head beneath her chin, loving the wriggling weight of him on her lap. It felt completely right and good.

Tomás had enough of the book and squirmed out of her lap to the floor. He toddled over to a plastic farmhouse populated with animals. He dropped to his stomach and banged a cow into the farmer with gusto.

She regretted the absence of his warm body yet enjoyed being able to look at him. He was so perfect with his wavy black hair and baby-smooth skin. Even the way the leg of his jeans was caught up on his little sock was adorable. And as he looked back at her and grinned a toothy grin, she felt a resurgence of her quest to have a child. It was the reason she was alive. It would fulfill everything.

Then why isn't it happening? Why haven't I gotten pregnant?

She knew the reason and pulled a pillow to her chest to protect herself from the truth. God was hesitant to give her a new baby because she hadn't done enough to protect the first one from harm.

If she wanted God to give her another chance with another baby, she had to earn his favor. She had to take whatever life threw at her and deal with it. She had to be strong and compliant and humble. And she couldn't complain. God hated complainers.

So did Mick. If she hadn't complained she would still be living at home, and she'd still have a chance to make the baby that would bring happiness into their lives.

I'll call him.

She spotted a phone on the end table, pulled it into her lap, and dialed. She'd make things right. She'd get home again. She had to.

Mick answered. "Yeah?"

Her heart flipped. "Mick. It's me."

"So?"

"Uh . . . how have you been?"

"What do you care?"

Her throat tightened with pending tears. "I'm really sorry I upset you, Mick."

"Whatever."

"Is everything working out with the . . . you know. . . the court?"

"I've got it covered. I gotta go."

"I'd like to see you."

"What for?"

The tears came. "Mick . . . I love you."

"You have a funny way of showing it."

Click.

Margery fumbled the phone into its stand, knocking over a picture on the table. She righted it, then pulled it into her lap. It was a photo of Tomás at about six months, dressed in a red velveteen outfit for Christmas, the bow from a package resting on his head. She wanted a baby to spoil at Christmas. She wanted pictures of children on her end tables. She'd plaster them all over the walls. She'd be the best mother ever. No one would love their baby more than Margery. No one needed a baby as much as she did.

Tomás came toward her, a tractor in hand. *"Rmm. Rmm,"* he said, making it run up her leg.

She scooped him up and held him close. Then she stood, found her purse, and tucked her coat under her arm. She opened the front door, then realized Tomás needed a jacket too. She looked around the living room, but there was no coat or sweater around. She raced up the stairs to his room with him bouncing on her hip. She found a jacket, but surrounded by his things, she thought of other items she'd need: diapers, clothes, wipes, a blanket. . . .

And food! Milk, his cup, bibs, a spoon, jars of junior baby food.

So much to do, so little time.

In order to work faster she set Tomás on the floor. She filled a diaper bag with supplies, grabbed the toddler, and headed to the kitchen where food was added. This rushed scavenging was becoming a habit, first at home this morning, and now this evening. Desperate times required desperate action. . . .

Tomás fussed and pushed against her shoulders, wanting down. "Want to go bye-bye?" she asked. She set him on the counter and put on his jacket. "Let's go bye-bye. We'll have fun. Yes?"

The way her heart beat in her chest, the way she was sweating, the way her breath came in ragged bursts . . . fun?

She couldn't think about that.

One last look around the room—there! His pacifier. She couldn't leave without his pacifier. Margery took Tomás out to her car. She didn't have a car seat but placed him in the passenger side and put the seat belt around him. It wasn't ideal, but it would have to do.

She ran around to the driver's side and got in, started the engine, and pulled away. "We're off, little buddy," she said. "Yay!"

He began to squirm.

"Sit still, bud."

He started to cry and pulled at the seat belt.

She tried to calm his busy hands. "Come on, buddy. You have to leave that on. I want you to be safe."

Honk!

Margery veered to the right, just missing a car in the other lane.

She veered to the left, just missing a parked car.

She straightened out. Safe, but shaken.

Too close.

Tomás was in full voice now, the sudden jerking adding fear to his frustrated cry. "I'm sorry, baby. I'm sorry. Shh. Shh. It'll be all right. Hold on, just a minute."

As soon as she could, Margery pulled to the curb and stopped the car. She undid her own seat belt and released the baby from his. "Come here, bud."

He didn't come to her, but slid onto the floor.

She patted the seat. "Come up here. Come on. Come give me a hug."

"No!"

He certainly had that word down.

She took the keys out of the ignition and jangled them. "Come play with these."

Tomás wasn't interested but poked the button on the glove compartment. "Ope. Ope."

"No, no, baby. Leave that alone." She remembered she had food in the diaper bag and reached into the backseat. "Want a cracker?"

That got him interested. "Come on, then." She got two out of the bag. He climbed onto the seat, but she held them just out of reach. "You have to sit down first."

He frowned. "Cack!"

"No cack until you sit down and get your seat belt on."

He stood on the seat facing backward and bounced—and whined. "Ca-a-a-ck!"

"No cack. Not until you sit down."

Suddenly, as if he'd deflated, he dropped onto the seat. "Good boy." Margery set the crackers safely out of his reach and buckled him in again. He took his reward greedily, taking one cracker in each hand. He was happy.

She was exhausted.

She started the car and pulled away from the curb, but within seconds realized she had no destination in mind. She had no place to go. For where could she take this child? She didn't have a home. She was living in her car.

He is not yours.

It was such a simple statement, but one that reeled in the logic that had so recently left her. It made her pause long enough to weigh what she was doing.

What *had* she been doing?

Margery brought a hand to her cheek and found it warm. She shook her head against the nearness of her crime. If Tomás had not rebelled against the seat belt, if the car had not honked her into reality, if . . . if . . . if . . .

She turned the corner and headed home, taking Tomás back where he belonged.

※ ※ ※

The restaurant had the most beautiful yellow mums on the table, yet not anything as pretty as the ones on Talia's desk.

Nesto tore off a piece of bread and ate it, sans butter. "Then Dr. Phil told them how to make it . . . work it . . ." He hunted for the English phrase.

"Make it work? Work it out?"

"That's it. Great show. You should have seen it."

"I was working." Talia hoped he'd get the full implications of her words.

He didn't, but went right into a play-by-play of another Dr. Phil show. Was he *that* clueless? Couldn't he see she wasn't interested? Talia tried to concentrate on her veal with mushroom sauce, but would have rather escaped to the restroom where she could find solace from this insipid small talk. She knew her husband didn't have anything to do all day but read and watch TV, but tonight's monologue disturbed her. It was obvious these shows had become the highlight of Nesto's life. When she'd been the one to stay home she hadn't let herself become so obsessed. Of course, she hadn't been sick either.

Guilt made her pay attention, smiling and nodding at all the right places. "That Dr. Phil seems to be a smart guy."

Nesto put his fork down. "You're not listening."

"Sure, I'm listening. You were talking about Dr. Phil and—"

"Earlier. I talked about Dr. Phil earlier. Now I'm talking about Oprah."

Since the excuse "I get them confused" wouldn't work, Talia found herself without defense. "Sorry," she said.

He pushed his plate away a few inches. "No, I'm the one who's sorry. I'm sorry I bore you."

"You don't bore me." She hoped the lie rang true.

Nesto rearranged the napkin in his lap. "I know I'm not the man I was, Talia. I know it's hard taking care of me, the house, Tomás. I am high work, high . . ."

"Maintenance?" It was not the time to fill in the blank.

"I'm more high maintenance than the baby. I'm pitiful. . . ."

She wanted to move around the table and hug him but knew it would be too conspicuous. Instead she extended her hand toward him. His hands were in his lap and she waited—and hoped—he would complete the connection.

He did not.

She pulled her hand away, taking a roll from the bread basket. Talia never would have imagined that she and Nesto would ever have trouble keeping a conversation going over dinner. They'd always been able to talk about anything. Nesto had prided himself on being up-to-date with the current events of the day.

Had prided himself. *Had.*

Now he never read the paper and refused to watch the news. "I don't want to be sad," he'd say. And watching dysfunctional families cheered him up? Maybe because their dysfunction made their own family's relationships look good?

If so, Nesto was kidding himself. In Talia's eyes their relationship was becoming a contender for Dr. Phil's waiting room. If they ever had a program on "Spouses of the Critically Ill" she'd sign up. It would be nice to get a professional's spin on what she was going through.

Not that Nesto wasn't going through anything. Sometimes she *was* guilty of having that slip her mind. He was the one who'd had the ability to work stripped away from him. He was the one who'd had to give up many facets of his life that defined his manhood. He was the one who could barely walk across the room without feeling pain. And ultimately he was the one who was facing, at best, the pain of a transplant and a lengthy recovery, and at worst, death.

So what if he didn't ask her about her day? Were a few extra chores around the house that big a deal? And so what if he couldn't make love to her anymore? She was being selfish. He was alive. And he *did* possess hope for the future. She couldn't let her petty concerns derail that hope. She couldn't let—

"Let's go!"

She blinked.

He tossed his linen napkin on his plate and raised a hand. "Waiter? Check, *por favor.*"

"Nesto, what's wrong? Why—?"

He flashed her a look as the waiter approached. "You know very well why. I'm alone all day with no one to talk to." He pointed at her. "When I do have an ear, you choose not to listen. *Eu sou frustrado.*"

The waiter looked concerned. "Is something unsatisfactory?"

"It's fine," Nesto said. "We're going. Check please."

"Would you like me to box up your meals?"

"No," Nesto said, "we're leaving n—" He suddenly put a hand to his chest and sucked in a breath.

Talia was around the table at his side in seconds. "Calm down, honey. Calm—"

His words came out in a pulled whisper. "I will not . . . calm . . . down!"

After scribbling in his black leather case, the waiter handed the check to Talia. "Is there anything I can do?"

"No, he'll be all right in a few minutes." She started to get her purse, but Nesto snatched the check from her hand.

"I'm the man. I'll pay." With fumbling fingers he retrieved his wallet from the inside pocket of his blazer. It took all of Talia's willpower not to offer help. Eventually he got out the correct amount. The waiter said good night and retreated.

Talia noticed they'd gained the discreet but curious eyes of the other diners. She hoped Nesto didn't notice. He was not one to like such attention.

No such luck. As Nesto rose from his chair, he saw he had an audience. "What are you looking at?" Talia moved to take his arm, but he shook her touch away. "I'll do it!"

The ride home was silent except for Nesto's heavy breathing and occasional moans. If only she had listened to *whatever* he'd wanted to talk about. If only she'd been the good wife who thought of her husband's needs before her own. If only this wasn't happening.

At home, Nesto refused her help, and once inside, fell into his recliner, trying awkwardly to cover himself with an afghan.

"Don't you want to go to bed?"

"No," he said, closing his eyes. "I'll sleep here."

Margery came downstairs, her finger to her lips, her face confused. "Hi," she said. "How was your dinner?"

"*Arruinado,*" Nesto said, engaging the footrest with a clatter.

"What?"

Talia smiled, hoping to make light of it. "Was Tomás a good boy?"

"The best. I just got him to sleep."

Talia wished she felt up to asking more about her son's evening, but she wanted Margery gone so she could deal with her husband. While stepping toward the door, she took some bills from her purse and pressed them into Margery's hand.

"This is too much," Margery said. "I was only here a short time."

"Take it as prepayment for next time," Talia said. She opened the door wide, ushering her out.

After Talia had closed the door, Nesto said, "Turn out the light."

"Don't be ridiculous," Talia said. "You know you'll sleep better in bed."

He opened one eye. "You'll sleep better with me not there."

Though she knew it was true—in theory—in reality she knew she'd sleep horribly, worrying about her husband downstairs. She pulled the afghan off him. "Come upstairs. For both our sakes."

"Give that back!"

The violence in his voice made her drape the afghan around him.

"Go to bed. Leave me alone." He snickered. "Alone. Get used to it."

"Nes—"

"Shh. I'm sleeping."

Talia stood there a moment, unsure of what to do. What *could* she do? She shut off the living-room light and headed upstairs. She got ready for bed and slid under the covers. It was strange not having Nesto there.

The remnants of anger played their tune. *It was his choice.*

And in a way, it might be wonderful. A night's sleep with no snoring, no heavy breathing . . .

Amidst that air of rebellion she scooted over to the middle of the bed and extended her arms and legs to the four corners. Room. Such a luxury.

A tragedy.

Within seconds she returned to her space. A lifetime of having all the space in the world loomed way too close and was way too possible.

She flung off the covers and headed downstairs. Her mother had always told her, "Don't go to bed mad." Never one to listen to her mother, she had to admit that this time her words sounded as potent as the wisdom of Solomon himself.

When she heard Nesto snoring, she changed her tread on the stairs to a tiptoe. She didn't want to wake him. He'd probably worn himself out.

Talia hesitated, looked at her husband, then back toward their room. Should she go back to bed and get some sleep herself?

In spite of the logic, she couldn't do it. Instead she tiptoed the rest of the way down the stairs. She adjusted the afghan around Nesto's arms, then curled up on the nearby couch.

The sound of his snoring was far better than the alternative.

❧ ❧ ❧

I nearly kidnapped Tomás.

Although Margery had managed to act normal when Talia and Nesto returned home, inside she'd been in utter turmoil. Once she'd gotten into her car—the very car where she'd taken the baby on a ride . . .

After driving a block she began shaking so badly she had to pull over. She shut the car off and let the silence press in around her.

"Why did I do it? Why?"

Although she'd had tough times in the past and had taken her share of chances, in the last few years Margery had come to a place where she was averse to taking risks. All she wanted was to live a life others might consider boring—dealing with a home, a family, and a job in an endless daily cycle. That was her ideal. If she could be a good person along the way, all the better.

Good people don't steal other people's children.

She squeezed her eyes shut against the memory, wishing she could erase it. It was so unlike her. So out of character. So . . . desperate.

Desperate times required desperate action.

Gladys had called her desperate. . . .

I deserve to act a bit desperate.

She thought through the events of the past few weeks: she'd changed jobs, Mick had been arrested, she'd been forced to steal his bail money—and had gotten caught. She'd been kicked out of her house and was now homeless, sleeping in her car. Marital reconciliation seemed a long shot. And tomorrow she had to sneak into the store and somehow take a shower without anyone knowing it.

But even beyond those crises was the horrible knowledge that all these things she'd worked for—marriage, home, and the chance to have a baby—were gone or were seriously at risk. She was totally and utterly alone. Who wouldn't want to escape? Who wouldn't be tempted by a darling, warm baby who represented everything good in the world? everything she didn't have . . . and might never have?

As her thoughts found resolution she took a cleansing breath, and within that one deep sigh and its release found a sense of self-forgiveness.

But not pity.

She'd get nowhere if she felt sorry for herself. She *would* survive. She *would* get through this.

And somehow she'd do it with dignity. It was a promise.

With that in mind, Margery started the car and headed home—to the motel parking lot.

❧ ❧ ❧

It had been a long day. By the time Gennifer got home from working late, Douglas's Mercedes was in the garage. She raced inside. "Douglas?"

"Up here. I just got home."

She took the stairs two at a time, nearly colliding with him on the landing.

"Hi," he said.

"Hi," she answered.

He kissed her on the cheek. "I was just going down to see if we had any steaks in the freezer. Do we?"

She glanced toward the bedroom. "I don't know."

Douglas headed downstairs. "Want one if we do?"

"Sure."

He paused four steps down. "Where's Sarah?"

"She's not here?" Gennifer asked.

"Her car's gone."

Gennifer hadn't noticed. "I don't know where she is."

His forehead furrowed. "Don't you keep track of her when I'm gone?"

"She's not a child, Douglas."

"Right. She's a teenager. Which means she needs more watching rather than less."

"You're the one who's gone all the time. Don't you dare get after me. I do more than my share around here and—"

He held up a hand, stopping her words. "Not tonight, okay?"

She took an odd pleasure in the suggestion that his trip had been a chore. "Did you have a bad trip?"

He continued down the stairs. "Actually, it was pretty good. I'm just tired."

Of me? Tired of me?

"I'll make those steaks."

She headed to the bedroom and immediately saw his suitcase by the window. But instead of feeling relief that she had just been given ample opportunity to do her last bit of sleuthing, she experienced a wave of trepidation. What if she found the necklace gone? The implications would change her life. Change everything. She'd be forced into the unenviable decision of deciding what to do next.

She walked into the closet, removing her navy blazer. She didn't have to know. She could let things be as they were. Maybe there was a logical explanation. Maybe Douglas had purchased the necklace as a favor to his boss in Chicago. The boss was going to give the necklace to his wife, and Douglas was simply the courier.

She missed the closet bar and the hanger fell to the floor.

As did the absurd scenario. There was no reason for Douglas to travel with a $5000 necklace in his carry-on unless *he'd* purchased it himself. To give to someone of his own choosing.

Her lawyer's deductive reasoning kicked in.

The defendant purchased the necklace in Iowa. Exhibit A: the call from Visa.

The defendant took said necklace with him on a trip to Chicago. Witness: his wife.

The defendant returned from Chicago. . . .

With or without the necklace?

She had to know.

Gennifer hesitated only long enough to confirm from the noises in the kitchen that Douglas was occupied. She approached the suitcase like a member of the bomb squad approaching a suspicious package. She unzipped it. She slipped her hand between the folds of the clothes. She dug deeper. She reached the bottom. She checked all the pockets.

It wasn't there.

Her heart raced. Even she couldn't twist the evidence. Even she couldn't find a loophole.

The defendant was guilty. Guilty as sin.

She stormed from the room and down the stairs, entering the kitchen, intent on confronting Douglas. Demanding the truth.

But then he looked up from the broiler and smiled at her. When he said, "I seasoned it just the way you like it" her fire fizzled. He couldn't be guilty. He was too nice. He was too polite. He was a good man.

She spotted her keys and purse on the counter where she'd tossed them. She grabbed them and headed out the door.

"Where are you going?"

"I have something to do."

"But your steak—"

Food was the last thing on her mind.

❧ ❧ ❧

Gennifer drove without knowing where she was going. How appropriate. She didn't know where she was going in her life either.

The whole thing seemed surreal. A pearl necklace? There, then not there? It didn't make sense. If only she'd never seen it in the first place.

Ignorance was bliss.

And the truth will set you free.

Both couldn't be right. A person couldn't embrace both at the same time.

Could they?

Her mind flashed with the image of Douglas giving the burgundy jewelry box to a pretty, curvy blonde who'd opened it and squealed, then wrapped her arms around his neck, smothering him with kisses.

Which he'd passionately returned.

"Stop it!" she yelled. The driver of the car next to her at the intersection glanced her way. *Mind your own business.* The light turned green and she was in motion again. As were her thoughts.

Douglas had a girlfriend? The idea was preposterous. Douglas wasn't a lady's man. He wasn't suave, debonair, or even that handsome. As far as romance went . . . it used to be better. After all, the man had given her a techno-gadget for her birthday.

She paused in the right lane as someone attempted to parallel park in front of her. For once, she wasn't impatient and played the polite card.

Polite. That was Douglas. Adding her favorite spices to their steaks . . . he'd always done his share of the chores. He was also conscientious, always calling to tell her when he arrived safely at his destination. Goodness, the man still opened the door for her when they went out. He was the perfect man for the perfect woman. What more could she ask for?

The image of the blonde returned, of Douglas opening the door for *her.* And maybe he hadn't been to Chicago at all. Maybe that had all been a ruse.

The car in front of her completed the parking maneuver, giving her free rein to move on.

Move on. Is that what she should do? Leave him? Let him have his mistress and good riddance? She could handle being alone. She enjoyed being alone. And now that Sarah was old enough to be caught up with her own activities, Gennifer had plenty of time. She didn't need to be bothered by other people's lives. She had enough to worry about.

Like her health. Last year, at her doctor's insistence, she'd let her name be put on a list for a kidney transplant. Yet she'd drawn the line when he'd wanted Sarah and Douglas tested to see if they could be a living donor; people *could* live with just one kidney. She wouldn't do that to them—play that guilt card, sympathy card, pity card. Put their health at risk. Besides, the scenario was impossible. They couldn't be tested because they didn't know she was sick. One of these days she *would* have to tell them.

And maybe *that* would get Douglas to leave his chippie.

Gennifer's attention was drawn to a playground and picnic area on her left. Was that Sarah's car parked on the street?

She slowed and looked past the row of cars to a brightly lit picnic shelter that was hung with the banner MENTOR MANIA! She spotted Sarah talking to a fiftysomething woman with nondescript, shoulder-length hair. Sarah smiled and hugged the woman. The woman patted her on the back. They separated, but the woman kept her arm around Sarah's waist.

And Sarah didn't sidle away.

Who was this woman with her arm around her daughter?

Gennifer's husband was finding comfort elsewhere. Her daughter was finding comfort elsewhere. Traitors, both of them.

She stepped on the gas to get away.

To go home?

To an unfaithful husband?

She headed back to work. Life made sense at work.

※ ※ ※

Angie turned her head to see what Sarah was looking at. A silver blue car was driving past. An expensive silver blue car. A Jaguar? The brunette who was driving had a boyish haircut. Sassy. Classy.

"Who's that?" Angie asked.

Sarah quickly looked away. "Uh . . . no one. I just like the car."

Yeah right. Angie watched as the girl took another look. "Is that your mother?"

"I want another piece of pie," Sarah said. "You want one?"

"No, I'm fine."

But as Sarah walked away, Angie noticed the girl glancing in the direction the car had gone. If the driver was her mother, why hadn't she stopped when she'd seen her daughter? And why had Sarah denied knowing her?

Gilmore Girls indeed.

※　※　※

When Gennifer got home she saw one place setting at the kitchen table. On it was a bone-cold steak, some asparagus spears, and a foil-wrapped baked potato. She'd completely forgotten she'd left Douglas making dinner—she looked at the clock on the microwave—two hours ago.

"What's wrong with me?" she whispered.

She looked upward when she heard movement in Sarah's room overhead. Why hadn't Sarah eaten the meal?

Because she was at a picnic. Getting cozy with . . . with . . .

With whom?

Gennifer set her guilt aside and zeroed in on her daughter's surreptitious behavior—which was not acceptable. She left the plate where it was and headed upstairs to confront her. As she passed the master bedroom, she noticed its door was ajar and the light was out. At least she wouldn't have to deal with Douglas tonight.

She hesitated outside Sarah's bedroom and put an ear to the door. Silence. It wasn't that late. Surely Sarah hadn't gone to bed.

Yet it wasn't that odd to have silence emanate from her daughter's room. Gennifer had always appreciated that Sarah wasn't into loud stereos. Not that Gennifer would have allowed it. Silence was platinum.

And regarding the picnic . . . usually Gennifer didn't care what Sarah did in her spare time—as long as it wasn't illegal or dangerous—so the fact that her curiosity had lingered was odd. Didn't she have enough to worry about?

But that didn't stop her from rapping her knuckle on the door. "Sarah?"

A rustle. Then, "Yeah?"

"Can I come in?"

Another rustle. "Sure."

She opened the door and found Sarah at her desk. In the past few months Gennifer's visits to her daughter's room had become less frequent. So much so, that now she wasn't even sure what to say. "What are you doing?"

"Nothing."

Gennifer despised that answer—and Sarah knew it. Gennifer adjusted the shade of a lamp on the dresser. How to broach the subject? It was like talking to a stranger. "I saw you today."

"I saw you too."

"You did?"

"Your car's hard to miss."

Gennifer wasn't sure if it was a cut or a compliment. She moved on. "What were you doing at the park?" *Hugging a strange woman?*

"I was at a picnic."

She remembered the Mentor Mania banner. "For what?"

"Just something at school."

"Was I supposed to be there?"

"No." Sarah turned toward her desk and opened a spiral notebook.

"Would you have come? You used to come . . ."

"I'd have to know about it in order to—"

"It's okay. You weren't invited."

Gennifer tried to ignore the slap. "The banner said Mentor Mania."

Sarah shrugged.

"Who was that woman with you?"

"What woman?"

Gennifer considered throwing something. Talk about a hostile witness. "The next-door-neighbor type. The blonde with the pageboy haircut. Fiftysomething, wearing the plaid jacket and the corduroys?" *The one who hugged you.*

"Oh. That's Angie. She's a friend."

A friend or a mentor? It was a logical conclusion, but Gennifer couldn't ask and risk setting the hurtful answer between them. Besides, it made no sense. Sarah didn't need a mentor. She had two parents who gave her everything. "It looked like you've known each other a long time."

"Not long."

And you hug her? "So . . . she's a teacher?"

Sarah turned around to look at her. "No." Her eyes were set for a challenge, as if she were asking for a fight.

Ask and you shall receive . . . "Don't make this difficult."

"Make what difficult?"

Gennifer threw up her hands. "Talking. Here I am, being polite, trying to engage you in some conversation and—"

"Don't tax yourself."

Gennifer took a step toward her. "You will not talk to me like that."

"Oh, that's right. Polite. We're engaging in polite conversation. How about we disengage?"

The fight went out of Gennifer. How could she make a prosecution witness writhe on the stand yet couldn't withstand a few barbs from her own child? She turned toward the door, yet had one more question. "What does this Angie person do?"

Sarah offered her the oddest smile. "She spends time with me."

Ouch.

The phone rang and Sarah answered it. "Oh, hi . . . well . . . okay . . ." She looked right at Gennifer. "No, I don't have to ask my mother. She doesn't care. Sunday's fine. It's not like we go to church or anything. Sunday at eleven. See ya." She hung up and pointed at her notebook. "I have homework. . . ."

"Who was that?"

"Angie."

Gennifer waited for more details. Nothing. She despised how Sarah was making her work for it. "What did she want?"

"We're doing something Sunday. Together."

"What?"

"Going downtown."

"To . . . ?"

Sarah turned her back on her mother and sat squarely at her desk. She opened her notebook. "We're serving lunch at a homeless shelter."

"Why?"

Sarah glared over her shoulder. "To help those in need. To think of someone other than ourselves. Angie is a good person. I'm happy to help."

Gennifer had already had enough of this Angie woman but couldn't think of a way to knock the saint from her pedestal. Plan B came into play.

"The shelter's in a bad part of town."

Sarah rolled her eyes. "We don't have many homeless people in the suburbs, Mother."

"It's not safe there."

"I'll be fine. Angie will be with me."

Gennifer suffered a quick thought—*I'll go with them*—but quickly discarded it. Spending her weekend serving up slop to the poor was not on her list of the top one thousand things she'd like to do.

Sarah picked up the phone and extended it toward her mom. "You want to call her? make yourself feel better? Or how about doing a background check using your police connections?"

"There's nothing wrong with being concerned, Sarah."

"Wrong, no. But you have to admit it's odd that *you're* concerned, Mother. It's not your style. Not lately anyway."

The lawyer was made speechless.

Sarah turned back to the desk. "Close the door on the way out, please."

Gennifer withdrew—and shut the door quietly behind her. What else could she do?

※　※　※

Margery settled into the backseat of her car in the parking lot of the Super 8. She'd parked next to another car, but not so close to the office entrance as the previous night. No one had bothered her then and until they did, it was a relief to have a place to go.

One less point of survival to deal with.

Yet she still had some bugs to work out regarding this homeless style of living. For one thing, boredom. With no home to hang out in during the hours between work and sleep, she had to find something to do. There were only so many evenings when Talia would need her

babysitting services—and Margery wasn't sure she wanted the temptation of Tomás in the near future. And without money, shopping was
pointless—and more than a little depressing. She couldn't afford to
see a movie, and restaurants didn't like nonordering loiterers. She'd
even considered sneaking back into work, but since the entire front of
the store was covered with windows, she couldn't hang out there. The
fantasy of getting stuck overnight in a department store full of clothes,
furniture, and electronics was one thing, but spending time amid
the cough syrups, greeting cards, and toilet paper of Neighbor's was
another.

She punched her pillow and tried not to think about it. She had
another twenty-four hours to come up with something different.

The seat was hard against her hip and she longed for a mattress. Or
a warm body. When was the last time she'd slept alone?

She let a puff of air escape. What a joke. No, she and Mick may not
have purposely spent nights apart but there had been plenty of evenings when Mick didn't show up, and she never knew where he was—
and didn't dare ask. She knew better than to rile him.

She pulled her purse close, needing to hug something against her
chest. Memories of little Tomás returned. If only she had a child, that
would make everything better. She would never be alone if she had a
child. They could be a duo. A pair. Her life would mean something if
she had a child to love.

She gently draped her hand over the purse, keeping it safe and
warm.

9

*God blesses those who mourn,
for they will be comforted.*

MATTHEW 5:4

Spinal meningitis. I didn't know what the big words meant, but I would never forget them.

Those two words took my best friend, Susie, away.

First Grammy, now Susie. Two too many people gone in my eleven years of life.

What surprised me the most was that Mama agreed I could go to the funeral. "If it'll stop your bawling, go. I'll drop you off."

Once inside the church, I didn't know what to do. The memories of Grammy's funeral had faded. I saw Susie's mama and daddy, but they were way up front, all huddled together crying, so I didn't feel right about going to ask if I could sit with them.

I saw a few of our classmates and thought about going to sit with them, but they were with their parents, so that didn't feel right either. So I slipped onto a bench in the back row and scooted over enough for two places. Maybe a couple would sit there and I could pretend I belonged to them.

I spotted a line of people to the left, at the back, and saw glimpses of the coffin. Susie was in there!

I turned my head away, looking forward. I couldn't see my friend. Not in a box.

But then I remembered some of the stuff Susie had told me about heaven during this last year, that by believing in that Jesus guy and admitting you'd done wrong in your life you got a surefire ticket there. I'd even gone up front in church one Sunday and told Jesus I was his.

Susie had told me heaven was full of light and music and angels and trees. We'd argued whether the trees would be greened up like springtime or all pretty colored like fall. I'd voted for spring and Susie voted for fall, and we'd decided to leave it up to Jesus to choose. Or maybe mix and match. Things like that could happen in heaven, Susie said.

Had said.

I looked toward the coffin again. My friend was gone and I needed to see her one more time. I needed to tell her I'd come to the funeral, tell her I remembered all about heaven and would see her there.

Going to glory.

I laughed and the people in front of me looked back. But it wasn't funny laughter; it was happy laughter. If Susie had gone to glory, she'd see Grammy! Although they'd never met in the here and now, I knew— just knew—they'd like each other bunches up in heaven.

I had to tell Susie that right away so I hurried to the line that was walking by the coffin. It was shorter now, as people were sitting down. Most people looked at Susie and cried, then moved on. But I didn't want to cry. I had good news for her.

Susie was wearing her red velveteen Christmas dress. Her hair looked pretty, but her skin looked kinda ashy like she needed fresh air. That's what she needed. And since it was fall . . .

I suddenly wondered if the trees in heaven would be fall trees since Susie had died in the fall. September sixth: 9–6. I hoped so. I wanted Susie to be right about the trees—for her sake.

There was a couple behind me, so I didn't have much time. I leaned as close as I could and whispered toward my best friend's ear. "It'll be okay, Susie. I'm here today, and better'n that, Grammy's up in heaven. So look for her. She's wearing a red dress too and is probably singing.

You'll like her. I promise." I couldn't think of anything else to say, and the people behind me were whispering between themselves, looking at me as if I were crazy. I only had time for one more thing, "Frog says hey."

I didn't go back to the bench in the back row after that. I didn't need to.

I went out the big doors into the sunshine and walked under the red fall trees.

10

Truthful words stand the test of time,
but lies are soon exposed.
PROVERBS 12:19

In theory, taking a shower with a handheld sprayer in a restroom that was tiled wall to wall was a good one. But in application . . .

Margery hung her change of clothes on the purse hook on the back of the door but when she got shampoo in her eyes, she jerked the spray and doused her clothes—and the towels.

Putting on damp clothes was the least of her worries. Her long wet hair would take hours to dry. When she'd stopped at home she had purposely left their hair dryer behind seeing's how Mick also used it. Margery had been sure the hand blower in the restroom would do the trick. The air-direction spout could be turned around so it blew upward. But it didn't have near the power of a hair dryer. She thought about grabbing one off the store's shelf, but using the water sprayer was pushing it. To use a hair dryer was too much—and the packaging was complicated with little twist ties around the cord and boxes within boxes. If only her hair were short, in one of those truly blow-dry styles.

The hand dryer shut off, punctuating the idea. Margery moved to the mirror. The only reason she'd kept her hair long was because Mick liked it that way.

And Mick's not around.

Time was running out. Gladys would be at work within the hour. If Margery was going to do this thing . . .

She knew right where the scissors were sold in the home-accessories aisle, right near the little packages of thread, needles, and pins. She made her way in the dark, then hurried back to the restroom. She combed through her hair, took a deep breath, held out a hunk of it, and cut.

There was no going back now.

Margery was surprised by the spring in her hair once its weight was gone. There were actually waves. The desire not to be stuck with a little-Dutch-boy bowl cut gave her courage and she cut further, making layers. Cutting the back was difficult but doable. She wasn't bad at this. Maybe she could go to beauty school. . . .

The whacking complete, she ran her fingers through her hair, fluffing it. It was genuinely cute. Bouncy. And nearly dry.

She nodded to her reflection. "Good choice, Margery."

Then she suddenly realized a lot of time had passed. She spun around, looking at the restroom that was still wet from the shower and which now was strewn with clumps and wisps of stray hair she'd dropped on the way from cut to trash. She gathered the towels and began the cleanup.

Suddenly, she heard the bell on the front door. Gladys! She held her breath and listened. She was thankful to hear Gladys in the pharmacy section of the store. But when Gladys inevitably went back to the office to get money for the register Margery would be doomed. The restroom was right next door.

Gladys was singing, "'Jeremiah was a bullfrog. . . .'"

Margery's only hope was to grab all her things and go out the delivery door. She'd never used that door because her key fit only the front, and now she wished she'd paid attention to whether it also had a bell attached to it.

Her memory grabbed on to the sound of a doorbell. The back door didn't have a bell when it opened, but it had a doorbell that delivery-men pushed when they wanted someone to open the door.

It might work.

If she left now.

With one final sweep of the towel over the floor, Margery shoved all the toiletries into her purse. She gathered her dirty clothes along with the wet towels, and readied herself to open the restroom door.

"'. . . singing, joy to the world . . .'"

Holding the center lock button so it wouldn't click, Margery turned the knob. The door opened without a sound. She exited and headed to her right, into the small storage room that held the delivery door. The room had no window and was dark. She ducked into the darkness and paused a moment, hoping her eyes would adjust quickly.

Gladys started the second verse as Margery made out the faint edges of boxes and shelves. The path to the door was clear.

Her movements were fluid and fast. There was no jangling bell. The early morning air was cold; she closed the door behind her with only the smallest click.

She ran to her car, dumping the items in the back. Once in the driver's seat, she pushed a hand against the beat of her pounding chest. That was too close.

Margery looked at the car's clock: 6:04. Why was Gladys at work so early?

It didn't matter. From now on, Margery would have to come even earlier.

※ ※ ※

Gladys shivered at a rush of cold air, froze in place, and looked in the direction of the store room. It was as if the back door had been opened.

That was ridiculous. She'd checked the door last night upon leaving.

She shivered again, though not from the cold. She needed to check the back and scanned the pharmacy for something to use as a weapon. There wasn't much. Would a burglar be afraid if she tossed a bottle of pills at him?

Pills. Drugs. Maybe someone was after drugs.

Gladys picked up her cell phone, ready to call 911. Weapon, weapon . . . she needed *something*.

She remembered on the customer side of the Drop-Off counter was self-defense pepper spray. She tiptoed around and was thankful the thing wasn't encased in some noisy wrapping. She readied her finger on the trigger and headed toward the back.

Local Pharmacist Overpowers Drug Thief. Film at eleven.

Gladys edged to the corner of the hall that led past her office and the restroom, and made her way into the storage room. The light from the pharmacy did not turn the corner, so darkness reigned.

But it would not be victorious.

Gladys had always hated movies where people heard a bump in the night and went to check on it—in the dark. She'd often found herself yelling at the screen, "Turn on the light, you doofus!" After all, a person could always switch the light back off. But surely, the knowledge gained by seeing who was there was more worthwhile than tiptoeing blindly into a black hole. Especially when one needed all the sight perks one could get.

True to her convictions, Gladys readied her pepper spray, strode around the corner, and flipped on the light in the storage room. The "Aha!" that came out of her mouth was unexpected, appropriate, but unheard by anyone else.

Because there was no one there. Gaining courage, Gladys looked into every corner and behind every stack of boxes. No drug thief present.

What about the door? It was shut. The lock in the doorknob was engaged.

But . . . the dead bolt was not.

Had someone left via this door? Had her early morning work surprised the seedy culprit who expected her to be in at a later hour?

Had he stolen anything?

She hadn't noticed anything amiss in the pharmacy, but there were other things to steal. Gladys marched into her office but found the money box intact. Next, she entered the main part of the store and flipped on all the lights. The register never contained more than a hundred dollars in change and it was all there. She strode up and down each aisle but found nothing out of place. Had she scared the thief off before he could steal anything?

Gladys stood in the middle of the candy aisle and let herself breathe. She rubbed her head. She needed some Excedrin and went into the restroom for some water.

But after taking the pills she noticed there were water droplets on the mirror. And there was a distinct shine on the wall to her left. She touched it. It was wet. Stepping back, she saw the hint of water on the floor.

Any stray moisture from yesterday would have long ago evaporated. Which meant the thief had used the restroom—and was messy about it. None of this made sense. The only thing Gladys was sure about was that she was going to call an alarm company.

Take that, you criminal.

❀ ❀ ❀

Gladys met Margery as she entered the front of the store for work. The older woman's face was pulled and her red hair seemed to glow especially bright.

"I'm so glad you're here." Gladys slipped a hand through Margery's arm and led her to the register. "I hate to worry you but we had a break-in last night and—"

"Break-in?" Margery's stomach tightened.

"Or break-out, or something," Gladys said. She took Margery's purse and put it away in the drawer under the counter. "I was here early and felt a cold rush of air, as if the back door had been opened. And it had."

"How do you know?"

"The dead bolt wasn't engaged. The dead bolt from the inside. I know I locked it last night."

Margery didn't remember unlocking any dead bolt when she'd escaped out the back, but she'd been running on adrenaline so it was entirely possible. "Are you sure you locked it?" she asked.

"I'm sure." Gladys paced in the checkout lane. "And there's more. The restroom was wet."

"What?"

"The walls and the floor, even the mirror. It was as if someone had used it. I don't know . . . maybe they bathed in it." Her eyes lit up. "Maybe a homeless person broke in and used the facilities."

You're way too close. Margery thought about the shower sprayer. She hadn't had time to put it back. "Did they take anything?"

"Not that I can see. But they would have if I hadn't shown up early."

Which led to another question. "Why were you here so early? We're not that busy, are we?"

Gladys stopped pacing and looked toward the pharmacy, then at Margery, then to the floor. "You may not know this, but my eyesight isn't very good."

Margery had guessed as much but only nodded.

"I'm finding the need to be extra careful. To check things twice. I wouldn't want anyone to get hurt because of a mistake I made. So I've decided to start coming in early."

So much for showers. Then Margery thought of a solution. "I could help you. Check things for you. I'd help however you need help. Then you wouldn't have to come in so early anymore."

"That's sweet of you, Margery, and I may take you up—" Gladys came close and touched her hair, obviously noticing it for the first time. "You cut it."

Margery fingered the nape of her neck. "Do you like it?"

"It's kind of cute. Bouncy."

"It's easy care."

Gladys laughed and pulled out a hank of her frizzy red do. "At least you can do something with yours. Mine has a mind of its own."

"It's beautiful," Margery said.

"It is what it is." Gladys started to walk away, then turned back. "Oh. What I was going to tell you was that I arranged for an alarm company to come in next week to install alarms on both doors. We'll need a code to get in."

"Code?"

"Keypad. I should have done it a long time ago. A pharmacy is too big a temptation nowadays." She straightened a Sale sign on some Bayer aspirin. "And if you don't mind, I think I'll be keeping the code to myself for a bit. No offense, but until I get used to it, until I feel safe again, I think it's best King and I are the only ones responsible. I hope you understand."

"Of course." Margery understood perfectly. She had an iffy reputation because she'd tried to steal from Gladys.

Yet not having the code affected her life in more drastic ways: the access to her shower had just been cut off.

As had her hair. She'd cut off her hair for nothing.

※ ※ ※

Angie handed her credit card to the clerk. She noticed the young woman's name tag: Margery. She looked at the girl with new eyes. Was this the babysitter Talia had talked about? There weren't that many Margerys in the world.

"Excuse me, but do you babysit for Talia Soza?"

The girl's eyes flashed. "Little Tomás, yes. I babysat for Talia last night."

"I'm Talia's mother. The baby's grandmother."

Margery shook her hand vigorously. "I'm so happy to meet you. Tomás is such a good little boy. Very sweet. And I bet you're excited for the new baby."

"Very." Angie signed the charge slip as Margery sacked her purchase.

"Are you going on a trip?" Margery asked.

Angie didn't understand.

Margery held up a travel-sized bottle of shampoo. The entire sack was full of trial-sized toiletries.

Angie laughed. "Those are for the homeless shelter. I ran out of hotel freebies to donate. I guess my husband and I need to go on another trip." She shook her head. "I can't imagine being homeless."

"Oh, I can," Margery said. "Not to have a place to sleep, to eat, to spend your time. My heart goes out to them."

"That's why I volunteer at the shelter."

"Doing what?"

"Whatever needs doing. A lot of times I serve meals. And talk to the people."

"I bet they're lonely."

Angie blinked. This was not the usual reaction. Most people nodded politely and said, "That's nice." But it was obvious Margery knew loneliness personally. And upon further study, there *was* a glow of compassion in her face. Angie decided to take a chance. "I'm going to serve lunch there tomorrow with a high school girl I'm mentoring. Would you like to come with us?"

Margery hesitated, then said, "I think I'd like that."

"I'll pick you up. What's your address?"

Margery fumbled the sack and nearly sent all the toiletries to the floor. She gathered the handles and handed them to Angie. "To make things easier, why don't you pick me up here."

"Quarter to eleven, then."

What a nice young woman. No wonder Talia likes her.

❈ ❈ ❈

Gennifer didn't usually go into work on a Saturday, but with the way things were at home . . .

She got out a file and had just read the first paragraph when she heard a noise, looked up, and saw her boss, Charles Chasen, in her doorway.

"Gennifer."

"Hello, Mr. Chasen." He was wearing a plaid shirt under a jeans jacket. She'd never seen him in anything but a suit. "I have a lot of work so I decided to come in and—"

He held up a hand. "You will never hear me complain about someone working hard. Carry on."

She looked down, then realized he was still in the doorway. "Yes?"

"Since you're here . . . I'd like a chance to talk to you about your schedule issues." He looked at his watch. "I have a few phone calls to make. Why don't you stop into my office in a half hour or so. Would that work for you?"

"Sure."

When he left her Gennifer felt her heart race into panic mode. With this one exchange, another problem was added to her burden. Charles Chasen was the partner who'd cornered her about coming in late three days a week. She'd lied and told him Sarah needed a ride to tutoring on those days, and had planned to come up with a better excuse. But with the Douglas-and-the-necklace fiasco she'd forgotten all about it. She couldn't get to work before nine because . . . ?

A blank.

She leaned her elbows on her desk and massaged the back of her neck. This was just great. Her health was bad and going to get worse, her marriage was in trouble, her daughter couldn't stand the sight of her, and now her career was teetering on the edge of a cliff.

So why fight it?

Gennifer grabbed a few dollars from her purse and strode to the vending machines in the office kitchen. It was like viewing a cornucopia of forbidden delights. She chose some potato chips, a Snickers bar, and a carton of chocolate milk. She returned to her office, leaned back in her chair, and put her feet up. Her ankles were swelling, as they often did between dialysis sessions. She opened the bag of chips and pulled out the first one. It was folded over, her favorite kind. She turned it around, studying its lusciousness. How long had it been since she'd had chips? The dialysis diet was a bore: high protein, low carbs, low sodium. She was lucky she wasn't diabetic or they would've taken sugar from her too. She moved the Snickers close, as well as the carton of milk. They were next.

She wasn't really hungry. Her appetite had also been a casualty of the disease. This wasn't about hunger; it was about the other kind of appetite—desire. Comfort. Decadence. It was about drowning her troubles in what used to be her four favorite food groups: fat, sugar, salt, and chemicals.

So there.

She carefully laid the chip on her tongue and enjoyed the tingle of the salt against her taste buds. Then the crispy crunch. Ahhh. This was the life.

Not anymore. You're going to pay for this Monday. Your electrolytes, minerals, and fluid measurements are going to be way off at dialysis. They'll know you were a bad girl, and your body is going to rebel.

So be it. The way she was feeling, rebellion of body might as well join the rebellion of her spirit, her emotions, and her intellect.

She cracked open the milk and took a big swig.

※ ※ ※

Charles Chasen stood when Gennifer entered his office. "Have a seat," he said. "Glad you could make it."

Was that a cut?

Charles settled in behind the desk. "Well then."

She smiled and nodded.

He picked up a pen. "How's the car situation going with your daughter?"

Fine collided with *We're working on it* smashed into . . .

The truth.

What else could she do? Her job was important to her. With her marriage and family in mutiny mode, she didn't have the strength to battle her career too. Maybe if she surrendered a smidgen of her coveted control to one, she would gain it back elsewhere.

Charles's face reflected her hesitation. "Is there a problem?"

"Yes." She crossed her legs and adjusted her khakis so they wouldn't wrinkle. "And no."

He set the pen aside. "Go on."

Gennifer took a deep breath. "I've been lying to you about my reason for being late three days a week."

His eyes hardened. "Oh?"

"The truth is, I have a kidney problem. Renal failure they call it. I'm on dialysis those mornings."

"Is that where they hook you up and clean out your system?"

"Pretty much." Since sympathy was vital, she added, "I need the procedure to survive."

"Oh my," Charles said. "I'm so sorry."

She shrugged, and actually liked the feeling of being the victim— the brave victim. This wasn't as bad as she'd expected.

He picked up his pen again. "So . . . how do you feel?"

Gennifer thought about her junk-food binge, but honestly could say, "At the moment, I feel fine." She uncrossed her legs and leaned toward his desk. "This does not and will not affect my work. The dialysis is successfully keeping everything under control. I'm fine. Really."

"What about a transplant? I was reading an article about those and—"

Yes. That. "I'm on a list."

"Good." He pointed his pen at her. "It's your duty to cover every base, grab on to every alternative."

"I'm trying."

"Please know that when the time comes, we're with you. You can take all the time you need."

"I can?"

"Of course." Chasen stood and came around the desk toward her. He pulled her into an awkward hug, then let go. "You're a valued member of this firm, Gennifer. We'll stand behind you. Just let us know what you need."

She felt tears threaten. She had not expected simple kindness. "Thank you. I appreciate—"

He pointed a finger at her, looking very much like a father chastising a child. "But no more fake excuses."

"Agreed." They shook hands; then she added, "I'd appreciate if you kept this between us, Mr. Chasen. At least for the time being."

He hesitated just a moment. "I think we can do that. And speaking of others . . . how are your husband and daughter taking it?"

The lie came quickly. "They're very supportive."

※　※　※

Gennifer entered her office in a far different mood from the way she'd exited fifteen minutes earlier. The burden that had been weighing her down was lighter now, and she was amazed at how good it felt to have someone know her secret.

Even if it wasn't her family.

The pity she'd so frantically avoided had not been condescending or embarrassing. Charles Chasen had shown true concern and a willingness to help. Maybe—just maybe—Douglas and Sarah would respond in kind.

Maybe it was time to tell them.

She'd have to think about it.

꙲ꙮ ꙲ꙮ ꙲ꙮ

Talia liked the Garden Atrium at the hotel where she worked. It was an open-air inner courtyard dotted with planters and benches, its greenery carefully maintained by the hotel staff. It was often booked for small receptions—when weather permitted.

Which left out today. Talia buttoned her coat and lifted the collar before taking out her PB and J sandwich. Good thing she was wearing pants and leather boots.

No, the good thing was, she was alone. She wasn't fit for human consumption today. Snappy, moody, with no patience whatsoever. She'd come this close to hanging up on a difficult client. That's when she'd grabbed her coat and lunch and escaped into the cold.

Cold Talia. Cold.

The memories of last night's aborted dinner with Nesto, with his ending up sleeping in his recliner . . . where was her empathy? Where was her common sense? Of course the man would talk about TV shows. He needed someone to talk to. Who was she to judge if his subject choices were good enough? And of course he wanted to pay for the check.

Of course she'd blown every point.

She took multiple bites, cramming her mouth with sandwich—if only it were a half-pound burger with the works. She shook her head, making crumbs fall. In disgust, she tossed the rest of her sandwich into a planter nearby.

"Halt! No littering allowed!"

It was Wade. She chewed furiously, covering her mouth with a hand, the peanut butter and soft bread making the process difficult. "I didn't hear you come out."

"You were too busy desecrating company property." He retrieved her discarded sandwich and opened it. "Peanut butter."

She swallowed with difficulty. "With apple jelly. I get tired of hotel food." *Expensive hotel food.*

He raised an eyebrow.

"Sorry. Actually, I felt the need for some comfort food." She patted her very pregnant belly. "It's for the baby."

"I can't remember the last time I had one of these."

"You don't know what you're missing."

He shocked her by brushing a piece of dirt off the bread and taking a bite. He chewed thoughtfully. "Not bad."

"I have another half I'll share with you—minus the dirt."

"I'll take you up on that." She scooted over and he sat on the bench beside her. She tore the sandwich in two and offered both sections. He took the smaller one.

"So. Why the cold-weather picnic?"

Talia realized Wade was wearing only his suit coat. She stood. "You must be freezing. You need to go inside."

He took her hand. "I'm plenty warm. Sit."

Once she was seated again he did not let go but placed their clasped hands on his knee. "You're having a bad day."

She laughed softly. "You noticed."

"Mr. Collins called back and asked if something was wrong."

And to think she'd almost hung up on him . . . "I'm so sorry. I shouldn't let my problems affect my work."

"No, you shouldn't. But it's not surprising you do."

She yanked her hand away and stood. "Because I'm an emotional woman? Because I'm not as professional as a man would be? Because—"

"Because you have a husband who's critically ill. Because you're having to deal with *dealing* alone."

She felt like a complete fool and sank onto the bench. "Sorry. Again. I wish I had a button I could push that would light a Sorry sign on my forehead."

"It *would* save time."

Talia relished the levity. She hadn't had enough levity. Hadn't had enough . . . of a lot of things.

"Anything I can do?" Wade asked.

Unfortunately, the initial answer to his question involved one of the not-enough issues in her life. She set that aside and said, "Just do what you're doing. Tolerate me. Listen to me. Don't fire me."

"I can handle that." Wade stood. "I'll leave you to your lunch."

"I'm done." She packed up the brown sack, choosing company over solitude.

❀ ❀ ❀

I can't believe I did that. I can't believe I ran out of gas.

Talia pulled into their driveway and stopped with a squeal of the tires, shoved the gearshift into park, and got out of the car. She stormed up the front walk, then suddenly realized she'd left Tomás in the backseat.

She tried to ignore the niggling feeling in her stomach. Running out of gas, then leaving her child strapped in the car were mistakes that heralded something far more serious, far deeper than her normal harried state of mind. The only blessing had been the fact she'd run out of gas *before* picking her son up at day care. She never would have been able to walk the three blocks to the gas station with him in tow.

Talia didn't need to use her key. Nesto met her at the door. "Where have you been?"

Usually she'd be quite willing to play the martyr by listing her woes. But not today. "Don't ask."

"I was ready to call the police."

She unzipped Tomás's jacket. "We're not that late."

"Over an hour."

"I ran out of gas." She didn't mention forgetting Tomás in the car.

"Why didn't you call?"

She didn't want to admit her cell phone was dead. She'd forgotten to recharge it. "Sorry." She tossed the jacket and her own coat on the back of the couch, went into the kitchen, and turned on the oven. "I made a casserole this morning. I'll preheat the oven and we'll be eating in forty-five minutes." She backtracked to the stairs. "Take care of Tomás while I change."

Talia didn't wait for him to object. Not that he would. But she didn't want anything to stop her from getting inside her room where she could close the door and . . .

Fall on the bed.

She closed her eyes. Maybe after a quick nap she'd wake up and be happy and kind and—

Mmmm. Sleep . . .

Talia's eyes shot open. She held her breath, unsure what had yanked her from her sleep.

"Talia! Come down here!"

She was on the stairs in seconds. Tomás was standing in a corner by his father's recliner, biting on the corner of a board book. He looked at her, then toward the kitchen.

It was only then, when she allowed herself a full breath, that she noticed a horrible smell emanating from that room. A foreign, nonfood type of smell.

She found Nesto in the kitchen with the oven door open, smoke rolling out.

"The Tupperware melted!"

Even as Talia was telling herself this was not possible, she saw the ocean of red plastic covering the bottom of the oven as well as the red stalactites hanging from the metal rack. Lemon mini-muffins dotted the top of the rack like survivors of a sinking ship.

"Did you check the oven before turning it on?"

Obviously not. And she always checked the oven. Her mind leap-frogged guilt and zeroed in on finding a solution. She grabbed hot pads and removed the rack, carefully balancing the unlucky muffins. "Open the door!" she told her husband. From the back stoop she tossed the hot rack into the grass.

Inside, she left the back door open to air out the place and tried to think of something she could use to scrape up the goo. She opened the utensil drawer and found a stainless-steel baker's scraper and grabbed the morning newspaper sitting on the counter. "Move!" she said to Nesto. She set the papers on the opened oven door and began scooping up the red mess with the scraper, transferring it to the newspaper.

"Don't get burned," Nesto said.

Duh. It was difficult maneuvering around the hot coils at the bottom of the oven, and her first inclination was to shut the oven door and pronounce, "We'll have to get a new one."

If only they could afford it.

She spotted Tomás in the doorway leading to the living room. "Hot!" he said, pointing to the oven.

"Yes, baby, it's hot." She looked at Nesto, moving a lock of hair out of her eyes with the back of her hand. "You two go outside. I don't want either of you breathing these fumes." She didn't want the baby breathing

them either, but at the moment that couldn't be helped. Nesto herded
Tomás into the front room. "Put on your jackets!" Talia called after
them.

What would they do without her?

She didn't want to know.

※ ※ ※

They went out to dinner—if McDonald's could be called "out." Talia
didn't feel much like eating, so she ordered herself a kid's meal. Tomás
was thrilled to get two toys.

In between bites of his chicken nuggets, Tomás climbed on the play
equipment. If only Talia had so much energy.

"Take care, Tomás," Nesto said.

Take care. It was the tagline of her life. *Talia Soza: Take care or be
square.*

Nesto took a bite of his grilled-chicken sandwich, then glanced at
his watch. "It's time for my medicine. Is it in your purse?"

Why would it be in my—?

Then she remembered. One of her tasks today was to pick up
Nesto's medicine at Neighbor's.

"You didn't forget, did you?" he asked.

Talia pressed a hand against her forehead. "I did. And they're
closed."

Nesto tapped the crystal of his watch. "I need it. You know that.
I *need—*"

"I know; I know. Maybe if I call Gladys . . ." She reached for her
purse, for her cell phone, which was still dead. She spotted a pay phone
on the wall and dug out some change. "I'll fix it, Nesto. Don't worry.
I'll fix it."

※ ※ ※

There was nothing Gladys liked better than homemade buttermilk biscuits slathered in butter and boysenberry preserves. The aroma emanating from her oven brought back memories of her mother's kitchen.
Her mom had not been a good cook, but she *could* make biscuits. They'd
eaten them a dozen ways: alone, with eggs, with creamed chipped beef,

creamed tuna, sausage gravy. They were definitely a multipurpose food. And more importantly, they were almost done.

Gladys checked the chicken breast in the George Foreman grill, and poured some lettuce from a bag into a bowl. Like her mother she chose her culinary adventures with a discerning eye. Cook and bake when you must, but otherwise . . . she saw no shame in taking advantage of shortcut cooking.

The timer on the oven buzzed and Gladys was there in seconds, hot pads ready. Out came the pan of biscuits, golden brown and inviting. With the flick of a finger, she flipped two onto her plate. Slicing them open was like opening an oyster and searching for the pearl. Rising steam heralded the coming delicacy. Gladys added the butter, loving how it liquefied upon contact. Then the preserves. Forget the chicken—*this* was the essence of the meal. The *pièce de résistance*. She couldn't wait to be seated. The biscuit called to her like a Siren calling Odysseus. She picked up the hot biscuit gingerly, careful not to drip the preserves. She took a bite, eager to savor—

Yuck! Gladys leaned over the sink and spit it out.

The bitter taste was so bad she had to cover it up with a swig of her Fresca.

Confused, she took a bite of another biscuit—sans butter and boy-senberries.

Yuck again.

Something had gone terribly wrong. Yet this was not a new recipe. Although she didn't know it by heart, she'd never had the biscuits not turn out.

Gladys picked up the daisy-edged recipe card and read through the ingredients. The words appeared a bit blurry, so she moved to the better light above the sink. Flour, buttermilk, salt. Check.

Three teaspoons baking powder . . .

Gladys looked to the sink where she'd tossed the dirty measuring spoons. The powder-encrusted tablespoon glared at her. She put the spoon to the tip of her tongue.

Yup. Bitter. That was the taste of the moment, all right.

The evidence was in. She'd used three *tablespoons*, not three *teaspoons*. A simple mistake. One anyone could make.

It had nothing to do with her eyes. Really, it didn't.

Gladys put the offending spoon back in the sink with the deliberate motion of a doctor working with operating-room equipment. Then she calmly walked over to the baking sheet of biscuits, picked it up . . .

And flung it across the room.

The pan crashed against the corner of the kitchen island, did a back-flip, nicked the fridge, and landed on the tile floor near a chair. The ten biscuits that had not been cannibalized abandoned ship—some sooner, some later, each one suffering a different degree of injury. Call 911. Paramedics needed.

The room responded with stunned silence. Even the fridge clicked off in shock, holding its breath in horror.

Like a drunk driver who'd just caused an accident, Gladys stared at the scene, uncomprehending. Then, realizing she was to blame, her legs gave out. She crumpled to the floor and began to sob. Long dormant tears forced their way to the surface. Given air, they let loose in sickening, wrenching wails.

Even as the sounds circled the room gaining speed and intensity, Gladys thought, *Surely this can't be coming from me.*

She shut her mouth. The sounds stopped, proving her wrong.

Surely they were. Surely these disturbing sounds had been hiding, suspended, just waiting to be released.

Surely she wasn't as in control as she'd thought she was.

Her legs protested the odd position and she moved them aside, allowing her bottom full access to the cold floor. She should get up. She should move as quickly as possible from this place of total despair to a familiar position, a posture and place that would remind her of all things normal, regular, and sane.

But she could not. During their escape, the wails had grabbed on to moderation, self-control, restraint, logic, and common sense, and had yanked them away from their safe core and hurled them into the room where they'd fallen into invisible and irretrievable piles of nothing-ness. Gladys leaned to the right, letting her shoulder find the floor. She curled up in a ball.

She was empty. She was hollow. She was spent.

She was done.

❊ ❊ ❊

Ring. Peace. *Ring.* Peace.

Gladys opened her eyes in time to hear the phone ring the third time.

Where am I?

In a split second she placed herself on the floor of the kitchen. In another second she remembered why.

Ring.

The fourth ring? In another two rings, the answering machine would kick in.

Even as she pushed herself to her feet, even as her muscles complained, Gladys considered ignoring it.

But it might be Aunt June. It might be about Mama.

Family duty won out. She reached the phone right after the fifth ring. "Yes?"

"Gladys! I'm so glad you're there. I tried calling the pharmacy, but it was closed and—"

"Talia?"

"Yes, I'm sorry. This is Talia."

Talia explained that she'd forgotten to get Nesto's medicine. She apologized profusely, but would be forever grateful . . .

"Don't worry about it. Meet me at the store."

Gladys hung up, glanced at the accident scene behind her, grabbed her purse, and headed out.

❊ ❊ ❊

If effusive thanks and apologies were turned into real money, Gladys would have reached millionaire status that night. Within ten minutes Talia—and Nesto—were taken care of.

A crisis averted. Thanks to Dr. Gladys Quigley.

That done, Gladys put the tools of her trade away, getting ready to leave. But when she shut off the light, she did not move toward the door. She wanted to move—she intended to move—but for some reason her body rebelled and stood fast.

In the dark.

In the empty store.

Then suddenly, she heard herself speak aloud. "What am I going to do?"

She looked up when the bell on the front door clanged. King entered, lit by the streetlight outside. "Gladys?"

She stepped toward the pharmacy window so he could see her. "Back here."

He closed the door and locked it. He didn't switch on the lights. "I saw the lights on, then go off. It's long past closing. Is everything all—?"

"Talia needed a prescription for Nesto."

"She couldn't get this during the day?"

"She forgot."

He walked through the store toward the pharmacy. "And you came to her rescue."

"I couldn't tell her no." *Do I have on any makeup at all? Did I cry it all off?* Why hadn't she cared about her looks when it had been Talia she was seeing? Hopefully, King would keep the lights out.

He came in the pharmacy. His hand reached for the switch.

"No!" she said. "Just keep it off. We don't want to appear open."

The glow of the streetlight had diminished intensity in the back, but there was enough. King took a step toward her, his head cocked. "Are you all right?"

Gladys reset the notepad and pen on the counter. "Long day."

He took a step closer. "And?"

She moved the pen from the side of the notepad to the top. "And it was a long day."

"Gladys . . ."

He was within touching distance now. His hand started to bridge the gap between them.

She stepped away. "Just go away, King. Leave me alone."

His hand froze in midair. Then he said, "Never."

"I can handle this."

"Handle what?"

"This."

"What's *this*?"

She sighed dramatically. He was not going to go away.

Do you really want him to?

Before she could weigh the pros and cons of opening up to her partner, she heard herself say, "I lost it this evening."

Blessedly, he did not ask what she'd lost. "'She was lost, but now she is found.'"

Gladys had no idea what he was talking about. "I threw a pan of biscuits across my kitchen."

His eyebrows rose. "Why?"

"Because they tasted awful."

"You're very hard on your food. I'm sure they were trying their best."

"It was my fault. I put in three tablespoons of baking powder instead of three teaspoons."

"That would do it."

He wasn't getting the significance. "Don't you see? I made a mistake."

"People do that."

"No, they don't! Most people can see the recipe card. Most people aren't losing their eyesight!"

He hesitated a moment, then took a step toward her. To comfort her.

She walked away from him, shaking her head. "No. Don't tell me it's going to be all right, or say something placating like I have a right to be upset."

"I wasn't going to say that."

She pointed a finger at him. "Yes you were. I know you."

At least he had the decency to shrug.

"The thing is, up until now I've handled everything life has thrown at me. And recently I've even handled an employee stealing from us, bad news from the eye doctor, my mother's illness, and the knowledge that someone broke into the store."

"That *is* a lot."

She went back to her list, needing to get it out. "I've handled all those things with strength and grace. But tonight when I messed up the biscuits . . ."

"You realized you can't do it all by yourself."

This was not what she wanted to hear. "I *can* do it. I *will* do it. I just don't know how."

He leaned against the counter, showing her his profile. "Have you prayed about this, Red?"

"God helps those who help themselves."

"Which you've done quite well at. As far as you're able. But now . . ."

She paced between two shelves of meds. "God wants *people* to work things out. Certainly he has enough to do handling the big stuff of the world. Wars, pestilence, tornadoes, making sure every college football team wins the big game."

"'If you seek him, you will find him.'"

"But I don't need to seek him."

"You don't? *You* don't?"

It sounded like a trick question. She wasn't sure how to respond.

"Do you actually think you get extra points for handling things yourself?"

She stopped at the end of the row. "Well . . . yeah. I don't want to be a weakling."

His jaw dropped. "So you think people who need God are weak?"

She shrugged. "Can't you see that I'm trying to give God a break? Give him time to help people who really need him?"

"Which isn't you."

It was a cocky statement. Gladys hesitated.

"Your hesitation shows at least a smidgen of wisdom," King said.

She put her hands on her hips. "Excuse me?"

"Ignorance and arrogance are close friends. It's best to avoid both."

"Are you calling me names?"

"You're a smart woman, Gladys. Or at least I thought you were. And if you'd jump down from your pedestal you'd realize what you need to do." He walked toward the front door.

"King? Come back here!"

"No thanks. I don't want to interfere where I'm not wanted." He unlocked the door, opened it, then looked back at her. "And neither does God."

11

Turn to me and have mercy,
for I am alone and in deep distress.

PSALM 25:16

Mama held the lottery ticket and glared at me. "Are you sure that's the number I should pick?"

I wasn't sure. Not at all, but since Mama had insisted I pick the number this time it made sense to choose 9696969696. "It's a good number," I said.

"Better be." Mama filled it in, chewing on her tongue. When she was done she held the ticket between us. "You don't want to know what will happen if this loses."

For once, Mama was right. I didn't want to know. She'd changed so much in the past couple of years since leaving Daddy. She was more negative, more desperate. She was still consumed with living the good life, getting rich, and having more, but there was a panic about her, like she had to have it *now*.

It didn't help that Daddy had remarried and had a good job in a town way out in California and Mama was still selling cosmetics. I liked Daddy's wife, Anne. She was nice and had taken me shopping for school clothes when they came to town to visit the one time. Mama got really mad when I came home with those clothes. "How do you rate?"

she'd yelled. "He gets a new house, a new job, a new town, a new wife, and I get nothing?"

I decided it wasn't the time to tell Mama that Anne was pregnant, that Daddy was getting a new kid too.

But to make amends, I took one of the sweaters back to the store and used the money to buy Mama a pretty blouse. She was a little better after that.

But she'd be even better if she won the lottery. I prayed that God would make that happen. For both our sakes.

*   *   *

Mama sat on the couch, put an arm around me, and pulled me so close our hips touched. I had never seen her so happy. "This is going to be great. I wish Ted could be here."

I had other wishes for my mother's newest boyfriend. A slow boat and China were involved. And various forms of torture.

The smiling lady on the TV made the balls in the machine jump. One by one, they were sucked into a tube. She displayed them like they were huge, round pearls. "The first number is 9."

Mama screamed. "Here we go!" She squeezed me tighter.

Another ball. The lady was all teeth and hair. And curves. "The second number is 6."

Another scream, but this time Mama kissed the top of my head. "I knew you could do it, Gigi! We're going to be rich! I'm going to do so much for you, girl. We'll get out of this stinkin' place and—"

The third number swooshed into the tube. I didn't need the lady to say what it was. It didn't matter. It wasn't a 9.

Mama sat perfectly still. And when the fourth number was also wrong . . . forget any more kisses, the arm around me, and sitting hip to hip. Mama stood over me, her face red.

As was the welt mark from the slap I got on my face. As were the finger marks that appeared on my arms after Mama grabbed me and shoved me across the room. As was the blood that trickled from the corner of my mouth, that dripped onto my knee as I cowered in the corner while Mama yelled at me.

"Why do I listen to you? You don't know anything. You and that stupid number. You're a freak and I don't know why I ever kept you around."

I needed to pick a new favorite color. Maybe blue.

Blue were the bruises . . .

※ ※ ※

I held my breath so I could listen to Mama's breathing as she slept on the couch. I hadn't moved from the corner, having learned that moving around—and especially trying to leave—only made things worse. Mama liked to have an audience when she got mad. And a victim. By staying put in the corner I was both. But that didn't mean I could relax. Making myself as small a target as possible was important.

Mama snored. After shoving me across the room she'd started drinking. I figured she was passed out but she'd fooled me before, springing to life when I moved too soon.

I'd wait a little longer.

I let my tongue find the broken skin at the corner of my mouth. There was a scab there. I noticed some dried smudges of blood on my knee, so I spit on my finger and cleaned them off.

After I'd heard Mama call me the bad names—the first time—I'd stopped listening and started planning. I didn't want to do this anymore. Today's beating was worse than the others, and now that Ted was around . . .

At twelve I didn't know the details of what a guy like that could do, but I knew the gist of it. Just the way he looked at me, all swarmy and schmoozy. It creeped me out. And from the things Mama had said tonight, I knew for sure if she had to choose between Ted and me, I was out.

So I might as well do the "outing" myself. Watching Mama drink the vodka, waiting for her to pass out, I'd made myself a mental list. Since it was summer, the backpack I usually used for school was empty. I'd fill it with a few clothes, a brush and toothbrush, a bag of beef jerky Mama had gotten for Ted, some graham crackers, and the bag of chocolate chips Mama had bought one weekend when she'd decided to make chocolate-chip cookies—which she'd never made because Ted had come over and they'd gone out. The food would get me through the night— especially since it was nearly morning. Plus, I'd take Grammy's pillow, and the pictures of Grammy and Susie I had on my dresser. With that in mind, I looked around the living room for any other pictures I wanted.

But there weren't any to choose from.

Not a single picture of anyone.

I looked harder. I knew there used to be one of my school pictures on the bookshelf. But it wasn't there. Why had Mama moved it?

It didn't matter. Gone was gone. But why hadn't I noticed till now? noticed that Mama and Ted wanted nothing to do with me? And neither did Daddy. He had a new life now, with a new, normal kid on the way. He hardly ever called, and he'd never asked me to come visit. Not that I blamed him. If I could get away and start over, I would too.

Speaking of . . . I raised my chin and looked defiantly at my mother. What was that old saying? "Kick me once, shame on you. Kick me twice, shame on me." I'd taken an awful lot of kicks. Twelve years' worth was more than enough.

Mama's snores seemed deeper. It was time to go. Where? I didn't know.

Away was good. Anywhere that wasn't nearby. For there was no good nearby here. Not in this house.

12

*In due season God will judge everyone,
both good and bad, for all their deeds.*

ECCLESIASTES 3:17

Unfortunately, no good fairies cleaned the kitchen while Gladys was sleeping. The night before, she'd come home from the store and her God discussion with King, and had marched right past the mess and up to bed.

Where she'd slept fitfully.

Her lack of a good night's sleep was God's doing; she knew it was. But if he thought he could niggle and nudge her into giving in . . .

Now, standing in the doorway leading to the kitchen, the biscuit debris assailed her, startling evidence of her meltdown over the baking powder.

She retrieved the baking sheet from its landing site near a chair, and in that one bending action, that one movement, was forced to face the truth.

Whom was she kidding? This mess was not caused by baking powder. It was caused by her inability to see the recipe. It was caused by the fact that she was going blind—and it really ticked her off.

But didn't she have a right to be mad?

She tossed the pan in the sink with a clatter and forced herself to take a breath. Her mind swam with thoughts she'd been fighting to avoid. Why couldn't God leave her alone? She was very willing to return the favor.

A couple more breaths in and out, a couple more attempts to clear her mind and think of anything else, made her take drastic action. She grabbed the edge of the counter and looked upward. "You want me to talk to you, God? Fine. You got it. But answer this: why are you doing this to me?"

The heavens did not offer an answer.

"Just as I thought." Gladys pulled the trash can from under the sink and moved to gather the biscuit remains. "There is no reason you're doing this except the fact that you can. You like to mess with people's lives; I know you do. Just when things are going good, you insist on stirring things up. You just love making people feel weak and needy."

She drilled a biscuit into the trash, then looked up from her work, pointing a finger for emphasis. "I am not playing into your game, God. I won't do it. I've handled everything you've tossed in my direction. All my life I've handled things and I'm going to continue to handle things. You gave me this brain and this will for a reason. You should be glad I'm willing to use them and not sit around and get mushy and woe-is-me about things."

Gladys looked at the mess on the floor, which showcased a prime example of a woe-is-me moment. She spread her arms to encompass the room. "This represents one weak slice of time. This does not represent a life—or a change in attitude. I'll get through this, God. You watch me. I'll get through it."

She concentrated on the cleanup. Yet she couldn't help but sense that the Almighty was looking down on her, watching. . . .

So be it.

※　※　※

Angie spotted Margery waiting outside Neighbor's and beeped the horn once.

Margery waved and got in the front seat. "Morning."

"Morning to you," Angie said. "Buckle up."

Margery fastened the seat belt across her chest as Angie pulled away. Her hand lingered on the leather upholstery. "This is a beautiful car."

"SUV," Angie said. Then she laughed. "My husband always corrects me when I call it a car."

"Guys and their cars . . . Mick would kill for an SUV like—"

When Margery broke off her sentence, Angie glanced in her direction and saw her redden.

"He'd love to have one, just like this," she said.

"Mick's your husband?"

Margery nodded quickly. "What's *your* husband's name?"

"Stanford. Stanford Sebastian Schuster."

"Is he nice?"

It was an odd question that was oddly difficult to answer. Was Stanford nice? "He's very patient with me."

"Patient?"

It was a stupid answer. She changed the subject. "Do you have any children, Margery?"

"Not yet."

"Give it time. Trying is half the fun."

Margery shook her head no.

"No?"

Margery gnawed on a fingernail, but managed to talk around it. "Mick and I are going through a tough time right now. But it'll be okay. I'm doing everything I can to make it okay."

Angie waited for her to explain.

"My husband and I are separated."

"I'm so sorry."

"I'm hoping he's innocent of the drug thing."

"Drug thing?"

Margery looked stricken. "Oh, dear. I thought you knew, that you'd talked to Gladys or . . . forget I said anything. I don't want you to think—"

"He was arrested?"

"Drugs. Dealing."

Angie didn't say anything.

"He told me he was innocent but . . ." Margery shook her head.

"I didn't know he was dealing. I always thought he was home when I was working at the Chug & Chew."

"You work there *and* Neighbor's?"

"No, no. I quit the bar to get a job with Gladys. I didn't like working there. It was awful."

"I can imagine." And she could—if she dredged up some long-dormant memories of another Angie in another time and place during her pre-Stanford years.

Margery sighed. "You and your husband have been married a long time, haven't you?"

"Thirty-one years."

"Wow."

"Not that it's been perfect. It was rough at the beginning. I was rough."

Margery laughed. "You? Rough?"

"Me, rough. Very rough. Stanford was my Henry Higgins."

"Who?"

"From *My Fair Lady. Pygmalion.*"

No response.

"The character Henry Higgins adopts a poor, uneducated girl as a project and makes her into a lady."

"Stanford did that with you?"

"He took me from a nothing clerk at Wal-Mart and made me into—" Angie caught her words. "Sorry. I . . . he . . . he taught me how to be a lady. A proper wife."

"He must love you a lot."

Angie was shocked by her own shrug. "He enjoys a challenge. He taught me what to wear, how to talk, and which fork to use. He made me over."

"An extreme makeover."

"The extremest—minus plastic surgery. Stanford is responsible for the life we have. I grew up poor and had an unstable family life. I pretty much raised myself and stayed out of my parents' way. Do you have any brothers or sisters?"

"There was just me," Margery said. "I think I was enough."

"My mother was enough for me," Angie said. "I started thinking about escape when I was little but hung around—probably too long. I felt responsible for her. She was rather pitiful."

Margery ran a hand along the dashboard. "How did you get out?"

"I got a scholarship to college. But I still had to pay some of my way by working as a waitress. That's where I met Stanford. Like I said, I was his Eliza Doolittle. He made me into what I am today. And I loved that I didn't have to work—to make a living."

"So you haven't had a paying job since?"

"None. I was plenty happy being a stay-at-home mom for my two children. But after they grew up, I got bored and began to get more involved in volunteer work."

"I bet he's proud of you."

Angie shrugged. "Stanford likes my volunteer work because it's the right thing to do, but he does *not* approve of me actually going to the shelter and seeing the needy people close up. He'll tell me, 'Just write a check, Angela.'" She sighed. "He can be quite the snob sometimes."

"Maybe he's worried about you getting hurt. It's not a good part of town."

She shook her head. "He doesn't want me to get my hands dirty." She smiled toward Margery, needing to lighten things up. "See? Everybody has troubles."

But Margery didn't give it up. She angled in the seat toward Angie. "Marriage is complicated, especially when it's messed up because of something that can't . . . what if it's not any one thing that's wrong? What if it just feels wrong even when it's supposedly right? What if . . . ?" She sighed. "It's hard to explain."

"Are things that bad?" Angie asked.

Her voice was soft. "Sometimes."

"You said you were separated. Are you getting a divorce?"

Margery shook her head vehemently. "I can't do that. Mick and I, we're meant to be. We're supposed to make a baby."

"That sounds a bit . . . archaic."

"What?"

"Old-fashioned. Outdated."

"I'm supposed to be a mother." Margery put a hand to her chest.

"I need to love a child. Especially because . . . I need to make up for the one I lost."

"Oh, Margery. You lost a baby?"

"It was born too soon."

"And it wasn't healthy?"

"I fell. Our daughter was born too soon and died. She was our special baby. The reason we got married. The reason we were brought together."

"So you were pregnant when . . . ?"

"I got pregnant, we got married, then I lost the baby."

They drove a block in silence. "Does Mick want a baby as much as you do?"

There was a moment of hesitation. "It'll work out. I know it will. Soon too. It has to happen soon."

"Why?"

"I feel the clock ticking."

"You can't rush these things, Margery. And sometimes the more stressed you are about it, the longer it takes."

"People say that. But I don't know how *not* to be stressed. Life is stressful."

"Then maybe . . . maybe you shouldn't be having a baby. If Mick's into drugs . . ."

"A baby. I have to have a baby."

Have to. What an odd way to put it.

When Angie pulled in front of Sarah's house, the subject was suitably changed as Margery reacted to the Mancowitz home. "Whoa."

She was right to be impressed. Sarah's house was a stately Georgian with red shutters. Yet it wasn't *that* big a house. Angie's was bigger. Margery's reaction made Angie wonder about her own housing situation. "It's nice, isn't it?"

"If Sarah's family is so rich, why does she need a mentor?"

"Rich kids have problems too," Angie said.

"Like what?"

Good question. "I'm not sure yet. Sarah puts on a good front; she's holding back. I think her parents are gone a lot."

"When I have a baby I'm staying home."

Angie thought of her daughter Talia who'd had to go back to work. "That's ideal but not always possible."

"So Sarah's mother *has* to work?"

Angie wanted to steer away from any economic differences between the two young women. "Sarah's a good girl who needs some one-on-one attention, someone to talk to. That's where I come in."

"I could have used someone like you when I was a teenager."

There was no time to ask for details because Sarah came outside. She hesitated when she saw another person in the car, and Angie suddenly questioned bringing Margery along without warning. But Sarah took it in stride and got in the backseat.

"Happy Sunday," Angie said.

"Hi."

Margery looked over her shoulder and made her own introduction. "I'm Margery. I'm coming along."

Angie delayed backing out of the driveway to explain. "Margery works at Neighbor's Drugstore. Yesterday, when I was in there, we got to talking and she offered to come with us."

"Are you poor?" Sarah asked.

"Sarah!" Angie couldn't believe the question—though Margery's clothing was nothing special and her hair did look as though it had been cut with a hacksaw.

Margery took it in stride. "Why do you say that?"

Sarah's blush revealed a welcome existence of shame. "I'm sorry. I just thought . . . since you're just a clerk and . . ." She waved her hands in the space between them. "Never mind. I'm sorry."

"Tact, Sarah. Tact would be a good thing to learn," Angie said.

The girl's eyebrows dipped together, nearly touching. "Maybe I'd better not go." She suddenly opened the car door, got out, and ran up the front walk toward her house.

Angie and Margery exchanged an incredulous look, then scrambled after her. Angie called out, "Sarah, come back."

"Sarah, it's okay," Margery said.

Sarah fumbled her key in the door. "I really blew it. What I said . . . it was mean. I didn't mean for it to be mean, and it was something my mom would say and I can't believe I said it, and—"

Margery put a hand on Sarah's, putting a stop to the fumbling. She waited until the girl looked at her. "It's okay. I know you didn't mean it. It's okay."

Angie was an outsider watching the exchange of emotions: Sarah's angst meeting Margery's forgiveness. Finally Sarah's shoulders slumped and she pulled her hand away. "I *am* sorry."

Margery nodded once, then held out her hand. "And I'm Margery."

Sarah smiled and shook her hand.

Quite a girl, that Margery.

❦ ❦ ❦

Gennifer edged the curtains aside and looked through the window. Douglas was in the front yard, raking leaves. He didn't have to do that. They had a yard service to mow and fertilize. With one phone call Gennifer could get them over to rake.

Suddenly, Douglas stopped raking. He rested both hands on the top of the rake's handle, lifted his face to the sky, took a deep breath, and closed his eyes.

Was he smiling?

For the first time Gennifer looked past the work, the chores, and the obvious, and noticed it was a lovely fall day. The leaves both on and off the trees were an artist's palette. The sky was undecided between blue and gray, a haze of clouds preventing sharp shadows. The scene was soft, intense, and full of spice. It was the kind of day for football and drinking hot chocolate. She wondered if the movie *Rudy* was on television.

Gennifer headed to the kitchen, filled with purpose. She remembered seeing some instant packets of hot chocolate in the pantry. Sure enough, there they were. *Add hot water*. She could do that.

And she did. But as she put on a jacket and carried the drinks toward the front door, she questioned what she was doing. This trip into nostalgia was worthy of a Hallmark commercial, but the reality was that her husband was having an affair. The reality was that Gennifer was seriously ill and had told her boss about it, but not her family. The reality was that their daughter was off with some busybody do-gooder, serving food at a shelter.

There was little right in the Mancowitz family. Real life was proving to be nothing like a movie. The person with good intentions never got carried off the field on the shoulders of teammates no matter how hard Gennifer tried to manipulate things.

The front door opened, making her step back. Douglas, his cheeks flushed from the cool air and the exertion, saw the beverages. "What's this?"

Gennifer smiled. "I saw you raking . . . I made hot chocolate."

His smile was genuine. "Thanks. I was just coming in for something to drink." He cocked his head toward the door. "Want to go sit on the step? It's pretty out."

The movie reel started up again.

※ ※ ※

Sitting on the step brought back memories. Talking. Planning their lives. Sharing their hopes. Loving each—

"I like raking leaves."

"I like having the leaves raked," she said.

They both sipped their hot chocolate—which was pretty tasty, considering it was instant.

Gennifer suddenly realized that now might be the perfect time to tell him about her sickness. If Douglas ever discovered that people at work knew about it before he did . . . no matter what was going on, she didn't want to hurt him. Not like that. She cupped her mug in her hands. "Douglas, I have—"

"Do you remember the time we went to New England in the fall?"

She did. She'd just taken a job at the firm, and she and Douglas had decided to go on a vacation before she started work. "It was beautiful up there."

"We loved Maine."

She nodded.

"Remember that room we got at the Bar Harbor Inn that had a

corner balcony with wicker rockers and a view of both the harbor and the islands?"

"Room 221."

He blinked. "You remember its number?"

She nodded, as surprised as he. "Remember getting pizza delivery from Geddy's because we didn't want to leave that balcony?"

"It was a great trip. We should do it again." He suddenly stood. "In fact, let's go."

"Go?"

He lowered himself to the step below her own, facing her. "Next week. I could take a couple days off, make it a four-day weekend."

She immediately thought of her dialysis appointments on Friday and Monday. She shook her head. "I . . . I don't . . ."

He studied her face a moment, then pushed against her leg to stand. "You don't have time. I know. You have things to do at work, innocent defendants you need to get off on some tricky lawyer glitch. Heaven knows your work is *the* most important thing in your life." He walked toward the leaves and picked up the rake. "Nice talking to you. Thanks for the hot chocolate."

What just happened?

It didn't matter. There was no way she could tell him about her disease right now.

She went inside.

※ ※ ※

Angie wasn't two steps into the shelter when the director, Josh Cashinski, ran up to her with a fervor beyond his usual welcome. He grabbed Angie's hand and pulled her back toward the kitchen. "I need your help. Now."

Angie motioned for the girls to follow. Josh talked as they walked. "The cook quit. Joe quit. I pulled Sheena in to help, but she's not used to cooking for a crowd."

"Who is?"

He stopped in the doorway. "You, I hope."

She had to laugh. "Me?"

With a sweep of his arm he encompassed the kitchen. "This is *not* my domain, Angie. Like I've told you before, I can open cans and stir, but I need someone to tell me which cans to open and what to stir."

Sheena held up a big bag of frozen corn. "Is this the boil-in-the-bag stuff?"

Josh took Angie's arm and whispered, "Help!"

She took a deep breath. "Show me the pantry."

Josh kissed her on the cheek and led her into an alcove full of shelves.

"What can I do?" Sarah asked.

"Me too," Margery said.

Angie had forgotten they were there. Proper introductions would have to wait. She shoved two huge cans of kidney beans into Margery's arms, and tomato sauce into Sarah's. To Josh she said, "Get me the biggest pot you got. We're making chili."

❦ ❦ ❦

Joy. It was such a simple thing.

In theory.

Not in practice.

While cooking the meal at the shelter—while cooking the chili and baking the corn bread—Angie felt the stirrings of true joy. And by its unexpected emergence, she realized how lacking it had been in her life.

With the help of the girls, Josh, and Sheena, dinner *was* served and enjoyed by fifty-seven people. Some even came back for seconds. As the cleanup crew did their stuff, Josh approached Angie. "My compliments to the chef!"

"Oh, you." She opened the refrigerator, moved some bags of lettuce, and set the jar of leftover chili on the refrigerator shelf. "It was a simple meal. Nothing fancy."

Josh pointed toward the main room. "Did you see them asking for fancy? Home cooking is good cooking. You did great."

"It *was* good," Margery said as she wiped off a counter.

Sarah tied the top of a trash bag. "I've never had corn bread."

Josh laughed. "My, my. Where have you been, girl?"

She shrugged. "I like it with honey. Lots of honey."

Josh put a hand to his chest, being dramatic. "'Kind words are like honey—sweet to the soul and healthy for the body.'" He bowed.

"You're just trying to get me to do this again," Angie said.

Josh blinked. He froze, then his face lit up. "That's it! I *do* want you here. You belong here."

Angie shook her head. "Josh, I was kidding . . ."

He took her hands. "I'm not! Take Joe's place. Three days a week."

"Three meals a day?" Even as she asked for this clarification, Angie's mind was shouting, *No, no, you can't do this.*

"Three a day. Nine meals total."

She let her body catch up with her doubts by shaking her head no. "I couldn't do that. I wouldn't know what to cook that many times a—"

"So you don't presently eat three meals a day?" Josh asked.

Margery laughed. "He's got you on that one, Angie."

Sarah moved close. "I'll help you."

"You have to go to school."

"I'll help you figure out the recipes and help down here when I can."

"So will I," Margery said.

Angie waved her hands, trying to stop their words. "I can't do it. I can't. My husband would never allow—"

Sheena raised a soapy hand from the sink. "Excuse me? Your husband will not *allow*? What century you living in, woman?"

"Yeah," Sarah said.

"Yeah," Josh said.

Angie noticed Margery didn't add her two cents' worth.

Josh untied her apron. "You go home right now and talk it over with hubby dearest." He wadded the apron into a ball. "If you tell me yes, I'll even get you your own special apron."

"One that says Kiss the Cook!"

"Sarah!" Actually Angie was pleased with Sarah's kidding. The girl had really come to life this afternoon.

As had she. As had she.

❧ ❧ ❧

Angie found him lying on the couch, watching golf.

That was a good thing. Golf was calm. It was better than finding him watching all-star wrestling. Not that he would. Ever. Golf was acceptable. Wrestling was . . . sweaty.

Had Angie ever seen Stanford sweat?

She heard him snore.

Ah. That made sense. Often when Stanford said, "I'm going to watch golf" he really meant "I'm going to take a nap." All those quiet pauses and the whispered commentary . . . Angie used to have the same thing happen while watching the old *Mission Impossible* show as a teenager. She'd see the initial scene where the boss man would get the assignment—should he decide to accept it—but then would inevitably slip off to sleep only to wake and find herself watching the local news.

Actually, she was glad he was asleep. Although spurred on by Josh, Margery, and Sarah, she knew there was no point in asking him if she could accept Josh's job offer. The answer would be—

Stanford lifted his head and looked at her. "You're back."

"I am."

He sat up and reached for a glass on the end table. It was empty. "Get me more tea, will you?"

"Sure." She took the glass and headed to the kitchen. Then she stopped. *What am I doing?* She returned to the couch. Stanford was sitting with his feet on the coffee table. He had the remote in his hand. "I've been offered a job."

He glanced at her. "Tea?"

She took a step closer. "I've been offered a job as a cook at the shelter. Three days a week."

His forehead tightened, proving he *had* heard. "The answer's no."

"Why?" She knew very well why.

Stanford put his feet on the floor and tossed the remote on the cushion nearby. "Because I need you here. At home."

A laugh escaped, surprising her. "To do what?"

"To do—?"

She strode to the space between husband and TV, leaving the coffee table as a buffer between them. "According to you I don't clean, cook, dress, speak, think, or even make love to your standards. You don't need me at home to do anything but provide you with a way to feel superior. In spite of what you think, I do have gifts. I do have something to offer the world. Something good."

He crossed his hands over his ample midsection. "At the shelter."

"Yes, at the—"

He laughed. "Actually, you do have something to offer the caliber of people at the city shelter. They, who have nothing, don't expect much." He picked up the remote. "Don't be dumb, Angela. Anybody can do that job, and it's not going to be you." He put his feet back on the coffee table, motioned her to move out of the way—which she did. Then he turned up the volume. A commercial for the newest, bestest car in the world came on. "I'm thinking of getting one of those," he said.

And Angie knew he would. What Stanford wanted, Stanford got. She walked away, her head and heart heavy.

"Talia called. They'll be here at seven for dinner," he said.

Dinner. She'd forgotten about their monthly family dinner.

Great. She had to cook again.

Her lack of joy revealed too much.

❧ ❧ ❧

Talia squirted toilet-bowl cleaner under the rim and watched the green gel ooze down the sides toward the water. While it did its work she tackled the ring of soap scum on the tub she'd ignored too long. Her seven-months'-pregnant belly made the maneuvering difficult, and she didn't like using the chemicals because of the baby, yet if *she* didn't do it . . .

If only they could afford a cleaning service. Every two weeks would be great. Let someone else clean the bathrooms and dust and vacuum. That would still leave her the laundry, the cooking, the constant picking up, the kitchen, the baby care . . . at least the yard was handled. Nesto's old buddies at the lawn business took care of that for free. One blessing among too many burdens—burdens that used to be blessings.

She turned on the water and rinsed the tub. She enjoyed the way the sides felt smooth now that she'd done her job. She rested on the edge of the tub and started to adjust the shower curtain to the inside when she noticed the bottom twelve inches of the curtain were dirty with soap scum. The curtain needed washing. And from this vantage point she noticed the baseboard could use dusting, and was that a cobweb dangling between the light fixture and the mirror?

It was too much. Never ending. Although she was handling the big chores, the details threatened to drag her under. "Don't sweat the small stuff"' was a good premise, but Talia knew the small stuff could grow to be big stuff and was often harder to control in the process. Small stuff like running out of gas, forgetting Tomás was in the backseat, melting Tupperware in the oven, forgetting to pick up Nesto's medicine . . .

She put her head in her hands, not even caring that they smelled like cleanser. That's what her life needed. A good cleansing. Bleaching. Scouring.

"What's wrong?" Nesto stood in the doorway.

"Just taking a break."

"You look like *you're* ready to break."

She stood, grabbed the toilet brush, and scrubbed the bowl, working up a froth. "I'm fine."

"'Come to me, all of you who are weary and carry heavy burdens, and I will give you rest.'"

Talia flushed the toilet. She did *not* feel like having him quote Jesus at her. "I'll be fine."

He turned sideways in the doorway. "Come here. Sit. Rest your weary—"

She stomped a foot, causing water to splatter from the wet brush. "I can't rest! Don't you see? I get done with ten things and there's twenty more waiting. It never ends, Nesto. Don't you get it? I can't rest, because if I do, we'll all go under. We'll drown. That's the ball game. You get it? Do you get what I'm trying to say here?"

His shoulders drooped as he nodded. "Sorry I'm such a burden."

The breath went out of her.

Talia knew she should counter his comment with "You aren't a burden, honey" or at least an "I'm sorry for blowing up like that."

But she didn't.

She flushed the toilet and tackled the sink.

While Nesto slunk away.

Bad girl. Bad Talia.

At the moment, that's who she was. And there wasn't a thing she could do to change it.

❦ ❦ ❦

They stood at the door to her parents' home.

"We don't need to go," Nesto whispered.

He was wrong. Their monthly dinners were nearly mandatory. Sure, they could miss, but the price was high. Too high. Keeping the family fantasy going kept her parents at bay the other twenty-nine days of the month when phone calls sufficed for bonding. In the few times Talia had forgone the monthly dinner, her mother had hounded her to reschedule: "Your father insists. Can't you do it to please him?" Why he insisted was beyond Talia. When they were there he always acted bored or distracted, and he still hadn't accepted Nesto. Yet even so, she'd found it was best to just do it. Besides, she wouldn't be any less exhausted a week from now.

She changed Tomás to her other hip and rang the doorbell.

Her father opened the door, a cell phone to his ear. He motioned them inside and disappeared into his oak-paneled office to the right of the entry. *Nice to see you too.*

Talia set Tomás down and took off his jacket. She was putting their coats in the entry closet when her mother came out of the kitchen. "You're here. I didn't hear the bell."

Talia nodded toward the office where the sounds of a phone conversation could be heard. "Dad let us in."

Her mother's forehead furrowed but relaxed when she saw her grandson. "Tomás, my baby boy. Come to Nana."

The light Talia saw exchanged between her mother and her son was the main reason Talia kept coming to dinner. With Nesto's mother far away in Portugal and his father deceased, it was important Tomás enjoyed the love of the grandparents who were close.

She glanced at her father's office. He was seated at the desk, still talking on the phone.

Grandparent. Singular. Talia could count on one hand the number of times her father had held Tomás. Even the times he looked—really looked—at his grandson seemed few and fleeting. Her father's eyes seemed to scan over the boy as if he were of no more consequence than a lamp or a coffee-table book on the art of John Singer Sargent.

Not that Talia expected more. Her father had never been an affectionate man. As a girl *if* she did what it took to please him she *might* have received the use of the family car or the chance to go to breakfast with her friends after prom. Any reward was directly related to good behavior. And all bad behavior cost. Big-time. Talia had often kidded (in private) that she should get a big piece of poster board and chart the specific debits and credits of her father's system. She'd call it the Love Balance Sheet. It would contain such tried-and-true entries as:

Mow the lawn = one hour of TV (and a microscopic assessment of each blade of grass)

Get an A on a test = new sweater (her mother picked out)

Come in late = 2 hours of chores (*plus* an hour lecture)

And her favorite:

Talk back = banishment to her bedroom (including periodic scoldings through the door)

It had taken Talia a long time to realize that banishment could be considered a reward, and as such, she had saved her moments of speaking her mind for times when being left alone was exactly what she desired. As far as the scoldings through the door? Earplugs and headphones covered that up quite nicely.

Her memories were interrupted by her father's voice: "But I told you, the order has to be there Friday."

At least he wasn't yelling at her—or her mother. Although Talia had hoped her father would warm to a grandchild—especially a male grandchild—she'd based her hope on an idealized wish list of what a family *should* be like. A grandfather running toward a grandchild, stooped low with arms outstretched to gather him up for smiles, hugs, and kisses . . .

Her father, phone still to his ear, got out of his desk chair and came toward the glass French doors that separated office from foyer. And closed them.

Never mind. One parent down, one to—

Her mother, in possession of Tomás, led them into the kitchen. Nesto found the nearest chair. Angie nodded toward the counter while nuzzling the child to her cheek. "Would you stir the spices into the ricotta, dear?" Her mother got Tomás an animal cracker and sat at the kitchen table with the boy in her lap. "Then spread a tablespoon of the mixture on those slices of roasted eggplant over there."

Talia looked at the serving tray where eggplant slices were positioned like the spokes of a wheel. "Whatever are you making, Mother?"

"Roasted Vegetable Napoleons. I got the recipe on the Internet."

But why? "You don't have to cook fancy for us. Nesto and I are fine with frozen vegetables."

"Canned vegetables are good too," Nesto said.

Angie shook her head. "Your father likes things fancy, so I make them fancy—" she sighed—"or at least I try." Her face brightened and her voice lowered. "But I have to tell you about a different kind of cooking. This noon, when I was at the shelter, I had to fill in for the cook who'd quit."

Talia's mother told them all about her chili-making experience using sweeping hand gestures and adjectives like *exciting, invigorating,* and *meaningful.* She took a final breath. "It was . . . fun."

Nesto nodded. "You seem very happy."

Angie's chest puffed up like a dandy. "Yes, I guess I was." Her smile faded. She pointed to the counter where bowls of vegetables lay sliced and ready. "Now, cover the ricotta with two potato slices and layer it with zucchini, onion, mozzarella, tomatoes, and end with the ricotta and eggplant."

Talia got to work. But she would not be so easily swayed from the issue at hand. "You said you *were* happy. Were."

Tomás wanted another cracker and Angie gave him one. It was fruitless to point out they were going to be eating dinner soon.

"I loved cooking that simple food—for people who appreciated every bite."

Talia sprinkled the cheese on the Napoleons. "As I said, you don't have to make fancy dishes like this for us."

"I know, honey. But as *I* said, they're not just for you."

Talia stopped working and looked over her shoulder. "You're not Dad's servant, Mother. Or his slave."

"Don't be silly."

Talia turned completely around to face her mother. "I wish it were silly."

"Your father took me out of pover—"

"Poverty and gave you a good life. Made you a lady. I know. We all know. And it's good to be grateful. But I get tired of watching you pay him back year after year, ignoring your own desires and preferences. Never having what you want, never getting to do what you want to—"

"They offered me a job at the shelter. As a cook."

Talia didn't know what to say.

Her mother put her lips to her grandson's head, then handily changed the subject. "Guess who I spent time with today?"

"Who?" Nesto asked.

"Your babysitter. Margery Lamborn. Margery helped at the shelter too. I also took Sarah, the high school girl I'm mentoring."

Too much information too fast. Talia raised a finger. "Back up. You were offered a job?"

His second cracker consumed, Tomás wriggled off his grandmother's lap while Angie pulled out a bin of measuring spoons, cups, and bowls. Toys and little boy took possession of the floor by the pantry.

"I'm not taking it," Angie said.

"Let me guess why."

"I *did* like getting the offer though."

"You don't have to do what Dad says. You *can* have your own opinion, your own life."

Angie sighed, her eyes skirting the room. "We need to get those in the oven. Just five minutes to melt the cheese. Nesto, would you please tell Stanford it's five minutes to dinner?"

Evasion was an Olympic sport at the Schuster residence.

13

For God himself has taught you to love one another.

I THESSALONIANS 4:9

Chico, Rags, and Boo-Boo huddled in a corner of the house playing gin, as they did every night when it was too cold to go out and beg for money.

Not that the house they shared with me and three other girls—Pearl, Shriek, and Toledo—was warm. It was abandoned and had a condemned sign on the door that said nobody could live here safely. Toledo said safety was relative. Having a roof and being around people you knew was better than being out in the open where strangers were everywhere and nobody could be trusted.

I wasn't exactly sure I could trust my six housemates, but after living in the house five months since running away from home—after living through a month of simply surviving on the streets—I was willing to take some chances. There was only so long a person could be alone—truly, truly alone—before they started thinking crazy thoughts about life that often had a lot to do with not living at all. And even with all Grammy's talk about dying being a natural thing . . . I didn't like such a feeling.

The fact that the house had an address on 96th Street

made it okay. Ninety-sixth with a red door. How could I not stay here? I'd settled in just fine—though I will say Grammy's Home Sweet Home pillow looked a bit fancy for the corner where I slept. Shriek had taken it for her own once, but I yelled at her and set her straight about that, and she'd never taken it since. Boundaries. That's what I was learning to do. Set boundaries.

After running away from Mama, I'd thought about calling Daddy. But since he'd been the one who'd pulled away from *me* the past few years, and since he had a new life and family, I was sure he (and his new wife) wouldn't take kindly to me popping into their lives, messing things up. Maybe I was wrong. Maybe I should've called.

Too late now. This mismatched bunch of people were my family now, and considering we watched out for each other, and nobody ever yelled at me or hit me or told me I was crazy, a freak, or a nobody, I was good with it. Good with them.

Actually, to the gang I *was* somebody. Pearl couldn't read very well and liked when I read to her. There were plenty of newspapers in the garbage, and we found a ripped up Perry Mason mystery that was missing the last fifty pages, but I made up an ending that was happy. The butler did it.

And Chico was real grateful when I sewed a button on his jacket. It was too big for the hole, but he made it work. A person needed a coat that could button in the winter. Some how, some way. Cold had a way of sneaking into any gap it could find. As it was, Chico was just getting over a bad cough.

Tonight, Toledo was the last one in, and as soon as she came in the door, everybody yelled, "Shut it!" because the air was so cold. We always did that, said that, even though everybody always shut the door as fast as they could. And honestly, having it open or shut didn't matter that much because there was a window in the back room that had two bullet holes in it which let in plenty of air.

Toledo held a brown sack. "Ladies and gentlemen, dinner is served!"

Rags looked up from the card playing. "What'd you get?"

She set the sack on the floor and opened it. "I got a whole tray of chips from the Mexican place that they was throwing out, and two cans of chili that has dents in 'em, a box of cornflakes with a smashed corner, and three apples." She took one out and polished it on her coat.

Everyone gathered round. It was a feast. Boo-Boo must've liked it because after we finished eating, he wiped the top of his bottle on his shirt and held it up in a toast. "To us. We ain't much, but we're plenty." Then he passed it around. I'd never tasted booze before—not that it wasn't offered and available but because seeing Mama drink so much had made me against it. But when it came time for me to take a swig on this very cold night, I decided to go ahead. I didn't want to hurt Boo-Boo's feelings and I wanted to be a part of the toast. I was thirteen now. Old enough.

It was nasty, awful stuff, but that wasn't the point. My family was having a party and I owed them.

Owed them everything.

14

The LORD *will stay with you as long as you stay with him!*
Whenever you seek him, you will find him.
But if you abandon him, he will abandon you.

2 CHRONICLES 15:2

Stanford muted the evening news. "Why can't they have these charity meetings during the daytime?"

Angie changed her wallet from her black to her camel-colored purse. "Because most people work. It's an early meeting. I should be home before eight."

He grunted and turned CNN back on.

Angie got in his sight line. "If you feel sorry for anyone, feel sorry for Talia. She's worked all day and now has to go *back* to work for this meeting."

"Hmm."

"You could help by going over there and spending the evening with Nesto and Tomás; save them the expense of a babysitter."

"I will not babysit an adult."

"A sick adult."

Stanford craned his neck to see the TV. "He and I have never gotten along; you know that."

"That's not his fault."

"Can I help it if I find it hard to respect a man who's uneducated?"

She put on some leather gloves. The weather had turned particularly nippy in the evenings. "He has plenty of education. But he chose to use his hands rather than sit at a desk . . . a college degree is not the problem— nor your objection. Nesto came from a poor background. That's what defines him in your eyes. But so did I. Or do you hold that against *me* too?"

He glanced at her, then tried to look around her at the news. "Don't be ridiculous."

It wasn't ridiculous. In Stanford's view of the world one fact would remain forever: his wife and his son-in-law were born poor. It was a vivid entry in their résumés that could be overcome but never erased. His daughter had married the wrong man. The fact that Stanford had also married poor was differentiated in that Stanford had molded poor Angela into a slightly flawed but acceptable version of a well-to-do woman. So far, Nesto had not risen far enough above his lowly beginnings. *That* was held against him, and would be until suitable progress was made up life's ladder of success.

Angie got in her SUV and headed for the meeting at the hotel, really wishing Stanford would be the one to babysit at the Soza household this evening. Talia had mentioned that Margery was coming over again.

Ever since Margery had told Angie about her husband's shady dealings she'd suffered her own bout of discriminatory judgments. Angie had even considered saying something to Talia and Nesto, but to do so would make her a hypocrite. Angie had seen Margery in action at the shelter. She was a good person. She had a good heart. Angie trusted Margery. Should a wife be held responsible for her husband's failings and faults?

Angie certainly hoped not.

Yet having someone in Margery's situation taking care of her grand-baby . . . *that* made it personal. What if Margery's husband found out where she was and stopped by? What if he brought some of his low-life friends with him? What if . . .

Angie shook her head, forcing the thoughts away. What-if questions were a staple of life. A person could get an ulcer over them.

Tomás would be fine. Margery could be trusted. Angie had to believe that.

I'm not sure about this.

Margery's wariness was twofold: being around Tomás again after she'd come close to running away with him coupled with the oddity of having the father, Nesto, there too. She'd only met him one time in passing. To spend an evening with him *and* his son . . .

Odd.

Margery rang the doorbell at the Soza residence. It was answered immediately by Talia, her coat already on, her keys in hand.

"Glad you're here. I need to go."

"Am I late?"

"No, I just thought of something I need to do before everyone gets to the meeting. You're fine. But I'm glad you're here."

With that awkward greeting, Margery went inside. Nesto sat in a recliner, reading Tomás a book.

"Tomás hasn't eaten yet. I hope you don't mind," Talia said.

Nesto raised a hand. "Not to worry, I *have* eaten."

Margery smiled. Maybe this wouldn't be so bad.

Talia was already out the door. "Nesto knows the ropes. Just be there to help when needed. Bye."

The slam of the door brought with it a swoosh of cool October air, as well as a distinctive silence, which was broken by Tomás pointing to his book and saying, "Moo!"

"Moo cow," Nesto said. He looked at Margery. "Sorry. My wife—" he waved his hands in the air like a tornado—"she rushes rather than walks, cries out rather than speaks."

It was a nice way to put it.

"Sit," he said.

Margery sat on the couch. "I like your accent."

"Portuguese. But I hope to be American soon—before it's too late."

Her teeth clicked together once.

"Sorry. I'm too blunt." He smiled. "I make Talia crazy."

She wasn't sure she should ask, but since he was so open about the possibility of dying . . . "What's wrong with you?"

"I need a new heart."

"A new one?"

He smiled. "Used. I hope to get a transplant."

"You're getting someone else's heart?"

"I hope so. If it's the right one."

"If someone dies."

He shrugged sheepishly. "That's the way it works."

She nodded. "I said I'd be a donor on my driver's license."

"Good for you."

"It seemed the right thing to do." Margery remembered the moment they'd asked her the question at the licensing bureau. *"Would you like to give the gift of life to someone by designating yourself an organ donor?"* The clerk had been so nice, so sincere in how he'd stated it. *"You'd be playing a part in a miracle."* So she'd signed up—but hadn't thought about it since.

Until now. Until meeting someone who was waiting . . .

Nesto readjusted Tomás on his lap. "It's hard to believe transplants are possible."

"It does sound weird."

"Miracles *are* weird. That's why they're miracles." He stroked Tomás's head, letting his fingers slide along his son's bangs, nudging them into place. "I hope I see the new baby."

Talia was very pregnant. Her due date couldn't be that far away, yet Nesto was afraid of not even seeing the baby?

Tomás looked back at his father and Nesto kissed him. "I'd like to see this one grow up too. Heaven may be great, but I'd like to be here a good while longer."

He was so casual in his mention of heaven that Margery asked, "Do you ever wonder what's *after*?"

"I don't wonder. I know."

"You do?"

"Sure. There is a heaven. It's better than here. God's there. Some of my family is there. Jesus is there."

Margery had also heard such things, but his certainty . . . "You *know* this."

"I know this." Tomás wanted down and Nesto made way for prodding elbows and knees. The little boy found his blocks on the floor nearby. "Do you go to church, Margery?"

"Not really."

"Ever?"

"A few times. A lifetime ago."

"Sorry to hear that."

Margery shrugged. "I did learn some of the big stuff when I was little: Jesus, Christmas, Easter, all that."

"*That's* a lot."

"One time when the pastor asked people up front, I went. I bowed down and said I was sorry and told Jesus I wanted to know him, that I believed in him."

"Then you know a lot. You believe a lot."

She shook her head. "I'm still not sure what it all means."

He pointed to his heart. "Were you sincere? Did you say it from here?"

She thought about it a moment. "Yes. But I'm afraid I haven't done much about it since. I try to be a good person. I try to do good."

"And you succeed. You're helping us."

"And I love doing it. But certainly whatever little I do, or whatever little I've done, isn't enough."

"Enough?"

"Well, enough to . . . to make me worthy. To make God love me. To earn his approval."

"You don't need to earn God's love. He loves you. Period." Nesto smiled. "You have a very big heart, Margery. A good heart. I'm sure God wishes more people had a heart as loving as yours. I'm sure he's very proud of you."

She felt herself redden and shook her head. "I want to do more."

Tomás tossed a block, then fell back with a cry.

"He's hungry," Nesto said.

Margery popped off the sofa. She'd forgotten all about feeding him. She took the child into the kitchen, put him in his high chair, and gave him some graham crackers and applesauce.

Nesto came in, walking slowly like an old man. Margery readied a chair for him and helped him sit. His breathing was heavy.

"Are you okay?"

"I just . . . need . . . to catch . . . my breath."

"You need a heart bad, don't you?"

"Bad."

Tomás pounded on the tray of his high chair. "Mo!"

Nesto smiled. "He wants more and wants it now." He reached toward the tray, but couldn't quite touch it. "Just like papa, right *o caro, meu pouco amor?*"

When Tomás grinned, some applesauce oozed onto his chin.

Nesto sat back, running a hand across the kitchen table as if finding comfort in its smoothness. "What does Margery want now?"

She stopped spooning more applesauce into Tomás's dish, the spoon in midair. "That's not a normal get-to-know-you question."

He shrugged. "I'm sick. So I ask. And hopefully you'll answer."

I want a baby, a home, a husband who loves me. That was the short list.

And yet, when Margery opened her mouth to answer, something completely unexpected came out. "I want to know why."

"Why?"

"Why things are the way they are." She added another question. "And what does it all mean?"

Nesto spread his arms wide. "You ask the question of the ages. What's the meaning of life?"

It made Margery feel good to know her question was not out of line. "So? How do we find out?"

Nesto narrowed his eyes. "Do you really want an answer?"

His intensity scared her. "Uh . . . yeah. Yes."

"Ask."

I thought I just did. "Ask?"

"Ask God to show you his plan for your life."

A snicker escaped and Margery put her fingers against her lips. "His plan. For my life." She put the refilled bowl of applesauce in front of Tomás. "I don't think so."

"I know so. A verse . . ." He took a fresh breath. "'The Lord will work out his plans for my life.' Not *our* plan. His. He *has* a plan. For me. For you. A good plan."

An old memory tagged the edge of Margery's thoughts. Her throat was tight. "Really?"

"Really."

NANCY MOSER / 185

Suddenly, Tomás hit his bowl with his hand, flipping it on end. Applesauce went everywhere. He started to cry.

Margery went to the rescue. "There, there, it's all right. It's all right." She took his bowl away and ran to the sink for a washcloth.

Nesto wiped applesauce from his own shirt. He looked up when she returned to the boy's mess. "It'll be all right, Margery. It will."

The intensity of his eyes indicated he was speaking of much more than the mess at hand. "I know," she said.

Best of all, after talking with Nesto . . . she believed it.

※ ※ ※

Talia had never been so well prepared for a fund-raising meeting. Was she trying to earn brownie points to make up for her recent less-than-stellar work?

Absolutely.

The conference room was set with glasses, pitchers of water, notepads, pens, and a neatly typed agenda. She had to admit that her mother's upcoming presence probably had a lot to do with her Type-A preparations. She'd never worked on a committee with her mother before, and she was eager for Angie Schuster to see she was good at her job, that she was a success. A harried, stressed-out success, but a success just the same. It didn't hurt that her mother had a reputation for never quite getting anything right. This evening was Talia's chance to prove she was *not* her mother.

Wade came in the room, his eyes scanning. "You look ready."

"I am. I have a coffee cart coming with an assortment of cookies."

"Everyone cooperates better with a cookie in their hand."

"It's a proven fact," she said.

Her mother appeared in the door. "Knock, knock? Am I the first one here?"

If nothing else her mother was always punctual. "Mother, I'd like you to meet my boss, Wade Hampton. Wade, this is my mother, Angie Schuster."

They shook hands and exchanged pleasantries. Talia had to admit her mother looked nice. She wore a peach wool blazer over a brown turtleneck and brown plaid pants, the image of the quintessential sub-urban volunteer. The string of pearls solidified her as middle-American.

Angie took a seat at the far side of the table, at the end. "Who's coming?"

Talia answered, "Troy represents the hospital; Donna, the state's organ-donation network; then you and Candice from the volunteer corps, and . . ." She looked at her notes.

Wade touched her arm. "And a lawyer, Gennifer Mancowitz."

"From . . . ?" Angie asked.

"Chasen, Grieb, and Caldwell. But she's here on her own. I mean, the firm is not officially sponsoring the event."

"Why not?" Angie asked.

The question caught Talia off guard. "I don't know. I—"

Angie hung her purse on the back of her chair. "Corporate sponsors are always handy when it comes to underwriting the expenses of fund-raising events."

Talia bristled. She knew this and she would get to it when the meeting got started. After all, she wasn't involved in this occasion solely as the hotel's event coordinator. She had a personal stake in the charity, in earning money to educate people about organ donations. If more people would sign up to be donors, her husband would have a better chance of surviving.

Her mother opened her red notebook that clashed with her peach blazer. "I'm familiar with everyone you mentioned, except Gennifer. What's her story? I'm just curious."

Why all the questions? Talia had never known her mother to assert herself like this. "She probably has a heart for charity."

Angie shook her head. "I'm betting there's more to it than that. She's either known someone who's needed an organ or someone who's given one. Most people have a reason behind their philanthropy."

Like a husband who won't let you work?

The meeting hadn't even started and Talia found herself weary. "I don't know her story, Mother. Perhaps you can ask her." Talia needed air and a chance to regroup. "I'll go check on the refreshments."

Wade touched her arm. "I'll do it. You stay here and chat with your mother."

"But—"

At his exit the room suffered an awkward silence. Talia straightened the pen at the head of the table.

"Is it difficult working with a boss who's interested in you?" Angie asked.

The pen flipped to the floor. "What are you talking about?"

Angie leaned back in her chair. "The way he touched your arm, looked at you . . . he's interested in you as a woman."

Talia picked up the pen. "Don't be ridiculous. He's my boss."

"Which puts you in a position of submission."

"Mother!" *If anyone was guilty of submission . . .*

Angie shrugged. "I've worked with a lot of men on a lot of committees. I'm not seeing things, Talia. Be careful."

Take care.

Troy and Donna came in together and chatted with Angie as if they were old chums. Wade returned with a uniformed waiter pushing the refreshment cart. People got coffee and cookies. Candice arrived. Talia welcomed the busyness.

After getting coffee, Wade announced, "We should probably get started."

Talia did the head count. "But we're missing Gennifer. . . ."

❦ ❦ ❦

Room 234. There it was.

Gennifer burst into the meeting room, out of breath. Four women and two men were in the process of being seated around a table. "Is this the meeting for the organ-donation benefit?"

A pregnant woman answered. "This is the place. Gennifer?"

"That's me. Sorry, I'm late. Court went a little long today."

"I'm Talia Soza. Come. Sit by me."

Talia introduced everyone around the table.

"Court. How exciting. What kind of cases do you handle?" asked Candice, one of the volunteers.

"Nothing glamorous today. An embezzlement, an assault, and a drug case. I pleaded out the last two."

"I don't like the idea of that," Troy said, with a cookie crumb on his chin. "Criminals should pay for their crimes, not have them bargained away."

Gennifer put her leather portfolio on the table. "Ideally that's achieved through the plea bargain. A level of justice without taking up the courts' time, or filling the overflowing prison system with the lesser offenders."

"My work would be a lot easier if some of the lesser offenders were taken off the streets." Angie, a middle-aged woman with a pageboy haircut, looked around the table as if waiting for everyone to agree. In Gennifer's eyes her main flaw was the string of pearls she wore around her neck. "I do some volunteering at the shelter downtown, so I deal with some of those offenders—and their victims."

Suddenly, Gennifer gasped. "Your name's Angie."

"Yes . . ."

"Are you . . . ? My daughter went to the shelter last Sunday with a woman named Angie and—"

"Sarah?"

"That's my daughter."

Angie beamed. "Sarah went with *me.* I'm her mentor."

Gennifer shook her head. "She doesn't need a mentor."

The smile faded and the woman faltered a bit. "I'm sorry you feel . . . but obviously, Sarah feels differently. As does the school."

The woman's words made Gennifer bristle. "You have no right to step in, to interfere—" *To wear pearls.*

Angie's cheeks flushed. "I don't interfere. I only go where I'm wanted. And needed. Where I'm asked to go."

Wade, one of the hotel reps, extended his hands, trying to calm them. "Ladies, please."

With a start Gennifer realized they'd been having their exchange in front of an audience.

Angie sat back in her chair. "Sorry."

They all looked at Gennifer. She had no choice but to say, "Excuse me."

Wade nodded to Talia, who held up a piece of paper. "If you'll all get out the agenda, we can get started."

It was not a good beginning.

❧ ❧ ❧

Talia went around the table collecting dirty coffee cups. She could feel herself smiling. Memories of seeing her mother standing up for herself against Gennifer's attacks returned. Her mother-the-doormat had a bit of fire in her? Her mother truly *was* a volunteer queen? A champion of the needy?

Very cool. And surprising.

Wade came back in the conference room.

"How do you think it went?" she asked.

He took a coffee cup out of her hand. "It went fine, but enough of this."

"I need to clean—"

"There's been a change of plans." He nudged her toward the door.

"But—"

He put his hands on her shoulders, looking into her eyes. "Your workday has ended, as of now. I have arranged for you to go to the spa and get the facial of your choice and a pedicure and manicure."

"But—"

He held up a finger. "No back talk. You're going. It's arranged."

Out of nowhere, tears threatened. "Wade, you don't have to do—"

"I want to do this. I want you to take a couple of hours and think only of yourself. You deserve it."

"But the babysitter. I have to get—"

"You'll be home way before you turn into a pumpkin." He turned her around and shoved her gently into the hall. "Now go."

She went.

❧ ❧ ❧

Ahhhhhhh.

So this was how the other half lived.

Talia let the rosemary water bubble around her feet and ankles. How could something as simple as hot water feel so luxurious? She closed her eyes against the muted light and let the piped-in sounds of a string quartet wrap her in its soothing mantle.

I bet people like Gennifer Mancowitz do this all the time.

She didn't know Gennifer beyond what she'd seen at the meeting, but the woman had an air about her that suggested that the finer things in life—perks like pedicures and facials—were prerequisites of day-to-day living. Talia didn't hold it against her. She didn't hold the rich in contempt, nor the poor. As long as a person worked hard and did their best, as long as they gave back a little of whatever they received . . .

Like her mother.

This evening Talia had seen her mother in a totally new light. Gone was the weak follower, the slave doing her husband's bidding. Present was a woman who faced the inequities of the world and tried to change them. Talia had never thought much of her mother's volunteer work, and had looked down on it as a mere trifle to fill her mother's empty days. But after witnessing Angie Schuster's confrontation with Gennifer, after seeing her mother reveal a fire in her belly toward charity work . . . Talia couldn't help but look at her with new respect.

With this new attitude, Talia's perception of her mother's activities moved from busywork to godly work. Angie gave back a huge percentage of what she received through her time, talent, and treasure. More than Talia did. More than anyone else Talia knew. The revelation both shamed and challenged her. She took a cleansing breath and made a decision. She'd be nicer to her mother. Treat her with the respect she deserved.

Talia felt a gentle touch on her foot. She opened her eyes to her pedicurist. "Are you ready to choose a polish color?"

Absolutely.

❦ ❦ ❦

Margery smiled at the three red chrysanthemum blossoms that sat tucked around the rearview mirror. She hadn't stolen them from Nesto's yard. When she'd left that night she'd admired the Soza plantings lining the front walk and Nesto had said, "Pinch off a few. Take them home and enjoy them."

And so she had. Taken them home.

Home sweet home. Funny how a few flowers made her happy. Funny how she could feel happy at all considering she was living in her car.

But she could. And she did.

Margery adjusted the pillow against the armrest of the back door of the car and pulled the blanket over her shoulder. She alternated ends of the motel parking lot every night, and tonight the overhead streetlight shone in from the left, from the feet end of her makeshift bed. She closed her eyes against its glare.

Her thoughts turned to Nesto. She could never—ever, ever, ever—remember having a conversation with anyone like the one she'd had tonight with him. She'd only known a few people who ever mentioned God. Certainly not her parents and certainly not Mick.

That wasn't entirely true. Mick mentioned God and Jesus all the time—just not in a nice way.

I've done the same thing. I need to stop that.

It was an odd thought, and something she'd never imagined thinking. People cussed all the time. So what? They were just words.

The Lord will work out his plans for my life.

She was proud for remembering *those* words. She'd never memorized a Bible verse before. It probably stuck with her because it was something she wanted to hear.

But was it true? Did God really have a plan? for her? She tried very hard to be a good person. Even when her life had been very, very bad she'd tried to be good. Do good. And while she was glad Nesto had told her she didn't need to earn God's love, she'd often felt God was proud of her. She saw his approval in little things, like the unexpected smile from an elderly woman at the grocery store when Margery helped her load her heavy bags. Or seeing an amazing sunset when she'd taken the garbage outside at the Chug & Chew. Or watching some birds dance around her neighbor's bird feeder in the morning when she was having a cup of coffee. Or having the rare nice guy leave her a huge tip just when the rent was coming due. God had always provided for her—in strange ways, for sure—but provided just the same.

Even now she had *enough*. She had a good job, was meeting good people. So what if she was sleeping in her car? It was an odd arrangement but it worked. And in a way, Margery felt more at peace now than she had in months. Could getting kicked out of the house have been a good thing? Another way of God providing for her? For she would never have gone on her own—never been brave enough to leave on her own. The way it happened was Mick's doing.

And as such, she was free.

Not a bad feeling, all in all.

※ ※ ※

Gladys had just sat down with a cup of Sleepy Time tea and was adjusting her headphones to listen to a little Fauré when the phone rang. Between chair and phone her stomach tightened. Coming this late in the evening it wasn't going to be a good call. She just knew it.

"Gladys."

It was Aunt June's standard greeting—or lack thereof.

"What's wrong?"

"She's gone! Your mother's gone!"

Gone?

"Dead, Gladys. She died an hour ago."

Gladys nearly laughed. This was absurd. "But she had medicine. I called the doctor personally. He was supposed to get her medicine."

"He did. But she got worse. Fast. This morning—"

"Why didn't you call sooner?"

"I was busy dealing with her, with things, with trying to make her better. I . . . you weren't here, Gladys. I was. I am. I had to deal with it. And I tried. I really, really tried."

June began to cry and Gladys felt horrible. She said the words her aunt needed to hear. "I'm sorry. I know you did all you could. You've always been there for her. For us. I'm sorry. But—" Gladys's own tears came—"but Mama . . ."

"I know. I know."

"She's gone."

"Yes, I know."

Gladys carried the phone back to her chair, sitting on the headphones but not caring. What did Fauré matter now? What did anything matter? Mama was gone.

"I'm making arrangements," June said. "I hope they're okay."

Gladys sat rigid. "I'm coming. Now."

"Not now. It's late. But do come, Gladys. I need you."

Gladys hit the phone's disconnect button and let it drop to her lap. Mama gone. There was always Mama. Mama always was.

Until God took her away.

Gladys jumped out of the chair. "You did this, God! You took her away just to get at me, didn't you?"

Her own words from Sunday morning came back to haunt her: *"I'll get through this, God. You watch me. I'll get through it."* The words had been said in response to her sight crisis, but remembering them now she saw them for what they were—a challenge for God to bring it on.

You asked for it; you got it.

One did not challenge the Almighty to a duel and win. Gladys sank back into the chair and pulled her knees to her chin. "What have I done?" She pressed her eyes against her knees, becoming as small as possible. "I'm sorry," she whispered. "I'm sorry. I didn't mean it. I take it back. Just bring Mama back. Don't punish her because of me. Bring her back."

But as her prayer fell away, as the silence of her house wrapped around her like a shroud, Gladys knew there were no take-backs. Her mother's illness had turned deadly because she had defied God.

She lifted her head, needing air. She looked around the house she loved. For the first time it did not bring her solace or pleasure. It was a silent house. Dead. Still.

And empty.

Suddenly, she needed to fill it. She could not be alone with God. Not now. Not after what she'd done . . . what he'd done. She picked up the phone and punched in some numbers.

"King here."

"Mama died and it's all my fault."

"I'll be right over."

🌺 🌺 🌺

Gladys was not a hugger. Never had been. But when she answered the door to King and he opened his arms to her . . .

She'd forgotten the comfort that could be found in a soft shoulder.

They stood in the open doorway with the autumn breeze rushing in around them, and for once Gladys didn't care if the furnace kicked on, didn't care if she was heating the outside. At that moment she couldn't move and didn't want to. She'd found her rock and clung to it like a drowning woman washed up from the sea.

Finally, her rock spoke. "Come."

She let herself be led inside and let King close the door against the cold and let him take her to the couch where he eased her down to the cushions. He took his place beside her, where she again found his shoulder and arms. His heartbeat was oddly reassuring that life did exist. Life did go on.

For her. For him.

But not for Mama.

New tears began and he stroked her hair. Gladys was grateful he allowed the moment to linger before he asked the question she knew was inevitable.

Finally, it came. "What do you mean it's all your fault?"

In the time between her phone call summoning him here and his arrival, she'd thought about what to say, how much to tell him, how to couch the truth so he wouldn't hate her or judge her or call her a fool.

But in that time she also realized there was no side road and no safe place to hide. This was King, her business partner, her confidant, her friend. He deserved the truth. If he couldn't handle it and she lost him, so be it. She had to tell someone. Or die.

Gladys readied herself to answer his question by sitting up and moving away, putting a full cushion between them. "Remember when you found me at the store after hours, in the dark?"

"Of course."

"Remember how you got after me for not letting God be a part of my life?"

"I do."

She pulled a throw pillow to her chest. "The next morning I challenged God to a showdown. I told him to give me his best shot."

King let a chuckle escape. He immediately squelched it with a hand, but it was too late.

She hit him with the pillow. "You're laughing at me?"

He set the pillow aside and moved closer. "I'm laughing at your gumption, your fire, your—"

"Stupidity. I know it was stupid. But I didn't think God would take Mama because of—"

King took her hand in both of his. "No, Red, no. I assure you God did not have your mother die to teach you a lesson or to win. He's not a God who needs to win; he's a God who loves, who saves us from ourselves."

She nodded. "By proving I was an idiot? By proving he's the boss?"

King's smile was kind. "That you learned those things is great, but I assure you he did not take your mother's life for that reason."

"Then why did she go from medium-sick to dead-sick so quickly? Friday I got a call she was sick, Saturday you reminded me to pray, Sunday morning I told God very adamantly that he and I being chummy was a no-go, and today, Tuesday, Mama's dead. You tell me what all that means. You give me another explanation. I dare you."

King raised his left eyebrow. "Dare?"

Oops. Gladys pulled her hand free from his and stood. "See how arrogant I am? Always daring, always confronting, always challenging."

"Always trying very hard to get things right."

She pointed down at him. "Don't give me attributes I don't deserve. I'm finally admitting my faults. Don't you dare water them down."

He laughed.

Gladys tossed her hands in the air. "I'm hopeless. Completely hopeless."

"Actually, I believe you've just proved yourself the opposite."

"You're doing it again. Trying to make me feel good about myself. You need to stop that. I'm on a roll here."

"Sorry to distract you. Have at it."

Suddenly given free rein to rant, disparage, and call herself down, Gladys was out of words. She fell into the armchair. "I'm done."

"Actually, you're just beginning. At a beginning."

"My mother's dead. It's the end."

"I'm not talking about her. I'm talking about you. About where you're at right now. With God."

Him again. She wrapped her arms around her torso. "I've told him I'm sorry."

"An admirable start."

"I told him I didn't mean it."

"He knows that."

"So?"

King moved from the couch to sit on the edge of the coffee table in front of her. "So . . . now you talk to him. No drawing lines in the sand, no confrontation, no arrogance. Just you and him. One-on-one. From where you are now, in the midst of your anger, your grief, your confusion, and your brokenness."

"I don't know what to say. I don't know what to ask."

"There are no magic words, Red. Just begin. He'll fill in the silence."

She could do that. She had to do that. She had nothing else she could do.

Gladys looked into the eyes of the man seated before her. "So it's not my fault Mama is dead?"

"It's not your fault." King stood. "Now, I'll make us some tea and leave you two alone."

Just the way he said it, as if God were real and viable and *here.*

Gladys watched him go, watched the swinging door of the kitchen stop its movement, leaving her totally alone with *him.*

But where to begin?

She ended her slump and leaned forward, resting her elbows on her knees. She bowed her head, having no idea what to say.

"God? It's me, Gladys."

King was right. God filled in the silence.

※ ※ ※

"I'm going with you," King said.

Gladys looked up from her fresh mug of Sleepy Time and shook her head. "The store. Someone needs to—"

"The store can survive a few days without us. I'll call Bernice to come in tomorrow and help out Margery. The store can be open and just have the pharmacy closed."

She'd never considered such a thing. And yet Bernice—the weekend and evening clerk—*had* been with them for years. She'd do just fine being in charge. "I could go alone," Gladys said.

"But you won't." King had been working at the computer on the kitchen desk. He hit the Enter button with a flourish. "There. It's done. Our plane leaves at eleven tomorrow morning. You'll be with Aunt June by three. I've always wanted to meet your aunt."

"I would have liked for you to meet my mother."

He tapped his heart. "I feel I do know her. I love the stories you've told me about the travels of the Terrible Trio and your odd beginning together, three females making a life."

Duo now. The Daring Duo? She sipped her tea. "We certainly were a unique band of females. Unmarried. Always harried." She smiled. "That's what Aunt June used to say."

"Still says. You still have *her*, Red. Remember that." He stood. "You need to get to bed, get some sleep. It's going to be a long day tomorrow." He held out his hand and she let him pull her to standing. "You need help?"

"No more than the considerable help you've given me already. Thank you."

He kissed her cheek. "Anytime. I'm honored you called me."

"Who else would I call?"

His eyes showed surprise, but also pleasure.

Tomorrow. Until tomorrow.

🌺 🌺 🌺

Knocking. Margery heard knocking in her dreams.

It didn't fit and she tried to push it away. Get back to the story.

"Hey! Hey you!"

Those words definitely didn't fit. She opened her eyes and saw a man at the window of her car, knocking on the glass with a knuckle. She sat up.

"You! Come out of there!"

No way.

He knocked harder. "Now! You want me to call the police?"

She noticed a name tag on his shirt with the motel logo on it. That made her feel a bit safer—but still in trouble. She unlocked the door and got out, pulling the blanket with her. She tried to untangle it from her legs and got off balance, bumping into him.

He pushed her into the car. "You want to sleep? You pay for a room."

She pulled the blanket to her chest. "It was late and I—" Actually, she didn't know what time it was.

"I don't want to hear it." He reached through the back door of the car, unlocked the driver's door, and opened it. "Go. Get outta here." He grabbed the blanket from her, tossed it in the backseat, and slammed the door.

She got in the driver's seat but couldn't find her purse.

"Come on! Get going."

"The keys. I need the keys." She spotted her purse behind the passenger seat.

"I'm counting to three. One . . ."

Fingers met keys. She fumbled for the right one.

"Two . . ."

She had it upside down, but flipped it around and into the ignition.

"Three!" He slammed his hand on the hood of the car at the same moment the motor roared to life.

She put the car in reverse and backed out, nearly hitting a car parked behind her. As the man ran toward her, she put it in drive and peeled out of the parking lot onto the street.

Margery had never *peeled* anywhere in her life, and with her huge car, the back end fishtailed and nearly ran into a car parked on the street.

Calm down!

A stoplight shone red up ahead. Good. A place to recoup and regroup. She jerked the car to a stop and in the nonmotion, discovered her heart throbbing in her throat. From sleep to exile in thirty seconds. She looked toward the mums, but they'd fallen from their perch and were strewn on the floor of the passenger side.

The light turned green but Margery didn't want to move. She didn't know where to go. Right? Left? Straight? Her nightly resting spots were gone. Two places tried. Two places denied. What now? Another parking lot?

A car honked and she had to move forward. But with each block a weariness entered the car and seeped inside her being until even holding the steering wheel was a struggle.

Her earlier acceptance of her situation fell away. Feeling free and provided for while she was sleeping in her car? Who was she kidding? Margery wanted a real bed. She wanted a kitchen and real food. She wanted a real shower. Gladys's new alarm system was being installed in three days and Margery wouldn't have the code, so any hope of continuing to use the store bathroom would be completely gone. She didn't want to sneak around anymore. She wanted a life.

She wanted a home.

Home.

Could she go back to *her* home? Dare she even try? Would Mick let her in? Did she really want him to?

"What choice do I have?" she asked aloud.

The fact there was no one to answer was her answer.

She turned north.

True north?

North.

※ ※ ※

Margery had not been back to their trailer since she'd snuck in and gotten a few essentials last Friday. She'd parked a block away then and had slipped in by foot. But this time, at this time of night, with her intention to stay, she drove up the street that bisected the trailer park. She spotted Mick's truck in the parking space near the front door and her stomach flipped. Would he make a scene? Would he yell? Would he throw her out again? Had he missed her at all?

Had she missed him?

Of course. She was his wife. He was her husband. Spouses were supposed to miss each other. It was a rule.

As she got closer, as she got ready to pull in beside Mick's truck, she noticed there was another car parked in front of Mick's vehicle. A red compact. She didn't recognize it. And why would it be parked in front of Mick's—

Movement in the lit living-room window caught her eye. The miniblinds were open and Margery saw Mick standing with a drink in his hands. He was smiling, looking down, talking to someone who must have been sitting on the couch.

The person belonging to the red car? Maybe someone from work?

Suddenly, Mick pulled the person from the couch to standing—into his arms. Into a passionate kiss. Hand in her hair, pulling her close. Then Mick put the drink down and they both disappeared from sight—until the top third of Mick's torso reappeared. Margery watched as he pulled off his T-shirt and flung it across the room.

She didn't wait to see more.

※ ※ ※

Margery was numb. There were no feelings. Too many feelings.

She couldn't go on. The world was too heavy. The car . . . she let go of the wheel and felt a moment's peace in the letting go—

She grabbed it back, nearly missing a light pole.

No. No. No. That wasn't the answer. She wasn't sure why, but no. Just no.

She'd driven into a residential area. Trees canopied the street. Front walks edged with fall flowers were lit by the friendly lights of front porches. Wind chimes tinkled and nylon flags appliquéd with pumpkins and leaves billowed gracefully. Only a few windows were lit from the inside, and a few blue television screens shone through sheer curtains, flashing, flickering, advertising "normal." This was normal. This was the life she'd always wanted. She hadn't wanted the life she'd ended up with. She hadn't wanted a dead child, a bad marriage, a beater car, a broken-down trailer. She'd wanted this. All this.

Help me, God. Please help me.

Knowing what she didn't have—and probably never would have—didn't help her mood. She couldn't go on. She pulled to the side of the street. No more. No more driving. What would come next she wasn't sure, but whatever it was had to happen right here in the land of normal.

Margery turned off the car. The sudden silence made her suck in her breath as she entered the gap between what had been and what was.

She leaned back, finding the support of the car's seat a comfort. She didn't have to go any farther. She could stay right here. Here was good.

Here was doable. Here was all she had. She closed her eyes but the nothingness scared her and she opened them again.

She noticed a car to her left, one house up. It was a red VW Bug with a black stripe on the side.

Gladys had a red VW Bug with a black stripe on the side.

She opened the car door and found herself walking toward the house. The outside light was on. The living-room light was on. Inviting her in?

She saw the address, black against the white clapboard: 9600.

And suddenly, at the sight of that number, her past rushed to meet her. How odd that now of all times, her very own special number had reintroduced itself into her consciousness. Yes, yes, ninety-six . . . this was the place. A good place. Within reach.

The good nearby.

🏵 🏵 🏵

The doorbell? Who would be ringing the doorbell at this hour?

Not that Gladys had been asleep. Despite King's reminder that tomorrow—today—was going to be a long day, she hadn't been able to even doze.

Mama was gone. God wasn't.

And now someone was at the door?

She approached warily, wishing she had more substantial curtains between herself and the night visitor. She hugged the entertainment center to get directly in front of the door where she could look out the peephole.

Margery?

All fear vanished and she opened the door wide. "Margery. What are you doing out at this time of night?"

Margery's shoulders drooped as if the frame of her torso had given way. Her voice was a ragged whisper. "I need help."

Tears started and Gladys drew her inside to the couch, in much the same way King had comforted her only hours before. After Margery had settled down, had wiped her eyes, and blown her nose, it was time to ask the question: "What's wrong?"

Margery's story was short but read like a soap opera. Dealing with an abusive husband, being kicked out of her own home, living in her car, finding out Mick was fooling around.

"How long have you been living in your car?"

"Since the day I bailed Mick out. Since the day I tried to steal from you."

Almost since the first day she'd come to work. A litany of not-so-kind thoughts about Margery's rumpled appearance brought with it a curtain of guilt. How would Gladys look if she were living out of her car? She had another thought. "Bathing. Food. How—?"

"I showered in the bathroom at the store."

"With what?"

Margery looked to her lap as if this next were her greatest shame. "I borrowed a hand sprayer from aisle 4." She looked up, touching Gladys's hand. "I'll pay for it." Again, she looked away. "I hadn't thought I'd be away from home so long."

Gladys's mind sped ahead to the alarm that was being installed Friday. "The alarm . . . how were you planning to shower after the keypad was installed?"

She shrugged. "I hadn't gotten that far."

Gladys blinked. "But the keypad . . . I'm having it installed because I thought someone was in the store that one morning and . . . that was you?"

Margery nodded. "You nearly caught me. I didn't hurt anything. I brought some towels that I'd snuck out of my house and cleaned up after myself. Other than using the sprayer . . . I tried to be careful. And I didn't take anything. Nothing. I know I nearly stole from you before to get the bail money, but since then . . ." She raised her right hand. "I haven't stolen from you, Gladys. I wouldn't. I won't. No matter what."

Gladys lowered Margery's arm to her lap. "I believe you."

Margery let out a breath. "I'm glad I'm working for you. I like it there. And since I'm getting a paycheck now, since Mick's not going to let . . . I'll get myself an apartment. I will." Her forehead crumpled, and she raised a hand in an attempt to block her emotions from Gladys's eyes. "I shouldn't be here but I have no place to go. My friends . . ." She shook her head. "I don't have any *real* friends. None I want to be around. None that would take me in, and . . ."

Gladys put her arm around Margery's shoulders. "You can stay here.

I have an extra room sitting empty. And I'll help you find a place of your own. We'll work it out."

The tears started again and Margery drew Gladys into a grateful hug. "Thank you. I won't be a bother. I can help, doing chores, cooking, whatever you need."

Gladys took Margery's hands in her own. "What I need is for you to promise me one thing."

"What?"

"Promise me you won't go back to Mick. Ever. He's bad news."

"I know."

"So? Do you promise?"

Gladys was not thrilled at her hesitation.

"Yes," Margery said. "I promise."

"Then it's settled. Come on. I'll show you your room."

Only after she'd gotten Margery settled into the guest room did Gladys remember one small detail: in less than twelve hours she was leaving to go to her mother's funeral. Leaving a needy woman alone in her house. A needy woman who had a husband who was a criminal— among other things. Could she trust Margery?

Do I have a choice?

Gladys had definitely gone above and beyond the role of boss. What had she gotten herself in for by letting Margery Lamborn into her life?

❊ ❊ ❊

The moonlight cut a path over the window seat, over a potted plant on the floor, and over the bed in Gladys's guest room. It bisected Margery, rising over the left side of her body, making its way across her middle, and falling over the other side, leaving the upper half in the light, and the lower half in darkness. Two distinct halves of a whole.

Such was her life. Her old life with Mick was veiled in shadow, dipped in darkness. She'd been blind with him. So much of the past seemed muddled. Every thought, every emotion. How often had she thought one thing, only to have reality prove the opposite?

Mick and I loved each other.

Mick had kicked her out and was with another woman.

We had a home; we were making a life.

They'd had an address, nothing more.

We've been together forever.

They rarely saw each other.

We have a history.

A bad history.

Things will get better.

They'd been living in a rut.

Once we have a baby . . .

They would never have a baby.

With a start, Margery sat up in bed.

It was true. Without Mick in her life there would be no baby. She'd never known anyone else, had never been with anyone else. She'd surrendered all her dreams to this one man.

Dreams he had crushed and crumpled. Trampled on. Spit on.

"Fool!" The word came out in a rush of air, barely audible, yet shouted just the same.

With a sharp shake of her head she vowed to be a fool no more. As of right now, Margery was starting fresh in this pretty red-and-white room with a quilt on the bed and the moonlight streaming through the windows. The house at 9600 . . .

Her number: 96. It had been a long time since she'd allowed herself to think about it. Her entire childhood had been filled with ninety-six. It had seemed important to her then, driving her, guiding her like a beacon of light leading somewhere (but who knew where?)

Margery turned on her side and snuggled into the pillow. It smelled of spring flowers and was soft against her cheek. The mattress was heaven compared to the seat of the car.

She was in a good place now. A better place. It was time to think ahead, not wallow in the present or worry about the past. What did she have to lose by embracing normal?

Maybe it would lift her up where she belonged.

15

The righteous person faces many troubles,
but the LORD comes to the rescue each time.

PSALM 34:19

He had the prettiest smile.

The kid was a couple years older so I was happy he paid any attention to me at all. The fact that we met while Dumpster diving made our relationship special from the very beginning. Weird, but special just the same.

I was at the Dumpster first, when he strolled up, his hands in the pockets of his jeans. "Want a boost?" He cupped his hands, creating a foothold.

I eyed him a moment, sizing him up. He looked harmless enough. His clothes were pretty clean even though his hair was greasy. If I'd seen him in school, I would've talked to him. If I ever went to school. I hadn't been for over a year now, not since I'd run away. "Sure," I said. "You boost me up and I'll hand things over."

"Deal."

I was hoping to find a ton of goodies in the Dumpster to share with him, but the pickings were slim. After getting a half-eaten burger and fries in a Styrofoam carryout box, and a box of Cheerios that was still a third full, I climbed out.

"This isn't much," he said, examining the burger.

"But it was on top, meaning it's not too old. Probably last night's. Split it. I'm hungry."

With another look under the bun, the boy shrugged and tore the burger in two, giving me the bigger half. We sat on some crates to eat, but didn't talk much. I'd learned most runaways didn't want to talk much at first. I was okay with it. Just being around another teenager—with a pretty smile—was good enough. So much was good enough now. . . .

When we finished he tossed the trash back in the Dumpster. He wiped his palms on his jeans. "I need sweets."

"Sorry, there wasn't anything in—"

"Come on." He walked out of the alley toward the street. He looked back to see if I was following. "You coming?"

Of course.

We went into Brady's Grocery. I used the restroom there sometimes when they were really busy and the clerks didn't have time to notice me, but I'd never been in there to shop. You need money to shop. But if *he* had money and was willing to spend it on me . . .

He stopped at the candy aisle. It had been a long time since I'd had candy. Snickers was my favorite.

But then, suddenly, he crammed two candy bars into the front of his T-shirt and shoved two toward me.

"Run!" he said.

I should've dropped the bars, but I didn't think that fast, and stuffed them in my pocket and ran out.

Just as a cop was going by.

I was arrested for stealing two Zagnut candy bars—that I didn't even like.

The kid got away.

My arrest led me to the Department of Children's Services. I wasn't sure when I made the decision to tell them my parents were dead, but when they asked, that's what came out of my mouth. But when I heard the lady on the phone mention care in a foster home, I panicked. I'd met plenty of kids on the street who'd been in foster homes—some of them in *many* foster homes—and I didn't want that.

A kid named Sherwood had told me he knew about a family who

collected kids and kept them in closets just to get the money from the government. Sherwood said his foster father had daddled with him. And another kid said he'd run away from his foster home 'cause they'd tried to feed him poison and had even killed one of the girls living there. Another true story had a family selling the teenage girls to a sex-slave operation in Thailand. I couldn't go to a foster home. I wouldn't.

So I jumped out of my chair near the lady's desk and yelled, "No! I won't go!"

The DCF lady stood up too. She was a big lady whose breath smelled like coffee. "Sit down, Gigi. Now."

I took hold of the back of my chair and shoved it over. "No!" I couldn't believe I'd done that. But then I started swiping and shoving everything. All the files on the lady's desk, the pencils in a cup, the plant in the corner—which was dying anyway . . .

The lady screamed for help and two men came running. They stepped over the stuff on the floor and grabbed hold of me. Hard.

"Let go! Let go!"

The more I struggled, the tighter they held on. One guy's grip pinched my skin and I knew it would leave bruises. With my arms out of commission, I used my feet—both of them at the same time. Which sent me toward the floor, dragging the guys with me. One guy fell and hit his head on the corner of the desk, but the other one held on, pulling me up. "Call County!" he said. "We need to ninety-six her."

Ninety-six?

I stopped fighting. I didn't know what *ninety-six her* meant but I knew everything was going to be all right.

But it wasn't.

※　※　※

Turns out *ninety-six her* meant putting me in a loony bin for ninety-six hours for observation. My screaming fit was to blame. But if it stopped them from sending me to foster care it was worth it.

Maybe.

After seeing all the certifiable crazies in the hospital, I decided to cooperate real fast. No more fighting. No more screaming. I even threw in a few "Yes, ma'ams" and "No, sirs" like Grammy used to have me say.

Actually, other than the patients, it wasn't that bad a place. Truth was, I was tired of the streets. Tired of never knowing where or what I was going to eat, or who to trust, and finding that a lot of the time I didn't much care. So the clean soft beds of the hospital, with real pillows and blankets—and plenty of time to sleep without being afraid? It wasn't a bad thing. And when I woke up? There was real food that wasn't leftovers or from a dented can. There were doctors and nurses in bright-colored outfits who talked in quiet voices, smiled a lot, and asked me about my life. One of the women had a red smock printed with smiling frogs. *Hey, Frog.* Plus the floor was black-and-white checked, just like Grammy's kitchen.

I kept my parents dead in my stories, and added Grammy's and Susie's deaths to make the doctors feel sorry for me. A regular doctor—a lady—looked me over and said I checked out okay. I knew that. I wasn't sick. And I hadn't been daddled with—though there had been the one time when a junkie yanked me behind a Dumpster and nearly raped me. I'd hit him over the head with a piece of wood and run like crazy.

I didn't tell them anything about that 'cause I wasn't sure if I'd killed the guy. I didn't need them looking into that and arresting me. This place, surrounded by sickos, was bad enough. Jail, surrounded by criminals, would be worse.

So I picked and choosed what I told the doctors. But when I heard the psycho doctor talk to a nurse about foster care again, I made a quick decision and "undeaded" my parents.

"Your parents aren't dead?"

"No, sir. I made that up." Best to come clean.

"Why'd you tell me they were dead?"

I shrugged, not wanting to let him know I was scared of the whole foster thing. Government places probably didn't like to hear kids talk bad about other government places.

The doctor crossed his legs, and the heel of the loafer on his hangy leg slipped off. With a quick move of his ankle, he snapped it back into place. "Tell me about your parents."

I knew the truth would never work. I thought of Susie's parents and started talking. "My dad is a teacher." Susie's dad had taught math.

"And your mother?"

"My mom stays home and takes care of me." *Oh, I'll take care of you, all right, Gigi.*

"So why did you run away from home?"

Another partial truth. "I wasn't doing too good, and then Susie died. I loved Susie. She was my best friend ever."

"I'm sorry you lost her."

I nodded, then said, "Can you call my mom now? I want to go home."

His face lit up like he'd won a prize. "I think we can do that. What's her name and number?"

I looked at it this way: I'd had a nice vacation at the hospital, and the bill that was due had to be paid by going home.

I could always leave again and find my other family on 96th Street. Look for another house with a red door. I knew I *could* make it on my own. I wasn't a kid anymore.

The streets had taken care of that.

16

*People are born for trouble as readily as sparks fly up from a fire.
If I were you, I would go to God and present my case to him.
He does great things too marvelous to understand.*

JOB 5:7-9

The bagel popped up in the toaster. Margery hummed as she spread strawberry cream cheese on top. Her cinnamon-apple tea steeped in a cup on the breakfast table next to the morning paper, next to a blooming pink African violet, next to a napkin holder created by two halves of the leaning Tower of Pisa. On the wall was a black-and-white poster of the Eiffel Tower as seen through two open French doors leading to a balcony with a fancy black railing. Come out. Relax. See the world.

Forget the world of Paris and Pisa. Margery liked this world, right here.

Very, very much.

She sat at the table and ate her breakfast. During the last three days Margery had been living a dream. When Gladys had told her she was leaving town with King to go to her mother's funeral the morning after Margery arrived on her doorstep, Margery had been floored. For Gladys to let her stay while she was leaving town, while she was

going through such a sad time . . . it made Margery even more deter-
mined to make Gladys proud.

Left alone in Gladys's house, going to work at the store with Bernice, taking care of things while Gladys was gone . . . it was a great
feeling to be trusted. And it was a great feeling to live in such a nice
house. It wasn't a big house. Not fancy. There wasn't a single chair
Margery was uncomfortable sitting in—or that wasn't comfortable *to*
sit in. She'd tried each and every one. The rooms were small and full
of furniture and things from around the world. Like Gladys's poster-
papered office at work, it was impossible to *not* know that the home's
owner liked to travel. There were wooden East Indian elephants on the
bookshelf in the living room between a plate on a stand picturing the
Golden Gate Bridge and a book that featured the Sistine Chapel. India
to San Francisco to Rome. Not a hop, skip, and a jump close to each
other. How wonderful to have been to all those places, to have touched
and smelled and heard . . .

Margery had never been much of anywhere. She'd moved around a
lot, but never to anyplace exotic. She *had* been to St. Louis once, but
that didn't count because she couldn't remember anything but having
an ice-cream cone and getting in trouble for dripping it on her shirt. In
ten years of marriage she and Mick had never taken a vacation. Neither
one of them had ever been at a job long enough to earn any paid time
off—not that places like the Chug & Chew cared much about employee
benefits. Margery felt lucky to have health insurance through Mick's
job at the garage—that is, if he still had that job.

Seeing him the other night at the trailer . . . she closed her eyes and
pushed past the image of him taking off his shirt and tossing it across
the room, and zeroed in on the fact that he was even there. There,
meaning *not* in jail.

What had happened to the drug charge against him? Had he gotten
a lawyer? Had he gone to court yet? Was he cleared? Was he innocent?

She snickered and wiped a crumb off her lip. Innocence was not one
of Mick's character traits. Never had been.

So why am I with him?

Ninety-six.

Odd how she'd thought about that number twice in the past few days after so many years ignoring it, avoiding it. But it was true. She'd first been attracted to Mick because he had the number 96 on his football jersey. Margery had been actively looking for the number back then, and though she'd discovered it wasn't always associated with good things, it had never been *bad*.

Just confusing.

Like the year she tried to stay at 96 pounds, nearly starving herself to do it.

Like the time in sixth grade when she kept getting 96s on her tests in school.

Like the time Mick had gotten a speeding ticket for going 96 in a 65-mile-per-hour zone.

Some good things. Some not so good.

Which category did Mick fall into? Had she been so caught up in the ninety-six business that she'd married the wrong man? The fact that they'd graduated, married, and were on their way to having a baby in 1996 had added to her certainty that being Mrs. Mick Lamborn was meant to be.

So why had things turned out so badly?

The timer on the oven buzzed. Gladys was due home today and Margery had made her a fruit-cocktail cake. It was one of Grammy's old recipes. As she took it out of the oven the room filled with a luscious smell of fruit and spices. She would frost it with broiled coconut frosting when she got home from work.

Margery put her breakfast dishes in the dishwasher and swiped a cloth one more time over the counter. She would not abuse Gladys's kindness. Last night she'd even vacuumed and had taken out the garbage. She'd earn her keep.

This house at 9600 was a good place. It was a good sign of better things to come.

🌿 🌿 🌿

Talia put a fresh supply of toddler diapers in her son's diaper bag. She spoke to Nesto as he sat in his recliner behind her. "There's tuna salad in the fridge, and open up a can of soup if you want. I set your medicine on the counter. I might be a little late getting home after work because I have a doctor's appointment and they're doing an ultrasound and—"

"Do me a favor," he said.

His voice was weak, causing her to turn toward him. His color wasn't good this morning and his breathing was heavier than usual. Why hadn't she noticed until now?

"Are you doing okay?"

"I'm fine," he said. "Just do me a favor."

She lifted Tomás onto her hip. "If I can."

"Find out the sex of the baby."

"But we agreed we didn't want to know. We want to be surprised."

He held out his hand and smiled so wistfully she felt compelled to go to him. "I want to know. Now."

Her throat tightened. "Nesto, you're scaring me."

He closed his eyes and slowly opened them again. "I want to know if it's a boy or a girl, so I can imagine the future."

Tomás squirmed in Talia's arms. She let him down and knelt beside her husband, pulling his hand to her chest. "You don't need to imagine. You'll be here. Years and years you'll be here."

Nesto nodded, but she knew it was for her benefit. Suddenly all the to-dos and selfish thoughts fell away and she was forced to once again face the possibility of life without him.

She dropped her head onto his knees and he stroked her hair. "I love you, *meu amor*," he said.

Which is exactly why the pain was so great.

※ ※ ※

King took a box of her mother's things to the car, leaving Gladys alone to say good-bye to Aunt June.

"Are you sure you don't want to come back with me?" Gladys asked. "I have a spare bedroom." *Or I did have . . .*

"Thanks, but no. My life's here. What's left of it anyway." June gripped the wood armrests of the tapestry chair the Terrible Trio had found in an antique store in Edinburgh. Martha Quigley had bought it because the arms curved into swans' heads. She'd laughed with joy upon seeing it and had not quibbled one bit about the price. This one piece of furniture was very much like Gladys's mother, flowing and delicate yet functional, with its own unique style and grace. It held a place of honor in the small room June had shared with Martha, right next to June's sturdy morris chair.

Yesterday June had offered to have the swan chair shipped to Gladys. But from the way June was stroking the arms now, Gladys knew she'd made the right decision in declining the offer. She wondered if June would ever sit in her morris chair again.

"The service was nice, don't you think?" It was the fourth or fifth time June had asked.

"Yes, very nice."

June began humming the song that had been sung, a beautiful piece called "Where Your Glory Dwells," which spoke of being in the presence of God in heaven. It had brought Gladys to tears more than anything else at the service.

Gladys looked toward the door. King was waiting outside, being the kind, considerate man that he—

"He loves you."

Gladys blinked. "What?"

June pointed toward the door. "King. He loves you."

Gladys laughed. "I don't think so. I'm fifteen years older than he is."

"So?"

"That's a lot of years. I'm not . . . I mean I never . . . I don't need—"

June crossed her arms, giving Gladys the challenging smirk she'd seen her entire life. "Certainly you weren't going to finish that sentence by saying you don't need love?"

Certainly I was. Gladys closed her mouth with a snap of her teeth.

June motioned Gladys closer, extending her hand until Gladys took it. The veins in the top of June's hand were three dimensional. "Over the years your mother and I discussed how we might not have done right by you, bringing you up in a household of women who weren't in any hurry to find men to fill their lives—not that any were beating down the doors once your father left, mind you, but you might have gotten the idea that needing, loving, and committing to a man was a bad thing. It isn't."

"I know that. I've had my chances."

"Hmm." June sat back, leaving Gladys's hand dangling.

"Quit looking at me that way," Gladys said. "I'm a big girl, three times past the age of consent. If I'd wanted the spouse-kids-picket-fence thing I would have made it happen. I didn't. I'm perfectly content."

"Glad to hear it." June's face did not reflect her words.

"I'm serious."

"Glad to hear it."

"Why don't you believe me?"

Gladys watched June look around the tiny room that was all that was left of two lives—now down to one. "I don't want you to have regrets," June said. "Your mother and I have been very happy all these years. She's the best sister a woman could have. But I'd be lying if I said we didn't have regrets. Twenty years more than you." She looked at Gladys. "It's never too late, you know."

Gladys snickered.

"I'll admit for some things, there is a time limit." June leaned forward again, pointing a finger. "But in other things—like love—time's not an issue. Unless you waste it. And from what I see coming out of King's eyes when he looks at you, from the muscles in his hands twitching when he wants to touch you . . ."

"Oh please . . ."

June flipped a hand in the air. "Go ahead. Ignore me. Ignore the wisdom of my years. Ignore what your mother wanted for you."

"My mother never met King."

"But she wanted you to be happy. And I'm telling you, that man is aching to make you happy."

"But I'm going blind."

"Not if you do something about it. Which you will. Today. You're going to call the doctor and get your name on that transplant list."

"I am?"

"You are. No arguing. You are going to do what you have to do. So there's that excuse washed down the dirty drain. You'll get your sight back fresh and new. And you'll be happy with a man who loves you."

"You've got it all figured out for me, don't you?"

"You betcha."

"Perfect sight, and the perfect man."

"I think you'd settle for better sight and a good man. 'Cuz he's not perfect, you know."

Gladys put a hand to her chest in mock surprise. "He's not?"

Aunt June aimed a finger at her. "Maybe that's your problem: waiting for perfect. If that's the case, you'd better give up, because *that* ain't ever going to happen."

"I'm not waiting for anything. It's just that I don't want—"

June stood, teetering a bit at the effort. Gladys held out her hand to steady her, but June shooed her away. "Go on! Get outta here. I've done all I can, and if you insist on being a total nudzh . . . you always were a stubborn thing, but I never thought you were stupid."

Gladys didn't want to part like this. "June, I've listened. I have, but—"

June pushed her toward the door. "But nothing. Go on. Thanks for coming. Keep in touch. But don't be surprised when that wonderful man out there finds someone else—'cause he will. Good ones like that need to share their love. Unlike some people."

Gladys was out in the hall. "But—"

June shut the door in her face.

※ ※ ※

King leaned against the rental car, but stood up straight when Gladys came out of the retirement home. His expression turned to concern and he took a step toward her. "Are you all right?"

With a quick move she fended off his touch—his touch that had gained new meaning, if June was right. "I just want to get home."

"Your wish is my command."

He opened the door and helped her in. The gentleman. Always the gentleman willing to do anything to help. To please her. To love her?

He went around to the driver's side and got in.

King was in love with her? It was absurd. They were business partners. Period. They rarely saw each other because they often worked opposite shifts—except for King's recent habit of coming in early before his shift started.

It was an act of polite attention and concern for the business. Surely not love.

Why not love?

She looked at him as he drove. He looked back and smiled in a gentle way. He *was* a handsome man. Not a hunk, as the kids would say nowadays, but Jimmy Stewart handsome. And certainly Jimmy Stewart charming. And nice. A good guy . . .

Who could *not* be interested in a woman her age. June was leading her astray, caught up in memories and regrets of her own, and seeing things where there was nothing to see.

"I like your aunt," King said.

"She likes you too."

"She's feisty . . . a character."

"Correct on both accounts."

He turned onto the on-ramp for the interstate that would take them to the airport. "I called the store," King said. "Bernice says everything is going great. Margery has really stepped up to the plate."

"Good, good." Business talk.

They shared a business connection.

That was it.

❧ ❧ ❧

After leaving the comfort of Nesto's lap, after leaving Tomás off at day care, Talia was in overdrive, not thinking about tasks but coasting through them, just assuming she was on the right road and going the speed limit.

Her thoughts of Nesto—of death, of pain, of loneliness—were obstacles as real as rocks and rain, and it took all her power—such as it was—to not end up in the ditch. Somehow she got to work safely. Somehow she made one minute move into the next.

"I love you, meu amor." Her husband's simple declaration was a mantra underlying every other thought. He *did* love her. She knew it with her entire being. And she loved him. Yet recently she'd felt herself pulling away, preparing herself for the worst, protecting herself. Loving him too much would hurt too much. Would she be able to bear it? She'd have to, for Tomás and for the baby. Yet how could she?

Don't worry about tomorrow, for tomorrow will bring its own worries.
Today's trouble is enough for today.

She nodded at the Bible verse she'd heard many times, knowing it was true, yet not being able to let go.

Let go and let God.

She leaned her elbows on her desk and covered her face with her hands. If she was having trouble handling the *thought* of being without Nesto how could she ever hope to handle the reality of it?

Suddenly, she felt a touch on the back of her neck. She turned around.

"Penny for your thoughts?" Wade asked.

She couldn't even say anything, but found her head shaking no, no, no, no.

"Is it Nesto?"

At her nod, he helped her to her feet and led her into his office. With one swift movement, he pulled her into his arms. Even as she thought *no* she found herself resting her head against his shoulder.

"There, there," he said. "I'm so sorry you're hurting. So sorry."

"I love him so much," she said into Wade's suit coat.

He put a hand to the back of her head. "I know. I know."

It felt so good to be held.

※　※　※

Angie stopped as soon as she entered her daughter's office with the list of florists. There, straight ahead, in plain sight in Wade's adjoining office, was her daughter in her boss's arms. Closer than close. She watched a moment longer, long enough to see Wade's lips graze Talia's hair.

She'd seen enough. Talia could deny the attraction all she wanted. Seeing was believing.

※　※　※

Talia carefully ran a tissue under her bottom lashes after telling Wade there could be nothing between them. "Thank you for being so understanding, Wade. I'm sorry if I've led you on. I don't like being a needy woman, and I really appreciate your friendship. But . . ."

"And I yours. I'm just sorry . . ." He didn't need to fill in the blanks, and she was glad when he moved back to his desk, creating the proper distance between them. A part of her hated to see him go. But it was for the best. She'd been teasing the edge of impropriety too long. It wasn't fair to either of them, and moreover, it wasn't right. After he'd comforted her she'd told him so. It was something she should have done the first time they'd had contact beyond the norm.

In truth she'd welcomed his attention. Wade was a handsome man by any standards. He obviously thought she was an attractive women—even in her very pregnant state—and he'd offered a few lingering looks and special smiles. Who wouldn't react to such interest?

Talia was human. She was vulnerable. But she was also going to do the right thing. Up until now she'd been playing a game. She'd allowed herself to play what-if? with her boss. Sure, the thoughts had only been fleeting. But they *had* existed. What if they could be together? What if she didn't have a sick husband? What if she sought a little pleasure? Was that so bad?

No. But it wasn't good either.

And it wasn't real. Running away from what *was* real was cowardly—and of no use.

So now it was time. Time to live in the here and now, accept what was, and deal with it. Be at peace with as many people as possible but not let anyone—anyone—drag her down.

"I'm leaving for my doctor's appointment now," Talia told Wade. "If that's all right?"

He pulled a file front and center and didn't even look up. "See you tomorrow."

Talia would have liked a more personable ending to the conversation, but she realized the time of dipping into the what-if world was indeed gone.

So be it.

❀ ❀ ❀

"Boon!"

Tomás pointed to the pink "It's a Girl" balloon bobbing in the front seat of the car. "*Balloon*, that's right, sweetie. Isn't it pretty?"

Talia checked the cake on the seat next to her. Through the cellophane on the top of the box she could see the pink writing: *It's a Girl!* There would certainly be a celebration at the Soza house tonight.

Talia had publicly said she didn't care if the baby was a boy or a girl—adding the trite though true line, "As long as it's healthy." But during the ultrasound when the doctor had told her, "Looks like you have yourself a little girl here," she'd felt a surge of happiness that rivaled her joy at Tomás's birth. A boy and a girl. Perfection.

She pulled into their driveway and decided to take Tomás in first. Nesto was not in his recliner. "Nesto?"

No answer.

She set Tomás down by his toys and went to the kitchen. He wasn't there either. She ran toward the stairway. "Nesto?"

No answer.

She raced up the stairs, past Tomás's empty room, to the master bedroom. He wasn't in bed. Her thoughts sped to an emergency. Had he called 911? Had they come and taken him to the hos—?

She heard the toilet flush. Moments later, Nesto came out of the master bathroom. "Oh, hi," he said.

Oh, hi? Talia put a hand to her chest, calming her heart. "I couldn't find you."

"I was—" he looked toward the bathroom—"busy."

"Are you okay?" she asked.

He came close and kissed her. "So? You have news?"

This wasn't how she'd played it out in her mind. She'd find him in his recliner, set Tomás on the floor close by, then bring in the balloon and cake in a triumphant show.

"Mama?" It was Tomás's where-are-you? tone.

"I'll be right there, sweetie," she called. "Let's go downstairs."

"Tell me here," Nesto said.

"No. Come downstairs."

"It's good news?"

What? "Yes," she said, taking his arm. "It's very good news." She whispered in his ear, "We're having a baby."

"Ha-ha. Funny."

"Be patient. Let me do this the way I want to do it."

She helped him down the stairs. Tomás met them on the bottom step, reaching up for his papa. "Wait till Papa gets seated, little one."

Once Nesto was in his recliner with Tomás on his lap, Talia went out to the car. She removed the cake from the box, licking a bit of frosting off the edge of her hand. She went up the front walk, the balloon flowing behind her. She paused at the door. "Are you ready?"

"Ready!" Nesto said.

She made a grand entrance, just as she'd planned. "Surprise! It's a girl!"

Nesto's eyes lit up—and teared up. *"Uma menina. Uma menina pequeña."*

Talia set the cake on the coffee table and knelt beside her husband's recliner for the second time that day. "Yes. A girl. A little girl," she whispered.

They kissed each other, then Tomás.

"Boon!"

Talia tied the balloon around his little wrist. He got off his papa's lap and marched around the room, the balloon dancing with the motion.

Talia slid her arms around her husband's neck. "Are you happy?"

He nodded. "I can see her. She has *bonito* skin like her mama."

"And big brown eyes like her papa."

"Arcelia," Nesto said.

Talia sat up. "That isn't one of the names we've been thinking about."

He shrugged. "It means treasure. She's our treasure for the future."

Arcelia.

Yes, indeed, Talia had much to treasure.

🐜 🐜 🐜

Make the frosting for the cake, sweep the front porch, have water ready for hot tea . . .

After spending the day at work, Margery entered Gladys's house going over her mental to-do list. If Gladys's flight was on time it had already landed. She would be home any minute and Margery wanted things perfect.

She hung her coat in the front closet and paused to retrieve a few stray gloves that had fallen from the shelf to the floor.

There was a knock on the door, startling her. Disappointing her. She hadn't even started on her list. But as she put her hand on the doorknob she had an odd thought, even as she swung the door wide: *Why would Gladys knock?* But the completion of the movement beat the completion of the thought, and—

"Mick!"

He pushed his way past her, taking possession of the living room in a few steps. He did a three-sixty, his eyes taking everything in. "Nice digs. How'd you manage this?"

"How'd you find me?"

He nabbed a crystal shamrock from the mantel, turning it over in his hands. "I followed you from work."

She realized she still had the front door open. She opened it farther. "You need to go."

He put the shamrock down, sat on the couch with a bounce. "Not bad. You sleeping with the guy?"

"What?"

"To live here. He's not making you pay rent, is he? Because you *could* barter. If you were smart, you'd barter."

Margery was repulsed. For him to think . . . to suggest, as if it were no big deal . . . The door was still open. Cold air flowed in. Obviously he wasn't going anywhere until he was ready. She closed it, but didn't move closer. "What do you want, Mick?"

He patted the cushion beside him. "Come sit by me."

She shook her head.

"Come on. I forgive you for whatever you've had to do to get here, but *I* need you now. I want you back."

She thought of his fling with the floozy on the couch. Their couch. "No you don't."

He didn't do a very good version of *stricken.* "Of course I do. Why would you doubt me?"

She wanted to mention the other woman and shove it in his face, but that would stir things up and take time. Gladys was on her way home. Margery made speed her priority. "I'm not ready to come back yet, Mick. But maybe. Soon."

He grabbed a pillow with one hand and heaved it at her, hitting her chest. "You think this is better? You think this guy is going to keep you around? You're not that good, Marg."

Her breathing turned heavy. She needed him out. Now. And she wouldn't go back to him. A few days ago she might have, but after her promise to Gladys and after experiencing what normal felt like . . .

Everything had changed, and more would change—in a bad way— if she didn't find a way to get rid of him.

"How's your trial going?" Making him mad was a risk, but he'd stormed out often enough. Maybe—just maybe—he'd do it now.

But instead of pouncing on her words, he relaxed against the cushions, spreading his arms across the back of the couch. "It's done. Got myself a lawyer who got me off."

"You're free?"

"As a bird."

When she felt a surge of disappointment, Margery realized the extent that her love for him had faded. She gathered another question. "So you're back at work. You're—"

He laughed. "Yes, well. Whatever." He stood. "Enough old-home week. I don't have time for this."

Neither do I. She wanted this over, yet braced herself for whatever he was about to say. It couldn't be good.

"You work at a drugstore."

She didn't know what to say to this. "Yes . . ."

"They trust you there."

One plus one was going to equal . . . "Not really." She realized he didn't know she'd tried to steal the bail money. He'd kicked her out of the house before she'd told him. "I'm working real hard to earn their trust and—"

He crossed the room, wearing his I-want-something face. She took a step back but he kept coming until one hand was on her shoulder. The other cupped her cheek, making its way behind her neck, pulling her—

Even as she reacted, she knew it would make things worse, but his touch . . . she jerked away and sidled around him, taking a place near the couch he'd just left.

His eyes widened in surprise, which was quickly replaced by anger. He dropped his hands, which had frozen in their touch-Margery position. "Let's get to the point. You work in a drugstore. I need drugs. You're going to get them for me."

Shock mixed with sadness. So he *was* into drugs. The charge against him was valid. He should be in jail.

But he was free. And standing in front of her.

"There's no cocaine there. Just prescriptions. Medicine."

"Drugs. It's not what I'm used to dealing, but there's still a market. There's a market for almost everything." He pulled a list from his pocket and shoved it into her hands. "Here's what I need. Here's what you're going to get for me."

She didn't even look at it. "You want me to steal?" She swallowed, then gave him back the note. "I can't do that, Mick. I can't."

He grabbed her wrist and twisted, making her knees buckle. "You will. I've given you ten years of my life—wasted ten years with you. I've got a good thing going now that will get me out of the hellhole I've been living in. And if you don't want to be with me, at least you'll help me."

"Let go!"

He leaned into her ear, his breath hot. "I will never let you go. And this is nothing compared to what will happen if you don't do as I say."

She heard the sound of a car pull into the driveway.

So did he. He bit her earlobe before his hand found her chin and squeezed. "Be a good girl, Gigi." His smile made her sick. "And maybe I'll leave you alone."

Her eyes darted to the front walk. Gladys was coming. "Please," she whispered.

"Then do it." He let her go with a shove and took a step back, just as the front door opened.

Gladys saw Margery; then her eyes moved to Mick. "Oh. Hello."

Margery had no idea if words would come out, but she made a try of it. "Gladys, this—" she cleared her throat, trying again—"this is my husband, Mick."

Suddenly Margery saw the charm of the man she married emerge, and the transformation chilled her far more than his recent words or muscling.

His smile was broad. He wiped a hand on his jeans and held it toward Gladys. "Nice to meet you, Gladys. Margery has told me so much about you."

Gladys's eyes flitted from him to Margery and back. "She's told me so much about you too."

Mick flashed Margery a look, but the fake smile remained.

King entered the opened door with a suitcase, taking in the room with a single sweep of his eyes. "Hi."

"You need some help?" Mick asked.

King stammered a moment, then said, "There's a box in the backseat that needs to come in."

Mick looked at the list in his hand, shoved it into his shirt pocket, and was out the door.

Gladys was immediately at Margery's side. "You okay?"

She shook her head no, her eyes on the window, watching Mick. "Just get him to go."

With a single nod, King moved onto the porch and met Mick halfway. He took the box. "Thanks for the help."

"No problem." Mick looked past him into the house.

Margery moved out of his sight line.

King held his ground, a barrier between sidewalk and door. "Thanks for helping, Mick. Have a nice evening."

"But Margery and I were having a nice visit."

"We're tired from our trip. Perhaps another time."

A pause, then Mick said, "Tell Margery I'll be in touch."

"Will do." King held his ground until Mick walked away. Then he came inside and shut the door.

Margery rushed toward it, bolted it, and hid behind it.

"Goodness, Margery," Gladys said as she took a step toward her. "You're shaking."

Margery's legs gave out and she melted onto the floor.

Gladys was immediately at her side. "King, get some water." To Margery she said, "Come on. Let's get you over to the couch."

Margery let herself be led. King appeared with the water, and

Margery took a sip even though she felt no need for it. Gladys sat beside her and King sat in the chair close by.

"Did he hurt you?" Gladys asked.

She shook her head, though her wrist and chin burned from his rough touch.

"What did he want?" King asked. Before she could answer, he added, "I thought he was in jail."

"He got out." Margery stood and moved away from them. "He followed me from work. He found me here. I have to leave. I can't have him . . . I can't involve you." She rushed to the guest room and opened a drawer, ready to pack. Then she realized she'd brought her clothes in by hand and didn't have a suitcase. She'd have to carry them out. She grabbed an armload but King and Gladys blocked the door. "Please move," she said. "I have to—"

King took some of the clothes away, making the rest of them fall.

Gladys put a hand on her shoulder. "Just stop. You're not going anywhere."

The pile of clothes divided them, as did so much more. Much, much more. Margery stepped back and sat on the end of the bed. If only she could disappear. "You don't understand. I have to leave. I can't work for you anymore."

"Why not?" King asked.

She shook her head. To tell them what Mick wanted her to do would imply she was the kind of person who would do it. Steal.

Which she was. She'd stolen before. From them. Or would have, if Gladys hadn't caught her first.

She told a different truth. "He wants me back."

Gladys raised her chin defiantly. "He can't have you."

"He won't give up. He'll dog me. He knows where I'm staying. He knows where I work. It's best I go away."

"Go where?" King asked.

That was the clincher. "I don't know. I've never been anywhere." She looked at Gladys. "Not like you."

Gladys sat beside her and put an arm around her shoulders. "And you're not going anywhere now, not like this. I will not have you driving to some strange town, living in your car again."

"But he knows where—"

"We'll make sure people are always around you," King said. "We'll protect you."

"You can't."

Gladys's voice softened. "Do you really think he'd hurt you?"

Margery thought back to the times Mick had gotten physical. He'd never hit her. Just grabbed her. Pushed her. That didn't count, did it? "Not really." But she wasn't sure if that was a truthful answer. She wasn't sure about anything anymore. Just a few days ago she'd wanted to start a family with him.

"We could get a restraining order," King said. "Then he'd have to stay away."

"Those things don't work," Gladys said.

"It might work."

Margery shook her head, knowing Gladys was right. Mick would do what Mick wanted to do. But suddenly, the other truth returned and Margery didn't have the strength to beat it back a second time. "He wants me to steal drugs for him."

"From the store?" King asked.

She nodded, feeling an absurd relief at getting it out. Maybe they *could* help. Maybe there was a way she could stay.

"Which drugs does he want?" Gladys asked, then flipped a hand at her own question. "You don't need to answer that. I know."

Margery was glad because she didn't know. She'd never looked at Mick's list and he'd never given it back to her.

King looked at Margery. "Did the alarm company come today?"

Yes! "Yes, they did. Bernice has the code."

"That'll keep him out," King said.

"But that won't keep him from wanting Margery to steal *for* him."

The room went silent. They were back to the beginning.

Gladys squeezed her shoulders. "You're not going anywhere. You're staying in my house and you're working at the store."

"And," King added, "you are not going to be alone."

Gladys looked at him. "Tomorrow's the weekend. She doesn't work, but *we* do."

Margery thought of something. "I told Angie I'd go to the shelter with her and volunteer."

"Good," Gladys said. "As long as you're with trustworthy people. Afterwards, you call me when you're on your way home and I'll leave work and come here to be with you."

"That's a lot of trouble," Margery said.

Gladys winked at her. "You're worth it."

Margery knew *that* wasn't true.

✾ ✾ ✾

Gladys heard a sound. She lifted her head off the pillow and listened. Hearing nothing but the furnace, she let herself relax.

Kind of. Sort of.

Yet she knew it wasn't merely this drama with Margery and Mick that kept her from sleep. There were the grieving thoughts of her mother . . .

And pleasant thoughts of King.

If only he hadn't gone with her to the funeral. If only he hadn't met Aunt June, June never would have said those things about him, and Gladys wouldn't know he was interested in her.

Liar.

She knew. She'd known for a long time, if she were honest with herself. Not that King had ever done anything improper. He'd never made a pass at her, never said anything suggestive—other than kidding her about being the only woman for him.

Gladys sat up with a start. He *had* said such a thing many times, the last time when she'd pushed him about the blind date he *didn't* have with Mandy Thomason. *"What do I need with her? I have a beautiful, smart, funny woman right here."*

He was always saying such things, and up to now she'd brushed them off as merely a ploy to disarm her and get her to change the subject. But according to Aunt June . . .

King was serious. He really did think she was beautiful, smart, and funny.

She lay back down and pulled a pillow into a hug.

But she didn't sleep.

❋ ❋ ❋

Gennifer turned off the TV. She'd had it on for an hour but hadn't seen any of it. Inane jabber. Noise.

Company. That was the truth of it. She'd had it on for company.

After coming home from work—to an empty house—she'd found a note from Sarah: *I'm out.*

The lack of details bothered her. For a while. Yet what did it really matter if Sarah was at a movie, at a friend's house, or with Angie Schuster? Sarah had her own life and wasn't interested in Gennifer, so Gennifer didn't need to be interested in her.

But she's my daughter.

She tossed the remote on the coffee table where it bounced and landed on the Oriental rug. She left it there.

After her dialysis this morning she hadn't felt well. Drained. Achy. Sick. Throughout the day her physical state had affected her emotional state and she'd snapped at people, had zero tolerance for the normal insanities of the law, and had left work as early as possible.

To come home to an empty house.

To be honest, her first reaction had been one of relief. She didn't feel up to dealing with Sarah's petulance and disregard, and certainly wasn't up to interacting with her two-timing husband. The three members of the Mancowitz family were spending the evening doing what they did best lately: going their separate ways.

They'd better get used to it. With her declining health she might not be around much longer.

Her sudden lack of optimism was annoying yet hard to shake. Sure, the doctor talked a good talk, being upbeat about a transplant. But even when that happened, *if* it happened, there would be a time of recovery when Gennifer would have to take it easy. So the fact her family got along fine without her was a good thing.

Especially if she died.

At that happy thought, she moved to the kitchen. Ice cream. Ice cream would be good right now. She got out the French vanilla, ignoring the pistachio nut that was Douglas's favorite. Yuck. Green ice cream? With nuts?

She grabbed a spoon and sat at the kitchen table to eat out of the carton, relishing being a purist. Vanilla—good vanilla ice cream—was as gourmet as any bizarre flavor Douglas preferred.

She looked at the clock on the microwave. Ten thirty. She guessed he wasn't coming home from his business trip tonight. It was kind of embarrassing not to *know* what day he was coming home. He'd probably told her, but the fact she'd not digested that vital piece of information was telling. Yet ever since the special time they'd shared last weekend when he'd impulsively asked her to go to Maine, and she'd hesitated, and he'd gotten mad . . . things had pretty much shut down.

Not that things ever ran smoothly anymore.

The sound of a car in the drive interrupted her thoughts. She went to the kitchen window and watched as Douglas pulled into the garage. Disappointment popped its evil head. What happened to the good lawyer, the good wife, the good mother? She wasn't good at much of anything anymore.

A memory intruded: her mother meeting her father at the door every night, kissing him on the cheek, and asking, "How was your day?" And her father's standard line, "Fine. Just fine."

Perfection. Something she'd tried so hard to attain . . .

Gennifer returned to her chair before the back door opened. She did not get up.

Douglas did a double take upon seeing her. "I thought you'd be asleep."

Just the way he said it . . . she rose. "You hoped I'd be asleep so you could sneak in and not have to deal with me?"

He put his suitcase down and closed the door. "Where did that come from?"

She pushed in her chair and stood behind it. "How's your lover doing?"

He stopped with one arm of his coat off.

Gennifer gripped the back of the chair. "I know about her, Douglas. I know you gave her an expensive necklace. Pearls, no less."

He looked at her the briefest of moments, then finished removing his coat. "You've been sneaking through my things?"

"I hardly think my sneaking compares with yours. How long has this been going on?"

Douglas picked up his suitcase and moved past her toward the stairs. "We're not doing this."

She grabbed his arm as he passed. "Can't stand being caught, eh?"

He shook off her grip. "I haven't been caught doing anything."

"I may not have caught you in bed, but I found the necklace. Just like . . ." She blinked. *Just like what?*

He set the suitcase down near the staircase and faced her. "Actually, your jealousy might be considered a good thing."

"How so?"

"It means you *are* capable of feeling. You actually have emotions. I was beginning to wonder."

Gennifer ran to the front door and opened it. "Get out! Leave! It's what you want."

He picked up his suitcase a second time and headed up the stairs. "No thanks. I'm tired from my trip. It's a big house. You can keep the master bedroom. I'll move into the guest room." He paused on the third step. "We rarely see each other anyway, so it shouldn't affect much." He looked up the stairs. "Is Sarah in her room?"

"She's out." She hoped he wouldn't ask more.

Thankfully, he only nodded and went upstairs. "Night."

Gennifer stood, immobile. That was it? The big confrontation about his having an affair was over? Nothing had been resolved. Nothing had even been admitted. There had to be more. There *had* been more . . . before.

Much more.

In her mind, Gennifer heard a shot. She cringed.

She shook the sound away and went up to bed. The door to the guest room was closed.

It could be worse. Much worse.

❧ ❧ ❧

Angie and Stanford sat in the family room and watched the evening news. Angie was in a mood, knew it, and even embraced it as her due. Ever since catching her daughter and Wade in an embrace she'd been bothered—though not for the reason she'd expected.

She wasn't appalled. Wasn't disgusted. Wasn't incensed.

She was jealous.

Angie was well aware their situations were very different. Talia was young and dealing with the pressures of an ailing husband who probably couldn't meet her emotional and physical needs. Angie was middle-aged and dealing with a difficult husband who *wouldn't* meet hers.

There was the difference. Stanford *could* be a good husband in all ways—if he wanted to. Nesto couldn't.

It was Stanford's choice. And he chose no. No affection. No kind words. No real love.

No job for Angie . . .

She was sick of it. And once she'd entered that mind-set while making dinner—when, in a moment of extreme rebellion she'd made herself a cherry pie instead of his favorite pumpkin—everything Stanford did all evening added fuel to the fire. The way he complained about the salmon being tough; the way he was appalled she hadn't made *his* favorite pie; the way he didn't bring his dishes to the dishwasher; the way he spent the entire evening on the phone, wandering the house as he talked, invading every room where she tried to escape for some silence like a male cat marking its territory. It was as if he had a need to be present—or be a presence—in every moment of her free evening. He possessed a listen-to-me-talk-I'm-so-important attitude. Which in her mood she interpolated into an and-you-are-not-important subtext.

As the evening wore on Angie had begun to take note of any eye contact he made *with* her, any word said *to* her. By the time the late news came on, his slate was clean. Bare. No entries made. Stanford had managed to go through the entire evening from dinner to bedtime without once looking at her or speaking to her.

Until . . .

He took off his reading glasses, set them on top of the latest *Forbes* he'd been reading, stood, and looked her way.

May the heavens open . . .

"Coming?" he said.

She knew what that meant. It was Stanford's version of foreplay.

Angie set her feet on the trunk that served as their coffee table with a decided *thud-thud*. She picked up a *Good Housekeeping*. "No thanks."

"Excuse me?"

She turned the page. "No thank you."

His right eyebrow rose. "What's got into *you*?"

You sweet talker, you . . .

Angie flipped the pages loudly. "I must admit I find your timing odd."

He glanced at the clock on the VCR. "It's bedtime. What's odd about that?"

"I find it odd that, after ignoring me the entire evening, you suddenly realize I exist—and want to, shall we say, interact?"

He rolled his eyes. "Don't be petulant."

Her feet hit the floor. "Oooh. Big word. I'm not sure you should expect someone as uneducated as me to understand what it means."

"Your lack of formal education has been addressed long ago—and rectified. I gave you the life education that made up for your pitiful past."

She gave him a standing ovation. "Bravo! The magnanimous man changes the wallflower to a rose—and makes her pay for the privilege."

He pointed a finger at her. "You should be grateful."

A brief moment of clarity made her acknowledge this. She softened her tone. "I *am* grateful. I've been grateful for thirty-one years. But how long before the debt is paid and you treat me as an equal, not a project?"

He stood speechless. Then he said, "Don't be ridiculous. You're my wife."

It rang as a title, not a consecrated vow. A position filled, not a calling.

"You don't respect me, Stanford. You don't want to be around me. You tolerate me."

"Of course I respect you and want you around." He shook his head. "It's getting late. What do you want out of all this?"

What *did* she want? Having to put it into words—words Stanford would respond to—was difficult, and Angie realized she should have thought this through before she started.

He picked up his glasses and magazine. "If you can't express it, how can I guess—"

"I want to be loved."

"You are loved."

She made a mental edit. "I want to *feel* loved."

He folded the glasses and put them in his shirt pocket, his head shaking. "I can't make you *feel* anything, Angela. That's under your control, not mine."

She took a step toward him, wanting to touch him but not daring to. "You're the one in control, Stanford. If you expressed this love you say you have for me . . . if you were more demonstrative. If you hugged me, kissed me . . ."

"I do all those things."

"In the bedroom. But how about in the kitchen when I'm cooking dinner? Or on the deck when I'm reading?"

"You want to have sex in the kitchen and on the deck?"

She sighed in exasperation. "I'm not talking about sex. I'm talking about attention. Touch me, look at me, talk to me as if I'm the most important person in the world."

"Don't ask me to be something I'm not."

"You asked me to be something I wasn't."

"That was different."

"How?"

"I asked you to be something better than what you were. I made you better."

"I want you to be something better than what you are. I want you—I want us—to pay attention to each other more."

His upper lip curled in a disturbing rendition of Elvis. "I don't like when you play the whiney, needy type, Angela."

"Well . . . I am needy. In this I am."

He shook his head, disgusted. "I am not a touchy-feely man. You know that."

She touched his arm. "But you could be. Couldn't you? For me?"

He looked down at her, but his eyes were neutral, just as they always were. Only his work made his eyes light up.

Angie did not.

The revelation made her legs weak even while anger sparked in the pit of her stomach. "For me?" she repeated, giving him one more chance.

He stepped back, shook his head, and turned toward the stairs. "We'll talk about this tomorrow. I have a big deal being finalized in an early meeting. I need to get to bed."

Angie took her own step back, creating even more distance between them. "And I need to go."

He stopped and looked over his shoulder at her. "What?"

She hadn't meant to say the G word, but it seemed to be the logical progression from his rejection of her . . . to her rejecting him.

Going. Leaving him.

She hurried toward the kitchen, gathering her coat and purse along the way. Even as she opened the door her thoughts raced: *What am I doing?*

But she couldn't stop, and that fact alone, scared her. She'd never done this before. Never threatened to leave. Never walked out. Maybe if she had . . .

Once in the garage, her spine tingled with the thought of his coming after her. Chasing her.

Her tingles were wasted because Stanford Sebastian Schuster did not open the door and call after her. He did not plead with her to stay. Or even demand that she "get back in here!"

As the garage door rattled open, as she started the car, the door between garage and house remained closed.

He was letting her go.

Right or wrong, there was no turning back now.

※ ※ ※

Talia was just getting into bed when she heard the doorbell. She glanced at Nesto, who was already asleep. Who could be visiting at this hour?

She wrapped a robe over her nightgown and hurried downstairs, wishing she had a husband who could be the brave one to handle a mysterious caller late at night.

She approached the door warily, edging up to its sheer-covered window.

"Talia? It's me. Mom."

She opened the door with a finger to her lips. "What are you doing here? I was getting into bed."

"I left your father."

The words could not have been more shocking than if her mother had said, "I'm going to take tap-dance lessons." Actually, the latter would have been more feasible.

"Can I come in?"

Talia let her inside, then remembered her family sleeping upstairs. "Let's go to the kitchen. I'll make tea," she whispered.

Talia put a kettle of water on the stove and got out a box of assorted tea bags. She held them up to her mother, who waved away her choice. Talia chose a soothing chamomile. While waiting for the water to boil, she sat. "So what happened?"

"He doesn't love me."

"Of course he does." As soon as she said it, Talia realized it was a trite response—and not entirely correct. She wasn't sure if her father truly loved anyone. Other than himself. Other than his work.

Her mother fingered the edge of the navy placemat. "I saw you and Wade today."

Talia dropped a tea bag.

Angie leaned across the table. "Do you love *him*?"

"Mother . . ."

Angie sat back. "So it's just a fling?"

Talia ran a hand through her hair. "I can't believe you saw. I hope no one else saw."

"You'd better hope that." Angie tapped a coral-painted fingernail on the table. "You never answered my question. Is it just a fling?"

Talia's heart pushed against her expanded belly. She sat up straighter, trying to give it room. "You were right about there being a chemistry between us. I'd played innocent, pretending it was nothing, taking his comfort when I needed it."

"So you *were* tempted?"

Talia hesitated, then said, "Wade gave me attention. He made me feel special."

"Exactly. That's exactly why I left your father."

"Someone else is giving you attention, making you feel—?"

"In a way. A different way." Her mother told Talia about their argument. Nothing was said that Talia didn't already know. And agree with. Her father was a cold man. Always had been. In fact . . .

"But this job offer from Josh at the shelter . . ."

"You're not interested in this Josh, are—?"

"No, no," Angie said. "Nothing like that. There's no romance involved."

"You liked cooking there that much?"

"It's not about the cooking—not *just* about the cooking. It's about the respect." She put her hands to her chest. "I feel whole there. Complete. As if I'm doing what I am destined to do."

Talia remembered the fire she'd seen in her mother at the meeting for the fund-raiser. "You are good at this sort of thing, Mother."

"How do you know?"

Good point. "At the meeting when you stood up to Gennifer when she got after you for mentoring her daughter . . ."

"I shouldn't have done that."

"It was wonderful. You were helping a girl in need and defended her. I was very proud of you."

"You were?"

"Before that meeting I hadn't realized how good you are at the volunteer stuff. You're an expert. You know what you're talking about. And you come alive when you're talking about it."

Her mother's eyes met Talia's. Angie's were teary. "You're proud of me?"

The need in her mother's voice made Talia's heart break. She'd never thought to compliment her mother before, to build her up—or even considered that her mother *needed* those things from her. "I am very proud of you," Talia said. "Very proud."

With a nod her mother moved on. "The thing is, I don't want cherry pie instead of pumpkin. I want peace."

Talia was lost. "A piece of pie?"

Her mother ran a hand over her forehead. "This afternoon while making dinner I started to make your father a pumpkin pie."

"His favorite."

"I hate pumpkin pie."

"Then why do you always make it?"

"Because he likes it."

"My mother, always the giver . . ."

She shook her head vehemently. "Not today. Because instead of making the pumpkin pie I made *my* favorite pie."

Talia thought a moment. "I have no idea which pie is your favorite."

"Because I never make it. I can't remember the last time I did. It's cherry."

"Why did you do it today?"

"Selfishness."

Talia laughed. "I hardly think making one cherry pie in all these years is selfish."

"But it was!" Angie sprang out of her chair and paced the room, the movement fueling her words. "It seems that all I can do is act in extremes. Either I'm bowing down to someone else's wishes at the cost of my own, or I do what I want and feel horrible about it." She stopped pacing. "I want peace. P-E-A-C-E. I want a balance between giving too much and not at all. I felt the possibility of that balance when I was cooking at the shelter."

"Then you should take the job."

"*Should* and *could* are two different things." She returned to her chair, slumping into it as if her pacing had burned away her spark.

The water on the stove rolled in the kettle. Talia got up and poured two cups, then returned to her seat.

Angie dunked her tea bag . . . up and down, up and down. "I don't know what I'm doing. One minute your father and I were watching the news and the next, I'm here." She took a sip and looked at Talia over the rim of her mug. "But I think I want to stay here. At least tonight. Would that be all right?"

Talia said, "Of course you can stay" but her mind swam with dumb logistics. She hadn't been in the guest room in ages. Was it decent or could her mother write her name in the dust on the dresser? Whatever condition it was in, it would have to do.

Her mother needed her.

Join the needy club. There was always room for one more.

17

A prudent person foresees danger and takes precautions.
The simpleton goes blindly on and suffers the consequences.
PROVERBS 22:3

He was number 96.

That wasn't the only reason I was attracted to him, but it was the first reason.

Me being at a football game at all was a miracle. Since leaving the hospital and voluntarily moving back home to escape the foster-care system . . .

Mama had been mad I'd run away, and me staying away a year had turned that mad to furious. Yet from the first moment I walked in the door I could tell she'd gotten used to me being gone.

In my absence Ted had moved in. "Hey, Gigi, nice to see you." His voice made my skin crawl and his eyes lingered . . . they made me want to wrap a blanket around myself. I had no clue what Mama saw in him. Yet it was clear by the way she hung on his arm that she did. I could only imagine the mixed feelings she must have felt when my doctor had called and told her to come get me.

Since I found Ted smarmy, I found ways to be away from home as much as possible. I worked two jobs plus going to school. Add studying to the mix and I was only home to sleep. I didn't have time for fun stuff.

So going to a football game that night was something new. A whim. I didn't even like football.

But during fourth hour on Friday, when we were forced to go to a pep rally for the big game against the Knights, when the girl sitting next to me on the bleachers said, "You want to go to the game with me tonight?" I said yes. I wasn't into the whole rah-rah school-spirit thing, but once I got there and sat in the middle of a crowd wearing blue and white, eating popcorn and hot dogs, chanting with the cheerleaders . . . it was kind of fun. America, apple pie, and all that.

Number 96 was the kicker. After he made the first extra point, he took off his helmet as he ran to the sidelines. Even from the stands I could tell he wasn't very big. The players on defense loomed over him, but he was cute in a sweaty-guy kind of way.

I turned to the girl next to me—her name turned out to be Suzy, which was close enough to Susie to make me like her. "What's the kicker's name?"

She knew right away, even without looking at him. "That's Mick Lamborn. He's in my math class. He flunked the last test."

I didn't care. I wasn't good at math either. I felt Suzy's eyes. "What?"

She grinned at me. "You like him?"

"I don't even know him."

"You wanna meet him?"

"Sure."

Why not? What could it hurt?

❧ ❧ ❧

Luckily, Suzy's math class was right before lunch, so Monday at the scheduled time I hurried out of American history and ran to room 342. Suzy was waiting for me and motioned me over. She was standing with Mick, and he looked in my direction as I came closer. Suzy would never win a prize for being subtle.

Mick's face had sharp features. His nose was kind of pointy and his eyes were small. But his shoulders looked strong. I was in the market for some strong shoulders I could rely on. I was getting weary of handling life by myself. Mama was no help whatsoever and needed handling just like the chores and the bills. And Daddy had his own life with his new family in another state.

Not that I was going to pounce on the poor guy, ask him to marry me and take me away or anything dumb like that, but wide strong shoulders were always a good thing. Especially if those shoulders wore the number 96.

"Come on, Gigi," Suzy said.

I moved faster until I was standing right beside him.

"You wanted to meet me?" he asked.

I flashed Suzy a look, then smiled at him. What could I say but, "Yeah."

He spread his arms, holding a notebook with one outstretched hand. "Here I am."

Here you are. I couldn't pinpoint why I was so attracted to him, but there was no denying the pull to my insides from just being close.

Suzy took hold of my arm and said, "This is Gigi."

Mick wrinkled his nose. "Gigi?"

He didn't like my name. Not a good start. "Actually, it's Margery."

The wrinkle left him and was replaced by a smile. "Margery. Marg. Better."

I vowed to never be Gigi again.

"Want to go eat?" he asked.

Anything. Anything.

18

Let us hold tightly without wavering to the hope we affirm,
for God can be trusted to keep his promise.
Let us think of ways to motivate one another
to acts of love and good works.

HEBREWS 10:23-24

Angie opened her eyes and wondered where she was, yet within a breath she remembered. She was in Talia's guest room. And it was 8:15.

She heard voices below. The family was up. They'd let her sleep. She wondered what Nesto would think about his mother-in-law being in residence.

She turned on a bedside light, then indulged herself a moment longer by snuggling back into the covers, her hand beneath her cheek. The glow of the lamp revealed a layer of dust on the wood and on the top of the clock, but she pushed such judgmental thoughts aside. That was a Stanford observation. Talia had taken her in. Beggars can't be choosers.

And as of last night, she was the biggest beggar of them all. She'd practically begged Stanford to love her—the way she wanted to be loved. Memories of their argument were cloaked in embarrassment. She'd never talked to him like that before. She remembered his comment, said in disdain: *"I don't like when you play the whiney, needy type, Angela."*

And her answer: *"Well . . . I am needy. In this I am."*

She closed her eyes. Was it so bad to *need*? to want something she didn't have? Or was that a case of envy? coveting? "Thou shalt not covet."

She should be content. She had way more than most people. She didn't have to worry about money, a roof over her head, or even buying the latest fashions each season. She and Stanford had traveled to exotic places most people only dreamed about. Their house had way more square footage than a couple with no children at home needed. So what if she didn't get as many hugs and kisses as she wanted? She had no right to *want* anything. She was provided for. That should be enough.

But it wasn't. God help her, it wasn't.

Angie turned over and faced the wall.

❊ ❊ ❊

"Mother, you're up."

There was the slightest bit of impatience in Talia's voice and Angie felt the need to make amends. "Sorry. I hope you didn't wait breakfast on me."

Angie needn't have worried. The breakfast table was set with cereal boxes. Cold cereal. Angie couldn't remember the last time Stanford had allowed the Schuster residence to succumb to Post Toasties or Cinnamon Toast Crunch. Yet Angie loved cereal.

"Sit," Nesto said, patting the place she'd sat in the night before. "There's coffee."

"Just what I need." She got herself a cup and freshened Nesto's and Talia's before sitting.

For the first time she noticed Talia was completely dressed. "Are you going somewhere? It's Saturday."

"Actually . . ." Talia hesitated. "I have some errands and I was hoping you could help with Tomás."

It wasn't that Angie minded spending time with her grandson, but for Talia to just assume . . . "I'm going to the shelter to serve lunch today. With Margery and Sarah."

"I'll be back way before that," Talia said, putting on her jacket. "Just an hour would help tremendously. Ninety minutes, tops."

"No problem," Angie said.

The look of relief on her daughter's face made Angie glad she hadn't balked. For the poor girl to be excited about ninety minutes? Perhaps things were even more stressful for Talia than she'd thought.

Talia kissed her child and husband and was out the door. Nesto moved the boxes of cereal within Angie's reach. "There's Life in the pantry . . . ," he said.

"This is fine." She chose the Toasties box because it didn't have a cartoon character on the front. Tomás held a piece of cereal in her direction. "For me?" she asked.

"Gee!"

She popped it in her mouth. The cinnamon-and-sugar coating was good. Perhaps she'd been hasty in her choice. But she couldn't very well pour the Toasties back in the box.

Nesto grinned. "You can have two bowls. I won't tell."

Angie hadn't realized her expression had mirrored her craving. "Maybe I will."

He raised a spoon. "It's like the country song 'Live Like You Were Dying.'"

The milk she poured on her cereal slopped over the bowl. How could he be so cavalier about dying?

Nesto pressed a napkin to the spill. "Do I make you uneasy?" he asked.

"No, of course not." She looked down. "I was uneasy before you said a word." She glanced up. "I'm sure Talia's told you I left her father."

"I'm so sorry."

Angie had expected him to say more. "I know it will be hard for people to understand—my leaving after all these years—but I've come to the end of my abilities. I try and try to earn Stanford's respect and love, and get nowhere. There's nothing more I can do."

"You're right."

"What?"

"The best things are not earned. They are given. Free."

Angie huffed. "Not from my experience."

"I'm sorry to hear that."

She sighed and ate a single flake from her bowl. "You'll have to forgive me but I'm feeling very cynical right now. Nothing's free. Nothing."

"Love is. It should be."

Angie smiled. "What planet are you from, Nesto? Don't you know that every smidgen, every iota of love has a price tag and has to be earned?"

He shook his head. "That's not right."

"But that's the way it is." Where should she begin? "If I want Stanford to go to a fund-raiser event with me, it costs me a steak dinner with his favorite twice-baked potatoes, a pumpkin pie, and . . . well . . . a few other things."

"He won't go just to please you?"

She laughed.

His head was shaking again. He wasn't convinced?

"If I want to borrow his headphones when I take a walk, it means at least an hour of running his errands in return." She got to the bottom line. "If I want a good day tomorrow, I have to earn it today. It takes hours of prep work to ensure peace in the Schuster residence." Angie realized she was crying. She flicked the tears away. "I'm sorry. I shouldn't air our dirty laundry like this."

"You're sharing. You need to share."

"But what good does it do? It won't change anything. Like I said, all good things cost. All good things have to be earned through tons and tons of work."

"Not all good things."

"Name one."

Nesto hesitated, then said, *"Vida eternal."*

"Eternal?" It sounded prettier when he said it.

"And *vida* is life. Life eternal."

Eternal life. "Oh please. As if I want this life to go on and on and on forever."

"Not here, but life after this one. In heaven. We don't earn our way to heaven. It's a gift."

A huge, disgusted laugh broke through her anger. "Come on, Nesto. Don't be naïve. We're supposed to fear God, which means he can get mad if we're not good. It means we have to earn his love, just like I have to earn Stanford's. Why do you think I do all this stuff for my husband—and for others too? Why do you think I bend over backward? To earn brownie points with God. To make sure I get to heaven."

Nesto's jaw dropped.

She pointed at it. "Why that look? Don't tell me you don't do good things to earn God's love?"

"I want him to be proud of me, but I don't do things to earn his love. He loves me, no matter what."

Angie felt another laugh threaten, but held it back. "So if I throw all propriety to the wind and become a serial killer he'll love me?"

Nesto retrieved a piece of Tomás's cereal from the floor. "He'd be sad, but he *would* love you."

"Then what incentive does anyone have to do good, be good, act good?"

"We do good because we want to. We choose it. Out of free will."

She snickered. "How much simpler life would be if God *made* us do what we're supposed to do."

"He wants us to *choose*. It means much more that way."

It might mean more but it was also much harder.

Nesto set his coffee aside, giving his words room. "If we could earn a way to heaven by doing good, we'd try—" he looked to the ceiling—"one up?"

"To one-up each other. Yes, I suppose we would. Whoever has the longest do-good list wins."

He wiped some milk from his son's chin. "There's pride in that. 'Salvation is not a reward for the good things we have done, so none of us can boast about it.'"

Angie pushed her bowl away an inch. This was very confusing. She *was* hoping to get to heaven by earning it. She *did* hope God was impressed with all her volunteer work and all her self-sacrifice in regard to Stanford. Yet if Nesto was right, the truth upon which she'd based her life was faulty. All her volunteering, all her good deeds . . . they might earn her God's approval, but they wouldn't earn her a way to heaven.

Heaven was a gift? Nesto made it sound so easy. Had she been complicating her life? making things harder than they really were?

Nesto reached across the table and touched her hand. "Are you okay?"

She slid her hand out from under his and took her bowl to the sink. "You've just given me a lot to think about, that's all. About heaven, about life, about . . ."

"Your husband?"

"We'll work it out," Angie said.

"You do that. Life's too short."

Nesto should know.

❊   ❊   ❊

Angie slipped upstairs to Talia's and Nesto's master bedroom to use the phone. Nesto was in the living room playing with Tomás. She'd made the excuse that she was going upstairs to make her bed.

It was already made.

She was going to follow through with the statement she'd made to Nesto about her marriage to Stanford: *"We'll work it out."* Four words casually tossed into the air, implying a mysterious sleight of hand that was based on nothing more than desire, determination, and blind hope. The specifics of how they'd work it out eluded her.

She sat on the edge of the bed and drew the phone into her lap. How could she get Stanford to love unconditionally? How could she even explain what that was? Nesto had explained it to her, but Nesto was eloquent. And Nesto had explained it to Angie by using God examples. That would not go over well with Stanford.

She assumed Stanford believed in God, but she wasn't completely certain. They periodically went to church, and when they did, Stanford always put a nice-sized check in the collection plate. But when she'd sneak a peek at him during the service at a moment when *she* was moved or touched in some way—to see if *he* was moved or touched—she'd invariably find him checking out the stained-glass windows or his manicure or the insides of his eyelids. And when Christians were portrayed badly in movies or on television—which they often were—Stanford was always quick to add, "I hate when they act all high-and-mighty like that. Or over the top like crazed zealots."

They. As in not *him*. Which made Angie wonder if her husband considered himself a Christian at all.

If he wasn't that, then what was he?

His own man. A self-made man who'd made her into a Stanford-made wife.

A Stepford wife? A robotic woman who did exactly as she was told? who achieved her husband's standard of perfection in every way?

"That's certainly not me."

Angie was startled to hear her thought said aloud. But that didn't make it any less true. No matter how hard she tried she would never be perfect. Never please Stanford. Never measure up.

The big question was, would he—did he—love her anyway?

It was time to find out.

She dialed home. When the phone rang two, then three times, she was almost reliev—

"Hello?"

"Hi," she said, proving the limited extent of her communication skills.

"Oh. It's you."

"I . . . I . . ." *Oh, dear.* Why had she called again?

"Where should I send your clothes?"

Angie moved the phone to her other ear. "I . . ."

"Come on, Angela. I don't have all day."

She hung up, her hands shaking. Forget discussing the finer points of unconditional love with her husband. There was no love present at all. Zero. Zilch. Nada. He wanted her to move out.

You are *out*.

Angie shook her head. No, she wasn't *out*. She was *away*. There was a difference.

Oh, God, what should I do?

"Angie?" It was Nesto's voice calling from downstairs.

"Coming."

Angie left behind the uncertainties of her marriage and went to love the ones she was with. As unconditionally as possible.

❦ ❦ ❦

Gennifer looked up from her mug of coffee as Sarah came into the kitchen. She did a double take because Sarah was carrying an armload of clothes from her closet.

"What are you doing?"

"Cleaning out some things." Sarah dumped the clothes on the kitchen table, then headed back upstairs.

Gennifer noticed a blouse and skirt she'd given her daughter for her last birthday. Tommy Hilfiger. She'd seen Sarah wear the outfit just a few weeks earlier.

Gennifer hurried into the front hall and called up the stairs. "Sarah? What's going—?"

Sarah appeared, struggling with two boxes. "You could help, Mother."

Gennifer rushed up the stairs and took the top box. It was full of books. She spotted *Little Women* and *Gone With the Wind.* They took the boxes into the kitchen. Gennifer set hers on the nearest counter. "Sarah, I demand to know what's going on." She picked up *Little Women.* "You love this book. These books."

Sarah was rearranging the items in her box. Gennifer spotted a CD player, a half dozen CDs, a funky orange-and-chrome alarm clock, and a little zipper case Gennifer knew contained Sarah's favorite hair bands and barrettes.

"Sarah? Answer me."

With a sigh, Sarah looked up. "I do love those books. And I love these things too. And the clothes. But that's the problem. I love them too much. There are so many people down at the shelter who don't have any—"

"You are not taking these things to the shelter!"

Sarah lifted her chin. "I am so. You gave these things to *me.* They are my things. Right?"

"Technically, yes, but that doesn't mean you have the right to give—"

"Technically, it does." She slipped the CD player between a stuffed bear and three Beanie Babies. "We have so much . . ."

"So you're going to just give it all away?"

Sarah stroked the head of the bear. Years before she'd bought it with her Christmas money and named it Max. "Not all of it," Sarah said softly. "I'd like to, but I just can't."

Suddenly, Sarah began to cry. Gennifer watched as her daughter fought for control—and won. "I'm going to the shelter now. To take these things. And to serve lunch."

"With Angie?" Gennifer hated the disdain in her voice but she wasn't awake enough to be subtle.

"And Margery." Sarah grabbed a banana. "Why did Dad sleep in the guest room last night?"

None of your business. "We had an argument. We'll be fine."

"You're not messing things up with him, are you?"

Gennifer felt her jaw drop. "How dare you say—"

A car horn honked outside. "Would you hold the door for me?"

In shock, Gennifer did as she was asked, but as soon as the door closed, she left her coffee behind and went back to bed. The oblivion of sleep was the only medicine worth anything right now.

❀ ❀ ❀

"You don't have to go," Gladys told Margery. "The shelter can serve the meat loaf and peas without you."

Margery zipped her navy hooded sweatshirt. "I'll be fine. Angie is picking me up. And Sarah will be there too."

"A middle-aged volunteer and a teenager. Quite the battery of body-guards."

Margery appreciated Gladys's concern, but . . . "Mick's my husband. He's not going to hurt me." A quick thought surfaced: *but he has.* She put her purse on her shoulder. "He doesn't even know I volunteer down there. Besides, he doesn't want me; he wants drugs."

"You'll be in a bad part of town, won't you?"

This conversation wasn't going anywhere. "I'll be back about two." She put a hand on Gladys's shoulder. "Don't worry so much. I'll be fine."

✻ ✻ ✻

"Don't worry so much. I'll be fine."

Margery's words haunted Gladys all morning at work. The odd thing was, her thoughts didn't revolve around Margery and her loser husband Mick, but around herself.

I'll be fine.

But would she?

Gladys dumped a new shipment of amber-colored prescription bottles in the Plexiglas box for easy access. The rattle of plastic against plastic corresponded nicely with the rattle of her thoughts.

"My, my," King said from across the room. "What did those vials ever do to you?"

"I'm testy today, all right? Can't a woman be testy in peace?"

"I'm not sure *testy* and *peace* can even live in the same sentence, but I'm certainly not going to argue with you."

"Good." She wadded up the empty bag from the vials and stuffed it in the trash can, pushing deep.

Bill, a regular customer, came up to the Drop-Off counter. Gladys would have preferred King handle him—since Bill had a penchant for talking in great detail about his Boston Terrier Abby and Gladys wasn't in the mood—but since Gladys was closest, there was no way she could gracefully hide in a corner and let King handle him.

Best to get it over with. "Morning, Bill."

"Morning, Gladys. How you doing?"

"I'm—"

King suddenly appeared at her shoulder. "She's testy, so watch out."

Gladys couldn't believe he'd said such a thing. "I am not testy. I'm fine."

As soon as she said the key word *fine*, Gladys went into overdrive. She heard King's and Bill's banter, and was even aware that Bill shared Abby's latest escapade, but was very glad when King filled the prescription. She wouldn't have been able to do it. For with the cue word *fine* she'd left testy behind and entered the Twilight Zone.

You are not fine, and you will not be fine, not until you take care of things. What things?

You know very well what things. Your eyes.

She had no idea what had brought that on. Her eyes hadn't suddenly gotten worse. She'd adjusted her lifestyle at home and at work to accommodate this weakness. Why was she even thinking about them at all?

King was at his workstation, filling Bill's prescription. He glanced in her direction. "You okay?"

"Fine. I'm fine."

There it was again. *Fine.*

And with its sounding, her heart started beating as if someone had just cussed at her.

Fine was not a bad word. It was a fine word. *Although it is a four-letter word . . .*

King finished the prescription and called Bill back to the counter. He went over the side effects of the drug, and they exchanged a few final pleasantries. "Do what you have to do, Bill. That's the only way to handle such a thing."

"That's the plan," Bill said. "Bye, Gladys."

Absently, she waved good-bye.

"Do what you have to do."

Those weren't just King's words. They'd been Aunt June's words too. Because things were not fine and they would not be fine until Gladys did what she had to—

"Hey, Red, is there a reason you're putting the cap *on* an empty pill bottle—and taking it *off*—over and over?"

Gladys looked down at the pill container in her hands. When had she picked it up?

It didn't matter. She had to do what she had to do. Now.

She set the bottle on the counter. "I'm going to call the doctor and get on the list for the corneal transplant."

King's expression went from confusion to recognition to confusion again. "That's great, but why now?"

"Because I have to do what I have to do." Suddenly her words spilled out, as if an inner dam had burst. "I am *not* fine, and I've kidded myself too long. I'm not going to get better without a transplant, and I can't get a transplant without being on the list, so why don't I put myself *on* the list? I am real great about giving Margery advice, telling her to do what needs to be done. I'm all brave on her behalf, but then I don't apply it to my own life. Physician, heal yourself and all that. I have to do what I have to do because I need all the help I can get." She took a much-needed breath.

King mimicked her breath. Then he handed her the phone. "Do it."

"Now?"

"Now."

"But . . . it's Saturday. I'm not even sure if Dr. Moss's office is open."

"Do it."

"You're being bossy," she said.

"I'm just trying to help you do what you need to do, because you need all the help you can get."

How could she argue with that? She took the phone and dialed.

❋ ❋ ❋

While Margery wiped off a table at the shelter to make it ready for the next meal, she couldn't help but notice the wonderful camaraderie between Angie, Sarah, and the administrator, Josh, as they served the last of the food. They were laughing as if they'd known each other for years, and Sarah had even gotten them singing "Java Jive." Angie's voice wasn't good at all, but Sarah's was a rich alto that complemented Josh's bass. Besides making each other smile, they were making the people at the shelter happy.

One of the homeless men pointed at them with his fork, "You guys know 'Operator'?"

The trio looked at each other, then Sarah broke out with "'Operator, give me in-for-ma-shun . . .'"

The other two joined in, pretending the serving spoons were microphones. The food line stopped, but no one seemed to mind. How did a teenager like Sarah know old Manhattan Transfer songs?

What did it matter? It was a great day. Margery couldn't remember the last time she'd had such fun. It was a release from the recent tension and the latest crises with Mick. She was glad she wasn't working at Neighbor's until Monday, but she had no idea what she'd do if he showed up there. As long as she kept people around her, as long as she didn't go anywhere by herself . . .

Maybe Mick was bluffing. Maybe he'd been in a mood last night at Gladys's. Or maybe he'd been high and had scared her because he *could*. He'd never been a real loving guy, but in the past year he'd become even less so. Although she hadn't realized he was into the drug scene, it did explain the change in him. The gruffness. The impatience. The frenzy. The mood changes. The pulling away.

The meal complete, she overheard Angie exchange a few words with Josh. "I nearly forgot! Sarah brought a bunch of clothes and books. They're in the car."

"Super," Josh said. "I'll get—"

"I'll go," Sarah said, heading toward the alley behind the shelter. She went through the kitchen.

Margery took her bucket of sudsy water into the back, then suddenly stopped. And shivered.

What brought that on?

She looked toward the back door Sarah had used moments before. The first time they'd come to serve a meal, Angie mentioned how Josh had suggested she park in the alley to get her fancy SUV out of sight. At the time Margery had even considered offering to driver her clunker, but had forgotten about it when this week's carpooling had been discussed.

A fancy SUV that oozed money. A teenage girl alone.

The shiver returned and Margery bolted for the door.

Margery pulled up short when she saw Sarah standing beneath the opened hatch of the SUV, talking to Mick.

He looked up and smiled. "Hiya, Marg."

Sarah's body was tense, the back of her legs pressed against the bumper of the SUV. She held a box of books as a barrier. Her eyes screamed for help.

"Sarah, go inside and—"

Mick yanked Sarah away from the canopy of the car's hatch. He held her arm with one hand and draped another around her shoulder, pulling her close. She stumbled and nearly dropped the box.

He spoke directly into her ear. "You all right, sweet thing? We wouldn't want anything to happen to you."

His grin made Margery cringe. Who was this man? Where was the Mick she married?

She tried to smile supportively to Sarah. Calm was the key. Keep it calm. "What can I do for you, Mick?"

He moved the arm he'd put on Sarah's shoulder to the back of her neck, and used his other hand to dig into the pocket of his shirt. He pulled out a piece of paper. "This. My wish list. You didn't take it last night."

She didn't want it but there was no way she could refuse without making him mad. She held out her hand, but didn't move closer. If he had to move, maybe he'd let go of Sarah. . . .

"No," he said, grinning. "Come get it."

She looked at Sarah, whose eyes were black with fright. Margery suffered a rush of fear. She started to move toward Mick, then stood her ground. "First, let her go. She's not in this."

He laughed. "She is now." He yanked her head close and kissed it. "Is that box getting heavy, sweet thing?"

"A little," Sarah said softly.

"Then tell my wife to come get this list and I'll let you go."

Sarah started to cry. Margery wanted to die. "Mick! Let her go!"

"Not until you—"

The box started to slip.

Sarah tried to stop it.

Mick tightened his grip on the back of her neck.

Sarah yelped in pain.

He heaved her sideways toward the car.

Her head hit the edge of the hatchback.

She bounced off and sprawled to the ground. A gash spurted blood.

"Mick!"

He froze for the briefest moment, then ran. Twenty feet away, he called after her. "I'll be back. You *will* do this, Margery. You will get me what I need. You owe me."

Margery ran to the door of the shelter, flung it open, and screamed for help.

Gennifer and Douglas ran through the doors of the ER. Gennifer reached the reception desk first. "Our daughter. Sarah Mancowitz. Where is she?"

The woman pointed toward some double doors. "Room 4."

Gennifer began to run again, but Douglas took her hand. "We're here now. Calm down."

She shook his hand away, but did slow to a walk. They found Sarah unconscious, her head bandaged, and her Old Navy sweatshirt covered with blood. Gennifer ran to her side and took her hand. "Oh, honey, honey . . ." She turned to Douglas, who was standing on the opposite side of the bed. "Where's the doctor? They've just left her here. Alone."

"I'm sure they'll be back. She has the bandage . . ."

"I want them here! Now. Find someone!"

He left and Gennifer gazed down at her daughter's immobile face. She looked at her arms and hands. There was no evidence of injuries other than her bandaged head. And the blood on her sweatshirt.

Where is that doctor?

Douglas returned. "They'll be here in a minute. But while I was out, a woman named Angie came up to me and said—"

"Angie? Angie's here?"

"She was with Sarah at the shelter and—"

"I know who she is!" With another glance to Sarah, Gennifer made a decision. "Come. Stand by her. I'll be right back."

"But the doctor will be here soon and—"

"I'll be right back."

Gennifer backtracked to the double doors leading to the ER's entrance. In the adjoining waiting room she spotted Angie Schuster— and Margery from the drugstore.

"You!" Gennifer said.

Angie stood. She held a cup of coffee, as did Margery. "How is she doing?" Angie asked.

With a swipe of her hand Gennifer knocked the cup out of Angie's hand sending coffee everywhere. She shoved a finger in her face. "You're the cause of all this!"

No one moved. Then Margery stepped forward. "No, she isn't. I am."

The woman from the front desk came over. "What's going on here?" she asked.

"None of your business," Gennifer said.

"If you don't behave, I'll call security."

Angie pressed her hands against the air. "It's fine. We'll clean up the mess. If you can get some towels . . ."

Angie's calm incensed Gennifer, plus she had no intention of cleaning up anything. She turned to the hospital worker. "Maybe you'd better call security, because this woman is the reason my daughter's in that room unconscious."

Margery shook her head. "It's not Angie's fault. Mick hurt Sarah because of me."

Mick?

The worker slipped away. Margery kept talking while she dabbed at a soggy magazine with a flimsy napkin. "Mick's my husband and he followed me to the shelter. He wants me to do—" she cupped the soaked napkin in the palm of her hand—"Mick's not himself. He's gotten into drugs and Sarah got in the middle. He was there because of me. Angie's not to blame."

Suddenly Gennifer realized why the name Mick sounded familiar. "Is your husband Mick Lamborn?"

"You know him?"

"I was his lawyer." Gennifer immediately wished she could take the words back.

"You're the one who got him off?" Margery said.

Gennifer looked toward the double doors. "I have to get back."

"Just know how sorry we are," Angie said. "We're praying for her."

Whatever.

✳ ✳ ✳

They admitted Sarah into a room. Although they'd stitched the gash in her head, they were concerned about swelling around her brain.

Concerned? What an understatement.

Gennifer shivered at the very thought of anything being wrong with her daughter's brain. Her only child. Her baby.

She sat beside Sarah's bed, her head in her hands. How could this have happened? Although Gennifer had eased up on blaming Angie completely, the meddling woman still had to take some responsibility for Sarah's injury.

Of course if you'd been a better mother, Sarah would never have gotten hooked up with a mentor.

Gennifer still didn't understand the mentor thing. She and Douglas provided for all of Sarah's needs. She wanted for nothing.

Apparently she needed something. . . .

Was it nothing that they'd given Sarah independence? The girl should have been grateful. Gennifer had been forced to learn independence the hard way. Sarah had it easy. Way easy. The suggestion that Sarah might not have wanted that much independence . . . Gennifer couldn't fathom such a thing.

You're to blame. You were the one who got Mick Lamborn off.

Gennifer hung her head low and grasped the back of her neck. She was only doing her job. Pleading out saved the taxpayers beaucoup bucks over the cost of a trial.

But you put a felon back on the streets—where he could hurt your daughter. Where he could have killed . . .

When her cell phone rang she grabbed her purse and moved into the hall. It was the office. Why would they be calling her on a Saturday? She considered not answering it, but needed to tell them about Sarah. She wouldn't be in on Monday. Her daughter needed her.

"Gennifer, Matt Breezley here."

Matt. She liked Matt. He'd pass on her news. "I'm glad you called—"

"Sorry to bother you on the weekend, but I've been working at the office and picked up the phone here. A dumb thing to do, but it turns out a client of yours has been arrested and—"

She had no patience for any of this. "Someone else needs to handle it. My daughter's been assaulted. I'm in the hospital with her now."

"Oh, Gennifer, I'm so sorry. Is she going to be okay?"

She has to be okay. "She's still unconscious."

"Don't worry about a thing here, Gennifer. I'll take care of it. You take care of your daughter."

Gennifer hung up and returned to the room, but being still was not an option. Her previous guilt was infused with rising anger at Mick, at herself, and at the system that made it possible for cretins like Lamborn to get off. Ever. Throw away the key. Strap him down for a lethal injection. Do anything to ensure he burn in—

"Gennifer?"

She saw Dr. Brandon in the doorway. He was her kidney doctor. Pleasantries. She knew she was expected to exchange pleasantries like *hello*.

It was not possible. With surprise she realized she had a tear on her cheek and swiped it away.

He saw it and came close. "Are you okay?"

No. Yes. She managed a nod.

"When I saw the name *Mancowitz* . . ." He looked at Sarah. "Your daughter?"

Gennifer nodded again and moved to Sarah's bedside.

Dr. Brandon joined her on the other side. His eyes showed his usual compassion. "A mugging?" he asked.

She didn't want to get into anything where she might have to admit her culpability. "It's more complicated than that, but generally, yes."

He patted Sarah's unmoving hand, then looked at Gennifer. "Stress isn't good for you, you know."

"I know."

"Last week your numbers weren't what we'd like them to be, so if you start to feel bad, come in."

"I will." Gennifer looked past him to the door. Douglas came in carrying two cups of coffee. Gennifer's stomach found a new reason to tighten. Since her husband didn't know about her kidney problems, he'd never met Dr. Brandon and—

Dr. Brandon looked over his shoulder, then met Douglas halfway. "You must be Gennifer's husband."

"I'm Douglas."

They shook hands. "Nice to meet you. I'm Dr. Brandon."

"Are you taking care of Sarah now?" Douglas asked.

"No, no, I'm your wife's nephrologist." He smiled toward Gennifer. "We're hoping for a transplant real soon." He crossed fingers on both hands. "But you can help me help her now by easing her stress as much as possible." He glanced at Sarah. "Not always easy, but we want Gennifer to be in good condition when a kidney becomes avail—"

Gennifer stepped between the two men, leading Dr. Brandon toward the door. "Thanks so much for stopping in."

"No problem." He paused in the hall. "Remember to come see me if you start feeling poorly."

Yes, yes. Her health was the least of her concerns right now.

Looking from the hall back into the hospital room, Gennifer had the urge to run down the long corridors. Move to Brazil if necessary. Anything to avoid Douglas's glare.

"Gennifer? What is he talking about?"

There was no way out. She was trapped. Everything that had defined her identity was being attacked.

So be it. She had no more defenses.

A defense lawyer with no defense.

How ironic.

☙ ☙ ☙

Window-shopping was not the most obvious choice of setting or activity when one was being forced to spill their secrets—secrets that had the capacity to completely change lives. But it was better than doing it in a hospital waiting room, a stairwell, a car, or the worst choice—back home.

Window-shopping in a mall near the hospital provided Gennifer two things she desperately needed: movement and company. There was no way she could tell Douglas all the truths she had to tell him while seated or while they were alone. Public spaces were good. Public spaces were safe. Public spaces were the coward's way out.

So be it. After facing the crisis of Sarah's injuries Gennifer had completely lost the ability to fight the good fight, present a stiff upper lip, or win one for the Gipper. The jig was up and all bets were on the table.

Or soon would be.

She was thankful Douglas had not given her a hard time about her request to walk in the mall. "If it'll get the truth out of you . . ."

Once they entered the happy land of shopping heaven, Gennifer felt a bit surreal. How could she talk of life-and-death matters to the sound of canned music, the sight of smartly dressed mannequins, Day-Glo SALE! signs, and the smells of freshly baked cookies and sesame chicken?

You asked for it; you got it.

She had no choice. Her time was up. And she was glad.

They turned right onto the main drag. The pennants and jerseys of college teams cheered her on from a sports store. *You can do it! Go team!* She was at the goal line. It was fourth down with inches to go . . . should she try for three points or six?

She decided on the whole shebang. "My kidneys are failing. I need a transplant. I've been on dialysis for a year." There. The basics were out.

Douglas stopped walking and faced her. "I heard the doctor mention a transplant. But that's not possible. For you to be sick . . . I would have known."

"Want proof?" She pulled up her left sleeve to reveal the dialysis portal in her forearm. "This is where it all happens. They created this fistula that provides a straight-shot hookup to the veins that lead to my heart. They hook me up to the machine, clean me out, and send me on my way. Three times a week."

His fingers moved to touch it, but stopped short. "Does it hurt?"

She put her sleeve down, covering it. "It can get uncomfortable. But I have to do it. I don't have a choice."

"You could've told me. You should've told me. Why didn't you—?"

"I'll admit to the *should've* part. Whether I *could've* told you is another question."

He shoved his hands in his pockets and looked at the floor as he walked. "I don't understand why you didn't feel you could trust me."

Trust was not a good word choice at the moment because it conjured up thoughts of his infidelity. Douglas must have figured that out too because he quickly added, "On this. You could have trusted me on this."

Gennifer didn't push the point. They'd move to talk of his mistress soon enough. She zeroed in on the real reason she'd kept the secret, the reason that was dogging her like a lurking shadow. "I am a prideful woman. I didn't want to be thought of as weak or needy. I've always been able to take care of myself."

"I'm sure you can—and apparently you have. That's not the point. I want to know why you felt you couldn't let Sarah and me in. If only you'd done that, I—"

She finished his sentence for him. "You wouldn't have had an affair?"

Unfortunately, it was at that moment they passed a lingerie store with its windows full of frilly, skimpy things. She kept her eyes straight ahead. When Douglas looked in her direction, she saw his eyes skim past her to the pretties in the window. But to his credit, he also looked away.

"A person needs to feel needed, Gen."

"So you'd prefer me weak and inept?"

He stopped, forcing her to backtrack to face him. "Do you really think needing someone makes you weak and stupid?" he asked.

Gennifer smiled at an elderly woman walking past. It was obvious by the distaste on her face that she'd heard his last three words. Gennifer took her husband's arm and started them walking again. "How about this? *I* don't like feeling needy. It's not a condemnation of others who need."

Douglas snickered. "'Others who need.' If that phrase isn't dripping with disdain . . ."

She removed her hand from his arm. "If you want to get into an argument over semantics and definitions, then let's save it for another time. I'm trying to tell you how I feel, and why I've done what I've done. I don't need—"

"Ha! You don't need!"

She sighed dramatically, but knew they'd reached a place where they could move on.

At least that was her plan until Douglas said, "I don't want a divorce."

Had she missed something? He'd said it as if he'd truly considered that option, as if they'd talked about it. Which they hadn't.

Had they?

Her mind was a jumble as they turned the corner in front of one of the anchor department stores. In the past two days they'd had a row about his mistress, and now this argument about her keeping her illness a secret. Two secrets that certainly had the power to divide a marriage permanently. Yet she'd never thought of divorce.

"We've both been in the wrong," he said.

"Yes." That much she *could* say.

He stopped again to face her, making a teenager behind them do a quick sidestep. "I'm sorry I hurt you," he said. "I'm sorry I was unfaithful."

His face was so sincere, so full of angst. She believed him.

"It was wrong. I'll break it off."

"You don't have to do that."

The words surprised Gennifer as much as they did Douglas. He was the first to snap out of it. "So you *want* a divorce?"

What a mess. She started walking. "No, I don't."

He hurried to catch up, taking her arm. "Then why did you say such a thing? I don't *have* to break it off . . . don't you love me?"

Her heart started to pump. "You obviously don't love me," she said.

"Of course I do."

"Which is why you have a mistress?"

"I just told you it's complicated. Dorothy came into my—"

Gennifer laughed and lowered her voice as they neared a crowd. "Dorothy?"

"What's so funny?"

"I expected Tiffany or Gabrielle or even Muffy. Not Dorothy."

"Don't laugh at her like that."

She raised her hands, feeling relief that the discussion had at least moved to the status of a more normal argument. She was a lawyer. She could handle argument. "Sorry to offend."

They parted to pass on opposite sides of a mother pushing a stroller. "This discussion is not happening," he said.

"I'm afraid it is." She adjusted her purse on her shoulder, making it secure. She liked feeling in control again.

"The point is, I never stopped loving you, Gen. I met Dorothy by accident. She works for one of the companies I service—"

Gennifer huffed. "*Service* is a good word . . ."

Douglas shook his head. "We only got involved after I felt you with-drawing—even more than your usual preoccupation and distance—"

"Oooh. You're making me feel all warm and fuzzy inside."

An old man in front of them dropped his sacks. Douglas helped him pick them up. They continued walking. "The point is, now that I know what you've been going through with your dialysis . . . your coldness makes sense. You were pulling away because you couldn't deal with more than that. Something had to give. Sarah and I were that something."

"Thanks for the psychoanalysis, Doctor Mancowitz."

"It makes sense," he said.

It did. But hearing him figure her out in such a logical manner . . . she was the logical one. Why hadn't she been able to dissect her own actions—and their consequences?

As they passed a bookstore, she had to one-up him. She couldn't leave him with this victory. "So my pulling away gave you no choice but to have an affair—and give your bimbo a $5000 necklace?"

"How do you know how much it cost?"

"Visa called, questioning the large out-of-town purchase."

"Oh."

"Just doing their job."

"To answer your other question, no, your actions did not give me the right to have an affair." He glanced her way. "I did try to talk to you about things. You do remember that, don't you? I did ask you what was wrong."

"Yes, you did." She licked her finger and made a mark in the air. "One point for Douglas."

Suddenly he pulled her into the alcove of a jewelry store, out of the walking traffic. He took her hands in his. "I'm sorry, Gen. I was wrong. It won't happen again. I really would like things to get back to normal."

She pulled her hands away. *Normal. What is that?*

"We had a good life for a while," he said. "We were as happy as any fifties sitcom. I was Ward Cleaver and you were my June." He pointed over her shoulder at a jewelry showcase. "I should have given the pearls to you. . . ."

Gennifer turned her head. The entire case was full of pearls. Strings and strings of pearls. And suddenly, it rushed back like a television show turned on in the middle of a scene. A horrible scene being played out over pearls.

She moved away from the display, her head shaking back and forth.

"Gen? What's wrong?"

"I don't want pearls. Never, ever pearls. I can't . . ."

He glanced at the display case, confused. "What do you have against pearls?"

Her back reached the opposite side of the alcove, causing her movement to be deflected to the right. Away. Get away from the pearls . . .

"I can't. I can't."

She raced into the main flow of shoppers, bumping against them, needing to get far, far away from the pearls that had made everything so horribly wrong.

"Gen!"

She knew Douglas was running after her, but she didn't stop. She couldn't be caught. She couldn't be caught looking, seeing, witnessing . . .

But he did catch her, his hands pulling her to a halt. "Gen? You have to tell me what's wrong. Why did you run? What are you running from?"

A fortysomething man stopped beside them, his eyes intent on her. "Are you okay, miss? Is he bothering you?"

The man's concern moved her and brought her back to the present. She blinked, seeing the hubbub and bright colors of the shopping mall. A safe, happy, family kind of place. "I'm fine," she told the man. "This is my husband."

The man looked at Douglas. "My question stands. Are you okay? Is he bothering you?"

"Hey, bud," Douglas said. "I'm her husband. Everything's fine."

"It doesn't look fine," the man said.

Gennifer realized if she didn't do something to defuse the moment the two might come to blows. She put a hand on the man's arm. "Truly, I'm fine. I really appreciate your concern and bravery. Our daughter is in the hospital and I'm just a bit overwrought."

His face softened. "Oh. I'm so sorry."

"Thanks for your concern," Douglas said, though he didn't look as if he meant it at all. "But as the lady said, she's fine."

The man gave Gennifer one last look, nodded, and walked away.

Douglas led her to a nearby bench. "Enough walking, enough running. You have to tell me what got into you back there. Why did you flip out over some pearls?"

And then, without planning for it, without thinking about it, the past presented itself front and center. "My mother was killed over a string of pearls."

Douglas did not react for a good ten seconds. Finally he said, "I thought she died of cancer when you were thirteen."

Gennifer straightened her shoulders. "I lied. About that and other things. Lots of other things."

"Gen . . . I'm not sure I want to hear any more."

"But you're going to hear it. That stupid string of pearls dredged it up in me, so you're going to hear it all. I'm tired of secrets. I'm just so, so tired." She leaned against the hard back of the bench and pressed her fingers on the space between her eyes. Did she really want to do this? What could it help?

What could it hurt?

Douglas took her hand. "Tell me."

The compassion in his voice urged her to begin. "My family *was* very much like the Cleavers on TV. My mother baked bread, starched my father's shirts, and we went to church every Sunday, where I'd sit between the two of them, never once suspecting they were living a lie. Acting out a part."

"That involved pearls."

"Douglas. Please."

He raised his hands in surrender. "Continue."

"When I was thirteen everything came to a climax when my father discovered a string of pearls my mother had received as a gift. From her lover."

"Oh . . ."

"The similarities are haunting, aren't they?"

He didn't move.

"Upon finding the pearls and confronting my mother, they had their first fight—at least the first I'd ever witnessed." Suddenly, Gennifer wished they were home, doing this in the living room, where she could

THE GOOD NEARBY / 270

pull her knees to her chest and make herself as small as possible. "The things they said to each other were horrible, nasty, hurtful things." She blinked the memory of the words away and looked at her husband. "Then my father got out a gun—" she paused for effect—"and he shot her. Killed her."

Stevie Wonder sang "For Once in My Life" in the speakers overhead.

"You saw it happen?" Douglas asked.

Gennifer raised her hands, gripping imaginary rungs. "I watched from the stairs." She dropped her hands and looked at Douglas. "When he shot her, he saw me, and for just a moment, I thought he was going to shoot me too. Get rid of the witness."

"Surely, he wouldn't have . . ."

She nodded strongly. "He should have. I testified against him."

"He's in jail?"

"Was. He got fifteen years, voluntary manslaughter. I assume he's out now."

"You don't know?"

She wrapped her arms close, feeling cold. "I don't know and don't care to know."

"You told me he was dead. Heart attack."

"It's what I wished for him."

"Don't say that."

She sprang from the bench and pointed down at him. "Don't tell me to care about my father! Don't tell me to have loving thoughts and care about him. I won't do it. I won't."

He gently pulled her down to the bench, his arm cradling her shoulders. "I'm sorry. I had no right . . ."

She dug her face into his chest. "No, no right."

They held on to each other—for dear life.

※ ※ ※

Back at home, Gennifer felt slightly foolish curled up in Douglas's lap, his arms surrounding her like protective wings. But she didn't move. In fact, she lay very still so the moment would last.

Her mind wasn't as cooperative as her body in accepting the comfort, in letting someone else be the strong one. It sped from one thought to another, as if panicked by the outer display of weakness. It did not like feeling vulnerable. Yet every time one of these flustered thoughts pushed its way front and center, she forced it back. Not now. Not this moment. She'd been forced to be strong and invincible for too long. Her battlements were scarred and the moat was dry. Letting Douglas in on the truth had lowered the drawbridge protecting who she pretended to be, to let him see who she was.

And joy of joys, shock of all shocks, he still wanted to hold her. In spite of everything.

"I love you," he whispered into her hair.

She began to cry and pressed deeper into the crook of his neck. She didn't deserve his love, yet she believed him.

Perhaps for the first time, she believed him.

※ ※ ※

Gladys met Margery at the door. They didn't speak until the sound of Angie's car had faded. Then Gladys said, "Are you okay?"

Margery didn't respond with words but by falling into the nearest chair.

"Would you like some tea?"

Tea. Always tea. Until moving in with Gladys, Margery had never had tea. She shook her head and pulled a tasseled pillow to her chest. If only it were Grammy's pillow. But that was long gone, left a lifetime ago in the house with the red door and bullet holes in the windows.

Gladys perched on the edge of the couch, silent, but waiting.

Although Margery had called from the hospital and told her Sarah had been hurt, she hadn't gone into details. Now, Gladys deserved a full explanation.

Margery pulled in the deepest breath she could manage. "It was Mick's doing. He showed up at the shelter."

Gladys slapped her thigh. "I was afraid of that. The way you hedged all my questions. Did he hurt you?"

"Not me. Just poor Sarah."

"That's Gennifer Mancowitz's daughter, right?"

"She's only seventeen."

"Tell me how it happened. Tell me everything."

Margery reluctantly told the story, ending with, "Mick didn't mean to hurt her. If anything he wanted to hurt me. Sarah just got in the way."

Suddenly, Gladys sprang from her chair and dead-bolted the door and started to close the front curtains.

"You don't have to do that, Gladys. We heard they arrested him. He's in jail."

Gladys returned to her seat but left the curtains closed. "Until some flashy-dashy lawyer gets him out on bail." She gave Margery a pointed glare.

"Don't look at me," Margery said. "I'm not bailing him out."

"Older and wiser. Good girl."

Margery thought of something. "But want to hear something ironic? Sarah's mother was Mick's lawyer. Gennifer's the one who got him off the drug charge so he was out there, able to—"

"Hurt her daughter. Wow. She must feel like dirt."

"At the very least." Margery didn't care much how Gennifer felt. She only hoped Mick's next lawyer wouldn't be so good at getting him off.

"At least we don't have to worry about Mick wanting you to steal drugs from me anymore."

"If he stays in jail. If they can keep him there."

Gladys didn't say anything for a moment, then stood. "*I* need tea. And so do you. I'll get us some."

As soon as Gladys left the room, Margery tried to relax. But she couldn't. She suddenly felt very dirty.

She went to the bathroom and turned on the hot water full blast. She stared at it, mesmerized by its sight and sound. When it began to steam she immersed her hands, then pushed the pump on the soap dispenser once, twice . . . over and over until she held a golden puddle in her palm. It was so pretty. . . .

She turned the water to a reasonable level and carefully let some hot water mix with the gold puddle. Bubbles burst forth.

She laughed.

Laughed? It was such a foreign sound.

But the feeling lingered.

Gleefully Margery rubbed her hands together, creating a exuberant lather. Fingers met palms met wrists with joyful abandon as she washed the day away.

She caught a glimpse of her face in the mirror and found herself smiling. She brought the frothy lather to her cheeks, not wanting them to miss out on the fun. Soon her forehead, chin, and nose joined the party. It was so smooth, so creamy, so silky, so . . . fresh and pure.

As is my life. Now.

The idea shocked her so much she froze, her hands caught in mid-swirl against her cheeks. Only the water made noise. Only her eyes moved, not seeing her reflection, but reacting to the details of her thoughts.

So many bad things had happened during the past month. Her rather ordinary, totally unremarkable life had been disrupted in a dozen ways. Some bad, some good. But . . .

The good was outweighing the bad right now. Margery wasn't homeless anymore. She had a good place to stay, a good job, and good friends. Mick had been the cause of many of her problems, and now he'd dug himself a hole that would hopefully keep him in jail. It was the best thing for him.

For her.

"I need him gone."

The words were barely audible above the water. She needed to hear them clearly so she shut off the faucet, looked at herself in the mirror, and repeated the words a second time—with feeling. "I need him gone."

There was no hesitation in her voice, no weakness, no doubt. Not so long ago she'd been desperate to get back together with him in order to have a baby.

Margery shook her head at the thought. "No baby." These were hard words to say. She'd spent her entire life with this goal in mind. Ever since she was seven and Grammy had told her she'd be married and have a baby someday. But had she been so focused on that, that she'd let it override logic and common sense?

Yes.

"I need Mick gone and he *is* gone." She leaned toward the reflection of her soap-swirled face and whispered, "He's gone and I'm free. I'm free—and safe."

She held her breath a moment to let the idea sink in.

So this is what peace feels like. It nearly made her giddy.

She let out the breath, then took a new one—her first breath as a free woman. As a free person. Had she *ever* been free before this moment?

"Margery? You okay?" It was Gladys's voice.

"I'm fine. I'll be out in a minute."

Margery allowed herself one last look at this silly, wonderful, absurd woman in the mirror. Then she turned on the water and washed the soapy mask away, taking with it all that was dead and dirty and stifling. As she patted her face dry she relished the tautness of her skin, proof that it was as clean as it could be.

As was her heart. As was . . . her life.

She went to the living room and found that Gladys had placed a steaming mug emblazoned with the Statue of Liberty near her chair. How appropriate.

"Gracious sakes, girl. You're practically glowing. What happened?"

Margery let out a laugh, pleased that her new attitude showed. "I just realized that I'm not afraid anymore. I'm free."

"Because Mick's in custody?"

Though Margery nodded, she knew it was more than that. "I've been afraid for a very, very long time."

Gladys did not argue nor ask for further explanation. Gladys was good that way—knowing when to speak and when to remain silent.

"Everything's as it should be, Gladys. I know it."

The older woman laughed too, making her red hair dance. She nodded toward the bathroom. "What did you *do* in there? Here I thought I'd be comforting you, and you've got yourself together all by yourself. It appears you're stronger than you thought, young lady."

Margery liked that. "I am. And I know things are going to be right from now on. Just as they should be." She got an idea. "In fact, I think this deserves a celebration. I'm starved. How about Chinese food? I'll fly *and* I'll buy."

"I never turn down dinner. Go for it," Gladys said.

And Margery would go for it. Life was good, life was full of promise, and it was starting *now*.

19

*God speaks again and again,
though people do not recognize it.*

JOB 33:14

I loved him. Mick was everything to me. And tonight was
the night I'd prove it.

We'd been going out for six months and Mick had
been after me to have sex with him since the second date.
Somehow I'd held off—and held him off. It wasn't easy. He
was very persistent and very sexy, and I felt my defenses
giving in.

I mean . . . if we loved each other, the sex part couldn't
be wrong.

Could it?

That night, on my sixteenth birthday, I'd decided to do
it. Become a woman. I hadn't told Mick my plan of surrender—just in case I wanted to back out—but I think he
sensed it because he brought me a yellow rose when he
picked me up for school in the morning. I took the flower
to my room real fast (wishing it were red) and set it on the
shelf in my closet so Mama wouldn't see it. Not that she
would've taken it or anything, but she was strange sometimes, getting mad when she saw me getting something
nice. Like she was jealous.

Mama had a boyfriend too. George something-or-other. He was better than Ted had been, and worse than Klaus. I liked Klaus—he was funny—but he hadn't lasted more than a month. He didn't like Mama's drinking. George did his own share of boozing. When she passed out he was usually close behind. I often found them sprawled in the living room, or even in bed together in Mama's room. It was kind of disgusting, but passed out and quiet was better than awake and mean. That's one reason I had two jobs. The money was always needed, but more than that, it got me out of the house so I didn't have to see . . . didn't have to deal with all that.

Actually, since dating Mick, I'd cut back on my hours at the Pump-n-Eat so I could spend time with him. And I was thinking about quitting my job at Burger Madness completely. Then Mick and I could really spend time together. Mick always wanted to party, and I drank with him some of the time. But I wasn't going to be like Mama. Nothing like that. I went along so I wouldn't disappoint Mick.

For my birthday he picked me up and we went to a movie *The Arrival* with Charlie Sheen. I was kind of disappointed he didn't have a present for me. Was the rose *it?* I don't know why I expected more. It was dumb to expect more. Hadn't I learned that by now? At least Mick had remembered, which was more than Mama did.

He did get me popcorn *and* some Skittles, so that was special. And he did let me dig my face into his arm when the people in the movie turned into weird aliens with knee joints that pointed backwards. That was gross.

I'm glad Mick wasn't the kind who ever wanted to discuss a movie afterward, because I wouldn't have been able to say much. I saw the whole show in flashes, paying attention for a few minutes, then letting my mind wander.

I kept thinking about Grammy and was looking for signs that where I was and what I was doing were okay with her. Okay with God too, if I got right down to it. No matter what had happened the past few years, all the hard stuff, the scary stuff, I'd always been able to depend on something good popping up, reminding me that I'd be okay.

They were dumb things really: seeing a checkered floor like Grammy's kitchen, or something pretty and red. Meeting someone named

Susie, hearing a hymn, seeing a stuffed frog, smelling a turkey dinner like that one I'd had during my first—and only—visit to Grammy's house. I'd forget about looking for signs for a while, but then things would go bad and suddenly I'd see something that would remind me of good times, of good people in my life, and I'd feel better. Like Grammy or Susie or even God himself was hugging me, right then and there.

I'd been looking for such things a lot lately, but there was nothing out there. It kinda scared me.

But maybe they were there and I just wasn't seeing them. I *was* kind of busy. Being with Mick, trying to please him . . . that's what took my time lately. Took my thoughts too.

Like now. I wasn't watching the movie. I was too busy thinking about doing *it.*

I wasn't stupid. I'd had health class in school, so I knew what went where and all that. Actually I'd learned plenty about sex stuff from living on the street and living in the 96 house with Chico, Toledo, and the rest. Saw too much. And Mama was never one to be discreet about such things. I was just glad I had my own room where we lived now. At least I had a place to go when she and her boyfriend wanted to get friendly.

As the credits rolled and everybody stood up I knew it was my turn now.

✲ ✲ ✲

I'd heard about girls doing it in the backseat of a car, but since Mick only had a pickup . . .

I lost my virginity in the bed of the pickup. Bed. Funny. Ha-ha. Although I didn't enjoy it much, that was okay, because Mick *really* loved me now, and that was worth anything. When I snuggled into his shoulder the world was good and I had a future. I was destined to be Mrs. Mick Lamborn and have a baby. I was destined to be happy, just like Grammy had predicted. Mick made me remember something else Grammy had said about my life: that I would be the good nearby to someone, that I would make a difference. I would be everything to Mick. Everything good.

When Mick took me home after doing it, I didn't want to leave him. In Mick's pickup, in his world, were hope and love and affection, and—

Mick took a final swig of his beer and tossed it behind the seat with the rest of the empties. "What you waiting for, Marg? Get out. I gotta get home too."

Tears threatened.

Even in the dark of the truck he must've seen them, because he leaned over, kissed my cheek, and said, "Happy birthday."

"Thanks."

"And . . . and thank you. For . . . you know."

I looked at him, hoping . . . "Was it okay?"

"It'll get better." He winked. "Practice makes perfect, you know."

I got one more kiss from him and then he was gone.

I found Mama on the couch. She opened one eye and mumbled, "Oh, you," before falling back into her drunken sleep.

Oh. Me. Happy birthday to oh me.

But then I remembered my time in the back of the truck. It wasn't just me anymore. Not *just* me.

Mick was mine now. Number 96 was mine. Forever and ever.

20

Whenever someone turns to the Lord, the veil is taken away.
For the Lord is the Spirit,
and wherever the Spirit of the Lord is, there is freedom.

2 CORINTHIANS 3:16-17

Gladys and Margery sat at the kitchen table, reading the morning paper.

The phone rang.

"Hello, Red."

"Hi, King." Gladys glanced at the clock on the microwave. It was seven fifteen. "You're lucky we're up."

"No, you're lucky you're up, because I'm inviting both you and Margery to go to church with me this morning."

"Goody."

"Be nice."

"You ask every week. And every week I say no."

"But maybe not today, right?"

"Why not today?"

"Exactly."

He was exasperating. "Maybe we don't want to go to church." She nodded at Margery to get her support.

But Margery surprised her by saying, "I'll go."

"You will?"

King said, "You will what?"

Gladys put her hand over the receiver. "You want to go to church with King?"

"It might be nice."

With a sigh Gladys gave in to the two against one. She uncovered the receiver. "You win. What time?"

🌺 🌺 🌺

When was the last time?

Margery tried to think back. She'd gone to church with Susie quite a few times, but when Susie had died, so had Margery's churchgoing. Susie's funeral? Had that been the last time?

It's not that she hadn't thought about it off and on. But the one time she'd brought it up to Mick, he'd laughed and pulled her close, saying, "Aren't I enough man for you? You don't need any Jesus in your life. You got me."

She hadn't argued with him. What was the point? And though she could've gone by herself, Mick would have seen that as a slap in the face and made her pay. A person shouldn't have to pay such a price to go to church.

But now, with Mick safely locked away in jail, she was free to go, and this freedom added to her other new feelings of liberation.

Margery looked to her left where Gladys sat next to King on the pew. She couldn't think of two people she'd rather be seated with. They'd both been so nice to her, taking her in, helping her through some of the rough spots.

King draped his arm over the back of the pew behind Gladys's shoulders. She didn't seem to notice, but he caught Margery looking and smiled. Margery smiled back. They sure were an odd couple—there had to at least be ten years between them, with Gladys being the older—but there was something right about them too. Like a cake that was tasty in itself getting a layer of frosting that made it something special.

The choir stood, their blue robes and green satin stoles a happy combination. They sang a short song. Then everyone stood and recited lines that were printed in the bulletin before telling each other hello and shaking hands. Margery felt awkward because she didn't know anybody.

"Is that Margery?" asked a lady in the pew behind them.

Margery turned around and saw Adele Connors, a customer from the drugstore. "Hello, Mrs. Connors," she said.

"Hello, yourself." She put a finger on Gladys's shoulder. "This girl's a keeper, Gladys." She put a hand under her bobbed hair. "See how shiny my hair is? All because I used that shampoo you suggested, Margery."

Her hair did look nice. "I'm glad you like it."

Some more music started and people got out their hymnbooks. Gladys handed her one. "Number 96," she whispered.

Ninety-six?

Margery fumbled to the right page, missing the chance to sing the first line. But as soon as she heard the hymn start, she lost all ability to sing.

> *Abide with me; fast falls the eventide;*
> *The darkness deepens; Lord, with me abide!*
> *When other helpers fail and comforts flee,*
> *Help of the helpless, O abide with me.*

It was Grammy's favorite hymn! The one she'd often sung or hummed. And it was the hymn that had been sung that first time Margery had gone to church with Susie. That Sunday she'd first been introduced to Frog.

Hey, Frog.

Amazingly, Margery found she knew some of the words. How was that possible? She hadn't sung it in nearly twenty years. When the next verse started, she joined in.

> *I fear no foe, with thee at hand to bless;*
> *Ills have no weight, and tears no bitterness.*
> *Where is death's sting? Where, grave, thy victory?*
> *I triumph still, if thou abide with me.*

As the music surrounded her with its comforting arms, Margery wasn't in church with Gladys and King anymore. She was standing beside Grammy and Susie, sharing the hymnal between them—though Grammy didn't look at the words at all, but sang them with her eyes closed and her face lifted to heaven.

They're both in heaven now.

Margery looked upward too, hoping that if Susie and Grammy were looking down, they'd spot her. *Hey, Grammy! Hey, Susie! It's me! I'm back in church! I miss you both so terribly much.*

Margery felt Gladys's eyes, and after a shared glance, looked down at the songbook.

> *Hold thou thy cross before my closing eyes;*
> *Shine through the gloom and point me to the skies;*
> *Heaven's morning breaks, and earth's vain shadows flee;*
> *In life, in death, O Lord, abide with me.*

Margery wished they'd sing it again. Now that she'd made the connection she wanted to drink in every word. Lacking an encore, when everyone sat and the service moved on, it continued without her. She kept the hymnbook open and read the words again. Suddenly, they weren't just words she'd heard in her youth; they were words that had meaning. For here. For now.

When other helpers fail and comforts flee, Help of the helpless, O abide with me.

She'd certainly been without help, without comfort. But this song was calling God the help of the helpless. And she knew he was. He always had been. Even in her darkest times she'd felt a calming presence and found some glimmer of comfort. Though she might not have realized it was God back then, now . . .

The next lines about having no foes and not being afraid about anything . . . *ills have no weight* . . . that wasn't true. She was afraid of plenty and—

No. That wasn't true. She *had* been afraid. She *had* cried bitter tears. But no more. As of yesterday everything had changed. And though the start of the change had been Mick's being arrested, Margery sensed there was more to it than that. She'd certainly been plenty scared of Mick lately, but there'd been much more to fear than just him.

Fear she'd never have a baby.

Fear she'd be stuck at the Chug & Chew forever.

Fear she'd never have a decent place to live.

Fear she wouldn't have enough money for food.

Fear she'd never find normal.

Fear her life would be for nothing.

The fears were falling away, one by one—if not finding complete elimination, at least fading to an acceptable size.

She looked to the words *Where is death's sting? Where, grave, thy victory?*

Margery had experienced death with Grammy and Susie. But she'd never been afraid of death. Death was not a fear. Had never been a fear. Her parents had thought she was crazy because of that.

I triumph still, if thou abide with me.

She looked up from the words, yet she didn't focus on anything in the sanctuary. *If people need God to deal with their fear of death and I've never feared death, then he* has *been with me all this time.*

Yet something bothered her. Her life had been far from easy, and if God was around, weren't things supposed to be all sweetness and full of good things?

She wasn't sure about that.

Back to the final verse: *Hold thou thy cross before my closing eyes.*

She looked up at the cross on the wall behind the preacher and remembered another cross behind another altar in another church. Susie's church where she had gone up to the front and told Jesus she was his. It was so long ago and she'd forgotten about it for so long . . . did it still count?

Margery felt the need to make sure. She closed her eyes and remembered the rest of the words: *Shine through the gloom and point me to the skies; Heaven's morning breaks, and earth's vain shadows flee; In life, in death, O Lord, abide with me.*

She felt a stirring inside as if she were being pulled out of any problems into something bigger. Grander. And right. She was being pointed to the skies with heaven breaking before her, to a place where there were no shadows. To a place where she could be with God, and he with her. A good place. A good nearby.

She felt Gladys's shoulder bump into hers. "What are you smiling about?" Gladys asked.

She hadn't realized she was smiling. "Nothing," Margery whispered back.

Plenty.

※ ※ ※

Margery's gestures were expansive as they sat in the booth at the restaurant after church. Gladys had never seen her like this.

"But the words to the song," Margery said, "you can't know how they made me remember Grammy and Susie. The words did something to me." She grabbed the fabric of her blouse at her midsection. "In here."

Gladys wished she could remember the words to "Abide with Me" but they were not in her memory bank.

King closed his menu. "You're glowing from the inside out."

Margery beamed. "I am?"

"Absolutely."

Glowing from the inside out. Gladys herself had said that to Margery just the night before. When was the last time Gladys had felt that way? Had she *ever* felt that way? Her time with God last Tuesday had been more of a battle and coming to terms of surrender than a glory-glory time.

"Gladys, you seem upset," Margery said.

Gladys looked at her two tablemates. "Sorry. I'm really happy for you."

"But?"

It would sound petty. "You're so cheery. So caught up in the joy-in-the-morning kind of stuff. From my experience . . ." *Such as it is.* Gladys focused on the menu. "I'm just hungry, that's all. What are you two having?"

"I shouldn't have gone on and on. I'm sorry," Margery said.

"Nonsense," King said. "That's why we have friends—so we can share with each other." He turned his head and looked at Gladys. "Right?"

She forced a nod.

Margery didn't look convinced. "It's just that feeling like I did today . . . I haven't felt that way since I was little, before everything turned crazy with Grammy and Susie dying, and running away and . . . I realize now that God was with me back then. He was taking care of me. I remember feeling it, seeing it, but once Mick came into my life . . ."

"Everything changed?" King asked.

"He'd get annoyed when I'd notice something good in the middle of the bad. He'd say it was dumb, that I was being a Pollyanna, that it wasn't good at all, and certainly not set there just for me. He called everything a coincidence and told me to stop it."

"Stop looking for God?"

She shrugged. "Not in so many words, but now I see that's what happened. I got so wrapped up in seeing what Mick wanted me to see . . ."

"He blinded you. He was a roadblock for you. He got you sidetracked from seeing God and—" King hesitated—"and maybe even from being who God wants you to be."

Margery nodded and her eyes flitted across the table, as if she were skimming through incident after incident in her past, seeing the truth for the first time. "Years ago, when I was tiny, Grammy told me I would do good. I might not change the entire world, but I could change the world of the people close around me." She looked up and blinked twice. "She said I'd be the good nearby."

"The what?"

"The good nearby. Good that's close around us. All around. Doing good for people who are nearby." She looked at King, then at Gladys. "Like you two. You are the good nearby more than I am. You've done so much good for me. To me."

Gladys felt embarrassed. "We've just done what needed to be done. Nothing that spec—"

Margery put a hand on hers. "*Very* special. Where would I be right now without your good help?"

Gladys tried to think of an answer but couldn't.

Margery withdrew her hand. "I can't believe I'm remembering all this stuff. After all these years."

"God has lifted the veil from your eyes. 'I was blind, and now I can see!'" King quoted.

Gladys took the words literally. *Hopefully . . . someday soon . . .*

Margery was speaking again. "I guess you're right about me getting sidetracked by Mick. I felt like I needed to be *his* good nearby, no matter how bad things got or how bad he treated me." She shook her head, then looked at King. "Hearing that 'Abide with Me' song again . . . that wasn't a coincidence, was it?"

"There's no such thing," King said.

Gladys let out a huff. "Pooh to that."

"To what?" King asked.

She hadn't meant to start something. "Pooh to there being no such thing as a coincidence. Coincidences happen by the dozens every day."

King shook his head. "God things happen by the dozens every day."

"By luck, not by any divine intervention."

King looked at her incredulously. Then he turned his attention to Margery. "What happened to you today was a blessing from God himself. A message for you alone. It was his hand guiding you back to your roots. Letting you know it's not too late to start over. Gladys and I heard the same song—as did hundreds of other people—and no one else got out of it what you did. You are important to God—every issue, moment, thought, act, and breath of your life is important to him and—" he took a fresh breath—"and Gladys is wrong."

He looked at Gladys and she at him. "How am I supposed to respond to that?" Gladys asked.

"Ask me why you're wrong."

She shook her head. "I'm not sure I want to hear this."

"Chicken?"

Never. Gladys angled her body toward his. "Fine. Why am I wrong?"

"How's this for starters? 'What is the price of two sparrows—one copper coin? But not a single sparrow can fall to the ground without your Father knowing it. And the very hairs on your head are all numbered. So don't be afraid; you are more valuable to God than a whole flock of sparrows.'"

"Oooh," Margery said softly.

King closed his eyes and recited: "'I knew you before I formed you in your mother's womb. Before you were born I set you apart.'" He opened them. "Pretty cool, huh?"

Gladys crossed her arms. "Have you been saving those verses just for me?"

"Just for me," he said. He smiled and bumped his shoulder into hers. "But I'm willing to share."

Margery's eyes were lit up like beacons. "I know that last one! Grammy told it to me when I was little. She said it means my life is important and has purpose."

King jumped on it. "The same verse received from two sources . . . God obviously wants you to take it to heart."

Oh please. Gladys rolled her eyes.

Margery sat back as if King's words possessed the power to push her there.

The effect of his words on Gladys was different. She felt deflated. Although she and God had come to terms, her time with him had not been joyous and he hadn't given *her* any cool verse.

Why not?

She was certainly more educated than Margery, of better social standing, with a greater worldview and experience. She wasn't a thief, the wife of a violent drug dealer, and had never slept in her car. Why would God give Margery a verse *and* a moment that made her all glowy and happy—and not give as much to Gladys?

The waitress came. The conversation moved on to other things.

But Gladys's question remained.

❧ ❧ ❧

Gennifer fingered the collar of her shirt as she looked out the window of Sarah's hospital room. Douglas sat in a chair, flipping through a magazine.

Suddenly, Douglas snapped the pages shut. "I feel so useless."

"You got that right," Gennifer said.

Douglas set the magazine on the floor, rested his arms on his thighs, clasped his hands, then sat back, his hands gripping the arms of the chair. "You think we should pray or something?"

Gennifer left the window's view and looked at him, incredulous. "What brought that on?"

"In interviews and articles you hear people say things like 'God answered our prayers.'" He took a breath. "We haven't prayed. Maybe if we did, she'd wake up."

"Boy, your conversion was easy. See a couple thank-the-Lord interviews and they've got you."

"I'm not converted. But I don't want to *not* do something that might help. And what can it hurt?"

He had a point. But next came the real problem. "So, let's say we agree to do this. Do you have *any* idea how to go about it?"

He bit his lip. "I was hoping you—"

Gennifer laughed. "Why would you think I know anything about prayer?"

He hesitated. "You're a lawyer; you're good with words."

He was right of course, but she also had the feeling that eloquence wasn't a prayer requirement. If that were so, a lot of people would be out of luck.

Douglas slapped the arms of the chair. "So. You want to start?"

"Being your idea, I defer to you."

He wiped his palms on his pants. "Okay then. For the sake of getting it done . . ." He clasped his hands and hung them between his knees. He closed his eyes and bowed his head.

Gennifer clasped her hands in front of her body and lowered her head too. But she didn't close her eyes. That was going too far this first time out. If God didn't like it, so be it.

"God?" Douglas began.

Gennifer thought that was a little abrupt, and probably would have gone with *Lord*, but she supposed *God* was better than *To whom it may concern.*

"Our daughter's hurt. She's unconscious and we're worried about her. She's a good girl and she didn't deserve to go through this."

Was that a cut? A subtle jab at Gennifer's part in Mick's attack?

"Please make her well. All the way well. If you do that, we'd be so happy. And we're going to do better at being a family too."

Gennifer didn't think he needed to go there. This wasn't a time for confession. Just ask God to heal Sarah and sign off. At least that's how she would have handled it.

With a deep sigh and a squirm in his seat, Douglas added, "And I want to say that I'm sorry for being unfaithful to Gennifer. And she's sorry for not telling me she was sick."

Gennifer wasn't exactly comfortable having Douglas apologize *for* her.

"We're both sorry for doing things that pulled the family apart. We've confessed it to each other, and we've promised to be honest with each other, and nice and attentive and . . ."

He didn't need to give God a laundry list of their faults.

Enough already.

"Anyway, take care of Sarah. Bring her back to us."

Finally, an ending.

"Oh . . . and one more thing, God. Heal Gennifer too. She's really sick and we want her well. We want her to be around a long time so we all can be a real family. Amen."

Gennifer felt his eyes, but she couldn't look at him. Not after that last bit. She'd never had anyone pray for her. She found it hard to breathe. Not that she really believed God was listening, but to hear her own husband say such things, ask for such things . . .

"Uhhhhhh."

They turned toward the bed. Sarah let out a breath and took a new one. Her eyes fluttered.

"Sarah!" Douglas ran to her side.

Gennifer took her hand. "Come on, honey. Wake up. Open your eyes."

And she did. As if she'd heard her mother's order.

As if God . . .

Gennifer didn't think about that now. She was too busy hugging her daughter.

❀ ❀ ❀

Talia stood at the mirror in the master bathroom and applied her lipstick. Working weekends was the pits. Friday nights and Saturdays were bad enough, but Sundays?

It couldn't be helped. Someone had to work in this family.

Not fair. And not nice. Thinking snide comments was a part of the old Talia. The new Talia . . .

Was still resentful. *Great.*

She heard the doorbell. With her mother off to visit Sarah at the hospital, Talia had been forced to call Margery to babysit. Husband-sit.

Hmm.

What she'd heard about Margery in the last twenty-four hours was shocking. It was Margery's criminal husband who'd hurt her mother's mentee. Since when did soft-spoken Margery from the drugstore have a criminal for a husband? Talia had been trusting her family to this woman and no one had thought to tell Talia about any of this?

And you didn't ask. You were so desperate for help . . .

Talia fastened the clasp of her watch and searched the jewelry box for her silver hoop earrings. Actually, Talia knew she shouldn't hold Margery accountable for her husband's sins. The girl was obviously trying to start over. And Gladys *had* been the one to recommend her.

But still. For a woman to choose to marry such a man in the first place . . . that showed bad judgment. And if Margery had bad judgment in that, she might have bad judgment in other areas.

Talia found her earrings and headed downstairs, seeking—and finding—rationalization along the way. Margery's husband was in jail. As far as Talia knew Margery had never done anything wrong. It would be okay.

Talia found Margery on the floor with Tomás, driving a Little People car up the ramp of the play garage, making the appropriate car sounds. Tomás watched, his mouth open, enraptured. Nesto sat in his chair nearby, beaming. What a lovely family picture.

Except Talia wasn't in it. Margery was. Talia's stomach grabbed oddly.

Nesto looked up. "Hey, *meu amor*. Margery's here."

"I see that." She transferred her wallet and makeup case from her black purse to the brown one. "I hate to leave you with the dinner duty again, Margery, but it can't be helped."

"I don't mind."

Talia put a sticky note on the doorjamb leading to the kitchen. "There's a hamburger-and-rice casserole ready to pop in the oven. Three-fifty for forty-five minutes. Tomás loves it."

"Me too," Nesto said.

Talia corrected herself. "The boys love it. There's Jell-O in the fridge. Feel free to slice a banana in it." She thought of her cell phone.

Where had she left it? There it was, by the mail. "Sorry, I didn't have time to make any dessert. You'll have to make do."

"Maybe we could make some cookies," Margery said. "Would that be okay?"

Before Talia could answer, Nesto said, "Oatmeal raisin."

"We're out of raisins," Talia said.

"Do you have nuts?" Margery asked.

"Top shelf of the pantry."

Margery turned to Nesto. "Do you like nuts?"

"I'm nuts about them."

Since when had Nesto gained a witty bone?

Talia gathered her things and left. Happy family sounds drifted after her.

❦ ❦ ❦

Angie turned into the hospital parking lot and did a double take. Driving out in a pale blue Jaguar was Gennifer Mancowitz and her husband. The one thing that had kept her from coming to see Sarah again was the chance of running into the angry mother. At least now the coast was clear.

As she approached Sarah's room, she heard a glorious sound— Sarah's voice.

Angie rushed inside. A hospital attendant was putting a tray of food on the wheeled bed table.

"Hi," Sarah said.

"You're okay," Angie said.

"I'm hungry." Sarah pointed to the food.

"That's a good sign," the attendant said to Sarah. "You going to be all right now?"

"Angie can help if I need it."

Angie felt a lump in her throat. The attendant left and Sarah removed a silver cover from a bowl of broth. "Smells good."

Angie hurried to help, moving the lid, offering her the napkin, taking the plastic wrap off the bowl of orange Jell-O.

Sarah took a spoonful. "Not bad."

"So you still trust me?" Angie asked. She hadn't meant to blurt it out like that.

"Why wouldn't I?"

"I'm sorry all this happened. I—"

"Mom and Dad were here when I woke up."

Angie nodded. "I saw them leaving the parking lot."

"I heard them praying. In my sleep. They don't pray."

"Apparently they do. For you."

"I woke up," Sarah said.

"I'm glad."

"I love orange Jell-O." She looked up at Angie. "How do you make Jell-O for fifty people?"

"Why would you want to—?"

"Not me. You. At the shelter with your new job. Everybody likes Jell-O, but how do you make it for so many people?"

Angie moved the glass of apple juice closer so Sarah could reach it. "I've decided not to take the job."

A spoonful of Jell-O stopped in midair, hanging precariously above the broth. "Why not?"

Her previous reason—because Stanford said she couldn't—was limp and without strength. Besides, now that she was on her own she could do what she wanted.

"You have to do it. Take the job."

"Why?"

"Because most people wouldn't." Sarah took a bite of Jell-O. "My mother wouldn't."

Angie did not want to come between Sarah and her mother. "But she does other things to help—"

"But not that." Sarah's eyes were deep with intensity, making her look older than her seventeen years. "Most people don't want to go to the shelter. You do. You don't mind. You were happy helping."

And there it was. Said so simply yet armed with the strength of truth. Then suddenly, out of the annals of Angie's memories, came words from Stanford that completely contradicted Sarah's words: *"Anybody can do that job."*

Perhaps anybody *could* do the job, but *would* they? *Did* they?

"Weren't you happy there?" Sarah asked.

"I was."

Sarah set down her spoon. "That proves it's right."

Maybe it did. Maybe it was that simple.

"I'm going back," Sarah said, taking up the spoon again. "You said
I could help figure out the menus. As soon as I'm out of here, I'll go
online and get you recipes for a crowd." Sarah picked up a plastic water
pitcher. "Can you get me some more water, please?"

And that was that.

᠅ ᠅ ᠅

Josh Cashinski's bear hug could have broken ribs. Angie was happy for
his exuberance, but relieved when he let her go.

"You won't be sorry," he said, then immediately amended his words.
"Actually, you probably will have bucketloads of second, third, and tenth
thoughts—maybe even hourly during mealtime—but hold on to this:
you've made the right decision. I know it."

"Thank—"

He took her arm and led her toward the kitchen. "Come on. It's time
for the chef to get a grand tour."

And that, was also that.

And more than that, it was good. Very good.

᠅ ᠅ ᠅

Gennifer was exhausted. But even though she and Douglas were home
for a respite from the hospital, even though they'd both decided to take
naps—Gennifer upstairs, and Douglas in the living room below—she
couldn't sleep. So much had happened. Too much for her mind to release.

After trying for a half hour, she decided to go downstairs. Maybe
a bowl of soup would calm her. But when she reached the top of the
stairs, she heard Douglas's voice. Just his voice. He must have been on
the phone in the kitchen. And by his hushed tone, he wasn't talking to
the hospital or to anyone at work.

Instinctively, she tiptoed down a few steps, then froze, listening.

"I'm sorry. I never meant to hurt you, Dorothy. But I love my wife.

Always have. And now that she's open to loving me back, letting me in; now that we've found each other again . . ."

Gennifer pressed a hand against her chest. He loved her. Everything he'd said before was true. Sincere. Real. He *did* want things to work.

"I know," he continued. "And it was wrong. I've done so many things wrong. That's why it has to stop. Now. Again, I'm sorry, I really—"

Dorothy must have hung up on him because he didn't finish the sentence. Suddenly he appeared in the doorway between kitchen and living room. Gennifer's muscles tensed, but it was too late to flee.

"Hi," she said.

"Hi."

They shared an awkward silence. Might as well get to the point. "I heard."

"I'm glad."

She came down the stairs. "Want some soup?"

He waited for her in the doorway. When she passed by, he took her hand and kissed her cheek.

❦ ❦ ❦

Gennifer didn't want to call into work, but she knew she should.

And so she did.

When Matt Breezley had called her yesterday, saying one of her clients had been arrested, she'd been of no mind to handle it. But today, with Sarah awake and better . . .

She sat at the desk in the kitchen, got out her address book, and called Matt at home. He'd be able to give her an update.

Matt answered after the second ring. "Matt, Gennifer here. About my client . . . just checking in."

"How's your daughter?"

"She's much, much better. Thanks. That's why I'm call—"

"Don't worry about work, Gennifer. I got it handled. Cory Roberts has already met with Mr. Lamborn and—"

"Lamborn? Mick Lamborn?"

"Your client. He was arrested yesterday for assault and—"

Gennifer stood up. "He was arrested for assaulting my daughter!"

"No . . ."

Was that all he could say? "We can't defend him! He nearly killed Sarah."

"It's too late," Matt said. "Cory's got it handled. He appears before the judge tomorrow and—"

"You're not listening to me, Matt. The firm cannot represent him. He's scum. He's a repulsive person. He's evil."

"He was your client, Gennifer."

The knife Matt had just thrust collapsed her breathing.

"I know this is odd, Gennifer. It's downright bizarre. But the point is, he was your client and he asked for you. We handled it. Bottom line? The man deserves a defense."

"He deserves nothing. He deserves to die."

"I know you're upset. And I understand why you feel this way, but—"

"I can't do this anymore."

"You don't have to see him, Gennifer. Cory will handle it."

"I quit."

Dead air hung between them. Gennifer was as shocked by her words as Matt must have been. Just to make sure she'd said them, she repeated them. "I quit. I resign."

"You're upset. I under—"

"I'm more than upset. I'm disgusted—at myself more than anyone. And I'm tired, Matt. I'm sick and tired of defending guilty people."

"Guilty people need defending, to make sure they get a fair—"

She laughed sarcastically. "Fair? What we do is fair? We go out of our way to win, to find loopholes, and then we congratulate each other when we get our clients off on a technicality, when we should be sharpening the key to lock them up, away from the society and the rules they abuse."

"You sound like a prosecutor."

Then it hit her. The next logical step. A step she had never even considered before, yet one that seemed perfect and good and right.

"Thank you for the career advice, Matt. You're absolutely right. I'll call the DA's office tomorrow morning, first thing."

"Don't be crazy, Gennifer. You're nearly a partner. At the DA's office you'll only make a pittance compared to what you make now."

"Do no harm," she said.

"That's a doctor's motto."

So it is. "Well, now it's mine."

She hung up and sat immobile. *What have I done?*

Suddenly, she heard slow and steady clapping. She turned and saw Douglas standing in the doorway. "Bravo!" he said.

"I quit my job."

"Good for you."

"Really?"

He hugged her and whispered into her ear, "I'm very proud of you." His words helped. They helped a little. But still . . .

What had she done?

※ ※ ※

The anniversary brunch for the Thompson family was to be in the Gardenia Ballroom—the small ballroom—tomorrow. Before heading there to check on the table setup, Talia stopped by her office to get the two posters she'd had made to put on easels that would direct the guests from the lobby to the celebration.

As it was Sunday and her office was officially closed, she had to use her key. She found the posters behind the door and gave them one final proofing: *Bennie and Margery Thompson: 50th Anniversary Brunch.*

The wife's name leaped out at her, leading her thoughts back to the Margery she'd left at home. Taking care of her family. Her stomach tugged. Again.

Talia shrugged it off as an overreaction, locked up the office, and headed to the ballroom.

The room was abuzz with men setting chairs around tables, and women employees setting the lavender tablecloths with the hotel's silver-trimmed bone china. The silver with the lavender was an attractive combination.

Missing were the centerpieces. Being a brunch, they needed to be delivered by this evening.

Talia started flipping pages on her clipboard to get the phone number for the florist, when a woman appeared, pushing a cart of floral arrangements.

"Just in time," Talia said.

"Sorry," the woman said. "We're running late." She let go of the cart, stood erect, and extended her hand. "Hi, I'm Margery, from Candlelight Florists."

Margery?

Talia discovered that upon hearing the woman's name, she'd withdrawn her own hand. With effort she extended it again and made the proper greetings.

"How do you like the arrangements?" Margery asked.

A single carnation in a cheap vase would have elicited a compliment from Talia. Fortunately for the Thompsons, the centerpieces were lush and lovely. "You did a great job," Talia managed. "Go ahead and set them."

Two Margerys in the span of ten minutes. If that wasn't a nudge, Talia didn't know what was.

She had to get home. As soon as possible.

Margery was sad to leave. After dinner, Nesto had suggested they play Scrabble. He couldn't believe she'd never played before. So they'd played two games—and Margery had even won one with the word *quieted*. They'd laughed when Nesto had tried to use Portuguese words. She loved hearing another language. She'd taken Spanish one year in high school, but couldn't remember anything much beyond, *"Hola! Mi nombre es Paco."* She admired people who could speak more than one language. Nesto even taught her how to say, "I won the game" in Portuguese: *Eu ganhei o jogo.*

"It's sleeting out there," Talia said, shaking off her coat before hanging it up.

"Be careful," Nesto said.

Margery put on her coat and glanced out the window toward a streetlight. Diagonal slits of rain were coming down hard. She shivered. To leave this warm and cozy place . . . at least she wasn't sleeping in her car anymore.

Nesto stood to see her out. "Thanks for the games," he said.

Margery smiled. *"Eu ganhei o jogo."*

He laughed and held up one finger. *"Somente um jogo.* Just one game. I won the other one. This session is tied. We'll play again."

"You're on." She opened the door. "Night."

Suddenly—or as suddenly as Nesto could move—he came toward her with arms wide.

Margery accepted his hug.

He pulled back. "Good-bye, Margery. *Deus seja com você.* God be with you."

Amen.

🕷 🕷 🕷

Talia waited until Nesto returned to his recliner. When he was settled, she pounced. "What was all that about?"

"What?"

"The hug, the Portuguese, sharing what were obviously inside jokes?" She pointed to the Scrabble board on a TV tray. "Since when do you play Scrabble?"

"I'm tired of TV."

"You should be in bed."

"I was having fun."

"I don't think I'm going to have Margery come anymore," she said.

"Why not?"

"You heard my mother talk about what happened to Sarah. Margery's husband is guilty. He was arrested. He's been arrested before."

"That's not Margery."

"Close enough."

Nesto shook his head. "She's sweet." He put a hand on his heart. "She has a good heart. I like her."

"Obviously."

Nesto looked at her, confused.

Talia picked up a stuffed bear with blue ears. "I saw how chummy you two have become. It makes me think . . . I mean . . . are you two . . . ?"

She knew it was a stupid—if not a horrible—question, but since it had slipped out she wanted him to answer. To deny everything. To make her feel better. Wanted. Needed. Desired even.

Talia was glad Nesto took the effort to stand and come to her. Considering he'd left his perch to hug Margery, it was the least he could do.

He pulled her into his arms. "I love *you*, Talia. Margery is like a little sister. A friend. She needs a friend."

The feel of his arms pressing her close made all the doubts of the day fade away. She leaned her head on his shoulder and closed her eyes. "Sorry. I'm just tired. So very, very tired."

They stood a moment, swaying just a little, two becoming one. Talia was willing to stay there a long, long time. She missed feeling close to him. Truly close.

Then Nesto pulled back and lifted her chin with a finger. "I know how to make everything better. Want a cookie?"

That was not what she had in mind.

Nesto pulled her toward the kitchen. "Margery made them."

Talia couldn't win.

☙ ☙ ☙

The evening spent babysitting at the Sozas' had been the perfect end to a great day. How come some days seemed so full, while others sped past as if they were empty? All days did *not* contain twenty-four hours.

She smiled as she drove toward Gladys's. This had definitely been a thirty-six-hour, twenty-four-hour day. The odd thing was that it had become extraordinary because of one decision. When she'd gotten up this morning she hadn't planned to go to church. Neither had Gladys. Yet because King had called, because Gladys had let herself be talked into it . . .

Margery's life had changed. Forever. It truly was a God thing.

The sleet pinged against the windshield. She turned the wipers on high just in time to see—

A car coming fast on her right.

Braking.

Sliding.

A tree! No! Not a tree!

She turned the wheel but had no control.

No, no! Yes! I'm going to hit. I'm—

Pain.

Then nothing.

21

Graduating high school, getting married, and having a baby in one year was a lot to handle. Most people would've spread it out a bit. But I didn't mind all of it happening together. Not when the year was 1996. That made it perfect and put a sparkle star on each and every event. As if God wanted it that way.

Mick wanted to wait to get married until we graduated, so it was planned for the day after. Nothing fancy. Mama said we didn't need any rigmarole, so I wore the graduation dress that I'd found on sale at Penney's for 70 percent off and got a bouquet at the grocery store. The ladies at the store were real nice, and put a red ribbon around it to match my dress. I baked a cake and bought a tube of red frosting so I could make curlicues around the top. I tried making some flowers, but they didn't work. I wrote *Mick and Margery* and made the outline of a heart. It was pretty. I also got some Hawaiian punch and pretty, matching paper plates, cups, and napkins.

Neither Mick nor I belonged to a church, so we got

married at the courthouse. I wished I'd kept going to Susie's church, but I'd never been back since her funeral. Mama was supposed to be at the wedding, but she didn't show up. Mick's mom was there. And Suzy from school came but she didn't stay for cake. Her family was in town for her graduation so she had stuff to do.

But big or little, it worked, and we were married. Me, a married woman, just like Grammy and I had dreamed. Mrs. Mick Lamborn.

An hour later, Mick pulled us into the parking lot of the Wonder-Fall Inn. Mick said they had a pool, a hot tub, and free food and drinks during happy hour. That sounded good. I just wanted to relax. The baby was due in seven weeks and it was moving around a lot, like it was excited too.

When we got our room key, Mick opened the door, but I didn't go in. I wanted him to carry me over the threshold like I'd seen them do in the movies.

"Don't be dumb, Marg. With the baby you're heavy."

He was right so I followed him inside, but he got the suitcases. The room was kind of pretty with a framed picture of a mountain above the bed. I went to the window. "Look, Mick! A balcony." I opened the door and went out. There were two white plastic chairs. I turned back to Mick. "Want to go swimming?"

Mick didn't hear me because he was on the bed, flipping through channels. I had to go back inside and ask again. "Want to go swimming?"

"They have HBO," he said.

"Swimming?"

He looked at me, his eyes scanning my belly. "What are you going to wear?"

I'd gotten a maternity swimsuit at the Nearly New Shop. "A swimsuit."

Mick's lip curled. "In public?"

My heart skipped. "Pregnant women wear swimsuits, Mick. All the time. Demi Moore even went naked on a magazine cover a few years ago. She looked beautiful."

"You're not her."

He might as well have slugged me in the stomach. I sank to the edge of the bed.

Mick popped to his feet. "Now, don't go getting all moody on me. Just because I made a little comment about you not being as pretty as some movie star."

He was right. I was being too sensitive. Nobody was as pretty as Demi Moore, and I *had* gained a lot of weight with the pregnancy. If Mick wasn't in the mood to be romantic on our honeymoon, I had only myself to blame. He'd wanted to wait until after the baby was born to be married. I was the one who'd insisted we do it first—so the baby had a proper last name. I should have been glad he'd agreed to marry me in the first place. He wouldn't have had to. So sometimes, it did seem like he really, really loved me.

But other times . . .

Mick went in the bathroom and I started to unpack. I'd splurged on a fancy baby blue nightie with lace around the neckline and hem.

I heard the toilet flush and Mick came out.

I held the nightie in front of me. "Do you like it?"

He blinked once, then reached for the remote, turning the TV off. "How about some dinner?"

❀ ❀ ❀

The restaurant was full so we put our name in. Mick wanted to wait in the bar. The stools were a little uncomfortable, but I liked the low lighting and the rows of glasses and decorative bottles.

"Two beers," Mick told the bartender.

"Can I see some ID, please?"

Mick flashed him a look. "Don't give me a hard time. We're on our honeymoon."

The bartender's eyes skirted over my belly.

Mick pointed a finger at him. "Don't."

"I still need to see IDs."

"Just give me and the lady a beer, okay?"

The bartender calmly wiped the inside of a glass with a towel. "She's pregnant. She shouldn't be drinking." He nodded toward a sign on the wall that warned against drinking during pregnancy.

I put my hand on Mick's arm. "Come on. Let's go wait in the other room."

"No!" He shoved my hand away, but in doing so, made me lose my balance.

I tried to catch myself, but the heel of my shoe got hooked in the rung of the stool. It toppled and I ended up on the floor.

Belly first.

A second after the pain, I thought, *The baby!*

Mick was at my side, yelling at the bartender. The bartender yelled for a doctor. People gathered round.

I rolled to my side. Mick took my hand. "You'll be okay. You'll be okay."

But the pain of the contraction told me different.

🥀 🥀 🥀

"I'm so sorry, Mrs. Lamborn," the doctor said. "Your daughter died a few minutes ago."

Daughter? The sedative made everything hazy. Dreamy. I hoped it was all a dream . . . the ambulance, the spinning lights, the gurney. The doctors in masks. The kind eyes.

The pain. Oh, the pain.

But no baby's cry. No happy, "It's a girl!"

The baby had been born and they'd stolen her away, leaving me behind. "Mick? Where's the baby? Mick? What's happening?"

Mick held my hand, but he had no answers. His eyes were panicked and sad.

The doctor patted my hand. "She was born too early. Her lungs weren't well enough formed. I'm so, so sorry."

Born too early. Born to die.

No! Not her. Not her. She was born, then died. . . .

And it's 1996. It's supposed to be a good year! This can't be happening.

I'd never seen Mick cry. I didn't like it. He was the strong one. He couldn't cry.

"I'm so sorry, Marg. So sorry."

I turned my face away from him. Sorry wasn't enough. Sorry wouldn't bring our daughter back.

"We can have another baby," he said.

Though I knew that was true, I didn't want to hear it. Only time would take care of the ache that carved me out inside. Only time would let me see beyond the pain of now and think about any kind of tomorrow.

Suddenly, Mick dipped his head against my hand. He began to sob.

He needs me.

How odd.

And yet the idea absorbed a bit of the ache and gave me strength. Mick needed me. We were man and wife. And though it would take a while to mourn our daughter, we *could* have another baby.

There was plenty of time for that.

Everything would be all right. We had the rest of our lives ahead of us.

22

Oh, how great are God's riches and wisdom and knowledge!
How impossible it is for us to understand his decisions and his ways!
ROMANS 11:33

"King, Margery's not home yet." Gladys heard a shuffling and jumbling of the phone and imagined King sitting up in bed. She gave him a moment to collect himself. But only a moment.

"What time is it?"

"Twelve twenty—AM."

"And she's not home?"

Gladys tried to be patient. "That's what I said. I've been waiting up, but I fell asleep. I just woke up and she still isn't here."

"Where was she last evening?"

"Talia's. She babysat."

"Have you called them?"

"I didn't want to wake them."

"So you decided to wake me?"

She wasn't in the mood. "If you don't want—"

"Stop. I'm here for you. Or I will be. Just give me a minute to get my brain in gear."

Gladys heard a car and rushed to the front window, pulling the sheer curtain aside. The car drove on by.

"Maybe she went back home—to her home?" King said. "After all, her husband is in jail so she *could* go—"

"We assume he's in jail. Maybe he got out."

"Do you think?"

"I *don't* think Margery would risk going back there in case he *could* get out. She seems done with him."

"She was in a good mood this morning after church," King said.

"Flying high. And she was upbeat about going to Talia's. She told me she likes Tomás and Nesto. Since he's so sick, he's there when she babysits."

"But maybe he had to go to the hospital and she stayed late to take care of the boy so Talia could go."

That was the first feasible scenario. And yet . . . "Why wouldn't she call?"

King's silence implied he was stumped. "Maybe she's not used to checking in? Who knows what kind of relationship she and Mick had. Maybe she's used to doing her own thing and isn't versed in the niceties of a polite phone call."

Gladys wasn't so sure. Even though Margery's background seemed lacking on the finer points of etiquette, she was a naturally polite girl. Conscientious. And appreciative. She would let Gladys know if she was going to be late. Gladys made a decision. "I'm calling the Sozas'."

"Call me back," King said.

Gladys found the number and dialed, preparing herself for an angry reception. Or maybe Margery herself would answer. *Please, please, please* . . .

"Hello?"

"Talia, sorry to wake you, but is Margery there?"

"Gladys?"

"Yes, yes. It's me. Is she there?"

"No. She left around eight. I—"

"Thanks." She hung up and called King back. "She left at eight. I'm calling hospitals."

"I'll be right over."

Gladys flipped to the Yellow Pages. My, the writing was tiny. . . . She got her magnifying glass and saw that Mercy Medical was the closest.

She dialed and asked if a Margery Lamborn had been admitted. She played her Dr. Quigley card to get the information.

"Lamborn . . . not admitted, Dr. Quigley. But she's here. In the ER," the worker said.

Yes? Gladys had never expected to get a yes. She'd hoped to call every hospital in the book and end up with a collection of no's. A yes?

"Was she in an accident?"

"I'm sorry. I'm not allowed to give out that infor—"

Gladys hung up and dialed King, hoping to catch him. She did. "Meet me at Mercy Medical."

Shoes . . . where are my shoes?

❧ ❧ ❧

Gladys and King pulled into the hospital parking lot within seconds of each other. She took his arm as they hurried inside, the ER doors opening by themselves. The first person she saw received her question. "Margery Lamborn. Where is she?"

"Are you her parents?"

Though it might be a stretch in King's case, if it got them inside, Gladys wasn't beyond fudging. "Yes."

The woman pointed to the right. "Room 3."

One, two . . .

A doctor was with her. He looked up.

"How is she?" Gladys asked. "What happened?"

The doctor answered the questions in reverse order. "Car accident. And we're still trying to determine how she is. There appear to be no internal injuries to her torso. Her vitals are satisfactory. But she has not regained consciousness. We're giving her medication for swelling on the brain and are taking her up for a CT scan to see the extent of the injuries." He put a hand on top of Margery's, as if easing *her* fears. "An orderly should be down momentarily."

A young woman with a clipboard appeared at the door. "Can one of you help with some of the paperwork, please?"

"I'll do that," King said. "Gladys, you go with her. I'll find you."

"After the test, we're admitting her to ICU on five. You can wait up there for the results." The doctor moved toward the door, touching Gladys's sleeve. "I'm very sorry. But we'll do our best for her."

But we'll do our best for her? *But?*

Everyone left, leaving Gladys alone with Margery. Moving close, she was amazed at how serene the girl looked. And unhurt. There were no marks on her. Not even a scratch. It looked as though she was sleeping. Yet for her to have been unconscious for so long was not good.

Gladys realized she didn't really know what time the accident had occurred, but from what Talia had told her, it must have happened soon after eight.

She took Margery's non-IV hand. To think of her being alone so long, with no friend or relative caring about her.

She's unconscious. She doesn't know she's been alone.

Gladys wasn't so sure. The capacity and capabilities of the human brain were largely unexplored. Who knew what coma patients knew or sensed? The hope that they were partially aware was proven every day by families talking to them, reading to them, trying desperately to engage them in some way as they waited for the eyes of their loved ones to open.

Gladys ran a hand along the edge of Margery's hair. Her funny, chopped-off hair, sacrificed to be easy care as she survived in her car. "Come on, girl. Things were going good for you. Come back to us. You have many, many better times ahead of you."

For the first time, Gladys noticed the beep of the monitoring machines. She watched the lines spike and move. Movement was good. As long as the lines moved . . .

Suddenly overcome with emotion, she clamped her eyes shut, fighting away tears. *Help her, God. Help her.*

She hoped God would listen to her. If he was who he said he was . . . and if he did talk to people like he'd talked to Margery in church . . .

She repeated her prayer again and again, covering all the bases.

※ ※ ※

Talia carried Tomás downstairs to eat breakfast and found Nesto standing at the front window, curtains parted, looking outside.

"What are you looking at?"

"Looking *for.*" He let the curtain fall back into place. "I'm looking for Margery."

Talia remembered the late-night phone call from Gladys. She'd gone right back to sleep. She kept her voice low, not wanting to wake her mother and bring her into the mix. "You haven't been awake all night worrying, have you?"

"Praying."

She felt a twinge of jealousy that this woman would elicit her husband's prayers, and guilt because she'd *not* felt compelled to pray. "I'm sure she's okay. She probably just went out after she left here, out to have some fun, and—"

"No." Nesto's voice was full of authority. "She wouldn't do that."

"What makes you think you know her that well?"

He hesitated only a moment. "When she left she was happy. And she's a stay-at-home type of girl. She lives with Gladys now."

"If it's worrying you so much, why don't you call Gladys? I'm sure she's up."

"I have. There's no answer."

Talia stopped with the kitchen door half open. "You already called her?"

He nodded and caught up with her. He took her hand. "Something isn't right. We need to pray."

She nodded at Tomás, sleepy in her arms. "Now?"

"Please." He held out his hand and she took it. He bowed his head until it nearly touched hers. "Father, we're worried about Margery. You know where she is. Take care of her. Keep her safe. Amen." He ended the prayer with a kiss to Talia's cheek and his son's head. "There. I feel better. 'The earnest prayer of a righteous person has great power and produces wonderful results.'"

Righteous? *She* wasn't even close. So would God hear *her* prayers?

Tomás was hungry. Good or bad, at the moment Talia had other things to think about besides her level of righteousness.

❧ ❧ ❧

"You going to get that, Talia?"

Talia looked toward Wade's office, then noticed that the phone on her desk was ringing. "Sorry." She answered it and dealt with a problem in the kitchen with a delivery of portobello mushrooms. And for a few moments after getting off the phone, she *did* concentrate on the scheduling and room assignments for an upcoming plumber's convention.

I have to do something about Margery. I have to get her out of our lives.

It irked her that someone who didn't have any education or breeding, who wasn't even that pretty, someone who had a husband in jail had connected with Nesto. The image of them laughing as if they were close friends made her jaw tighten.

But what would you do without her to take up the babysitting slack? Even though your mother has moved in, she's gone more than she's home.

With a shake of her head, Talia forced herself to look back at the convention scheduling. What was she doing wasting her time thinking of Margery? She had important things to do.

But the memory of seeing Nesto at the window this morning, watching for Margery . . . he shouldn't worry. It wasn't good for him.

She had a way to fix that. She flipped her card file of phone numbers and dialed Neighbor's Drugstore. She'd talk to Gladys—or even Margery herself—to be reassured that everything was all right, then call Nesto and get him to stop worrying. Maybe *then* she could get some real work done.

She dialed.

A man answered: "Neighbor's Drug, this is King. May I help you?"

"King, this is Talia Soza. Gladys called last night about Margery? Did you—?"

"Talia. So sorry. We should have called back but it's been crazy. After she left your house, Margery was in a car accident. She's in intensive care at Mercy Medical. Gladys is with her."

Talia's heart fell. "Accident?"

"She's in pretty bad shape. Head injuries." She heard a muffled, "I'll be with you in just a moment, ma'am." King's voice came back on the line, talking to Talia. "I have to go. With Gladys and Margery gone . . . I'll keep you posted."

"I'm going over there."

"That would be nice. Gladys could use the support."

Talia hung up and started to dial Nesto. Then she stopped. He'd been upset wondering what had happened, but he would be even more upset if he knew Margery was hurt. Yet Talia knew that even an awful known was often better than an unknown. She'd call and tell him, then assure him she would take care of it by going to the hospital.

It was a plan.

※ ※ ※

First Sarah and now Margery? Angie's young friends were dropping right and left. But as upset as she was by the news about Margery, Angie was afraid for Nesto. Ever since Talia had called he'd been sitting in his chair, perfectly still, looking out the window. He wasn't visibly upset, but he was so quiet. . . .

"Are you okay?" she asked him.

He blinked and turned his head in her direction, coming out of his reverie. Yet his face was at peace. It even held the slightest of smiles. "God is up to something."

Angie was horrified. "Two young women have been hurt in two days. If this is God's doing I wish he'd stop it."

Nesto shook his head. "No, you don't. God knows what he's doing."

She popped off the couch. "How can you say that?"

"He does. No matter what happens."

Angie was incredulous. "Surely you don't think God is behind this?"

"He allowed it to happen. There has to be a reason."

She waved her arms, wanting his absurd words to scatter. "I suppose you're one of those annoying people who say, 'It's all for the best' to grieving family at funerals."

"No. I give them a hug. I tell them I'm sorry."

She was relieved to hear it.

His eyes turned toward the window again, then moved back to Angie. "God is up to something."

As a woman she was used to gut feelings. Intuition. Whatever a person called it, it was a real commodity. So who could say that if a godly man like Nesto felt such a thing *it* wasn't real?

He smiled at her. "I'm glad you're here, Angie. I'm glad we can pray together."

Pray. Yes, she should pray. That she could do.

❧ ❧ ❧

As she drove to the hospital, Talia filled her car with a string of apt descriptions of her character. "I am the most selfish, mean, nasty, vicious, cruel . . ."

Unfortunately, there was no one to argue with her. Not that they could have, present or not. To waste the entire morning absorbed in her mental vendetta against Margery only to find out the woman was desperately hurt and unable to defend herself . . .

"I'm so sorry. So sorry."

Upon hearing the words—which *were* heartfelt—Talia realized she'd been saying them as a prayer. Luckily, God had been the only one aware of her horrible thoughts against Margery. The idea of someone else knowing the horrid condition of her heart made her cringe with awful could-have-beens. If she felt guilty now, how much deeper would it have been if she'd shared her pettiness with others?

But now, no one needed to know. Like the good person she was *not*, Talia would do the right thing by going to the hospital to show her support. She knew all the right words to say, and hopefully, the actual doing would rub off on her inner attitude and water down the guilt so she could at least live with herself. She'd get through this excruciating nibbling of her insides, the biting that accompanied every memory of her malicious thoughts.

Talia realized she wasn't sorry for the thoughts just because Margery was hurt but because they weren't deserved. She often called her father a snob for berating Nesto's humble background, yet she'd just proven herself to be every bit as unfair and bigoted against Margery.

Strong word *bigot*. But that's what she was. A jealous, petty bigot who took her frustrations out on an undeserving target.

"But I'm so stressed."

The words sounded as empty as they were. Everyone was stressed. Such was life. Everyone had a right to complain, but the fact that Talia did more than her share . . .

Suddenly a flood of tears threatened, and Talia pulled into the parking lot of a grocery store where she could let them come. Shame overwhelmed her. Not just for the bad things she'd thought about

Margery, but for her attitude in general. When was the last time she'd done something without complaining or being irritable? Even getting up in the morning, even getting Tomás up and going, then tackling her to-do list from the mundane to the major . . . nothing was done with joy or even a quiet acceptance. Everything elicited anger, bitterness, and constant complaining, vocal or internal. It was horrible being immersed in such discontent.

But as things were, how could she be otherwise? During this awful waiting for Nesto to get a heart and for life to get back to normal, contentment wasn't an option.

Was it?

And speaking of options . . . would they ever know normal again? Was it a possibility? Or would their lives continue on this merry-go-round of chaos?

Yes.

The simplicity of the word caused Talia to suck in a breath. Yes? This was going to continue?

She felt the baby kick and put a hand on her abdomen to comfort it.

The baby—their daughter—would be here soon, bringing with her all the accoutrements of new life. If Talia thought life was complicated now . . .

Come to me, all of you who are weary and carry heavy burdens, and I will give you rest.

She'd heard Nesto repeat the verse many times—the last time while she'd been scrubbing a toilet. Talia smiled bitterly at the previous non-divine location, though honestly, sitting in the parking lot of a Piggly Wiggly wasn't much better.

But maybe that was the point. No matter where she was or what she was doing, Jesus was saying, "Come to me." She didn't have to be in church or even in a particularly reverent state of mind for him to try to make contact.

. . . all of you . . .

Everyone. Anytime.

Talia gripped the steering wheel, leaned her forehead against her hands, and began. "Lord, I'm tired of waiting for things to get better. The key to all of it is Nesto's getting a heart. The way I see it, if he could get better, then everything else will get better. So answer that one, Lord. When? When is Nesto going to get a heart?"

She was quiet a moment, and was not surprised there was no answer. She was only slightly disturbed to find the thought *See? I knew you wouldn't answer* ticker-tape through her brain.

With a surge of sudden drama, she spread her hands toward the roof of the car, raised her face, and closed her eyes. "Here I am, God. I'm a messed-up, confused, often nasty woman. This is all I am at the moment. If there's anything better in me, I'm afraid it's hidden way down deep and you are just going to have to deal with it. I am what I am. So *here* I am. Do with me what you want. Frankly, I'm too tired to care."

She opened her eyes and lowered her hands. A little boy riding in his mother's grocery cart nearby stared at her. She waved. He waved back.

If God needed a witness to whatever transaction had just taken place, he had one. No age discrimination here.

Talia had to acknowledge she *did* feel better. She had no idea why, but would take what she could get.

And now that's exactly what she had to do. Get. To the hospital.

It was time to at least pretend she was a good person.

❧ ❧ ❧

"Are you sure you'll be okay alone with Tomás?" Angie asked Nesto.

"Go. Go see Margery—for me as well as for you."

Angie kissed him and her grandson and left. After praying with Nesto Angie had experienced an odd nudge to go to the hospital. For Margery's sake but also for Sarah's. Sarah was still recovering. If she found out through the hospital grapevine that Margery had been hurt . . .

She said another quick prayer—for green lights.

❧ ❧ ❧

When Angie knocked on the door of Sarah's hospital room, Sarah was buttoning a plaid shirt. She still had Steri-Strips on her face, and a bandage covered a cotton ball where the IV had pierced the back of her hand. She smiled over her shoulder. "Hey, Angie. I'm going home as soon as Mom and Dad get here from Mom's dialysis session."

"Dialysis?"

Sarah told her an amazing story about her mother's secret illness. As if the girl didn't have enough to deal with.

"I'm glad you're going home." Angie handed her a pair of socks.

"Mom isn't too keen on me going back to the shelter to help again, but I'm raring to go. I won't leave you and Margery in the lurch."

Angie perched herself on the edge of a nearby chair. There was no way to make this sound less than it was. "Margery's been hurt."

Sarah dropped a sock. "Did her husband beat *her* up too? I thought he was in jail."

"It wasn't her husband. He *is* in jail. You're safe from him. She was in a car accident. She's here."

Sarah stood. "Here? She's here at this hospital?"

"She is. Gladys is in the waiting room. I'm going to join her and—"

Sarah started putting her shoes on. "I have to see her."

Angie realized she'd started something she had no right to finish. "You can't just yet, hon. You have to wait for your mom and dad to get here and check you out."

Sarah looked at the clock. "But they won't be here for forty-five minutes. I can't wait that long. I—" she picked up the phone—"I can't wait."

❀ ❀ ❀

Gennifer looked up from her dialysis chair. Douglas smiled at her, then went back to his *Sports Illustrated*. She'd told him he didn't have to come with her to the Monday morning dialysis, but he'd insisted. He wanted to see what she had to go through three times a week. It was sweet—if not a bit unnerving.

After overhearing him break off his relationship with his girlfriend last night, this morning's special attention was further proof he was really going to try to make this marriage work. She had no more excuses. He was willing to commit, to do whatever it took.

Was she?

"I'm sorry this is so boring," she said. "Just a little longer."

He closed the magazine. "What do you do while you're here?"

"I read a lot. Talk with the other people." She'd introduced him to the regulars around the room. When she looked up, Marianne Bradley winked. Gennifer had never told them much about her family, so she knew they'd pummel her with questions next Wednesday. At least she'd have something good to say.

Her cell phone rang and she reached to answer it. At least she didn't have to worry about it being the office. She was now a free agent. "Hel—"

Her daughter's words came in a rush. "Margery has been in an accident. She's here at the hospital in intensive care."

"Margery? The woman whose husband hurt you?"

"Margery, my friend. I want to go see her but I can't until you check me out. When will you be here?"

Gennifer checked the time. "I have ten more minutes."

"Can't you go faster, Mom?"

"No, I can't go faster. But we'll be there as soon as we can."

She heard Sarah sigh. "Soon, Mom. Soon."

Gennifer hung up and answered Douglas's questions.

"Sarah doesn't need this stress when she's recovering herself," he said.

"But she's adamant. We need to get over there as soon as we can."

"Poor Margery," Douglas said. "To have a loser husband and then get in an accident?"

Another crisis. Just when things were looking up.

※ ※ ※

The TV in the waiting room intruded with an ad for shampoo. Gladys hadn't minded its company before, but now she found it to be like fingernails on the chalkboard of her nerves. She shut it off. The woman reading a magazine in the corner didn't seem to mind.

At that moment Talia Soza came in. "Gladys, how is she?"

"I'm waiting to hear."

Talia fell into a chair next to Gladys. "She has to be okay. I didn't mean any of the things . . ." She kept shaking her head.

Gladys had no idea what Talia was talking about. She pulled the young woman's hand into her lap.

❧ ❧ ❧

They all looked up when the doctor came into the waiting room:
Besides Gladys and Talia, the group had grown to include Angie; King;
Gennifer; her husband, Douglas; and their daughter, Sarah. The doc-
tor's eyes scanned the faces until he found Gladys. He came toward her.

Gladys stood. Her heart was in her throat.

"May I speak to you a minute, please?"

With a plaintive look to King, she followed the doctor into the hallway.

His face was grim. "On the admitting form you were listed as next
of kin."

"Oh."

"Are you her mother?"

"No. I'm just a friend. But—"

His eyes closed and he rubbed them with a weary hand. "We need
the next of kin."

"Her husband's in jail for assault. He's abusive. He doesn't care about
her. I do. She works for me and lives in my house. If you want me to
sign some papers that say I adopt her as a daughter, I'll do it. But the
fact is I'm as close to kin as you're going to get." Gladys realized she'd
said the whole thing in one breath and it had winded her.

The doctor smiled. "I believe you. And she's lucky to have someone
who cares as much as you." His face turned serious again. "Unfortunately
. . . things aren't going very well and some decisions need to be made."

She put a hand to her chest against the sudden expulsion of air.
"She's dying?"

"There's something I want to talk to you about."

❧ ❧ ❧

Just as Margery's friends had looked up when the doctor had entered
the waiting room, so they did again when Gladys returned.

King came to her. "What did he say?"

"You'll never believe it." She let her eyes scan each and every face.
"You'll never—ever—believe it."

23

I opened my eyes and found myself on a path. Flowers blanketed the ground on either side, nodding in a gentle breeze. Taller shrubs guarded the trunks of a multitude of trees that reached toward a vivid blue sky. The scent of honeysuckle, plumeria, and roses surrounded me. Birds sang amid the greenery and a yellow butterfly teased the air in front of me.

I laughed.

But then I realized I didn't know where to go. I looked behind me, yet didn't remember coming this far. How had I gotten here? And what was ahead?

Though I wasn't sure which way to walk, I didn't want to go back. Forward. Forward. Step forward.

I looked at my feet and found them bare. And my clothes . . . I wore an ivory dress made of voile. I extended my arms and watched as the breeze made the sleeves dance. I felt pretty. Even beautiful.

I heard a rustling in front of me and lowered my arms, waiting. I was not afraid. Somehow I knew that what lay ahead was a good thing.

I heard the voice of a woman singing: "'Hold thou thy cross before my closing eyes; Shine through the gloom and point me to the skies. . . .'"

Grammy? I wanted to run ahead, yet I didn't. I sensed I had all the time in the world and could—and should—savor everything. I would wait for the song to be finished; I would wait for Grammy to come into—

And there she was! Smiling and waving.

"'Heaven's morning breaks, and earth's vain shadows flee; In life, in death, O Lord, abide with me.'"

I pressed my hands to my lips, unable to fathom what was happening. To have Grammy—the most important person in my life—right in front of me.

Grammy put her hands on her hips. "Well? You going to hug me or not?"

I flung myself into her arms. I had never felt so safe. I could have stayed there forever.

It was Grammy who gently pushed me away. "Welcome, child. We've been waiting for you."

"We?"

Grammy turned in the direction from where she'd come. "You can come out now."

I watched as my best friend came toward me. "Susie!"

She smiled, but shushed me with a finger. She was carrying a bundle.

"Hey-de-ho, Gigi!" Susie whispered. "We heard you were coming."

When I went to hug her I saw that the bundle was a baby. A tiny newborn.

And then I knew. "Is this my daughter?"

"The very one."

My hands hovered above the pink bundle, aching to touch her, yet hesitant. "May I?" I asked Grammy.

"She's yours, child. She's your child. We've just been taking care of her until you could come."

I took my daughter in my arms for the very first time. The baby wiggled, adjusting herself to the new warmth. She opened her eyes and

I ran a finger along her cheek. "Hello, sweet one. I'm your mommy."
I raised her up to give her a kiss. "She's perfect."

"Of course she is," Grammy said. She winked at Susie. "But you ain't
seen nothing yet." She extended an arm toward the path.

"Where are we going?" I asked.

"The Father is waiting for you. Nearby."

"Father?"

Grammy slipped her hand through mine, touching the baby on her
nose. "He has a lot to tell you, child."

"About what?"

"About everything. About your life. About the ninety-six."

"He'll explain—?"

"Everything." We began to walk. "And let me say, it's guaranteed to
be quite a story. Guaranteed good in every way."

I had no words. It was more than good. And it was so very close.

It was the good nearby.

24

*When you put a seed into the ground,
it doesn't grow into a plant unless it dies first.
A different plant grows from each kind of seed.*

I CORINTHIANS 15:36, 38

Gladys checked the computer itinerary on the sixteen-day Best of Europe excursion: London, Paris, Lucerne, Venice, Florence, Rome . . . she wanted to get Vienna or Salzburg in there, but knew it might not be possible. Although she'd been to most of these cities with her mother and Aunt June—Rome was her all-time favorite—King had never been to Europe at all. That's why she didn't mind repeating herself. To be able to show him, to see it fresh and new with his eyes.

Ha. Fresh and new with her eyes. Her *new* eyes. Thanks to Margery.

She scrolled down the screen to see what sights were planned in Rome, thinking of her first meeting with Margery in the drugstore's office—the office that was plastered with posters of faraway places. Margery had mentioned that she hadn't even been on a plane.

Never would.

Gladys often felt guilty about that, about moving forward with her life when Margery had *no* life. About seeing things so clearly when the world had once been so indistinct. And it was more than just seeing clearly with her eyes. The past two months had been chock-full of new ways of looking at things.

"Boo!" King had come up from behind and dug into her rib cage.

"You startled me!"

"As intended." He leaned low and kissed her cheek before turning his attention to the screen. "What are you looking at, Red?"

"Sixteen days, six cities." She scrolled to the top and let him see the intro. "There are lots of options. Just tell me which cities are on your wish list."

He wrapped his arms around her, his cheek to hers. "I only want to be with you. Where is secondary."

"You are far too mushy."

"Get used to it." He let her go and leaned against the desk, facing her. "Actually, I have a proposition for you."

"I think you already did that by proposing."

He winked and crossed his arms. "What would you think about inviting two extra people along?"

"On our honeymoon?"

"On part of our honeymoon. If we're gone over two weeks, maybe they could join us for one of them."

He certainly had her curious. "Who did you have in mind?"

"June and Jason."

Her aunt and King's son. "Now there's an interesting pair."

"Actually, I think they'd enjoy each other immensely."

He was right about that. Between June's sarcasm and Jason's wit, the conversation would never be dull.

"Jason will be through with classes for the summer. He'll have a summer job, but if he can tell them up front he's going to be gone . . ."

"What about June's health?" Gladys asked.

"She's been doing okay. In spite of her initial bellyaching, that retirement home has given her a new lease on life. Now that the essentials like room and board are taken care of, she's getting to be quite the social butterfly. Don't you remember her last e-mail? She's signed up for a class on Shakespeare's sonnets and is taking samba lessons."

Shakespeare and samba. Yes, June was certainly behaving like her normal self. Gladys imagined the sound of her aunt's squeal when they told her she would be coming with them. "Can we call her now?"

King handed her the phone.

※ ※ ※

Talia's heart swelled with pride. To see her husband standing so proudly next to the other new citizens as they took the oath.

Twenty-two people repeated together: "I hereby declare, on oath, that I absolutely and entirely renounce and abjure all allegiance and fidelity to any foreign prince, potentate, state, or sovereignty, of whom or which I have heretofore been a subject or citizen; that I will support and defend the Constitution and laws of the United States of America against all enemies, foreign and domestic; that I will bear true faith and allegiance to the same . . ."

Arcelia Margery Soza made soft baby noises in Talia's arms. Tomás stood between Angie and Stanford, looking handsome in his tiny red bow tie and big-boy suit. He held his grandparents' hands but his eyes were on his new shoes. Why were children so fascinated with new shoes?

" . . . I take this obligation freely without any mental reservation or purpose of evasion, so help me God."

The room burst into applause and the new citizens beamed. Although Talia couldn't clap without rousting Arcelia, she clapped a hand against her side. *Bravo! Bravo!*

The new citizens dispersed to their families and there were hugs all around. Especially meaningful was seeing her father shake Nesto's hand and tell him congratulations. Ever since the heart transplant— where Nesto received Margery's heart—her father had been especially kind. Maybe her mother leaving him—even for that short time—shook him up. Sometimes that's what it took.

That's what it had taken for Talia. If only she could learn lessons without having to suffer embarrassment and pain. Her old penchant for playing the complaining martyr for attention's sake was pitiful when held against the true sacrifice of Margery Lamborn. Everything had been taken away from Margery, yet through that tragedy she'd been able to give so much to so many. Talia was making a concerted effort to be a better person, to show her gratitude for the miracle of Nesto's recovery, for having him present and healthy at the birth of their daughter.

She kissed the baby's forehead. Family was her focus. And doing what had to be done without complaint—or with as little complaint as possible. Yes, she was still working at the hotel, but as soon as Nesto got back to work full-time she hoped to stay home with the kids. Maybe someday she'd work outside the home again.

Nesto put his arm around her waist and pulled her close. She kissed his cheek. "Are you happy?" she asked.

He lifted Tomás into his arms before answering her. The little boy waved a small American flag. "I am better than that," Nesto said. "I am blessed."

Amen to that.

✿ ✿ ✿

Stanford opened the car door for his wife. "Thanks, hon," Angie said.

"No problem."

After getting inside, Angie watched him walk around the car toward the driver's side. It's not that her husband hadn't always opened doors for her. He'd always gone through the public motions of being a gentleman. But now . . . it was different. The niceties of their marriage carried extra layers, as if previously, Stanford had only been playing a part.

If he'd been guilty, so had she. How many times had she done things for him out of duty rather than love? The scales were heavily weighed on the duty side. It was one way to live a life, but not the best way.

They were living the best way now. Who would have thought after thirty-two years of marriage, things could change so drastically? Who would have thought—after his initial vehement reaction—that Stanford would respect Angie's getting a backbone? And who would have thought Angie could receive a portion of unconditional love from her husband by giving him some of her own?

Stanford got in the car. "Home?"

"Actually, I have to go to the grocery store and get supplies for the meals at the shelter tomorrow. But we can go home first. Then I'll take my car and—"

"Nonsense. I'll come help. Do you have your list?"

Good point. Angie looked in her purse. "Got it."

"Then let's go. And how 'bout stopping at the bakery and picking up some of that cherry strudel you love?"

Would wonders never cease?

※ ※ ※

Gennifer slipped a letter into a see-through page protector and patted it flat. She handed it to Sarah, who put it in the three-ring binder with the others. "There," she said to her daughter. "I think we're done."

Sarah clicked the notebook closed. "There sure are a ton of them."

"I've lost track. Would you count them, please?"

Sarah nodded and started counting the pages.

Meanwhile Gennifer checked on the plaque they'd had made to hang in the ER waiting room of the hospital:

> *In honor of*
> *Margery Lamborn (1979–2006)*
> *a woman set apart.*
> *Endings became new beginnings.*
> *We are the proof;*
> *Margery is the cause.*
> *She was the good nearby.*
> *That is our inspiration—and our aspiration.*

Gennifer still couldn't believe that she'd received one of Margery's kidneys. There was no way she could express her gratitude. For how did one say thank you for a miracle?

She polished a smudged fingerprint on the brass with the corner of her sweater. No one had asked her to do this for Margery. And seeking out and compiling a list of those who had benefited from her organs and tissues had been difficult. But letting them know who was behind their benefit had become a crusade.

When the letters started coming in, Gennifer had compiled them in a notebook. And at her own expense, she'd had a shelf created that would sit beneath the plaque and hold the notebook containing the letters. She hoped that maybe, while people were waiting to get news of their loved ones in the ER, they would take a moment to read about a woman who ended up helping . . .

"Ninety-six people," Sarah said. "There are ninety-six letters."

Gennifer nodded with satisfaction. "Ninety-six. That's a very good number."

A life of self is death.
The death of self is life.
ANONYMOUS

DISCUSSION QUESTIONS

1. Grammy is a bright light in little Gigi's dark world. Have you ever known such a person? How can you be such a person to someone else?

2. Gigi's parents take her to a doctor, wanting him to explain away her uniqueness. Is there a danger in this? What would you have done if you'd had such a child?

3. Gennifer keeps her illness a secret. Do you know of anyone who's kept a big secret? What were the results? Can the keeping of such secrets ever turn out well?

4. Talia is overwhelmed with work, home, and family responsibilities—a common situation. What practical advice could you give someone in this situation?

5. Poor Margery. One crisis after another. If you could get her in front of you for some one-on-one time, what would you say to her?

6. Angie has a stable life. Yet in what way is she not truly alive? What do you think is the balance between accepting what *is* and looking for what *could be*?

7. Most of the characters are caught up in playing a part. Go through them one by one and pinpoint the part they're playing: Margery, Gennifer, Angie, Talia, and Gladys.

8. Gladys has always been on her own. No husband, no kids. How has this independence become a roadblock to her faith?

9. Talia unexpectedly witnesses her mother's talent as a volunteer worker and gains new respect for her. Who in your life has surprised you with hidden talents? Isn't it about time you let them know how special they are?

10. In spite of extreme hardship, little Gigi has a good attitude about life. What is it about some people that enables them to rise above adversity, while others succumb to it? Which type of person are you?

11. Gladys goes above and beyond her position as employer to help Margery. Describe a time when you went out of your way to help someone—even reluctantly. And/or describe when someone went out of his or her way to help you.

12. Has there been a song, a verse, a color, an item in your life that has repeatedly offered you comfort? How can you see God's hand in this?

13. Do you know anyone who has donated organs or benefited from an organ transplant? Have you signed up to be an organ donor? Why or why not? (Do it today—information is in the back of this book.)

14. A challenge: Look around at the people in your life—the ones you see often, the ones nearby. See the good in them. Let them see the good in you. Be the good nearby in someone's life. Today. Tomorrow. From now on.

Dear Readers:

Whose life counts? Whose life doesn't?

That was the question that spurred *The Good Nearby*.

How many people do we see every day, but not see? not notice? And yet their lives may have more impact on the world than our own. Not because of the *big* things they do, but because of the *good* things they do, and the good people they *are*.

Sometimes I look at the celebrity magazines and marvel at how much interest movie stars generate. There are actually pages that showcase celebrities being ordinary people—buying groceries or pumping gas. It's absurd. Without much effort you and I could name dozens of "stars" who have been thrust into our consciousness by a media-ruled world.

But what about the lady at the bus stop who makes a point of asking about our kids? Or the jolly elderly man in the drive-through window of the burger joint who makes us forget the line was long? Or the stock boy who helps us find our favorite brand of kitty litter at the grocery store and even asks the name of our cat? How do they spend their time? What do they care about? What do they worry about? What is God's plan for their lives?

What is God's plan for yours?

We have a tendency to think life doesn't count for much unless we do something big and flashy. (It's the American way!) Yet the stooped grandmother who gives a child encouragement and a hug, the neighbor who—unasked—collects our newspapers while we're on vacation (because we forgot to stop delivery), the gardener who spreads mulch around the tulips in the park that make us smile and think hopeful thoughts of spring and new beginnings . . . these people do good every day. Little bits of good that add up to changed attitudes and changed lives. If we notice. If we allow ourselves to really *see* them and acknowledge their sparks of specialness.

These people are the good nearby. They *are* good and *do* good. We need to open our eyes—our eyes that usually skim past them—and recognize the blessings they offer. We need to accept those blessings, appreciate them, and give away some blessings of our own.

We need to *see* the good nearby . . . and *be* the good nearby.

That is my challenge to you.

So go. Change the world. One little bit of good at a time.

Nancy Moser

You have something priceless to give . . .

On any given day, there are over 91,000 people in the United States waiting for an organ—91,000 people whose life can be saved or radically improved by the gift of life. (For a real-time waiting list go to http://www.optn.org.)

Have you signed up to be an organ donor?

It's not difficult. While donated organs and tissue are shared at the national level, the laws that govern donation vary from state to state. Therefore, it is important for you to know what simple steps you can follow to ensure that your decision to be a donor is carried out. Visit www.donatelife.net for more information about organ donation and how to be an organ-and-tissue donor in your state.

   Once you have <u>decided</u> and <u>documented your decision</u> to become a donor, the most important step is <u>telling your family.</u> Most people support donation, but few have told family members of their decision to donate. Talking about donation is talking about the opportunity to give another person a second chance at life.

Give the gift of life

For more information about organ transplantation contact the United Network of Organ Donation at www.unos.org.

ABOUT THE AUTHOR

NANCY MOSER is the best-selling author of three books of inspirational humor and fourteen novels, including *The Seat Beside Me*, the Mustard Seed series, and the Christy Award–winning *Time Lottery*. She also coauthored the Sister Circle series with Campus Crusade cofounder Vonette Bright. Nancy is a motivational speaker, and information about her Said So Sister Seminar can be found at www.nancymoser.com and www.sistercircles.com. Nancy and her husband, Mark, have three children and live in the Midwest.

SCRIPTURE VERSES
in The Good Nearby

CHAPTER	TOPIC	VERSE
Prologue	Troubles	Ecclesiastes 8:6
Chapter 1	Purpose	Ephesians 4:16
	Purpose	Jeremiah 1:5
Chapter 2	Problems	Psalm 25:17
Chapter 3	Glory	1 Thessalonians 2:12
Chapter 4	Trials	Romans 5:3-4
Chapter 5	Invitation	Matthew 19:14
Chapter 6	Evil	Proverbs 3:7-8
Chapter 7	Hope	Revelation 21:4
Chapter 8	God's ways	Ecclesiastes 11:5
Chapter 9	Comfort	Matthew 5:4
Chapter 10	Truth	Proverbs 12:19
	Lost	Luke 15:32
	Seek	1 Chronicles 28:9
Chapter 11	Mercy	Psalm 25:16
Chapter 12	Judgment	Ecclesiastes 3:17
	Kindness	Proverbs 16:24
	Rest	Matthew 11:28
Chapter 13	Love	1 Thessalonians 4:9
Chapter 14	Seeking	2 Chronicles 15:2
	Purpose	Psalm 138:8
Chapter 15	Troubles	Psalm 34:19
Chapter 16	Troubles	Job 5:7-9
	Worry	Matthew 6:34
Chapter 17	Prudence	Proverbs 22:3
Chapter 18	Hope	Hebrews 10:23-24
	Covet	Exodus 20:17 (KJV)
	Salvation	Ephesians 2:9

Turn the page
for an exciting preview
of Nancy Moser's next book,

Solemnly Swear.

Available spring 2008
at a bookstore near you.

www.tyndalefiction.com

SOLEMNLY SWEAR

On her first day of jury duty Deidre Kelly soaked in every word of the lawyer's opening statements, knowing her husband Sig would want a play-by-play that evening. She was glad the judge had said they could take notes. She had trouble remembering three items to get at the store without writing them down, much less days and days of testimony.

The defendant—Patti McCoy—was a bitty thing who could have benefited from some beauty parlor expertise. There was natural beauty there, but with her minimal makeup, washed-out lips, and hair pulled back in a low ponytail, she blended into the background. Her position as a maid at the Country Comfort Resort and Spa was not a stretch. She was someone Deidre would have nodded at while passing in the hall, an invisible motel employee like she'd met a hundred times before. There, but not there. Although Patti had not spoken aloud as yet— would she be allowed to testify?—Deidre imagined her voice would be soft. "You'll have to speak up, Ms. McCoy. . . ."

Yes, indeed. The girl would have to speak up if she was going to get acquitted of this murder charge.

With a start Deidre realized Patti couldn't be acquitted. She *had* to be convicted.

Deidre's life depended on it.

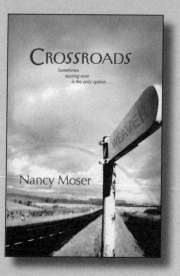

Turn the page for a preview of

Crossroads

by Nancy Moser.

Available now
at a bookstore near you.

TYNDALE
FICTION

CROSSROADS

Eighty-one-year-old Madeline stormed into the middle of Weaver's main intersection, positioned herself directly beneath its only traffic light, spread her arms wide, and screamed, "I will not allow it!" Just to make sure every atom and chromosome of every person within range heard her proclamation, she turned one-hundred-and-eighty degrees and did it again. "Do you hear me? I will not allow it!"

The light guiding the traffic traveling along Emma Street turned green, but there was no need for Madeline McHenry Weaver to move out of the way. The light could show its colors from now until Elvis returned and she would not have to move—for safety's sake anyway. Yet the truth was, she couldn't stand out here all day. If the heat of their Indian summer hot spell didn't get to her, her arthritis would. Annoying thing, getting old.

"You done yet?"

Web Stoddard sat at the corner, on a bench that skirted the town's only park, with one arm draped over its back, his overall-clad legs crossed. The shoelace on his right work boot was untied and teased the sidewalk. He slowly shooed a fly away as if he didn't have anything better to do.

Which he didn't.

Which brought Madeline back to the problem at hand.

She waved her arms expansively, ignoring the light turning red. "No, I'm not done yet. And I won't be done until people start listening to me."

His right ankle danced a figure eight. "No people to hear, Maddy. It's too late."

She stomped a foot. "It's not too late! It can't be."

Web nodded to the Weaver Mercantile opposite the bench. "Want to go sit at the soda fountain? I have a key."

"You have a key to every empty business in town. Don't abuse the privilege."

He nodded slowly, then grinned. "Want to go neck in the back of the hardware store?"

She crunched up her nose. "It smells like varnish and nails in there."

"Not a bad smell."

"You're obsessed with necking."

"When was the last time I mentioned it?"

She hated to be put on the spot. "But you *think* about it a lot."

"Last I heard, thinking tweren't a bad thing. And don't act like I'm pressuring you. The last time we kissed was 1942."

She looked past him toward the gazebo that sat in the middle of the town square. Even from here she could see that the floor was covered with the first sprinkling of gold, rust, and red leaves. Dead leaves. Blowing away, just like the town. Yet that's where she and Web had exchanged their last kiss. "October twenty-second, 1942."

He smiled. "You remembered."

"You were abandoning me, going off to war."

"You were supposed to wait for me."

Ouch.

She took two steps toward the bank that she and her husband Augustus had owned. Yet proximity or distance from Web wouldn't make the past right itself. But how dare he bring it up at a time like this? She put her hands on her hips and glared at him.

"Gracious day. What a look. What did I do?" Web said.

"Here I am worrying about Weaver and you . . ." She let her head wag like a disappointed mother.

He sat up straight and his loose lace became sandwiched between shoe and sidewalk. "You need to let the town go, Maddy."

She shook her head.

He patted the bench. "Come over here."

She crossed her arms, hugging herself. She didn't want to be scolded, or worse yet, placated. "I will not let Weaver die on me."

His voice softened. "It already has."

Her arms let loose, taking in the expanse of the main street. "The town's going to turn one hundred next year. We can't let it expire at ninety-nine. It's . . . it's sacrilegious."

He squinted his left eye.

"Scandalous?"

"You're overreacting, plus taking it way too personal."

"It *is* personal. I'm a Weaver." As soon as she said the words she wished she could take them back. Her becoming a Weaver was directly related to her not waiting for Web's safe return from World War II.

He was charitable and let it slide. "Nothing lasts forever. Not even a family line," he said.

Ah. Sure. Rub it in. If only she and Augustus had had children . . .

"It's just you and me, kid," Web said, doing a pitiful Humphrey Bogart imitation.

But he spoke the truth. They were the only lifers left in town . . . which made her remember, there used to be another. "I can't believe the Sidcowskys left. We went to high school with Marabel."

"You can't blame them for moving to Wichita to be closer to their grandchildren."

Madeline strode to the curb in front of Sidcowsky's Hardware and kicked it. The scuff in her shoe and pain in her toe were worth it. "They're traitors, the lot of them. Abandoning their lifeblood, their hometown that needs them. They are selfish beings, thinking nothing of the greater good, only thinking—"

"The Sidcowskys are good people, but they, like others, came to a crossroads and had to make a choice. The Sidcoswkys held on way beyond when others left."

Madeline would concede the point—privately. She did a lot of conceding in private. Although she hadn't let others see her panic, that *was* the emotion holding her in a stranglehold this past year. What had Queen Elizabeth called her horrible year when Windsor Castle burned and she endured the scandal and divorce of her wayward children? *Annus horribilus.* So it was.

Actually the demise of Weaver had not come about in a single year's time. The disease that had eaten away at its foundation had come slowly, like a cancer cell dividing and eating up the good, only making itself known when it was too late. Townspeople finding jobs elsewhere. People moving out, no one moving in. People getting greedy or panicking when business slowed. Closing up shop. Forgetting in their quest for more money, more success, and more happiness, all that Weaver stood for: family, tradition, safety, security, continuity.

Where was that continuity now? Where was the loyalty? It wasn't strictly a Weaver problem. People did not stay employed with one company their entire lives anymore. They didn't even stay in one neighborhood, but hopped houses and even spouses as if all were interchangeable and acceptable on the frantic road to happiness. The truth was, Weaver's demise had killed her husband. The doctor may have said it was his heart, but Madeline knew frustration and despair were the real—

"This town isn't the only town going through hard times, Maddy. People need to eat."

She pointed at the Sunshine Café on the opposite corner. "People could've eaten right there, until those quitters, the Andersons, moved out."

"Moved on, Maddy. People have to move on when they aren't making enough to live. Big towns with big stores and big jobs. That's what people need."

She watched a squirrel scamper diagonally from the park to the bank just a few feet in front of her. It didn't even hesitate. Even the rodents knew there was no need for a traffic light in Weaver anymore.

Her shoulders slumped. What she *needed* was a long soak in a lavender-scented bath. What she *needed* was time—more years to accomplish what she wanted to accomplish. "They don't *need* those things they're after, Web. They *want* them. Big difference."

He came toward her, right there in the street. She let him come. She could use a hug. In the three years since Augustus had died, she'd relied on Web's arms to make her feel better when the world was uncooperative. Her cheek found his shoulder. The clasp to his overall strap bit into it, but she didn't care.

"It's not your responsibility, Maddy." He put a hand on the back of her head and she closed her eyes to let the years slip away. Many, many years . . .

But then his words—instead of falling away as they gave comfort, hung back and started to jab like a bully offering a challenge.

Yes, she and Web had lived a lot of years here, shared a lot of history, but it wasn't time to rest on those laurels yet. There were too many years between them to brush off as being past and over. She may be old, but she wasn't dead yet.

She suddenly pushed away from him. "It *is* my responsibility, Web. You don't know . . ."

His faded blue eyes looked confused, as if he'd forgotten he'd just said those very words.

She repeated herself, growing impatient. "Weaver *is* my responsibility." She pointed at the street signs. "Emma Street is named after Augustus's great-grandmother, and Henry Avenue was named for *her* father. Every street in this town is named after a Weaver. They claimed it ninety-nine years ago and we've been here ever since. I'm the last Weaver standing and I will not go down without a fight!"

She noticed her arm was raised in a give-me-liberty-or-give-me-death position. She kept it there for effect.

"Ever hear of retirement, Maddy? Enjoying your golden years?"

She lowered her arm. "Oh pooh. Use it or lose it." She started walking toward the Weaver Garden on the far edge of the park, right across from the Weaver mansion. She often did her best cogitating among the flowers.

When she didn't hear footsteps coming after her she turned back and found Web still standing in the middle of the abandoned street. "You coming?"

He put his hands in his pockets. "Depends. Exactly *what* are you planning to do?"

"I'm going to save Weaver, silly. And after I do, we're going to have the best and biggest one-hundredth birthday celebration this town has ever seen." Web's shaking head riled her. "I *will* save Weaver, Web Stoddard. The question is: will you help me?"

Web's sigh was eaten up by the drone of the cicadas overhead. "What do you have in mind?"

Madeline had never let technicalities stop her before, and she certainly wasn't about to start now. She put her hands on her hips. "Are you in or out?"

"You need to explain—"

She took a step toward her best friend. "I don't need to do anything of the sort. I need a yes from you. Now."

"Before I even know the question?"

"Exactly."

"You're not being fair, Maddy."

She planted her feet dramatically and waited. *Come on, Web. Do this for me. For Weaver. For us.*

Web's head shook no even as he said, "Yes. Yes, I'm in."

Bravo.

It was a start.